Praise for US CONDUCTORS

"Michaels' book is based on the life of Lev Termen, the Russian-born inventor of the theremin, the most ethereal of musical instruments. As the narrative shifts countries and climates, from the glittery brightness of New York in the 1920s to the leaden cold of the Soviet Union under Stalin, the grace of Michaels' style makes these times and places seem entirely new. He succeeds at one of the hardest things a writer can do: he makes music seem to sing from the pages of a novel."
Scotiabank Giller Prize jury citation (Shauna Singh
Baldwin, Justin Cartwright and Francine Prose)

"What a debut. . . . A continent-spanning historical epic."
The Globe and Mail, Favourite Debuts of the Year

"The Giller jury got it right this time. . . . An exhilarating meditation on manipulation, whether it's scientific, musical or political. Michaels makes complex physics easy to understand while writing about music in ways that make you hear it. Brilliant." *NOW*

"There was enough intrigue in the real life of Russian musician and inventor Lev Sergeyvich Termen to make a fictionalization of his adventures seem superfluous. Hustled off to America by his government, the inventor of the theremin (an early electronic instrument that seems to pull sound out of thin air) meets legendary musicians, performs at Carnegie Hall, falls in love with a violinist and is pressed into service as a spy. On his wonderful music blog *Said the Gramophone*, Sean Michaels has made the maxim 'writing about music is like dancing about architecture' seem like a beautiful fantasy rather than an admonition. Here, in his debut novel, he focuses on the small moments that bring this man of ideas and ambition to vibrating life."

Jacob Ganz, editor, NPR Music (Best Book of 2014)

"Following the life of Leon Termen, the inventor of the theremin, *Us Conductors* takes the reader from Leningrad to New York City, from gulags to speakeasies, dance floors and concert stages to laboratories and cattle cars. *Us Conductors* stretches its arms to encompass nearly everything—it is an immigrant tale, an epic, a spy intrigue, a prison confession, an inventor's manual, a creation myth, and an obituary—but the electric current humming through its heart is an achingly resonant love story. Sean Michaels orchestrates his first novel like a virtuoso."

Anthony Marra, author of *A Constellation of Vital Phenomena*

"Carefully crafted and engaging. . . . The discussions on art are handled with delicacy and never overdone. . . . The story moves with a driving force that makes it difficult to put down." *Ottawa Review of Books*

"The Giller-winning tale of the theremin's invention saw so many Canadians swept up in the body electric of Sean Michaels's tender debut, *Us Conductors*." *National Post*

"Quirky gem of a book." Marsha Lederman, *The Globe and Mail*

"Michaels writes eloquently about the unsettling ecstasy of obsession and the airborne joy of musical discovery. This year's Giller jury got it right when it awarded Michaels Canada's top prize for fiction."

The Georgia Straight

US CONDUCTORS

IN WHICH I SEEK
the heart of Clara Rockmore,
MY ONE TRUE LOVE,
finest theremin player the world will ever know

SEAN MICHAELS

VINTAGE CANADA

VINTAGE CANADA EDITION, 2015

Copyright © 2014 Sean Michaels

Published in Canada by Vintage Canada, a division of Penguin Random House Canada
Limited, in 2015. Originally published in trade paperback in Canada by Random House
Canada, a division of Penguin Random House Canada Limited, in 2014.
Distributed by Penguin Random House Canada Limited, Toronto.

Vintage Canada with colophon is a registered trademark.

www.penguinrandomhouse.ca

Library and Archives Canada Cataloguing in Publication

Michaels, Sean, 1982–, author
Us conductors / Sean Michaels.

ISBN 978-0-345-81333-6
eBook ISBN 978-0-345-81334-3

I. Title.

PS8626.I17U83 2015   C813'.6   C2013-906321-8

Cover image: Jen Kiaba/Arcangel Images

Text design by CS Richardson

Image credits: Photo of Clara Rockmore by Skippy Adelman, year unknown.
Photo of Lev Termen, photographer unknown, 1924.

Printed and bound in the United States of America

2 4 6 8 9 7 5 3 1

Penguin
Random
House

VINTAGE CANADA

For Jan, Arlen and Robin Michaels

THIS BOOK IS MOSTLY INVENTIONS.

PART ONE

In memory, everything seems to happen to music.

Tennessee Williams, *The Glass Menagerie*

ONE

DIALS

I WAS LEON TERMEN before I was Dr Theremin, and before I was Leon, I was Lev Sergeyvich. The instrument that is now known as a theremin could as easily have been called a leon, a lyova, a sergeyvich. It could have been called a clara, after its greatest player. Pash liked "termenvox." He liked its connotations of science and authority. But this name always made me laugh. Termenvox—the voice of Termen. As if this device replicated my own voice. As if the theremin's trembling soprano were the song of this scientist from Leningrad.

I laughed at this notion, and yet in a way I think I also believed it. Not that the theremin emulated my voice, but that with it I gave voice to *something*. To the invisible. To the ether. I, Lev Sergeyvich Termen, mouthpiece of the universe.

That mouthpiece is now atop the sea, aboard a ship, in a rectangular cabin the size of an ensuite bathroom at New York's Plaza Hotel, the hotel that was once my home. This vessel is called the *Stary Bolshevik*. The walls are made of steel and painted eggshell blue. There is a cot in the corner, a frayed grey rug on the floor, and I sit in a folding chair before a desk that is also made of steel, also painted eggshell blue. The bare light bulb glows. When the weather is rough, as it is now, I am as sick as a dog. I clutch my sides and listen to the drawer beside my bed sliding open and slamming shut and sliding open. The room rocks. I go to the toilet in a tiny closet, and then I come back and stare at what I have written. Rows of symbols—qwe asd zxc, the the the, lt, cr, lt, cr (((((((((&. I wonder who will see these pages. Will I send them away, like a letter? Will I keep them in a safe? Will they drown one night, in seawater?

On the other side of the hall there is another room like this one, lit by its own incandescent bulb. It is filled with my equipment. Some of this equipment is delicate and easily damaged. When the waves heave, it would be reassuring to go across and unfasten the cases' clasps, check that all the wires are coiled, the batteries capped, the tubes intact. Check that my theremins still sing. For the last seventeen years, a day has rarely passed that I did not hear their sound. From Archangelsk to New Haven, in palaces and shacks, I travelled and taught, performed for long-shoremen and lords, and almost every night I was able to reach across the room and find the electrical field of one of my humble theremins, coaxing current into sound.

But the door to my cabin is locked. I do not have the key. Just a typewriter, just paper and ink, just this story to set down now, in solitude, as the distance widens between us.

WHEN I WAS FOURTEEN YEARS OLD, one of my teachers at the gymnasium introduced the class to Geisslers—glass cylinders, vacuum tubes. They came in wooden crates, wrapped individually, like wineglasses. I say like wineglasses but really to me they were like intricate conch shells, the kind of treasures that wash up on a beach.

Professor Vasilyev must have recognized my fascination, because one holiday he let me take a vacuum tube home. I kept it wrapped in butcher paper, strolling with it in my jacket pocket, one hand resting over it, and in my mind's eye it was an emerald. At home I experimented with wires and Fahnestock clips, spark coils, and the new lamp beside Grandmother's bed. While my parents thought I was practising piano and violin I was crouched over a wooden board, assembling circuits with brass screws. I knew to be careful: I had been tinkering with machines for years, phonographs and an old wireless set, Father's camera. At the end of the break I wrote Professor Vasilyev a long letter proposing a demonstration at the upcoming Family Day. I delivered the letter together with the vacuum tube—intact, undamaged—into his hands. He took more than a week to answer. I remember it was a Friday. He called me aside after class, drummed his fingers on the desktop, stared at me from under patchy eyebrows. "All right, Lev," he said.

On Family Day there were displays by the wrestling squad, the botanical club, one of the choirs, and a class recited parts of *Ilya Muromets* from memory. Vova Ivanov sang a song about seagulls. After this, Professor Vasilyev clambered onto the stage. In his gentle voice he explained to the audience that some of his students were about to distribute Geissler vacuum tubes. We were lined up and down the gymnasium aisles, crates of tubes at every corner. We passed them hand to hand as though we were building something together. Soon all of the parents and uncles and aunts and grandparents had Geissler tubes in their laps. They turned them over and over, like wineglasses, like seashells, like emeralds. Then Professor Vasilyev asked everyone to look up at the ceiling. What they saw were the sagging lines of four-teen criss-crossing copper wires. I had pinned them up myself as Professor Vasilyev held the ladder. We had hidden the induction coils in a broom closet.

The ceiling wires now flowed with electric current.

They made no sound.

"Please raise your Geissler tubes," said Professor Vasilyev.

One after another, they lifted their little glass tubes. They held them up with their fingertips. The feeling I had was the feeling you get as you pass through a gate and into a walled garden. As each vacuum tube entered the electrical field of my lacework of wires, one by one, the Geisslers began to glow.

I felt then what I have felt many times since. It is the moment you forget the electricity, the conducting metals and skipping electrons, the tubes and wires and fundamental principles; standing with hands in pockets you forget these things and for a hot, proud instant you think it is *you* who did this, who made the tubes glow, you clever mouse.

This is the hubris of the inventor. It is a monster that has devoured many scientists. I have strived to keep it at bay. Even in America, among ten thousand flatterers, I tried to concentrate on my machines, not their maker.

Perhaps if I had been prouder, this story would have turned out differently. Perhaps I would not be here, in a ship, plunging from New York back to Russia. Perhaps we would be together. If I were more of a showman. If I had told the right tale.

But Lev Sergeyvich Termen is not the voice of the ether. He is not the principle that turned glass into firefly. I am an instrument. I am a sound being sounded, music being made, blood, salt and water manipulated in air. I come from Leningrad. With my bare hands, I have killed one man. I was born on August 15,

1896, and at that instant I became an object moving through space toward you.

MY FIRST INVENTION was called "the radio watchman."

I was still a student, scarcely out of adolescence, and I invented a magical box. The radio watchman emits an invisible electro-magnetic field and then waits for a disruption. If a human body passes inside this field, the circuit closes and an alarm goes off.

Imagine a vigilant wireless set, keeping guard.

It was a small triumph to have devised something new. At Petrograd University my class was full of rivals and each of us wanted his own calling card. During my first semesters, the only thing distinguishing me from the other students was an uncom-mon interest in music theory. Twice weekly, I attended courses at the conservatory across town. Sometimes I jangled out Tchaikovsky's "Dance of the Sugar Plum Fairy" on the piano in the physics lounge. Nobody was impressed. But now I had a desk with a magical box, a bulb that flashed whenever I came near it. Classmates would stand just outside the watchman's field, as if by setting it off they were submitting to my success. Only Sasha came close and backed away, waved his arm or threw a shoe, testing what I'd done. Only Sasha wasn't intimidated; he was always so sure of his cleverness, that he was cleverer than I.

My friend was tall and thin, with an unknit brow. His life seemed effortless. The day I presented the radio watchman, he insisted on taking me out to celebrate. It was a winter night, one of those chill evenings when your vision is interrupted by ten thousand wild snowflakes. We were talking science. Probably Sasha was telling me about the paper he was writing. We ducked into a tavern near the grey Fontanka River, took two stools near the window, but the spirits hadn't even started flowing when a commotion blasted through from around the corner. Banging, shouts, and then the procession of a few hundred people, dark coats flying past our window, rippling banners, a gathered effort in the marchers' faces.

"Reds," Sasha said, without any disdain. We were Reds too. This was 1917. Both of us had mustered for protests at the university. Now we watched the parade of Communists and read their slogans and more than anything I remember feeling the rhythm of their drums, the clang of wooden spoons on iron pots.

"Should we join the rascals?" Sasha said. He was already a party member. I hesitated. It was one of those instants when you feel your youth. I glanced back into the safety of the tavern, where drunks were slouched against the tables. Then we threw on our coats and went outside. The mob was boisterous and happy. To be in a parade like that, bold and loud, owning the road, is a messy jubilation. The snow was still falling. The crowd was strident, casual. "Bread and land!" we shouted. We moved together through the city. "Bread and land and freedom!"

Suddenly there was disorder up ahead. The front of the procession stalled. We bumped into our neighbours. Sagging banners, yells, then two loud pops. "What is . . . ?" Sasha began to say, before a channel opened through the crowd.

There, at the square, a row of riflemen, their guns aimed straight through the snowstorm.

We bolted. Men and women were breaking in all directions, some toward but most of them away from the Imperial soldiers. Bodies pushed into us like shoving hands. Snow was still falling. Cold light. More pops, thin trails of smoke, dark coats, and now glimpses of green uniforms, gold buttons, then rising up, the terrifying silhouettes of horses, cavalry, and we ran and ran and ran, over torn earth, over ice, filled with raw, fierce terror. From the street ahead, another bang—deafening, like an explosion. Reality seemed to be on the diagonal; I was so scared I felt I might be sick. We dashed down a bright alley and I pulled Sasha into a half-open doorway. Pressed together, we caught our breath. "You all right?" I said, finally.

"Limbs intact. You?"

I swallowed, then let out a breath. The city's din had vanished. Before us just snowflakes.

Our bundled coats had pushed the door further ajar and we stood at the entrance to a long, wide room, lit with lanterns, a crackling stove. Eight or ten men, stripped to the waist, stood staring at us.

Most of them were Chinamen, or they looked like Chinamen. At first I thought it must be a dormitory, somewhere workers slept. But almost at once I realized no. It was a gym. Two of the men were holding long sticks, like shepherds' staves. The air smelled of sandalwood and sweat.

One of the Chinamen approached us, an older man maybe my father's age, barrel-chested, with a birthmark across his shoulder. "Good evening," he murmured. "Can I help you?"

"We, er . . ." Sasha said. "Well, we—"

"Please come in," he offered. We did and he pulled the door closed behind us. "It's cold." In the partial dark, the students eyed us. I felt very clumsy in my greatcoat.

"This is a gymnasium?" I asked.

"Yes. Training room. We call *kwoon*. Are you hurt?"

"No," Sasha and I said together.

A pair of men had lost interest in us and began to spar. One was Asian, the other Russian. They attacked each other in slow motion, with short, fluid punches, pirouetting kicks.

The man beside us called out something in Chinese.

"I tell them, 'Breathe like a child,'" he explained to us.

I watched them dodge and shift. "This is judo?"

"*Wing-chun kung-fu*," said the man.

"There are soldiers outside," Sasha said.

The man regarded him levelly. "You are Bolsheviks?" I noticed that he had bare feet. They all had bare feet.

"Yes," I said.

He nodded. "I also."

He shouted something at the students who still watched us. They laughed and fell back into their own practices.

"You're a communist?" Sasha said.

The man shrugged. "Yes."

Sticks swung in slow arcs.

"Would you . . . fight?" Sasha said.

The man scratched his belly. "Against soldiers with rifles?" he said. "What use would we be?"

"You might be of use."

The man, the teacher, *sifu*, clicked his tongue. "When you have the right tools—that is when you serve," he said.

A painting of a slender old man, mid-kick, hung on the wall beside us. He seemed to be floating above a lake. He looked serene.

We never went back to find the protesters, who had bravely rallied, evading the soldiers, gathering at the Winter Palace. They shouted long into the night. Instead we watched the men do kung-fu and then I followed Sasha back to the tavern, where we drank vodka and toasted our safety, pleased with our little adventure.

Only much later that night, lying in my sheets, did shame come and find me. It rose up from the floor like a mist. I kept seeing the whirl of the crowd, the way I had clutched my fists and run. My mindless fear. My premature departure.

I hadn't stayed to learn the ending.

❖

THE IDEA FOR THE THEREMIN came to me in 1921. It was Sasha's doing. I remember he was standing in the laboratory, still in his coat, dripping wet. I was on my hands and knees, soaking up the water with towels. Scenes like this were common in those days. To get to the Physico-Technical Institute, on the outskirts of Leningrad, you had to wedge your bicycle into the tram and ride forever. Past the library, over the Okhta River, under blue skies or grey skies or in the rain, pinned against a wall with a pedal in your neighbour's calf. You could recognize the other scientists by their bicycles. Chemists with their hands on the handlebars, biologists resting their briefcases in their bicycle baskets. The mathematicians always had the most elegant bikes, minimal and gleaming. Physicists usually had complicated ones: hand-rigged gear systems, precision brakes. I was not like the other physicists. My bicycle was ordinary, with a bell that played middle C.

Anyhow, you took the tram to Finlandskiy, the last stop, and extracted your bicycle from the train car, and saluted the driver, and off you would go—weaving eight kilometres along the dirt road, across the field and under a wide sky, through the green bends of the arboretum, fast, where birdcalls banish any heavy heart; then up the hill and panting, round the bend, coasting in low gear through the grounds of the Physico-Technical Institute, dodging bent boughs, passing students on their way to class. You'd leave your bicycle with Boris the skinny clerk and duck through the arches, saying hello to the charwomen Katerina and Nyusya, and ascend the marble staircase, past the landing, round the corner, and then you would find yourself, sweaty and alive, in the midst of all the lab's buzzing equipment.

In the winter you couldn't ride your bicycle, not in the snow and mud; and so you didn't bring your bicycle; and so on the tram the scientists were indistinguishable from the tailors, from the bankers, from the bookbinders, until you got off the tram and trudged a barren highway to the polytechnic, every path unmarked except by ice-encrusted footprints; and you'd walk forever across the arboretum's empty woods, and the institute's empty woods, over spaces where bushes had stood, in summer, and finally the bare trunks parted and you ducked through the arches, and said hello to Katerina and Nyusya, and climbed the slippery marble stairs, past the landing, round the corner, and if you were prudent you changed into a second pair of trousers and left the other on the radiator.

Sasha was not prudent. He stood before my latest experiment with caked ice melting from the soles of his boots, the cuffs of his trousers. I was on the floor, patting the tiles dry. Water was a dangerous thing in the laboratories of the Physico-Technical Institute.

"It's very clever," Sasha said.

"Thank you."

He tapped one of the dials with his fingernail. "This is the density?"

"Y—yes. Be careful. It's very sensitive."

Both of us had been at the Physico-Technical Institute for a couple of years. Sasha, the brilliant theorist, was already a senior researcher. I was less feted, coasting in on the fumes of my radio watchman. We worked together and apart: competitors, co-workers, scientists who sometimes went to concerts, or for cherry cake at Café du Nord, who talked of family and politics, of elementary particles. If I had mentioned my sister to him, it was to say that Helena seemed distant to me, a creature of another phylum. And if he had mentioned his own sister, Katia, it was not to reveal that she was pretty, or that she was unrelenting, like a flood; it was to describe a holiday they had shared as children, or the ham she had carved at New Year, while Sasha scored chestnuts.

I would learn for myself that blue-eyed Katia was pretty, that she was unrelenting.

I got up from the floor. Sasha was still peering at the same dial. "Very clever," he repeated.

I hoped he would say something to Ioffe, my supervisor.

"But alas for the blind man," Sasha said.

"What?"

"All these dials."

There *were* many dials. Splayed before us, the device was a disparate contraption of coiled wires, readouts, rubber piping and a hissing chamber with two suspended plates. The plates formed a circuit: electricity jumped from one to the other, through the air. When the chamber was filled with gas, the electricity's crackle changed, quickening or slowing. And thus it was able to measure the properties of various gases, particularly their dielectric constants. A dial read: 1.055.

"It's a calamity," Sasha said. "How will the blind man learn the dielectric constant of helium?"

"How is he to check his pocket watch?" I said.

"You mean he should ask his wife. Machines like this are the reason we don't see more blind physicists." The joke really entertained him. "Couldn't you rig something up? Make it spray a new scent for each gas?"

"So sulphur gas can smell of roses?"

He chuckled.

"It would be easier for it to make a sound," I said.

"If the constant's higher than 1.2—a puff of cinnamon and the sound of a barking dog."

"A tone," I said. "Actually . . ." I thought about this. "A pitch that reflects the conductivity?" I picked up my notebook. "By adjusting the temperature, the gas could be made to sing a song. Or just wave your hand . . ."

Sasha tapped his fingertips against the wall of the chamber, making the dials' needles wag. This made him laugh again. "But what about the frostbitten soldiers," he asked, "without any fingers?"

I was no longer paying attention. I watched the needles flicker, a tiny back-and-forth, as if they were gesturing for my attention, and an image came to me, strongly, the kind of intuition a scientist leans on. It was like a film loop, the same scene over and over: a man inside a bell jar, his hand hovering above a metal plate, and the metal plate singing. *La*, it sang. *Fa so la.*

I looked at my own small hand.

THE THEREMIN WAS MORE OR LESS a combination of its precedents: the soundless watchman, the hissing gas monitor. I was measuring human movements as if they were the fluctuations of a gas, and adding sound.

The early prototypes were variations of the metal plates I'd shown Sasha, with added oscillators and an earpiece. I demonstrated the concept to the department head, Abram Fedorovich Ioffe. My waggling hand sounded out something between a shrieking bumblebee and Massenet's "Élégie." Ioffe was tickled. "One day," he pronounced, "our orchestras will run on batteries."

In November 1921, I was invited to demonstrate the theremin before the institute's mechanical engineers and physicists, my first formal audience. I felt again like Lyova with a crate full of vacuum tubes. But these were not credulous *dedushki* and *babushki*; these men had invented and reinvented radio, sent complex messages through the air. They spoke the language of electricity. They'd not be dazzled by twinkling little lights.

I was nervous. All right—I was petrified. Beforehand, I shut myself in Ioffe's office. The sun had dipped behind the hills and filled the room with blue silhouettes. As I paced, the shadows skewed and reoriented themselves. I felt as though I was sabotaging something: the order in the room, its tranquillity, its dusk. I went to turn on the electric lamp on Ioffe's desk, but it was broken. I took a small screwdriver from my jacket pocket. I was partway through the repair when he knocked on the door and said through the wood, "It's time."

In the low-ceilinged hall I stood beside the apparatus. Twists of smoke rose from cigarettes. I named and indicated the transformer, the oscillator, the unlit vacuum tubes. I closed the cabinet, concealing the components. I cleared my throat. "And so," I said, and I turned the theremin on.

Here is the way you play a theremin:

You turn it on. Then you wait.

You wait for several reasons. You wait to give the tubes the chance to warm, like creatures taking their first breaths. You wait in order to heighten the audience's suspense. And, finally, you wait to magnify your own anticipation. It is a thrill and a terror. You stand before a cabinet and two antennas and immediately the space itself is activated, the room is charged, the atmosphere is alive. What was potential is potent. You imagine sparks, embers, tiny lightning flecks balanced in the vacant air.

You raise your hands.

Raise the right hand first, toward the pitch antenna, and you will hear it: DZEEEEOOOoo, a shocked electric coo, steadying into a long hymn. Raise the left hand, toward the volume antenna, and you will quiet it.

Move your hands again, and the device will sing.

My theremin is a musical instrument, an instrument of the air. Its two antennas rise up from a closed wooden box. The pitch antenna is tall and black, noble. The closer your right hand gets, the higher the theremin's tone. The second antenna controls volume. It is bent, looped, gold and horizontal. The closer you bring your left hand, the softer the instrument's song. The farther away, the louder it becomes. But always you are standing with your hands in the air, like a conductor. That is the secret of the theremin, after all: your body is a conductor.

My colleagues at the institute did not applaud that day. They simply *listened very carefully*. I played works by Minkus and Massenet. I performed Saint-Saëns's "The Swan." I remember looking out over the sheet music into rows of faces, mostly moustached, and seeing Andrey Andreyevich Korovin, a man I had never spoken to, a man I had only seen, his features like the scored bark of a tree. Andrey Andreyevich had worked in the metals lab for fifty years. He had sharp grey eyes and a thin mouth. He was listening to me. My hand was in the air and I was playing a low note. Andrey Andreyevich Korovin, a man I had never spoken to, appeared to be on the verge of tears.

The theremin has always been a machine with two strangenesses. There is the strangeness of the playing: palms flexing in empty space, as if you are pulling the strings of an invisible marionette. But the stranger strangeness is the sound. It is acute. It is at once unmodulated and modulating. It feels both still and frantic. For all my tweakings of timbre, the theremin cannot quite mimic the trumpet's joyous blast, the cello's steadying stroke. It is something Else.

Yes, the Elseness is what brings audiences to their feet. It is what inspires composers like Schillinger and Varèse. But there is no escaping the other part, too: like the pallor of an electric light bulb, like the heat of an electric stove, the theremin's sound is a stranger to the Earth.

I have escorted this stranger across the globe. For all the assembled multitudes, for Rockefeller, Gershwin, Shostakovich, cranky George Bernard Shaw, for wives and friends, enemies and lovers, lost hopes, and for empty rooms, I conducted the ether. In a hundred halls, Saint-Saëns's "Swan" floated like a ghost. The voice that was not a voice neither paused nor took a breath.

LATER, IN AMERICA, one of the RCA salesmen, Len Shewell, told me the story of selling a theremin to Charlie Chaplin. Len had been invited to Chaplin's vast mansion, a place done up in marble and ebony, as black and white as Chaplin's moving pictures. Len dragged his suitcase after the butler, through corridors with sharp corners, to a wide parlour where the Little Tramp reclined on a chaise longue. A vase of roses posed on every table, Len said, and the fireplace was roaring even on that August afternoon. Chaplin asked him to begin his demonstration and Len launched into his routine, but when the sounds started, *DZEEEEOOOoo*, Len's hand wavering by the pitch antenna, Chaplin gasped so loudly that Len turned off the machine.

"Is everything all right?" Len asked.

Chaplin was as pale as chalk. "No, yes, continue," he said.

The actor was plainly terrified. The best-known phantom in the world, a man who had made his fortune as an illusion projected onto silver screens—he was scared of this box of ghosts. Listening to Len's rendition of "The Star-Spangled Banner," his face leapt from horror to ardour and back. His eyebrows rose and fell as if they were on pulleys. He trembled. When Len was finished, Chaplin jumped to his feet, crossed the room, shook the salesman's hand. "I'll take one," he said, and with one finger he reached forward to touch the theremin's cabinet—as if it were a jaguar, a panther, a man-eating lion.

The sound of the theremin is simply pure electric current. It is the hymn of lightning as it hides in its cloud. The song never strains or falters; it persists, stays, keeps, lasts, lingers. It will never abandon you.

In that regard, it is better than any of us.

TWO

PINK ORANGE RED

BEFORE I CAME TO AMERICA, I toured my own country. It started fitfully—a week in Moscow, a few days in Smolensk, an excursion to Kazan. I huddled with researchers, smoothing schematics with my hands. I played the theremin for halls full of students. I visited the Kremlin one shining spring afternoon, to show my machine to Vladimir Ilyich Lenin (may his memory be illuminated). Then my mission changed: these discoveries aren't just for the academy, Lenin told me. They are for the people.

I went out by train. Men towed my equipment through what was then Nikolayevsky Station, past puzzled workers, into huge railway cars. I followed them in my best but shabby suit, Lenin's name on a card in my pocket. Demonstrations were arranged in tiny Russian towns, hamlets whose one electric light glowed wanly in the night. I slurped *shchi* with the leaders of local worker councils, farmers with weary faces, explaining why fires need oxygen, why lightning strikes. Tarussky's top cattle breeder wanted to learn why silver tarnishes. A woman in Shuya asked if radiators could cause freckles. I connected a theremin to a sputtering gas engine and as my instrument shrilled, the people rose to their feet, astonished, hands held over their hearts.

Back in Leningrad I was beginning to feel like a star. I spent weekdays at the institute, improving my devices, advancing my theories, feeling the satisfaction of the inventor who knows his inventions will be seen, will be wondered at, in open air. Sasha didn't want to hear any of my crowing. He became grumpy when I hung around his office doorway, unspooling anecdotes. "You can have your shepherds and milkmaids," he said. "I'll take the committee chairs and Nobel laureates."

One night, he stood me up. I had tickets to the ballet, but Sasha wasn't at home when I arrived to collect him. Instead, a pretty girl answered the door. She had dark eyelashes, an upward tilting chin, a soft assurance to her face. I imagined she was the type of person who writes down her dreams in the morning. Her arms were crowded with screwdrivers, pliers, a tin full of nails. She seemed vexed.

"Pardon me," I said. "I've come for Sasha."

"He's out."

I was surprised. "Out?"

"Yes, out. At the lab."

"I see," I said.

She examined me. "Are you Termen?"

"Yes. Lev Sergeyvich."

"He said to say sorry, he wanted to finish something."

"Ah," I said. I looked at the shined toes of my shoes.

"I'm Katia," she said. "His sister."

It was as if I saw her for the second time then. "Are those your tools?" I asked.

She rolled her eyes. "Sasha left his mess for me to tidy up."

"How rude of him," I said. "Would you like to go to the ballet?"

THE NEXT THREE YEARS were a time of self-creation. I was in a rush to be established—the sturdiness of my life, I thought, should match the heavy type that newspapers were using to print my name. There were so many elements to put in place: published papers; professional endorsements; applications for a new apartment, for a new laboratory; a wife. Eventually I quit the Physico-Technical Institute to work under my own supervision, in a shared lab overlooking the Neva. I moved into a new home. I invented better theremins. I made abrupt, titanic promises.

My parents disapproved of all these metamorphoses. The Revolution was fresh in their minds and they advocated steady advancement, sober restraint. They wanted me to be more like my sister, Helena, who was studying botany, obscurely cultivating a career. "We always taught you to keep your voice down," my father said, perched on a chair in my kitchen. "Whose attention are you in such a hurry to receive?"

Worse than my parents' disapproval was how little they cared about my accomplishments. Father could not be persuaded to flip through my write-ups in scientific bulletins, let alone to assist at a demonstration of the theremin. He sipped from a cup of strong tea and issued advice about how to start a family. "Patience, Lev. The main thing is patience." When I tried to show him the distance-vision prototype I was working on, it was only a few minutes before he became distracted by a squirrel scritching on the windowsill. He shouted through the glass, "Hello my friend! Hello!"

Finally I directed the explanation to my mother. "Good work, Lev," she murmured, without lifting her eyes from her knitting, without waiting for me to turn it on.

I had more and more reasons to stay at home and I found more and more reasons to go away. Sometimes Katia and I would have arguments by letter—underlined words and no signatures. I attended a conference in Nizhny Novgorod. I made a presentation to generals in Moscow. I came back from a visit to Kiev and found that my country had new ideas for me. They wanted to send me into western Europe. "Impress them with your machines," said a man from a dark corner of the interior ministry. "Our operative will do the rest." I faced Katia across our small table, ham on plates like little moons.

My new mission began with an appearance in Berlin. It was my first visit. I arrived in the mid-morning—weary, excited, dishevelled from the sleeper car. The streets were smeared with red and gold leaves. Lines snaked from the door of every bakery—it was some sort of national holiday. I was met by the eminent Dr Beirne, and we toured the National Academy. I demonstrated the theremin and the radio watchman to a classroom of physicists. They stroked their short silver beards. We took a carriage across town, to the Deutsche Oper, where the rest of my equipment was being stored. I went down into the basement. I met the man I call Pash.

Pash. That is how he introduced himself to me that day, so that is what I always called him. Pash. My operative. My handler. I was the communist magician, the conductor of the ether, sent out by the state to show off my great discoveries. And here was a man in an overcoat who travelled alongside, like a shadow, a larger shadow, filled with his own directives.

Pash had a gentle face, square and well formed, with blue irises like chips of stone. A kind face, and an ogre's back and shoulders, as if his body foresaw circumstances that demanded something more than clear, quick, handsome eyes.

We travelled together in Berlin, and then to other German cities—Cologne, Hamburg, Frankfurt. By the time we arrived in Dresden, the rest of the tour had sold out. Crowds filled the theatres. They called me "the Russian Edison"; they said I would transform the world. At the Tonhalle they applauded and applauded even after my presentation had finished, even after my second curtain call, even after the stagehands had raised the house lights and propped open the exits. They applauded, stamping their feet, shouting.

"Theremin!" they shouted. "Theremin, Theremin!"

Pash steered; I followed. From Germany we cut through to France, then over to England. Each city offered the same obstacle course of handshakes and expectation. First came someone from the Russian consulate or, in London's case, someone from the former Russian consulate. These someones were always tall, malnourished, jumpy. They were not sure why I had been sent, or under whose aegis I travelled. My companion particularly perplexed them.

"And you are . . . ?" said the someone from Paris.

Pash shrugged in his overcoat. "It doesn't matter."

The someone laughed at this, raised expectant eyebrows.

"Pash," Pash said finally.

"Pash?"

"Yes."

"But you are Dr Theremin's . . . that is, Dr Theremin is your—?"

"May I use your telephone?" Pash said, and then he took out his identity card, emblazoned with a particularly intricate and notorious seal, and the someone asked no further questions.

Pash made his calls. He asked the consulate man for reports, contacts, lists of local partners. I soon realized I was the diversion, Pash's pretext for opening bank accounts and trade offices. His briefcase filled with paper and wave after wave of visitors crashed down against us, in a blur of champagne bubbles.

Next came the dignitaries: mayors, ambassadors, lesser royalty, keen to meet Leningrad's wonder-worker. They spoke of welcome, of international cooperation. None of the nobles mentioned Russia's executed czar.

"Try the mussels," they said. "Try the flan. Try a banana." In London, the Earl of Shaftesbury flourished a curving yellow fruit. I watched him peel it. "Now," he pronounced, "anoint it with a scoop of ice cream."

After the dignitaries came the businessmen, with whom I had been instructed to seem polite but distracted. "Be soapstone," Pash had said, as our train clicked past Reims. "Promising but inscrutable—let them think you are a mystery to be drawn out."

My box of tricks was not a deception, simply physics. And yet the mission in Europe was to tantalize, plant seeds, dangle hooks. All these foreign entrepreneurs, seduced by the theremin: What would they trade for a share?

I smiled thinly at the Western wealthy. I kissed widows' hands. I smoked their sons' cigars. In time I derived a formula: my accord with a person was inversely proportional to the number of rings he or she was wearing.

At every stop, my favourite group was admitted last. Once the dignitaries, businessmen and socialites had cleared to the punch bowls, at last: the physicists, the chemists, the engineers, the doctors, the astronomers, the autodidacts and the musicians. I welcomed them with joy and relief. Pash had come to meet the chamber of commerce but I was here for this: to encounter men and women of refinement, intelligence, and curiosity. In Paris: Paul Valéry, the marquis de Polignac, the English ambassador John Rafe; in London, Julian Huxley, Sir Oliver Lodge, Maurice Ravel, the conductor Henry Wood. Not to mention John McEwen, principal of the Royal Academy of Music, and brilliant Ernest

Rutherford. Finally—finally!—we could talk about something besides the weather. This esteemed company discussed electricity, hypnosis, and Dmitri Shostakovich. At that time my English was much worse than it is today, and my French, non-existent. So I had interpreters. In Paris I was assisted by a lovely girl called Aurélie—the daughter of an émigré who taught at the polytechnic. Translating French interrogatives into Russian, Russian conjectures into French, she moved her miniature hands before her: tiny gestures that evoked the poses of birds. I remember the press conference where I announced that I would be going abroad at the end of the year: a "short trip," organized by Pash, to introduce my work to the Americans. A lure at the end of a line. Standing on a makeshift stage, in the bar of the Paris Opera, I found that I was apprehensive. Not just about the substance of my statement—where I was headed, why—but about my whole overblown situation. Equipment was being unloaded downstairs and instead of labouring among my crates and wires, I was here, leaning against a baby grand, making a speech to Valéry, Polignac, and a columnist for *Le Temps*. For a long, yawning moment I felt utterly outclassed. I did not know what kind of wine I had been drinking, or which term I should use when addressing the marquis. I was so nervous, and beside me Aurélie was so solemn, measuring each word as if it were a death sentence. Compulsively, I began to extemporize. I tried to provoke Aurélie, to unsettle her gravity, employing esoteric nouns and far-flung adjectives, inserting references to folk songs and fairy tales, Nevsky Prospekt vernacular, pops and crackles of onomatopoeia. Noticing a plate of biscuits, I said they smelled like Tulsky gingerbread, like the nave of the Church of the Annunciation, on Vasilievsky. "Such a perspicuously mnemonic aroma," I said. I wanted to make Aurélie smile. I wanted her to lower her hands that were like small birds and to comfort me with a smile. But solemn Aurélie simply stood in her neat black skirt and parroted my nonsense in pearly perfect French.

I wonder where Aurélie is now.

She has probably married a lawyer and taken his name.

WHEN I RETURNED TO LENINGRAD, the Physico-Technical Institute seemed unchanged. I came up the long road in a glossy white taxi; my driver wore gloves. Inside, the marble hall was almost empty; two students were disappearing up the staircase. "Helloooo!" I called, letting my voice echo. The students stared at me. Nyusya popped out of the charwomen's closet.

"Oh," she exclaimed. "Professor Termen, you're back!"

"Maybe so," I said.

I bumped into Ioffe outside the lab upstairs. "My boy!" said my former supervisor. "To what do we owe the pleasure?" He fetched the teapot and poured two mugs of tea; we sipped them standing. I told stories of my travels and he marvelled. "Rutherford himself!" he said. "What an age this is."

Later I found Sasha in his office, scowling into a book.

"Toc toc," I said, instead of knocking.

He looked up. I saw his gaze change, lengthening, sharpening, as he recognized me. "If it isn't our Wandering Dutchman," he said. "Are you finished your gallivanting? Back for some work?"

"It's good to see you," I said.

Sasha sniffed. His tall body was hunched over his book, almost protective. "How's my sister?"

"She's marvellous," I said.

He perused the page, then looked back at me. He seemed about to say something; but he did not open his lips. He shook his head, then finally said, "Do you wonder, Lev, whether the thing you're after is worth it?"

I scratched the back of my hand. "Doesn't everybody wonder that?"

Sasha smirked. It was as if I had said precisely what he expected me to say. He shifted in his chair and raised his chin. "No," he said.

IN DECEMBER 1927, Pash and I came to America on a ship called *Majestic*. The crossing was 13 days long. In a way, I had never been so free, not even at home. Here I was on the surface of the Atlantic Ocean, trapped in a small floating city, and treated like a movie star. "Go where you please, Dr Termen"; "Visit when you like, Dr Termen"; "To what do we owe this pleasure, Dr Termen?" When I stepped onto the bridge, every officer rose to his feet. The *Majestic* was like a maze with a thousand friendly exits: Lo, the kitchens! Aha, the map room! Look, here's where they keep the pets!

I did not know what to expect in the United States. I thought I would have to be on the lookout for Apaches. But I was also worried that eight weeks was not long enough to accomplish my mission. Pash did not wish to squander any time. Squared in stained red wing chairs, we sat beside the *Majestic*'s steamed fish buffet. Ostensibly my secretary, actually my supervisor, poring over lists of officials, academics, scientists, captains of industry, he quizzed me in whispered rapid fire:

"Arthur Feuerstack?"

"Director at G.E."

"Bert Grimes?"

"Regional director for Westinghouse."

"Jack Morgan?"

"J.P. Morgan & Co."

"Jimmy Walker?"

"Mayor of New York."

"Sergei V. Rachmaninoff?"

At this I laughed. "Genius."

Pash and his employers wanted me to slip like a hand into America's industrial pocket. The international press was already celebrating my discoveries: I simply had to appear, the exotic Russian. I would woo the Yankees not only with the theremin but also with my radio watchman, new television prototypes, any invention that caught their magpie eyes. While I collected invitations, Pash would secure patents, ink contracts, launch corporations, and generally sign so many deals that his colleagues would have a permanent channel in and out of the USA, a passage for smuggling sheaves of industrial secrets. As a proud patriot I'd accepted this mission without hesitation. But I had other concerns, too. That is: scientific discovery, exchanges of knowledge, meetings of minds. Also, a small but persistent thought had wormed its way into my head at a Paris press conference, when a little man in an olive jacket raised his hand and asked: "Do you imagine a theremin in every home?"

It was a beguiling idea. Consider the public good that could result. Around the world millions of workers who are fascinated by music are demoralized by the challenges of traditional instruments. Little is intuitive about the keys on a clarinet, the fretless neck of a cello. But the theremin! There is an innate simplicity to it. The closer your hand to the tall antenna, the higher the pitch; the farther away, the lower the pitch. Because it trusts the worker's own senses, not the knowledge locked away in the lessons and textbooks of the elites, the theremin becomes a revolutionary device—a levelling of the means of musical production.

Yes, I imagined a theremin in every home; not just the billions of new songs that would sing out, but the realization of millions of Americans, Englishmen, Spaniards, Siamese: *If we can do this, what else can we free people accomplish?*

Businessmen often point out that a theremin in every home would make me very rich. I am not a businessman. Money has never been a motivation.

I SPENT MUCH OF MY FREE TIME on the *Majestic* in the bowels of the ship. The engines of the vessel were not just marvels of engineering but finessed, subtle, ingenious marvels of engineering. Some of humanity's most agile thinkers had devoted decades to these behemoths, honing their components, increasing their efficiencies, and these are no wristwatches: they are huge! They haul small cities across seas.

Amid the steamy machinery, I was also able to hide from Pash and his damned quizzes. He was conspicuous down there, too big and lumbering, a giant jammed into an expensive Moscow suit. He made the men with coal dust on their faces scowl.

There were others I wished to avoid as well. At first I was happy to put up my feet in the first-class lounge and speak with fellow guests. The marvellous cellist Pablo Casals was on board, as was Jan Szigeti, the pianist from Lublin. We spoke about Tchaikovsky, acoustics, and standing ovations. But Szigeti became a nuisance. He followed me like a pet, standing too close, smelling of the saltwater he showered in. Smitten with my peculiar brand of celebrity, he wanted my opinion on all sorts of matters, from the crescent rolls at breakfast to the best makes of typewriter.

It was our own fault, really, Pash's and mine. As I have said, my English was then still very weak. So as we began to receive messages by wireless from America, we required a translator. Szigeti volunteered. There we were in the first-class lounge, chattering beside trays of steamed salmon, the wireless operator's transcripts clutched in Szigeti's puffy paws. He read them out to us. They all began with the words *Professor* or *Dr Theremin*; then they proceeded with several compliments; then a proposal—usually to do with a private party, at a chalet or on an island or at a "darling little apartment"; and finally, a figure. The lowest of these was $500, the highest, $6,100. As Szigeti converted from dollars to rubles, his eyes popped out of his head. "These are famous families!" he told us. "The Pittsburgh Clarks have a swimming pool the size of Slutsk!"

I found these invitations vaguely horrifying. I did not wish to privilege the privileged. I wished to remain as I was, and proudly so: a representative of the scientific community, and of the people of Russia.

But Pash was drawn to these offers like a magnet to a lockbox. It wasn't just the lure of the greenback; it was those sterling American names. With bovine Szigeti before us, we argued in glances: Pash keen, me dull. When Szigeti was elsewhere, we were more forthright. In those days I was still sometimes able to sway my minder, to persuade him he should listen to me. I leaned on sheer pragmatism. I told him we needed to play the long game, bore any suspicious Americans with our guileless communist chastity. "We mustn't look too eager," I said. "We have to hide our appetite for Fords, Victors, Rockefellers." I argued for us to keep to our plan, first demonstrating the theremin for my fellow scientists, academics, musicians, and a handful of journalists. After that, for the public at large. Finally—when we'd proven our priorities, cast off suspicion—"Then, Pash, you can go have a look at the Pittsburgh Clarks' pool."

Over the course of two late-night conversations, murmuring from spring-bed bunk to spring-bed bunk, I persuaded him. Thereafter, our audiences with Szigeti were less strained. The pianist translated the offer; I feigned indifference; Pash shrugged his giant shoulders; and only Szigeti, stammering, counted the zeroes.

THE ENGINE ROOMS ALSO provided a private place to do my kung-fu exercises. As sifu told me, my first week: *practise once a day, more will do no harm.*

He had not seemed surprised when I appeared again at his kwoon, two months after stumbling in with Sasha. There was no concern in his face; he came over casually. He watched me watching the sparring students—only three there that day. "You want to learn?" he said finally.

"I think so."

"You seem you think a lot."

It was partly the violence crashing through Leningrad in those days. It was partly the desire for physical activity: an order I could bring to my body. It was partly the grace of those fighters, their limbs that moved in deliberate lines. I wanted order, I wanted grace. I wanted to pass like a wind through any tempest.

So I began coming to the kwoon five or six times a week. I learned how to stand; I learned how to exhale. Sifu taught me the first form, "Little Idea," a sequence of gestures that seem like magic, summoning motions, not like any kind of combat. I stood with Lughur and Yu Wei and repeated the movements, repeated and repeated them, becoming taller, becoming clearer, ten thousand tiny refinements. Sometimes sifu called up a student, his birthmark glowing in the lantern light; five seconds of contest and then the simplest shift of weight, sifu pivoting his hips, a figure sent sprawling.

I improved. My body became lighter and stronger. I did push-ups beside the radiating stove. I squatted with Yu Wei, drinking tea, hearing tales of Peking. I laughed with Moritz, who had begun studying kung-fu during the war, when he was stationed in Tsingtao. "Even the Chinese monks know how to fight," he said. I couldn't visit the kwoon as often when I began travelling, but still I went. Sifu taught me the second form, "Sinking the Bridge," with its pivots and kicks. He taught me the third form, "Darting Fingers." He taught me as though I was the most fitting student, a natural son, and I left coins behind, in the box by the door.

Aboard the *Majestic*, travelling to America, I tried to maintain my practice. If Pash was out late or up early, I could use our cabin to run through the first and second forms. But usually I skipped down the ladders and across the catwalks to practise in a corner of the aft hydraulics chamber, an area the engine men nicknamed the "gym." Several of them were enthusiastic body-builders (admittedly, all bodybuilders are enthusiastic). They planted themselves beside the hydraulics chamber's heaving silos, feet flat on the grille, and lifted things: boxes, metal struts, barrels of lard. I worked beside them. It was easy to be self-conscious: I was a paid passenger, smaller than the strongmen, greaseless. I was also the only martial artist. And yet as soon as I slipped into horse pose, my insecurities fizzed away like vapour. There we were, shoulder to shoulder: sailors with sacks of coal raised over their heads, the scientist from Leningrad punching his wing-chun one-inch punch. It was hot. We sweated.

I stripped to my underpants before the third form, darting *biu jee*. Sometimes the space was too crowded to make many movements, but this was all right, this I embraced; the student needs new challenges. In the bowels of the *Majestic* I tried to breathe like a child.

Nevertheless, I had to come out sometimes, for messages, for meals, and, alas, most frequently, to be sick. At regular intervals I climbed up from the engine rooms, scurried down the aft corridor, flung open a door, and vomited into a toilet. Szigeti always seemed to be standing watch. As soon as my head poked up from the stairwell he would be over me: briny, excited, eager to talk. I'd trundle past him, breathing sideways, feeling every swaying slow motion of the ship. I kneeled by the porcelain. MADE IN TORONTO, it said. Szigeti stood quietly outside, leaning his head against the closed door, speaking in the tone of a lover. "Are you all right, Lyova?"

"Yes," I murmured.

Sometimes I would come out and he would be gone, and the only sign he had been there was the glass of seltzer water he'd left for me, gurgling, sad and alive.

NOW IT IS ELEVEN YEARS later and I am on a different ship, the *Stary Bolshevik*, and here too the waves fall and lift. I once proposed a device that would ameliorate a great boat's sway, balancing the bobbing seas, a sort of unbobber, but I could not find anybody to finance the prototype.

I am being taken back to Russia. Where once I roamed the *Majestic*'s decks, now I sit in a sealed cabin, its door locked from the outside. The ship's roster pretends I am the ship's log-keeper. Thus: I keep a log. This is a Skylark Mk II typewriter, made in

Saint Paul, Minnesota, a place I once visited. Under a red sky, I played Rimsky-Korsakov's "Song of India." The applause was like a net of fish being drawn from the brine.

When I was last atop the Atlantic, I imagined New York as a single row of gold and brass buildings, a panel of architecture nestled against the shore. Beyond these buildings—desert, cowboys, Indians. Ten thousand miles of sand, spurs, and feather headdresses. I was not seeking love or fortune, just a new frontier, just open country for young inventions, just a long, clear course to serve the Revolution.

In the end I found much more than that, and less.

WE LANDED IN NEW YORK on December 20, 1927. There were photographers, newsmen, a quartet of harpists. The harpists and the newsmen did not get along. At every angelic strum, the journalists' grimaces deepened, like retraced drawings. They shouldered past the musicians, blocking their view, blocking my view of them—and I was eager to see them, the Queens and Brooklyn harpists, the first American women on whom I had ever cast my eyes.

Of course I had no idea why there were harpists playing for us. The winds blew harshly from Ellis Island and we were all shivering as we left the ship, tucked into coats and hats. I had expected to go quietly to a car but instead—this small crowd. People yelling my name, yelling questions in squawky New York accents. Camera flashes going off. I was shocked. I was delighted. I strained to see the harpists. I had no idea Rudolph Wurlitzer had hired them to butter me up; I assumed that in America, harpists greet every ship. It was only later, plunging into a lunch at the Grove, also paid for by Wurlitzer, that I found out he was responsible. In his coughing Germanic English he said he had read an article about me, an interview in London, in which I spoke of my love for the harp. I have no idea what he was talking about. I have no love for the harp. "You spoke with such fine *arteeculation*, Dr Theremin," he said. He coughed. "You were like a *deeg*neetary for science."

He wanted a demonstration, of course he did; he wanted to license the theremin for his company. He had papers in a croco-dile-skin attaché, ready for me to sign right then and there. But I didn't; of course I didn't. I gave Pash a pre-emptive glare. I wanted to wait and see. I wanted to speak with other Yankee gentlemen. Perhaps things would have gone differently if I had signed with Mr Wurlitzer. Perhaps there would be a theremin in every home. He said he wanted to introduce me to Thomas Edison, "the Theremin of America!" At the Grove, 10:30 in the morning, he ordered a steak (well done).

One more recollection of our arrival: as we crossed the gang-plank to the pier, I could see the covered rows of the West Street Market, tables piled with sweet potatoes, buckets of oats, fish on ice. Men stood smoking. Horses waited. I gazed at these first tableaux of New York City and Pash gazed too, both of us new-comers, awed and curious. I glanced at my companion and abruptly I saw him darken, straighten, not because of me but because of something he had seen. Pash was suddenly more like himself. He stared out past the journalists, the musicians, to where the tugboats were docked, scuffed and beetle-like. A figure in a slate-grey trench coat stood on the timber pier, in the boats' wide shadows. He was tall. He was almost motionless. He looked as if someone had placed him there. Through binoculars, he watched us.

"Who is that?" I murmured.

Pash continued down the gangplank. It did not seem as if he was going to answer me. He put his hands in his pockets and lowered his head. I followed. "Pash?"

He looked back over his shoulder. "The enemy."

I HAD MY DEBUT on January 24. I performed in the Plaza Hotel's ballroom for scientists, academics, journalists and the rich. Many of the attendees' names were familiar from Pash's quizzes: Edsel Ford, Charles S. Guggenheimer, Vincent Astor. I spent much of the evening hiding from Szigeti behind piles of oysters, wedged into corners by Mr Downes from the *Times* or Mr Klein from the *Evening Post*. At the demonstration, Sergei V. Rachmaninoff and Arturo Toscanini sat in the same row, and my eyes were drawn to the composers' faces. These faces were grim. I watched them as I played Schubert's "Ave Maria," Offenbach's "Musette." From all around—gasps, murmurs, applause. But Rachmaninoff and Toscanini did not smile, did not yawn. They were imagining, I am certain, the chopping and splintering of ten thousand cellos, violins, and trumpets, rendered obsolete by the theremin's ethereal tone.

Later, outside the ballroom, the composers greeted me like an old friend. Rachmaninoff called the performance "singular." Toscanini said it was "magnificent." Yet in both men's voices there was this faint faraway tremor, the shiver of men who are shaking hands with their executioner.

I spent much of the next three months on tour: deep winter in Cleveland, Akron, Philadelphia, Detroit, Chicago. Back to New York, where I removed my mittens and made my first appearance at Carnegie Hall. For every demonstration, I brought three or four different devices as well as the Y-shaped loudspeakers

I call the cypresses, for their shape. I usually began with an introduction to electric conductivity, passing current through solutions in large crystal bowls. Charged with electricity, the acid chromate changed from summer orange to emerald green; the tourmaline pink permanganate solution went instantly as clear as glass. My apothecary vials were like a jeweller's cache.

I also rigged up a basic music-stand theremin whose antennas are hidden within the stand itself, invisible. (Although the instrument's sensitivity is dramatically reduced, it's an elegant illusion.) I brought my illumovox, with its spinning wheel of coloured slides, and set it beside an electric lantern at the foot of the stage, tilted up like a footlight. When connected to a theremin, it responds according to movements around the pitch antenna. As the music changes, the illumovox whirs, colour wheel spinning, and throws different shades of light onto the player's face. The low notes are bathed in burgundies, the highs in glimmering grass greens.

Throughout this early tour, I was frustrated by one unavoidable fact: there were just two thereminists in all of North America—Pash and me. We would roll into town with a small truck full of devices and yet I was forced to work with traditional accompanists—pianists and string quartets. The music was fine, certainly, but I was hampered by a lack of human resources. Pash's itinerary did not allow me to pause and recruit theremin pupils, let alone to train them.

He planned it this way, I think, because he liked being on stage. Pash was a manic-depressive spy, shunning and craving the spotlight. He could spend all week slinking in alleyways, in telephone boxes, but come Friday night he would put on his tuxedo and stride into the clouds of applause. He would introduce himself as Julius, or Yuri, or George, or Goreff, or Goldberg. I still called him Pash. Depending on whom we were speaking to, he was variously my business partner, my assistant, my friend, my cousin, or my ambiguous "liaison."

I do not know who taught Pash to play the theremin. I suppose he taught himself. The day we met, in Berlin, he already knew. I arrived in the cavernous basement of the Deutsche Oper, celestes and concertinas under heavy canvas sheets, and there was a man in a chocolate-brown suit leaning on one of my space-control devices. His grin sparkled in the electric lights. The man from the consulate didn't seem to want to touch him. "Call me Pash," Pash said. He smacked me on the shoulder. He said, "We are two men at the beginning of our careers."

He asked me if I wanted to hear a song. I did not know what to say. "What kind of song?" I said.

"Your kind of song."

"What do you mean?"

He hit the switch on the side of the theremin. *DZEEEEOOOoo.* I took a step back. I had never met another thereminist before. I had thought there were no other thereminists. He waggled his fingers like a magician.

He played Saint-Saëns's "The Swan." It was as if a stranger was lifting a pen to a clean white piece of paper and replicating my signature. I could not move. This time "The Swan" did not sound melancholy or serene; it sounded mortal. Like something that will die.

"Well?" he asked when he was finished. He had ruffled black hair, pale eyes; he played without vibrato.

I was still in shock. "When did you learn?"

"Sometime between seeing you perform for the second and third times."

I did not ask him which organization had obtained one of my devices for him to practise on. I asked him simply who he was.

"I am your temporary friend," he said.

In America, Pash was my accompanist. But behind closed doors he remained the man who gave me papers to sign, who interrogated me about whose hands I had shaken and how forcefully, who mucked about with seals and photographs and cheques and who announced one evening, just as we were polishing off two bowls of apricot compote, that he had extended our visas.

"How long?" I asked.

"Six months," he said, swallowing. "Aren't you going to thank me?"

Katia would not have thanked him. She would have stared at him with her gaze like drawing pins. Our parting had been so stilted it was almost theatre. I wondered how I would tell her I was staying. I wondered what Sasha was working on, with Ioffe, in Leningrad. I imagined them staying late at the laboratory, graphing the curves of new data, uncovering secrets of space and air, becoming closer, like father and son, while I rummaged in the pockets of America.

IN THE SUMMER OF 1928, I opened the first Theremin Studio at New York's Plaza Hotel, on West 59th Street. When I moved in, the suite consisted of a pair of bedrooms, a kitchen, a study, a dining room and a parlour. The place was full of air, well ventilated, like small gusts of wind were moving through the rooms. Everything was mauve, from the wallpaper to the lampshades. I could step to the bay window and see into Central Park, watch the swarms of insects that rose up from the woods at sunset.

Pash insisted that my home be my workspace: the personal and professional hidden behind the same heavy curtains. I used the study as my primary research site, an array of hanging wires and whirring instruments, manuals piled on the floor as they arrived from Leningrad. The dining room became our storage area: we set our plates on top of theremin cabinets, used the cypresses as a buffet. I stripped the apartment's largest closet, a walk-in pantry off the kitchen, of shelves, then nailed an etching of Leung Jan to the wall—an old man, kicking the sky. I used it as my private kwoon, twice and thrice daily, lunging into the corners where a previous tenant had piled potato sacks. I had intended to keep the parlour free for receiving guests, but its large size made it the place for real tinkering. Pash would arrive most nights before midnight, carrying an attaché case like a cake box in both hands, with papers to sign. I would be on hands and knees in the parlour, wrestling with a mechanism, grease congealing in the mauve carpet. The chandelier glimmered above us. This was America.

I slept in the second bedroom, in its king-sized bed. On one night table I had a jar filled with nuts and bolts. On the other, I had a jar of screwdrivers. The top shelf of my armoire held wire. I kept the most important electrical equipment piled under the window. Every morning I woke up, opened my eyes, and gazed at a long shelf of batteries.

SOMETIMES I AM LYING in my cot and I think: this place reminds me of the hold of a ship. And then of course I rub my eyes and remember I am indeed in the hold of a ship, and these groans are a ship's steel groans, and my dreams are the dreams of a sailor. By standing on my pillow I can look out through my porthole, onto the water. The sea is endless. When the moon is out, it leaves a path of light across the waves.

At mealtimes, a man appears at the door to my cabin. He is

the size of a polar bear, with the beard of a polar bear, the whiskers of a polar bear, a heavy white coat like that of a polar bear. His eyes are like a polar bear's eyes. Were it not for his hands, five-fingered, wide as 78s, I might well mistake him for a polar bear. But he is a man. He was born in Murmansk. His name is Red, which must be a joke.

My cabin door clangs open and Red is there, holding a tray of food. "Comrade?" he says, and I answer, amenably, "Hello, comrade." With this formality out of the way, he asks, "How are you, Lev?" And I say, "I am good, Red." He says, "Well, here is your feast." The feast is usually potatoes and meat, but it is indeed a feast. The cook of the *Stary Bolshevik* is very fine: he does much with potatoes and meat and his rack of spices. Red claims that years ago, the cook worked in the kitchen of the Czar; and so of course now he is the chef for a groaning grey cargo ship; here he feeds the workers, and me—whatever I am.

"Thank you!" I tell Red as I take the tray. He nods. "How goes the writing?" I tell him what I always do. I say: "It goes, it goes." Sometimes I ask if I might peek in on my equipment across the corridor. Every time, Red seems to genuinely consider this. His eyes roll up and to the left and in some old instinct, he bares his teeth. Then he inevitably answers, "I am sorry, no." And I smile, and he smiles.

"My regards to the captain," I say. Red nods his polar bear nod and gives me a thumbs-up. He picks up my dirty dishes with one giant dinner-plate hand. He turns and then looks back over his shoulder, as if to check whether I am following him. I am never following him; I am at my desk with my feast.

Red leaves and the door swings shut behind him. There is a simple pause, like the one in Chopin's op. 28, no. 7, a pause like the passing of autumn into winter, a pause like other pauses I have known, before Red locks the door.

❖

JOSEPH SCHILLINGER WALKED INTO the studio on a cool afternoon. I didn't hear him knock, didn't let him in. I was soldering. The blinds were drawn. I looked up and a small man was in the doorway, my desk lamp's glare reflected in his glasses. He had a slick of polished black hair and a brown bow tie. He stood as still and straight as a post.

I put down my soldering iron. "Yes?" I asked.

"Dr Theremin," he said. He smiled.

"Are you selling something?"

He rolled his eyes. "We met at the conservatory."

"Which conservatory?"

"The conservatory of music."

"Which conservatory of music?"

We were speaking in English. In Russian, he said: "The Conservatory of Music at the State University of Petrograd."

I turned the rod at the window and light broke through the blinds. It fell across Schillinger in a series of orderly bars. He wore an immaculate grey suit and fine, polished shoes. I did not remember him. He had something in each hand, palm up. "What are you holding?" I asked.

"They are for you," he said, and extended the gifts. In one hand, a tin wind-up frog. In the other, what looked like a dirty white billiard ball. He gave me the frog. "Try it," he said. I looked from the toy to him and back to the toy. I twisted the shiny crank and felt the springs inside tightening. I put the frog on the workbench and let go.

I expected it to jump across the table. It did not. For a long moment, as we listened to the mechanism coil, it did nothing at all. Then the frog turned one of its large, painted eyes around in its head, and it stared at me. Then it said, very loudly, "*Kva-kva.*"

My eyebrows jutted up in surprise.

"They have some kind of loudspeaker in there," Schillinger said.

"Remarkable."

He nodded.

I looked at the item in his other hand. "What's that?"

He put it down beside the frog. "A truffle mushroom."

"For cooking?" I asked.

He shrugged. "For whatever you like."

Schillinger became one of my first students in America. He joined Alexandra Stepanoff, a former soprano; and Rosemary Ilova, a former mezzo-soprano; and Anna Freeman, the daughter of Hoagy Freeman, who raced horses. Alexandra was dark, Rosemary was red-haired, and Anna was blonde. All had curls to the napes of their necks.

Schillinger arrived to lessons late, unapologetic, and always in a different outfit: a black jacket with black trousers and black slip-ons; a tan jacket with tan trousers and tan wing-tips; a brown jacket with black trousers and tan rain boots. Once, Frances, his wife, confided that he owned two hundred pairs of socks and alternated them according to a calculus of weather and season. She said he kept an almanac under the bed; crack the code and you could tell the date and the precise temperature from his sartorial permutation. She said this with a smile, a curl of hair at her lips. With the back of my fingers, I brushed it aside.

Later, I asked him. "Schillinger," I said, "is there an arithmetic to your fashion?"

And he said: "In sum, I try to look good."

So he arrived late, accidentally perhaps, but more likely it was deliberate. In the years to follow, when Schillinger taught classes at the studio—"New Forms in Musical Composition," "A Quantitative Analysis of Song"—he was always prompt. I think that in those early days he was simply being a gentleman, making sure that there was time for Alexandra, Rosemary and Anna to receive private instruction.

Schillinger took to the theremin with terrific speed. He was a composer, a scholar. He needed to hear something only once to be able to recall it at will. This was not true for the things he read: the *hearing* was important. Schillinger had learned English, French, Italian and German by ear, in conversation. His Hebrew— learned from a book—was apparently much worse. He was an amateur table tennis champion. He was a pacifist. He believed in a system of physical aesthetics, that music and art are governed by natural laws.

I said: "There is a formula for beauty?"

He answered: "More than one."

IN THOSE DAYS I HAD two main projects: building upon the commercial potential of the theremin and prototyping new devices. For the first, classes and demonstrations were the principal means. Show the businessmen the wonder of the "ether music" and the contracts should follow; sign the contracts and appease Pash, satisfy his employers, serve my state.

At the same time, I devised new schemas for the theremin's circuitry: lighter, simpler, cheaper. These were the adjectives that made RCA's and Wurlitzer's engineers' eyes light up. The marketing people, stocky men with fashionable eyeglasses, preferred a different word: *easy*. So Pash and I told them it was easy, my theremin: easy as apple pie. We showed them my students, lovely white arms in the air.

As the weeks passed, I began to fall for New York. I wandered through the Met, caught a foul ball at a Yankees game. I bicycled

through green, green Central Park, past chasing dogs, past rho-
dodendrons, past the lonely Indian chief in headdress, whom
the city had paid to paddle around in a canoe. I bought yellow
French's mustard and developed a taste for salted potato chips.
In a jazz club, in a cellar, I listened to a man play a drum solo.
My life's first drum solo. The whole world seemed in the process
of being rebuilt.

There seemed to be money everywhere. Pash's midnight
visits brought proposals, contracts, memoranda of understanding, but also commissions, advances, bankers' cheques. RCA
and Wurlitzer were both contending for the right to sell theremins across America. Eccentrics, heirs and engineers paid exor-
bitant sums for lessons, for recitals, for the chance to sit with
me at a table and discuss collaboration. Pash looked after my
bank account; he looked after my immigration status. Whatever
hidden business was transpiring on his side of our mission, it
was transpiring well. One night he came in with a cheap medal,
bought on 38th Street. He pinned it to my suspender strap. "For
unwitting services to the country," he said.

"I am not so unwitting as all that."

He gave me a stern look. "You are more unwitting than you
think."

Toward midsummer, I played Coney Island Stadium before
twenty thousand people. It was a Communist Party event. I
shook hands with union leaders, quipped in clumsy English.
The demonstration went well. There was nothing overtly ideo-
logical about my performance: it was political because of where
I had been born. After the concert Pash and I leaned on a wall
backstage, on either side of a drinking fountain. We were taking
this one small moment before going back into the fray. Out of
the hallway, almost invisibly out of it, came a tall man. He was
slender, handsome, in a slightly ill-fitting suit. He had a sweep of

blond hair and blue eyes like the flowers on a teacup. I thought he was a fan. "Hello," I said warily.

He was quite forward. "Pleased to meet you," he said, and shook my hand.

He nodded to Pash. "Hello," he said. "I'm sorry; I saw you onstage but I didn't catch your name."

"Yuri," said Pash. "You are?"

"Danny Finch," said the man. "I work with the U.S. government."

Instantly Pash was upright, his feet flat on the ground. His face was as relaxed as before but now the rest of him had joined the conversation. He was ready. He was alert.

"What do you do for the government?" Pash said evenly.

"I work for the State Department," Danny Finch replied.

I was confused. "Which state?"

"The State Department," he repeated.

Pash looked at me. His gaze was heavy, like an iron weight placed into my hands. I glanced back at Finch and at that moment I imagined a pair of binoculars around his neck.

Finch flashed an impulsive smile. "I wondered whether we could have a conversation sometime," he said to me. "I'm an admirer of your work."

"Perhaps." I was conscious of the way my lips touched and parted.

For one more moment, Danny Finch lingered. He seemed filled with cheerful, nervous energy, but at the same time I sensed this energy was not real; that his enthusiasm was deliberate, theatrical, and his heart was beating slowly.

"Right, well, have a good night," he said. He gave me his card.

"Goodbye," Pash said.

I added, awkwardly, "Yes."

Finch bowed his head to each of us, overly formal. He turned and disappeared around a corner. I held his business card in my hands. It read DANNY FINCH in block letters, with a Washington, DC, phone number. There was no seal or logo.

"Give me that," Pash said.

A few weeks later there was a concert sponsored by a hot-dog company at Lewisohn Stadium, to twelve thousand. Pash organized this after the Communist-run Coney Island gig, after the meeting with Danny Finch. We needed to demonstrate our bland bona fides: the Lewisohn concert was pure scientific spectacle. It was time for the theremin to become an assimilated, red-blooded American.

"As of today," Pash said, "we are done with hammer and sickle."

He joked about handing out American flags, recruiting baseball-player accompanists. I did not find this funny. He told me, "Put on your best smile." When I came out on stage, blinded by the lights, I felt as if I might be at the beach: wave upon wave of applause greeted me, like rolling surf. The New York Philharmonic sat behind me, poised. We performed Handel's "Largo," Mozart's "Ave Verum Corpus." Pash had wanted me to play "The Star-Spangled Banner."

"That's too much," I said.

"Maybe you're right," he agreed. "Just make sure everything's loud."

I had devised a series of new loudspeakers, mounted on trellises. They were deafening. Even in the stadium's open air, with dozens of string players sawing behind me, and trumpets blasting, the theremin sailed over it all. I felt as if I were commanding the winds. The audience's faces went on forever, like fields of wheat. I lifted one arm and the sound rose up; lowered it and there was a hush. Was I serving myself, or my country?

There were five minutes of sustained applause, five curtain calls, five women who fainted at the sounds of the machines.

AT SUMMER'S END I owned five tuxedos. It seemed that I was always either in my undershirt, stripping wire, or in black tie, receiving toasts. There was a queue of pupils. More and more, my visitors were dilettantes and star seekers, with little patience for practice. Women came with their husbands, balked at taking off their fur coats. I let them mill about. I stripped wire in my undershirt. I showed Alexandra Stepanoff how to hold her arms.

Gradually I collected about forty dedicated players. Although students' first lessons were always at fixed times and dates, there was an open door for advanced students. For a long time the city's only theremins were the ones that rested heavily in my apartment's master bedroom, or splayed in the parlour, so my pupils drifted in and out of the studio, practising on their own schedules, meeting to discuss scientific principles or alternate scales. They appeared at breakfast time, or after dinner. Henry Solomonoff, a gentle, doughy accountant, would often spend the whole weekend hanging around. "Where else am I gonna go?" he said, rubbing a plump cheek. "The track?"

The most dedicated was wealthy, serious Lucie Rosen, who came most days in the early afternoon and stayed until evening. She was skittish but proud; she worked alone, concentrated, careful, an auburn stole around her neck. She was gifted, but only in the way that hard work makes you gifted. Sometimes I would be in another room, plotting data or doing push-ups, and when I came in she would not even lift her eyes. She kept her kind, young gaze on the theremin's motionless antennas, her own two trembling hands.

Meanwhile, Schillinger recited his mystical poetry and lectured me on jazz. He was writing another tome about his theories of art. I tinkered with my television prototype, built cameras on a circuit, wired the rehearsal studio so I could watch my students from the bedroom. Occasionally I sat with Henry and each of us tried to write an anagram couplet, as I had been writing in Russian for years. I remember my first poem in English:

> *Wide United States,*
> *Wise and destitute.*

At night, after everyone had gone, I pushed rolls of parcel paper out over the floor, over empty snifters and packs of cigarettes, covering everything. With the day hiding under thick brown paper, distractions buried, I sketched with a short pencil, inventing things that did not yet exist. A device for ascertaining the height of an aeroplane; for finding veins of rock salt underground; a fingerboard theremin, with a neck like a cello, for bass notes. And in my wallpapered closet, surrounded by patterns of weaving ivy, I kicked, stooped, practised the *bong sao.*

And then one day I met you.

THREE

THE COLOUR OF SPRING

SNOW WAS FALLING in streamers on West 59th Street. The studio was nearly silent.

I stood at the window, looking into the flurries. Headlights flashed and went away, distant gestures of civilization. Heat lifted from the radiator. All my students had stayed home. There is weather all around us and then sometimes it interrupts our lives, as though a temporary new law has been passed.

There was a bell from downstairs.

I picked up my watch and went to the door to wait.

Dr Vinogradov wore a grey mohair coat and hat. He was accompanied by five other men, similarly dressed. They took off their hats. Two girls stood among them, shivering, heads lowered. You wore scraps of snow, as if you had been decorated by hand.

"Dr Theremin," said Vinogradov, "I hope you don't mind that I brought some guests."

"No," I said lightly.

Vinogradov was a friend of Schillinger. He taught chemistry at the New School. Often he would come to the studio and sit, eating *oreshki*, as I disassembled circuits. We would discuss metals. He loved the theremin but could not play it. Utterly tone-deaf, his hands swam aimlessly in the air.

"This is Mr Larramy," he said, "from the faculty of physics. Mr Gorev, from the Brooklyn Chamber Orchestra. Stanley Marbelcek, one of my postgrads."

We shook hands.

"Gary Kropnik. I play in the orchestra," said a man with sandy eyes.

"Trumpet," someone added.

"Mitchell Pelt. I work at ETT. I'm an old friend of Vlad's."

"Pleased to meet you," I said. I turned to you and your sister.

"And these are the Reisenberg girls," Vinogradov offered, wiping fog from his glasses.

You raised your head, Clara, and a drop of melted snow slipped down the centre of your face, from your brow to your chin.

"Nadia," said Nadia. I kissed Nadia's hand.

You cleared your throat. "Clara," you said, without moving your lips, as if the word were lifting unspoken from the floor.

You all left your boots piled by the door. They looked like kindly, resting things. I led the grand tour, scientists and musicians in socks and stockings. It was a parade of zing and spark, static electricity jumping from our fingertips. The light fixtures glowed orange and although it was noon, it felt like night. In the workshop the men admired my wire cutters, my jars of radiotron tubes. We looked upon the reproduction of Arnold Böcklin's *Die Toteninsel*, hanging above the fruit bowl. The image is of a strange island, a kind of relic, filled with tall trees; a boat approaches. "A tribute to mysteries," Vinogradov remarked. For me, the painting had always been an evocation of destinations. The places we're headed.

I took inventions from cabinets or kneeled beside them on the floor, and the group leaned in around me. The men drew on their cigarettes, Vinogradov on his pipe, while I explained the principles of conductivity and resistance. Nadia applauded my carpentry. But you were the one who seemed startled by every new idea, as if your world was not ready for it, as if I were knocking you off balance. You held my altimeter in the air and then lowered it to the ground. We all watched the needle flicker in your hands. Clara, you had such brown eyes.

We came to the theremins. New models, old models, models hidden in music stands or cabinets or bare on the carpet like dismantled engines. I blew sawdust from box tops, polished glass dials with a frayed sleeve. I had a keyboard prototype, with just two keys. Gorev played it, slipping back and forth between the two notes, as I calibrated a regular theremin. It sounded like two kettles, you said, side by side. "You mean like a viola," joked Kropnik. I didn't laugh but you did, a laugh like a tumbling kite.

Nadia was the first to try. She stood before the theremin's cabinet with me opposite, in mirrored pose. One of each of our arms was low, the other high. I leaned forward and flicked a switch. We could feel the buzz, the electromagnetic fields, the instrument's tiny stormy thrum. I brought one hand in toward the pitch antenna, showing Nadia how to proceed. She followed. *DZEEEEOOOoo*, said the device. You all jumped. Mitchell Pelt began to giggle. The theremin warbled with the nervous gestures of Nadia's hand. "Well, listen to that," someone said. I indicated she should mirror me and guided her through a very shaky "Frère Jacques." She was smiling wide but her eyes were serious. I could feel her frustration at the instrument's sensitivity, its jumpy vibrato. She was a pianist: she was used to pure, chosen notes. You sat in the corner, by the wall, with your legs folded beneath you.

Nadia motioned to you to join her but you shook your head. Kropnik pushed off from his chair and they tried playing together, he and Nadia. He interrupted her high note with a low, trembly bass. She rolled her eyes at him. You were smiling.

Nadia went to sit down beside you. She said: "This is a remarkable invention."

"It really is, professor," you said.

I asked you to call me Leon.

Gorev tried playing, then the rest of the men. Vinogradov played a rough version of "Jingle Bells," his tongue between his teeth, the rhythm unmistakeable but every note wrong. You got up, then, tucking a curl of brown hair behind your ear. The theremin greeted you. You held your hand in the air and it was a perfect D. I wondered where you came from, Clara Reisenberg. Then you moved your hand, sliding between notes, trying to poke out a melody but lost in glissando. Almost immediately you stepped away. "I would need to practise," you murmured.

I was going to say: "Come practise," but you said: "Please play something, Leon."

I played "The Swan." I remember the early twilight, the way certain windows were frosted, others steamed up, and others clear. Outside the glass, the blizzard was infinite and slow. I remember breathing, and seeing you all breathing, chests rising and falling, under the shelter of my roof. I remember our shadows slanting by the lamps, and touching. My hands passed through the air and I looked at you, just a girl. Already, I knew: You were so many things. I tried to make the room tremble. I tried to make it sing. I think it sang.

IN CERTAIN NEW YORK CIRCLES, you and your older sister were a sensation that winter. The Reisenberg girls, who emigrated from Lithuania as children; now 17 and 24, on violin and piano. I went with Schillinger to see you at Peveril Hall. The tickets said 7:30 but the concert must have begun at 7:00; the aisles were criss-crossed with latecomers and ushers. In the tumult of our arrival I did not look at the stage until we were seated, my gloves folded on my lap, my hat on my knee. You were in a spotlight, violin on your hip. Nadia was playing a solo. You listened to her with perfect patience. You were so serious, slim and pale, with almond-shaped eyes and a fighter's round jaw. You were always dry-eyed, playing music, listening to music. Nadia's cascades rang and jumped, scattered like skipped stones in the quiet of the hall. Ushers were still escorting latecomers like will-o-wisps, led by glimmers. I could not see the shape of your legs under your black dress, the arc of your ribs. You held your violin by the neck, its curves in silhouette.

When it was your turn, you played Mendelssohn. Your bow was a dragonfly. I felt my heart skimmed, skimmed, skimmed.

Schillinger turned to me and said, "They really are quite good."

AFTER THE CONCERT we followed Vinogradov backstage; three lumberers descending the short spiral staircase, hats in hands. The reception area was full of performers, patrons, students from the music school. Young people jostled together, spilling cups of peach punch. There were finger sandwiches. I watched a husky older man, pinioned in his tux, nervously opening and closing a set of opera glasses. Schillinger and I stood together until he went to get a slice of lemon cake. Gradually I found myself in a circle of music tutors from the institute who were gossiping and laughing but squinting as they laughed, as if hiding the fact that nothing was actually funny. I drifted toward a group of society women who were asking questions of a luthier. "Cherry wood," I heard him say.

Then I came across you, in a corner, among a ring of strangers. I was beside a girl in a translucent pink dress. Two young men were wearing sweaters and bright white trousers. A laugh had just subsided. Everyone was staring at the floor, at the circle of shoes, as if there were something important there. I imagined we had uncovered a turtle or a shard of clay pot.

After a long pause someone said, with a smile, "This party is dead anyway."

I could not tell if these were old friends or new ones. I tried to divine it from the way the bodies tilted toward each other and away. Someone recognized me and I remember I gave a quick little bow, my hands behind my back, and when I straightened you were looking at me with wry concentration, as if you couldn't tell if I was a joke or a riddle.

"Do you live in Moscow?" someone said.

"In Leningrad."

"Is that Petrograd?"

"Actually he lives at the Plaza," you said.

They all laughed. Was this funny? Everyone seemed so young. You set off a ping-pong of jokes and conversation, boys who held forth on rafting down the Mississippi River, a girl telling the story of a teacher who distrusted light bulbs. You stood with your head tipped very slightly forward, eyes flicking between faces, a narrow smile that would flash into place and then disappear. You were generous with your attention but not with your approval; as your friends told stories I saw you stare them down, patient, waiting for the value of all that talking. And when you were delighted—when someone's story revealed something or when they spoke a truth—you became almost solemn. You let your fascination express itself as stillness, steady stillness, like a lake gone smooth. Your violin sat in its case, near the points of your shoes. Only the corners of your lips showed your sparking heart.

At a certain point I told you I'd enjoyed the concert and you rubbed your elbow, smirking, only half contented. You said, "Thank you." You nodded twice, firmly, to yourself or else to me. You said, "I'm glad." Then Schillinger came over from where he had been speaking to your parents, and I looked to where they were standing, holding plates of lemon cake, proudly surveying the room, so capably elegant in their early middle age. I thought to myself, *She is fifteen years younger than you.* I decided I should go. So I made my farewells and left.

IN 1925—FOUR YEARS AFTER I met Vladimir Ilyich Lenin (may his memory be illuminated), four years after he gave me the card with his name that is still in my pocket, three years after his stroke, one year after Petrograd became Leningrad and our leader died, and two years before I went to New York and met you, Clara—I received a curious letter.

I had already been touring the theremin for several years. Zigzagging through Russia, attending conferences, making excursions to foreign universities. I returned from a visit to Kiev and found the correspondence waiting on the table by the door. It seemed so innocuous. The exterior had a stamp and my name, typewritten. A circle of paper was concealed inside an ingenious circular envelope, about as wide as my hand. On one side of the paper was again typed LEV SERGEYVICH TERMEN. On the other, these words: GOOD WORK. There was no signature.

I remember I immediately tucked the letter away, into a drawer. Like a note from a mistress or from someone trying to collect on a debt. Family had come over for supper; my parents were sitting in the cramped parlour with Katia and my aunt Eva. Father saw something in my face. "What is it?" he said.

"Nothing," I said. "An invitation to a colloquium."

A week later, I arrived home from the lab to find a similar postcard. LEV SERGEYVICH TERMEN, it said on one side; and on the other: WE SHOULD TALK, with a Moscow telephone number.

Again I put the missive in a drawer. I went back outside. The dusk felt early. I took my bicycle and headed to the kwoon, which was almost empty. Some of the lanterns had gone out. Perhaps sifu was having supper. I took off my shoes. I stared at the portrait of Leung Jan floating above a lake. I touched my right fist to my open left hand. Another student did the same. We skipped rope and did push-ups. Sifu arrived with Yu Wei, Lughur and some other students I didn't know. They took off their shoes and touched right fist to left palm. Sifu demonstrated falling. We all fell and got up and fell again. Then we practised *chi sao*, the hand dance, standing with partners and moving, always remaining wrist to wrist, flowing and following, sensitive. But I had no sensitivity that evening. I kept losing my position. I kept seeing, in my mind's eye, my typewritten name.

That night, I called the telephone number. A woman's voice answered. She asked my name. Then a man's voice came on the line. He asked when we could meet. Two weeks later, I went to see an old man at a rented office on Nevsky Prospekt. I am certain it was not the same man I'd spoken to on the telephone.

One week after that, I met another man at a café on Sadovaya Street. These men always seemed different and the same, like dominoes. They worked for the state. They asked me questions about my work, about its commercial potential, about Bolshevism. My answers seemed to please them. I met yet another man, this one short, very short, like a doll. He met me in a train carriage at Moskovsky Station. We were the only people on the train, which idled on the track. He had a table lamp in the carriage, and a small desk, like a doll's. It was not until I left, stepping from doorway to platform, that the train pulled away. It took the small man with it. He had asked me questions in Russian, Italian, French, English and German. I had never learned any German and I told him so. He asked me about my family. "Are you close with your parents?" he asked.

"No," I answered before I knew what I was saying.

The man did not seem surprised.

"Are you prepared to travel?"

"Yes."

He said, in a voice like a circular card being slipped into a circular envelope, "We would like to offer you a new responsibility."

In Leningrad that summer I felt so alone, standing beside Katia on the tram, sipping thin stew at my parents' apartment, wandering up to the Physico-Technical Institute, where I no longer had a lab. Even attending a lecture with a pretty student, an admirer, and strolling in Alexander Garden. Children rushed by me, officials clambered into a carriage, squirrels darted, a line of soldiers filed past the flower beds. The girl said something and I thought of Katia waiting for me. The sun refused to set. All around, lives were going on. I watched water pour out from the fountain and into the drain.

The men from the government called me a beacon for the Soviet people. They called me an adept.

These were not the same sort of people who had worked under Lenin. This was a different time. Our Dear Father, Iosif Vissarionovich, boomed from the wireless sets now, and when I'd met his generals, earlier that summer, they had been interested only in whether my distance-vision technology could be implemented, immediately, at our borders. All matters were reduced to directives, simple prescriptives. *Our country needs your help*, they said. *Our country needs you to travel to Western nations, arranging demonstrations, forming companies, filing patents, inking trade agreements. These contracts will allow Mother Russia to increase its influence, to diversify its investments, to multiply its channels of information and trade.* They explained all this. These different and same men looked at me with hooded eyes. On my next trip, they said, they would send me a handler. I practised *chi sao*, watching my partner, sensing my partner, moving with his movements. I walked in Alexander Garden with the pretty student. These men asked me, "Would you like to be a hero?"

A FEW YEARS LATER I sat with Mr Thorogood from RCA as he asked, "Would you like to be a millionaire?"

He opened his attaché case and I saw that it was almost empty. It contained two copies of a contract, which he withdrew, and a dozen pens, flashing like electric components. I wondered which was his favourite colour of ink. I liked dark green. Lenin was always said to write in red. Pash used either black or blue.

I didn't sign his contract. I told him I would be in touch. I told him I was a scientist. That night, at the Plaza restaurant, I conveyed our conversation to Pash. He was cracking crabs' terracotta shells with his bare hands, sopping crabmeat in butter.

His suit looked bulkier than it used to; I wondered if he was carrying a flask, or a gun.

Pash wiped his mouth with his sleeve and put down the fractured crab. "Let me tell you something, Lev," he said, "and listen very closely."

I remembered that I did not know where this man had come from: where he was born, where he was taught, which Moscow spire held the safe that held the dossier that held his real name. Whenever we dined, Pash's right hand did not stray far from his knife. "Thorogood asked you if you would like to be a millionaire?" Pash looked at me, dead straight. "Yes, you would."

ONE MORNING A CARD without a stamp arrived for me at the Plaza Hotel. LEON THEREMIN, it said. I slit open the envelope and found a printed drawing of an elephant, in pen and watercolour. The elephant seemed friendly and wise but very old, very tired, with hundreds of lines in his skin. In his trunk he held a lemon.

On the reverse of the card, below date and details, it read:

"DON'T FORGET!!"
YOU ARE CORDIALLY INVITED TO A LEMONADE SOCIAL
MARKING THE EIGHTEENTH BIRTHDAY
OF
MISS CLARA REISENBERG.

R.S.V.P.

I tapped the card against the counter, then found I was picking up the telephone receiver.

Our conversation began like this:

"Is that Clara?"

"Yes, who is this please?"

"This is Leon Theremin."

What did my name say to you? Did it speak merely of science, engineering, and that snowy afternoon? Did it say something else?

You said: "How is all that electricity doing, Leon?"

I could not attend the party. I had an appointment with RCA that same day, slated to go until dinner. Perhaps I could have cancelled it but really I was not sure what to do, at that moment, talking to you on the telephone. I hesitated. I invited you to tea, the day after. A tardy birthday. "Sure," you said. We both put down our phones.

The elephant seemed to be staring at me.

There were other girls, then. I don't mean Katia. I felt young, arriving in America. I felt new. There were flirtations, exchanges of affection. Discreet ministrations. My valentines were associates, students, chance acquaintances. One drowsy evening with a friend's ginger wife. I write this not to embarrass you, or out of a need to confess, but to say that in the week between that phone call and your visit to my apartment, every other face disappeared, at once, from my thoughts. It was as if I had plunged my head into a bucket of seltzer: everything fluttered up and then was gone.

On your eighteenth birthday, a collection of friends and family visited your parents' home for lemonade. You played charades and musical chairs. There was dancing. I am given to understand that Schillinger performed an air on his Arabian *mijwiz*. I was not present. I was with Pash and Mr Thorogood and later I was alone in my workshop, holding a screwdriver between my teeth, working on your birthday present.

You arrived at two the next day. I wondered if you would come alone but there you were with your mother and also a gang of friends, girls and their dates, all crowding together in my doorway. "Look at that," I said clumsily.

You smiled. You said: "Hi, Leon."

I had put on a new Paul Whiteman record. The maid had cleaned the carpets. The blinds were raised. My studio seemed like a chamber at the top of a tall tower. All the vases were filled with tulips. There was a telescope by the window, a large jade plant, a crate filled with piano keys, a tapestry in lace that depicted the makeup of an atom. Your group gathered twittering around each object. You seemed older than your friends. This time you were more careful in your admirations. You gazed at a childhood photograph of me, an old portrait from Leningrad. I was eleven or twelve, with a volume of the encyclopedia wedged clumsily under one arm. White stockings were hiked to my knees. In the camera's long exposure my face seemed ghostly, already distant.

"What were you scared of?" you asked.

"Nothing," I said.

You found Schillinger's frog and it chirped in your hand. You gave the happiest laugh. The lock of hair slipped from behind your ear.

"Have it," I said.

"You mean it?"

"Happy birthday."

I called everyone into the parlour. On a table sat a round, iced cake. I had supervised its assembly in the Plaza Hotel's kitchen. Now I stepped behind the rose-coloured confection and twisted together two trailing wires, closing the circuit. Your mother watched me as one would watch a magician, waiting. I moved away; I invited you to read the cake's inscription;

I felt a nervous thrill. You stepped closer. Beneath the strata of buttermilk, sugar and chocolate, a mechanism invisibly stirred. A motor whirred. The oscillator in the buried radio watchman sensed your body's electrical capacity, sent electricity along a wire into an illuminating vacuum tube, which set an axle spinning. The top layer of the cake swivelled clockwise on its axis, all the way around, a pastry shell on a hidden platform, a secret door—and revealed a copper birthday candle. The flame lit by itself, darted and danced. It wished.

"Oh!" you said. You clasped your hands, you bent, you blew it out.

"Happy Birthday," we sang.

It was you I felt in my electromagnetic field.

TWO MONTHS went by.

I REMEMBER I NOTICED a quarter on the pavement. I bent and picked it up, held it glinting in the lights of the Great White Way. There I was on Broadway, in the spring of 1929, a shining silver coin between my fingers. I slipped it into my pocket. I began to walk. I bumped into you.

"Pardon me," I said, shaking my head clear.

You tugged at the collar of your sky-blue coat. "No, no, it was my fault." You bent forward to walk on; and stopped. "Dr Theremin?"

I blinked. "Clara," I said.

"Hi."

"How are you?"

A smile grew on your face. "I'm good."

I had seen you only once since your birthday, at an anniversary party for the Kovalevs. You were with your parents. We waved across the room. The two of us had never had a private conversation. I would be out in the city, waiting for an elevator or passing through Central Park and I would recollect suddenly the angle of your gaze. I would wonder whether you ever thought of me. Now we stood facing each other on the sidewalk and you had swinging pearl earrings. I saw the slightest tremor in your brown eyes.

"It's a pretty night," I said.

"Yes."

Broadway is no place to stand still. We were being bumped and bounced by the throngs. Cars roared past, honking; men shouted after other men; you could hear the distant crash of trains. Signs shone over and around us, projected hazy words onto our raincoats. BARBERSH read the red letters on your left sleeve. A neon dollar sign hid in the gloss of my right shoe.

"Would you like to get a coffee?" I asked.

"Could we make it a drink?"

On the boat to New York, I had been told the city had no nightlife left. This was the scuttlebutt from the bankers and salesman aboard the *Majestic*. They raised toasts of vodka, burgundy and calvados, told me to sip the good stuff while I could. "Prohibition," complained a luggage baron from Tallinn, "has ruined the merry USA."

"It's not Prohibition," grumbled a jeweller from Omsk. "Drunks aren't afraid to break the rules. The trouble is *enforcement*."

All of their favourite bars were shuttered: a speakeasy discovered in springtime would disappear by the time they returned in fall. I am not much of a drinker, but it saddened me to imagine a city without taverns, without the free sound of a bottle being unstoppered.

But neither Prohibition nor enforcement had banished liquor from New York. Manhattan came alive after dark. I could stand at my apartment window and watch couples pirouetting into the street, into taxis. I could see the streaming lights of cabs heading east and west, and in the wee hours north, to Harlem. I had been in New York two months when I asked my new friends about drinking. Henry Solomonoff scribbled down the number for a bootlegger. "Cheap!" he said. "Rum, gin, rye. Seven bucks a bottle."

"But where do you go for . . ." I hesitated.

"For a good time?" Solomonoff laughed. "Get your coat."

Around Broadway, the speaks were tucked just down, just around, folded behind shopfronts. At some, visitors rang a bell and showed their face, or placed their hand flat against a frosted-glass window. At other doorways one had to murmur a pass-phrase. Although Schillinger kept a notebook of secret codes, I was not so thirsty that I required an almanac. I knew several spots, here and there, and in with my other papers I carried six or seven members' cards, but mostly I smiled, and I was polite, and my accent refuted any suspicion that I was a cop.

We went down into a place without a sign. Light fell from the windows in gauzy shafts. The bartender was dark and extremely handsome, but slight, as if proportioned for the dreams of a twelve-year-old girl. His name was Tony. Most bartenders' names were Tony. This one felt more like an Anthony. There were two other couples already there and a table with four men in suits. Schillinger called this place "The Blue Horse," for the murals that curved and galloped around the bar's other fittings. The images were dreamlike, surreal, visions from a Krazy Kat cartoon. A blue horse reared up at the left side of the bar, its mane like the tossing of the sea. You ordered a gin fizz, Clara, and I took a rum and Coke. The glasses were cold. We drank in near silence.

After a little while you asked whether I had baked any cakes recently. There were very fine creases at the corners of your eyes. You rested your elbow upon the table and your chin upon the heel of your hand and I noticed the curve where your jaw met your neck. I imagined your violin cradled there. I imagined snowflakes touching the wide white courtyard that lay outside our windows, growing up.

"I have been drawing," I told you. "These days, it is all drawings."

"I didn't know you drew."

A drawing was in my jacket pocket, folded into eighths. I took it out, opened it in the space between us. The paper crackled.

"The RCA Theremin," you read aloud from the corner.

"Shhh," I said, with false gravity. "These things are secret."

We looked at the arcs and contours and corners of my schematic. The table was painted with wet circles where our drinks had sat. Shreds of rubber eraser still clung to the page. This was a plan for the principal cabinet of the space-control device, the proposed RCA model. I would turn it in to the RCA engineers, this drawing and others like it, and they would take out their rulers and adding machines and materials books and spec manuals, and they would build prototypes, and ring up factory foremen, and perhaps they would even fly to hardwood forests, to nickel mines, to rap on tree trunks and chip at ore, evaluating whether all these things could be adequately smelted, sawed, and assembled into America's new favourite musical instrument.

You sipped your fizz. "If you were trapped in a snowy

wilderness, just you and a winter coat and a cabin full of electrical equipment—would you be able to build a theremin? Just with this plan?"

"If nothing were missing?" I asked.

"If nothing were missing."

"Then yes," I said.

YOU WERE IN THE CITY to meet an accompanist. He had ended the rehearsal early. He was young, you said, and arrogant. You were eighteen years old.

WHEN WE HAD FINISHED our drinks we went outside. The sky was a dark midnight blue, that strange nighttime blue of big cities, and it seemed so clean. Couples jostled past us, men in dinner jackets and women in dresses, hats, gold at their wrists. They were going dancing. We watched them. "Do you dance?" you said. It was just a question.

"I do," I said. I tried to speak with the same transparency. "Do you?"

Your face lit up. "Yes."

A moment passed. "Would you like to go dancing?"

You hesitated for a second. I don't know if it was because of me, or of some other beau, or the thought of your parents at home. Then your face seemed to apologize for the hesitation, and you said: "That'd be nice."

I glanced at the ground, where your feet stood beside my feet, and I thought the silly thought that in that second we were standing perfectly in our own footprints.

I took you to the Make-Believe. It had the largest ballroom in the world, a room as big as Rybinsk's town hall, the ceiling strung with paper lanterns and the walls done up in stars. We left our coats with the twins who kept the coats, I tipped the maître d', and he brought us straight to a table and we straight-away got up. For the first time in the history of the world, since the seas cooled and birds alighted in the trees, Clara Reisenberg and Lev Sergeyvich Termen danced together. There was no band at the Make-Believe—there were two gramophones and their minders, a man and a woman, a library of records visible from the floor. The couple moved back and forth across the shelves, choosing the next song. They chose swing from New York and swing from Chicago, swing from London and Paris and Montreal. We stepped together and apart, leapt, grinned. I clasped you in my arms and I threw you away.

Later, breathless, we leaned on the bar and drank long glasses of water. "Now what?" you asked. We grabbed our coats and went to the Roseland. The club was just heating up. A man tossed his partner three feet into the air. A woman slipped beneath her partner's legs and rose up like a geyser. You asked me where I had learned to dance. I told you in Leningrad, that we did not have jazz but the bands played other quick songs. You danced the Charleston and I followed. You reminded me of Katia—but just for an instant, the way the rain reminds you for a moment of a particular spring. I had been trying not to think of her, the woman who had followed me on a ship. She was in New Jersey. She was, I told myself, a million miles away.

I asked you where you'd learned to dance. You said you had always known and twirled in your skinny dress. The air seemed to whistle. I placed one hand at the small of your back and held one of yours with the other. You breathed against my chest and the source of that breath seemed so close by, rising and falling in smooth suddennesses. We were skipping ahead of our footprints. The band played a drumroll and my heart played a drumroll. You stepped on my toe. "Whoops," you said. The bandleader lifted his baton. The trumpeters premiered a rare new racket.

A little while after, you stood fanning your face with a menu. I was sweating in my suit. I couldn't tell the Roseland's painted flowers from its real ones. You put down the menu and massaged your right arm near the elbow. There was a shadow behind your eyes.

"What is it?" I asked.

"Nothing," you said. You shook your arm out and summoned a crooked grin. The grin was unpersuasive at first but then abruptly you seemed to believe it. The grin said: *Now what?* I looked around. The other dancers didn't seem real. They were paper dolls. I looked at my hands and then I looked at you.

We took a taxi to La Conga. We bought half pineapples full of juice and tipped gracious strangers' rum inside. I sipped through the straw and gazed out into the room, where the men's cufflinks were flashing in the lights. There was a woman on the little stage, backed by horns, gyrating to the flexing sax chords. She wore apples, pears and a banana on her head. My first pineapple had been at the Petrograd Agricultural Fair in 1921. My first banana had been in London, three years earlier, divided in two and served as a *split*. You had the hiccups. A man with a brush moustache was playing a pair of tall drums with the flats of his hands, sending the rhythm jumping into our shoulders and heels. We danced so hard my shoes came untied. It was not elegant, not deft, not courtly. We danced so hard my shoes came untied. I wondered if this was what it was like in Cuba. I decided that one day we should go; the two of us.

THAT SUMMER, WE MADE IT a habit. Once or twice a week I picked you up or you buzzed my door and off we'd whiz, in a taxicab or sometimes a subway car, through the rain or sunset. Perhaps I'd be tired after a long day of work, or you'd be bored, arm hurting from your hours of practice; but the moment we were side by side, looking at each other's dancing shoes, these reluctances would scatter. "To the Onyx!" we told the cabbie. "To the El Morocco!" "To the Nouveau Palais!"

We danced everywhere. We danced to Benny Goodman's band at the Philadelphia. We danced to Emile Coleman's lot at the Green Room. We danced at the Winter Garden, with its horses and clowns and circus stripes. At the Sugar Cane there were plank floorboards, hot barbecue; at the Strand roof, illicit champagne and ginger ale by the bottle. Men's jackets bulged with flasks, ladies' gin nestled against chair legs. At the Country Club we played ping-pong, we danced the Blackbottom with Belle Livingstone, luxuriant in red pyjamas, right beside us. We went to Harlem: to the Savoy, on Lenox Avenue; to the Cotton Club, where there were usherettes in pink hunting coats, and a band with a blind piano player, and coloured girls, dancing as if they had been listening to those songs all their lives. At Small's Paradise, where Charleston-ing waiters served Chinese food, the music was better than anywhere else. Negroes danced with whites as if the Revolution had come to America. We threw our partners, and caught them, and we darted and dipped and breathed hard. I felt richer than I ever had.

Sometimes we'd sit knee to knee and yell into each other's ears, through the hullabaloo. I remember your earrings dancing on your ears. I remember you told me you wanted to travel.

"Where will you go?" I said.

"I don't know," you shouted. "Anywhere, everywhere. Paris, Casablanca, Siam. Why not? I could hop on a tug to Bermuda, ride an elephant in India. I'm done school. I don't have any obligations, not really. Play some recitals, some premieres. Make some money and book a ticket to Calcutta."

"Beethoven on the Ganges," I murmured.

You leaned closer. "*What?*"

"Beethoven on the Ganges!" I yelled.

You grinned. The room was filled with happy tumult. "Or Stravinsky, or Dvořák. Wouldn't that make a scene?" You grabbed for your glass of cold something. "Where would *you* go, if you could travel?"

"Me?"

"You."

I laughed. "I came here, Clara. I'd come right here."

You clicked your tongue. "Leon, you look like you need an elephant."

Then we danced some more, circling and bumping on the floor, and there were moments in the songs when your face was merry, and moments when your face was serious, or far away.

I thought to myself:

There are twelve notes on the chromatic scale. But music is limitless.

FOR ALL OUR REVELS, there was one dance hall that we did not visit: Texas Guinan's 300 Club. We heard about it together, jammed into a cab with some friends of Schillinger's. They were stinking drunk. "How about Guinan's new place?" they said.

"Who?" I asked.

The man hiccupped. "So much for that!"

"What do you mean?" you said.

"Texas Guinan's 300 Club," mumbled the woman, "is the most extraordinary and exclusive spot in all the boroughs of New York."

"But you need an invitation to get in!" said her partner. "We figured mister Russian rocket scientist'd have one."

"No," I admitted.

The woman twisted in her seat. She dipped woozily, almost intimately, toward our faces. "It's got the best music, the best dancers, the best—everything. Live parrots." She burped. "Magnolias for sale, these Spanish guitarists who roam around. If you fall asleep the waiters blow trumpets in your ears!"

"Sounds like a good time, huh? It's the promised land," said the man. "Except the location is a *secret.*"

In the darkness of the cab you caught my eye, or I caught yours, and I decided: *I will find out where it is, and I will win an invitation from Texas Guinan, and then one day, Clara Reisenberg, when we have something to celebrate, I will take you to the 300 Club.*

I would save this pleasure; I would keep the treasure buried. We would have celebrations yet.

BY NIGHT IT WAS the foxtrot and the shimmy. By day it was deal-making. A dozen deals a week, signed with handshake and signature, with raised glass and copies in triplicate. There were rich deals and poor deals. Simple, speculative, ambitious, aggressive, convoluted and crazy deals. Some of them were big-deal deals. Some were not. We signed my soul away and then signed it right back, richer. Let RCA take the theremin: let them raise up billboards in Boston, Chicago, Detroit. "We are forming a new corporation," Pash would announce, flourishing paper, spraying ink, cracking champagne over the bow of a new entity: the Theremin Corporation, the Migos Corporation, the Theremin Patents Corporation. Corporations American, Panamanian, Canadian, real and false, shell companies and whatever hides in shells. The details were Pash's, the inventions mine. Every time I saw my handler, his silhouette seemed wider, taller, darker, as if it had been gone over in charcoal. I remember how he appeared at my door one night, when I was on my way out to see you.

"Where are you going?"

"Out," I said, cheerfully.

"Out where?"

I narrowed my eyes at him, a little mockingly. "On the town."

He didn't seem frightening, just formidable—an officer at peak efficiency. He wore a watch the colour of a Morgan dollar and a ring the colour of a Chervonet. His eyes had the glint of safety deposit boxes.

"A girl?" he asked.

"Yes," I said, and he nodded, without the slightest leer. I finished doing my tie. "Do you need me for something?"

He didn't answer. I took down my coat, put on my hat. "Pash?"

"I'll take care of it," he said.

So I left him there.

While you and I wheeled under chandeliers, I trusted Pash to take care of everything. While we whiled away our days, dreaming of dancing, he sold exclusive patent rights, licensed partial patent rights, engineered royalty payments, purchase options, dividends. The space-control theremin, the radio watchman, even my early television work—all of it split up, subdivided, sold and resold to men in windowless rooms. We jitterbugged beneath the Pirates' Den's netting and Pash wrote names in rows, and numbers in columns, and I never looked, never asked, because I was looking at and asking you.

At the Ritz-Carlton's Japanese Roof Garden, which was neither a garden nor on the roof, my pockets were stuffed with banknotes. You were at the other end of my arm. We ate gigantic Malpeque oysters and drank glasses of cold white wine. There was a gypsy guitarist. He strummed his instrument as though he was shaking a secret loose. We burst, midstep, into song.

In September, I gave you a theremin. I had painted small red flowers and small blue flowers and small pink flowers on the panels. I had drawn curlicues in gold ink. By lamplight, I had polished the antennas. I was resting against the kitchen counter as you stepped behind the device, balanced on heels, and you extended your right hand. The theremin yowled at you. You withdrew your hand. You looked at me. You extended your hand again, and again the theremin yowled. You were still looking at me. You were a violinist. You were a violinist with serious, dark eyes. I laughed at my own doggedness; your theremin stayed in a corner of my office. I took the violinist dancing.

At the end of October, America collapsed.

FOUR

TASTE THE FLOOR

IF THE APOCALYPSE COMES, I would not know. In this small steel room, in a boat, on the sea, there is no way to tell if a volcano has belched forth from under Budapest, if the waters have engulfed Venice, if the world has split in two along the line of the Greenwich meridian. Perhaps a leviathan has risen at Stockholm, or a behemoth at Lisbon, or all of Africa has melted, like crayons under a too-hot sun. I do not know. I rely on Red to bring me news. Red relies on the wireless. And if the radio goes dead? If there is a flood, an earthquake, a meteor? We would not know, bobbing here. The sirens would not wake us. The groans would not reach us. Nobody delivers the newspaper. The clouds gather, some days, and then on other days they do not. Red brings me food, and then on other days he does not. It has always been this way. This is not a military ship, strict and regimented. It is just a cargo boat travelling across the water, in which there was room to stow me.

I have not eaten in almost two days. Has Red forgotten me?

I wonder if there has been a mutiny. I wonder if there are coyotes outside my door.

IT WAS A LITTLE LIKE THIS, the 1929 Crash. I was alone in my apartment. I did not know that men in ties were leaping from Wall Street windowsills. I had begun creating the fingerboard theremin: a device that's played upright, like a sort of electric cello. I was searching for a slotted screwdriver. I had set it down somewhere and now I could not find it. I ransacked my rooms. I remember I knocked over a potted lily and then in frustration poured the rest of the soil out onto the carpet. I called down for an egg sandwich but no one picked up the phone. Finally, crazy with irritation, I marched downstairs, past the hotel's shuttered restaurant, and across the road to the hardware store, the excuse for a hardware store, the little shop on the corner that seemed to sell only brass doorknobs and nails for hanging pictures. The owner was stout, with two baby slaloms of black hair parted exactly in the middle.

"Slotted screwdriver," I said to him.

The expression on his face was one of terror and bewilderment. I did not know why.

"Is everything all right?" I asked.

He nodded. His eyes remained glazed, glazed like the patina on a porcelain fawn. "How many?" he said.

"How many what?"

"Screwdrivers."

I fixed him with my severest glower. He did not seem affected. "One," I said.

He nodded again. It was clear that something was affecting this mole-man. I couldn't tell if it was miracle or calamity. Had

he just been robbed? Was his wife in labour? I allowed my glower
to dissipate. "Please," I said.

The man found a screwdriver. He held it out to me like a
dagger. I grasped it by the end.

I paid and got the hell out of there. I went across to the bakery.
The door was locked. I rattled it. "Hello!" I called. I really wanted
an egg sandwich. I leaned my head against the door's glass. I
took a deep breath. With the screwdriver in my hand, I went back
into the Plaza Hotel, climbed the stairs to my room, let myself in.
I knelt beside a modulator and removed the mounting. I felt a
bloom of deep satisfaction. I disappeared into the afternoon.

It was nightfall when I looked up from the fingerboard theremin. The room was almost completely dark. I moved to stand
but my knees shrieked in pain; instead I hobbled to an armchair
and sat down. My eyes stung from squinting. I closed them. I
rested in the cushions. Behind my eyelids I could see the theremin revolving, doubling, connections joining.

I blinked and looked at the time. After eight o'clock. After
eight o'clock and not a single caller. Where was everybody?
Normally I would have four, six, ten visitors over the course of the
day: students, guests of students, Schillinger barging in with a
new chapter of his book. But there had been no one. My stomach
made a molten sound. I picked up the phone to ring up an egg
sandwich. Still no one was picking up. I sighed. I recalled the tin
of potato chips I had finished the night before. I hauled myself
to my feet and to a calendar, nailed to a closet door. Was it a holiday? Was it Presidents' Day? Armistice Day? American Easter?
Was it Halloween? Halloween was in October; that holiday with
carved squash and fancy costume. But it was not yet Halloween.
It was Tuesday, October 24. Outside my window, New York City
appeared normal. It was black and white and violet.

Pash came in then, without knocking. He had an enormous briefcase, the largest briefcase I had ever seen him carry, big enough that I could have curled up inside it. His face was drawn. He stopped at the edge of my living-room carpet. The rug was covered in earth and the remains of a potted lily. "What happened here?" he said.

"I have no idea."

We looked at each other.

"Did something happen out there?" I asked.

Pash showed me his teeth. It was a gesture of exasperation. He came toward me. He put down his briefcase. He snapped on the radio.

I stood and I listened.

THE CHANGES WERE HARD to categorize. Most of my students stayed away only for a couple of days. Henry Solomonoff started to visit even more often. Rosemary Ilova never came back.

I rang your house on Saturday afternoon. "She's not at home," your father said. He had the tone of a weary adventurer: respectful, but tired. "Would you like to leave a message?"

"For Clara?"

"Yes, for Clara."

"Tell her it was Leon."

"Which Leon, please?"

"Leon Theremin."

"Ah," he said. "The scientist."

"Yes."

"Will there be anything else?"

I drew a circle on the pad beside the phone. "Does one say 'Happy Halloween'?"

"What?" your father said. "You mean on Halloween?"

"Yes."

"I suppose."

I put down the pencil. "Please also wish her a happy Halloween."

I was restless. I went out into the city.

I wanted to do something with myself, with my body.

At first I thought maybe I was going to a club. Maybe I would go dancing, with strangers, while the markets shuddered. I walked south, downtown, but as I passed corner after corner I kept on walking, kept on into downtown, continuing under the sagging awnings and blurs of electric light, through clouds of steam; I found I was walking beyond midtown, beyond the nightclubs, past empty restaurants, darkened banks, old men dozing in cars; past Union Square, where a drunkard had just staggered out of the fountain; all the way to Chinatown, where many of the doorways were painted gold or red, and the people moved with a different tension in their shoulders, in their hips, as if they needed to stay unfamiliar to each other.

Above a stall selling jade trees I saw a sign that read WING-CHUN KUNG-FU.

Almost before thinking about it, I slipped inside.

In Leningrad, the kwoon had always seemed slightly illicit—the hideout for a group of bandits, a Far Eastern cult. There was less mystery here. The stairwell was coal-black stone, swept clean. The upstairs door was smoked glass, with a painted Chinese symbol. I went through and found a wide, square loft, high-ceilinged. The gym felt like a workshop, like a factory. A line of men repeated a sequence of low kicks. Two older students stood wrist to wrist, practising the hand dance. Behind them a group of children passed through the first form, half-expert, half-clumsy, facing a chrysanthemum shrine. The air smelled of frying oil and cut flowers. There were Negro students, Caucasian students, a tall turbaned Sikh talking to a boy who stood up to his chest.

The man who was their sifu saw me by the entrance. He approached me slowly, as if he wanted to give me enough time to examine him, or to prepare my greeting. He was older than my Leningrad sifu, older than my parents, old in the manner of the toothless old men who spent all day at the barber's. Only he wasn't toothless, he wasn't stooped; apart from a small paunch, his body was a straight line, a strong torso under drooping cheeks.

"Hello," I said, my voice vanishing in the room.

He nodded.

I bowed. I touched my right fist to my open left hand.

He gave half a smile and bowed as well. Then he crouched at my feet, where a marmalade-coloured cat was meandering. He picked the cat up. "Do you know kung-fu?" he said. His accent was mostly New York, only very faintly something else.

"Yes," I said.

"Where did you learn?"

"Russia."

This surprised him. "How much kung-fu is in Russia?"

"Not much."

He appraised me with his rheumy grey eyes. "What style?"

"Wing-chun."

"Hm." The cat was motionless in his arms. It blinked as he petted it. It seemed to be watching me too.

"Do you fight?" sifu said.

I considered this. I looked into the wide kwoon, where men were punching and kicking, pivoting, holding their fists like heavy lake stones. "That's not why I came," I said.

Sifu put down the cat. "Dollar twenty-five a month."

"You mean—?"

"Take off your shoes," he said. "We are open from ten to ten."
I was taking off my shoes. "Closed Sundays. I am sifu."

"Thank you, sifu."

"Jin!" he shouted. He rubbed his eyes with his wrist.

One of the men doing *chi sao* broke away from the hand
dance. He was close to my size, with a high waist. He had gentle
features. He jogged to where we were standing, sifu and me, the
to-dai, and the orange cat.

"Jin," sifu said, taking a step back, "see if you can knock this
Russian down."

I swallowed. "Hello," I said.

"Hello," Jin said.

He knocked me down, but only eventually. After we had
seen and evaded each other, touched and come apart. I had
missed this physicality, this duel.

As I hit the floor, I found I was smiling.

Jin remained in a defensive pose, *bai jong*.

I propped myself up on my hands.

"Good," sifu said.

FOR HALLOWEEN I WENT to Schillinger's and we carved
squash. He was spending much of his time in Cleveland, preparing the first major work for space-control theremin and
orchestra. The country didn't know yet the trouble it was in;
despite Wall Street's calamity, this concerto was due to premiere
in Cleveland in November, with a repeat performance in New
York. Schillinger named his piece the *Airphonic Suite*. He carved
an intricate happy face into the orange flesh of the squash. It
was grotesque in its happiness. "What is that thing?" Frances
asked him.

"It is the face of bliss," he said.

The other squash depicted a cat. Frances and I had designed it on paper. I held a ruler while she applied the knife, tongue hooked in the corner of her mouth, her red hair in a bun. There was a certain tension in the air. Schillinger had wanted to perform the theremin solo at the suite's premiere. The director of the Cleveland Orchestra preferred to have the inventor, which is to say myself, play the solo. When the director rang me I had no idea of Schillinger's desire—he had been in Cleveland, shivering over his pierogies. By the time he and I spoke, the composer and the soloist, it was too late; the contracts had been signed.

"I could play it badly," I suggested.

"Play it badly in Cleveland," he agreed, "but not in New York."

Rehearsals kept me in Cleveland for several weeks. Instead of billeting in Schillinger's rented cottage, the director put me in a hotel across the road from Terminal Tower, which was under construction. Every morning I would divide the curtains and look up at the skyscraper. Every morning it seemed taller. All this time I had been living in America, running my masters' errands, and this tower had been getting taller.

At the orchestra's first rehearsal, with loudspeakers wedged between the double bassists, I activated the theremin's coils. *DZEEEEOOOoo*, it said. There was an immediate brassy bang from the far side of the room. A French horn player had fainted. Her instrument lay on the floor, mouthpiece tilted toward the ceiling. My theremin meekly warbled. I switched it off. We gave her smelling salts.

People began to tell me I seemed distracted. I lost track of sheet music. I neglected to exit elevators. Cars honked as I stood at the corner of the street, forgetting to cross. "What's wrong with you?" Schillinger asked one day, after I brought a rehearsal to a standstill.

"I'm preoccupied."

"Preoccupied with what?"

"With Clara Reisenberg," I admitted.

"She's eighteen years old and she's miles away," he said. "Go dancing with someone else tonight. Clear your cloudy damn head."

I introduced myself to a secretary at the symphony, asked her out on a date, and forgot where we had agreed to meet.

On the train back to New York I resolved to try to keep my head clear. You were a dance partner, an eighteen-year-old girl. You were a diversion, and there was important work to attend to. I remembered Katia in New Jersey. Ten thousand waiting trees passed on the other side of the window.

Arriving in Manhattan, New York seemed more or less the same as when I had left it. A depression does not show itself instantly. The banks had not been replaced with soup kitchens. The clock towers had not stopped. But there were more men sitting in the streets, on stoops and curbs, even on that icy Tuesday. Like in the days after the Revolution settled, in Leningrad, weather seemed less important. People walked in the rain. They shivered in the sun. They scanned newsstands' newspaper headlines with fragile faces, awaiting disaster.

At the Plaza Hotel, they told me you had rung. I saw your name in the receptionist's neat hand, and it was as if I had been topped up to full strength. This inky blot was enough—wherever you were, you had wondered too. My question had lost its urgency. I did not call. I folded your name and put it in my pocket. I went back to work. I attended my meetings; I performed Schillinger's suite for a rapturous Manhattan crowd. I found other diversions. And when finally I dialled your number, feigning indifference, lying to myself, almost a month had passed.

"Where've you been hiding?" you said. Then you told me there was no time for dancing. You were going away with family, for a month.

"What are you doing on New Year's?" I asked.

"Haven't decided," you said. "Trying to find either the biggest bash or the smallest."

FOR NEW YEAR'S EVE a few of the studio regulars rented a hall in Brooklyn, hired a band to play Chopin and Ellington. Maybe it seemed as though the market was bouncing back—maybe Schillinger's friends just wanted to celebrate his airphonic success, the calling cards that had been left backstage by Steinways and Rockefellers. Maybe I wanted to see you.

We set up picnic tables and spotlights, a baby grand. I looped lanterns across the ceiling struts: lights that came on only when there were people underneath. We prepared baskets of snowballs, on ice, and bowls of chocolate coins. Then all at once the crowd was arriving: raucous, celebrating, tossing flowers onto our centrepieces of piled screws. The lights went on and off. Music flew out in a jumble. We started to sing, already hoarse. During the chorus of "Someone to Watch Over Me, " George Gershwin himself arrived, wearing a torn suit. Frances Schillinger kissed his cheeks.

"You're the inventor," Gershwin said. He had brought a bottle of real cognac and a plate of devilled eggs. The devilled eggs, he declared, he had made himself.

We toasted tomorrows. We got drunk. Gershwin asked me about Russia.

"Is the sky any different?" he asked.

"No," I said. "Not yet."

We swallowed devilled eggs. I taught Gershwin to dance the quickstep. I taught Frances to dance the quickstep. Schillinger wrested the piano from its player and plinked out some Sousa. We bleated along with the brass. We ate doughnuts, *blini*, barbecued frankfurters, poured frothy beer from a bootleg keg. We traded shoes. Bugs and Missy Rusk showed up, and they brought friends, but there was only a mild stir from the white crowd. We had met at a place in Harlem; he was a piano mover and she was a maid; now we passed each other the barbecue tongs. Bugs had brought me an anagram poem, neat block letters on a square of paper.

SWING YER HEART

NEW YEAR'S RIGHT

"Couldn't get 'New Year's night' to work," he said. "I tried for hours." They were the first Negros I had ever supped with, danced beside. They were earnest and hilarious at the same time.

I told him, "Nothing is more unjust than an anagram."

During every second of that stupid party, I was watching the door yawn open, watching the black night outside, watching and waiting for the girl I was trying not to wait for. My heart was swinging. When finally you appeared, I was so delighted that I couldn't bring myself to say so. You had come with two girl-friends. You had braided little leaves in your hair. I stayed in my corner, talking to whomever was in front of me, glancing across the hall to see if you were having fun. Glancing at those leaves in your hair. At last I touched your elbow as a waltz came on.

"Might I?" I asked.

"You might," you said.

We waltzed. You didn't care about my compliments. You murmured the words as we stepped and unstepped to the song. Around us there were bowls of punch, women in fur, men with flushed faces pouring drinks. *Each of these drinks is lawless,* I thought. I wanted to reach up and pull the light green leaves down across your eyes. Even in our slowest steps you were secretly quick: it was in your looking, your mouth that could not conceal your thoughts. You asked, "Are you used to a different New Year's?"

"What do you mean?"

"From Russia," you said.

"We celebrated on another day."

"And does it feel the same?"

I loved the sharpened curiosity in your voice. This was not an exchange of metaphors. You wanted to know if it felt different, the old Russian New Year.

"I don't remember," I said honestly.

"I think it probably felt the same." You seemed about to lay your chin on my shoulder but then you did not; you craned your neck to rest it on your own shoulder, looking out into the room. "New Year's is so arbitrary. It's what makes it nice. A party just because we want it. A date that's special because we say it is."

"An invention," I said.

"Like the automobile," you agreed. "Like the cotton gin."

"Like the waltz."

"Like the waltz," you said, and straightaway the song ended. Those leaves were in your hair. Abruptly, you looked at your watch and cursed and said, "Oh we need to dash."

I was caught completely off guard. "Why?"

"My friend Sadie—she wants to meet this . . ." You shook your head. "It's a long story." You rubbed your lips. You called to your girlfriends and soon you were gathering your coats. You glanced at me over your shoulder. Then you all went out into the night, to catch a cab.

—

Ten minutes later, you came back. You were alone. You found me beside a platter of potato chips.

"You'll ruin your figure," you said.

"You came back," I said.

"I did. And you didn't go anywhere."

"I stayed," I said.

"What were you doing?"

I drew a breath. "I was inventing a new calendar."

AT MIDNIGHT SCHILLINGER CLIMBED up on the piano bench and held aloft his pocket watch. He bellowed for quiet.

"It's only 11:52!" shouted Rosalyn, one of my new pupils, in a green dress. The band was still playing.

"Not by my time!" Schillinger yelled. "Twelve! Eleven!"

A commotion rippled through the hall.

"Ten! Nine!"

It was not until "Eight!" that we agreed to abide by his chronology.

"Seven!" you answered.

"Six!" I yelled. I found I was so happy, shouting numbers.

"Five!

Four!

Three!

Two!

One!"

And then it was the new year. Bells rang, streamers flew, champagne popped, lovers veered toward each other. I looked at you and you were scrutinizing me with your forceful brown eyes. I felt a wisp of something rising up through my chest. I bent toward your face. In that instant someone hit me in the back of the head with a snowball. Our heads clonked together and the world humbly shattered and a laugh knocked from your lips. I wheeled. I was searching for the culprit. There was no culprit, just a party, a hall of thronging movement and a dozen whizzing snowballs that I had helped prepare.

When I turned back to you, you were smiling still, ear to ear, loosened.

"Happy New Year, Leon."

"Happy New Year," I said.

You looked over at where George Gershwin was pretending to cross-country ski.

"Which new year do you want?" I said.

"All of them," you replied. "Why not?"

IF I PLOTTED A GRAPH with all the good news from my first two years in America, it would be a long, silver, upward-curving line.

But beginning in early 1930, it became a different picture. A graph of winter temperatures, perhaps. A downward slope. Decline.

"Things are not so good," said RCA's Mr Thorogood. Even the ink in his pens had faded.

The RCA Theremin had debuted at the Radio World's Fair in September 1929. Over the next eight months, salesmen took the theremin on the road, demonstrating it to audiences in Illinois, Texas and California. They paid former pupils to perform as guest soloists, visiting virtuosos, ambassadors for the instrument's ease of use. RCA paid the Marx Brothers to have a go, paid Ripley's Believe It or Not to introduce a new act, launched a weekly theremin radio program, at 7:15 on Saturday nights, sending ether song across the country. There were ads in newspapers, ads in magazines, ads on the radio and in the polished windows of music stores.

But as the device cooed at Harpo, as families listened bewilderedly to the radio, RCA's plan was failing. America was enamoured with my invention: it festooned small-town newspapers, drew crowds in places where priests and sluggers were the customary idols. Yet the people did not themselves wish to own theremins. They were too busy worrying about their wages, saving food stamps, clamouring for the repeal of Prohibition. This was too elaborate a contraption.

MEANWHILE, PASH HAD GONE MISSING.

I could not find him. Our customary relationship relied on his finding me. He had eagle's eyes, bat's ears, a bloodhound's nose; I'd be sitting at the movies, at the zoo, trying a Flatbush Sacher torte—all at once his hand would clap my shoulder. "Comrade," he'd say in his bootblack voice. He might have papers for me to sign, news from the motherland, instructions from his employers. He might simply be lonely and wish to talk—long monologues on Kuril scallops or Russia's bandy league. I do not know if Pash had any friends. I do not know if I was his friend.

But he had been missing since Black Tuesday. That night he had had a look in his eyes: not the look of a man recalling something but the look of a man recalling he would recall something. The something was grim. He left without saying goodbye.

You, too, seemed to step away from my life in the weeks and months after we counted down to one. The next time I saw you, you were crossing the street near the opera. I called to you, waved with both hands. Beside me, men were using pitchforks to heft sacks onto a flatbed truck. I shouted again. You stopped and saw me. You smiled. You hesitated. I saw you see the men who were lifting those stinking sacks, and me in shirtsleeves, and you mouthed something. Then the truck started to reverse and I had to move out of the way and when I looked up you were gone.

You went away on tour for huge swathes of 1930. Was it an intentional absence? I don't know. Had I ruined something somehow? The country was falling apart and you were playing your violin in Illinois. When we did see each other we were careful with our faces. We had come very near to each other and now every look reminded us of this. Sometimes too much seems promised.

In November I knew you were back. I rang your house.

"She's out with that lawyer," your sister said. Nadia spoke to me as if we were accomplices. "I don't trust alliterative names," she said.

"What?"

"Robert Rockmore."

I said just: "Oh."

"They're at Texas Guinan's."

I said again, "Oh."

So you had gone to Texas Guinan's.

While you were flying by taxi from paradise to paradise, with another man, I was counting my change. I was riding the subway to the kwoon in Chinatown. The USA's economy had gone limp, like a flag that is brought indoors. First the RCA devices were rebranded as "budget" Victor Theremins. We released plans for an updated model—a little cheaper, a little simpler, with a loudspeaker built into the cabinet. These were not beautiful or subtle instruments. They were clumsy. But they looked a little like radios—familiar, easy, bestselling radios. At the Providence Home Progress Expo they called this new design "the most amazing invention of modern times."

Unfortunately, the most amazing invention of modern times never went on sale. On a Monday morning I received a letter from the De Forest Radio Company of Passaic, New Jersey. The letter was on rich, thick paper, paper the colour of a stork. Its letterhead showed the elegant names of three Baltimore lawyers. The signatures were equally elegant. The rest of the words were typed. Everything was spelled correctly. They informed me that the De Forest Radio Company of New Jersey was in possession of several patents concerning vacuum tubes and synthetic sound.

RCA also received a copy of this letter. Their legal team called me to a conference room uptown, where the light cut through the curtains. The sun was in my eyes. My muscles ached from the morning's workout regimen. They asked me questions. They showed me schematics. The inventor Lee De Forest had taken out patents, decades before, governing the musical use of vacuum tubes. "I was in Russia," I said. "This is unrelated." They said it didn't matter. They said it was related. They said that De Forest had been sitting on these patents, waiting for us, like a bandit. "This is an ambush, plain and simple," they said, and I wished that Pash was there. RCA sent me home. They sent me a letter, on thin, flimsy paper. *Decisions such as these*, Mr Thorogood wrote, *do not reflect anything except the jurisprudential realities*. RCA settled with De Forest. Every RCA and Victor Theremin was removed from the market.

In all of America, just 485 of my devices had been sold.

WHAT DO YOU DO when you are going broke? You search for your patron. Winter was blowing in and Pash was out there somewhere. But I could not reach him at his telephone number. He did not answer my mail. Three times I visited the apartment that was not really his apartment, where I knew he occasionally stayed. There was no answer, just scuffs and creaking behind the walnut door. As a co-director of the Theremin Corporation, his signature was often needed; I faked it.

One day I went to the covert Soviet consulate in midtown. I waited thirty minutes for a someone to emerge, spidery, from a grey door. I asked him: "What am I to be doing?"

He replied: "Please go back to your laboratory, Dr Termen."

When I came outside I felt all of the city's steely ambivalence. Office windows reflected clouds. Down the street, construction clanged. I stepped between cars, scanning for a friend, for a bus, for something to smile at. On the corner, a black car purred. I looked away and then looked back, squinting. Behind the wheel sat a tall, lean man with a sweep of blond hair. His binoculars were raised, and trained on me.

I ran.

At home I balanced in a green leather chair, a recliner that collapsed if the occupant leaned too far forward or too far back. I had set up a snapping, whirring television device in the corner of my bedroom; it projected the rehearsal rooms in jerky light, glowing squares, triangles, rectangles. I watched students arrive and disappear. I did not go to see Schillinger or Frances. I did not visit with my most loyal students, like Lucie Rosen or Henry Solomonoff, who were now teaching the others. I sat on the cusp of collapse and imagined the receding silhouettes of you and of Pash. My life had paused on each of you, for a moment. Where was it headed now? I sparred with partners at the kwoon, knocked them to the floor. I imagined Pash in an alleyway, swinging at Danny Finch. I walked home through flurries. A courier arrived with a new U.S. visa: what spirit had renewed it?

Late at night, when the students had left, I ate small, simple meals, enjoying the movement of a knife through an onion, the division into two pearly parts. My bank account was like an emptying vault: income depended on loans, patents, future sales. There were no loans, no new patents, no future sales. No one was buying a thing and I owed the Plaza Hotel two months' rent. Their envelopes collected like fallen leaves on the end table by the door. I did not know where I would get the money. I thought of Sasha in Leningrad, reviewing new data. I thought of Katia growing older in New Jersey, but did not call her, just sat in my recliner and watched the students' arms, like semaphore, signalling that I had more yet to do.

At night I dreamed of sums, but mostly of subtractions.

It was an acquaintance who saved me. One evening Walter Rosen came up to the studio with Lucie, and when she went into the practice room to run her scales, Walter stood meditative in the vestibule. I could see him on my rickety television, like a bit player in a movie. He wore a jacket and waistcoat. He had pouches under his eyes. He crossed to my bedroom door and knocked.

"Who is it?" I said.

"Walter Tower Rosen," he said.

I tugged the television's plug from the wall socket. The projector died away. "Come in," I told him. We had spoken only twice, three times before.

"Hello," he said.

"Hello."

He seemed to be waiting for me to stand up.

I rose and shook his hand.

"Lucie is my wife," he said.

"Of course I remember."

Walter was a lawyer. The first time he and Lucie came to visit, he said the instruments sounded like "Spanish birds."

I wondered if Walter thought I was sleeping with his wife.

"How can I help you?" I said, hands balled in my pockets.

"Dr Theremin, I understand you are having some financial difficulty."

I did not react. He did not seem to need me to.

"Lucie has been talking to me about this for some time, although to be honest I didn't realize how serious it was until I ran into Douglas Hollingworth at the bank and he told me about your line of credit."

"This is somewhat embarrassing," I said after a long pause.

"Nonsense. Happens to the best of us." He seemed to be looking over the room: piles and stacks and jars. He gave a gentle smile. I realized suddenly that this smile was genuine; it was gentle because it was genuine. "Lucie had her second recital last week. It was superb. Everyone says so. There is no question that you are doing important work."

Did he want her to receive more private lessons? To have a theremin built?

"Lucie is a fine pupil," I said.

"When capital runs out, one requires investors, simple as that. It's obvious you have the ideas. All you need is the space in which to develop them. Yes?"

"Yes," I said carefully.

"We live on West 54th Street. Do you know it?"

"It's around the corner," I said.

"We wanted to invite you to move into number 37."

"To move into?" I said.

"We live next door, but 37 is vacant. You could move your studio."

"*This* studio?"

"That's the notion," said Walter. He shrugged, as if he were apologizing. "Just until you get back on your feet. Don't worry about rent; the current tenants are just a few dusty insects. Moths don't pay rent either. For us it's the best of both worlds: I can ask you to explain the scientific principles I read about in the papers; Lucie can practise or have repairs done. Then when your troubles are behind you, you'll be able to find your own space."

"Of course," I said.

"Perhaps we can even have dinner together!"

I looked at this man, guileless, accommodating.

I said, "I do not know how I can repay you for this."

He waved his hand. "Dr Theremin, it is good for the spirit to be able to help a mensch."

"A *mensch*?" I didn't recognize the expression.

"A *mensch*," Rosen said, "is what we all aspire to be."

YESTERDAY, RED APPEARED with a plate of sardines. "Hello comrade," he said. He did not explain why he had stopped bringing food to my door. He said he was sorry he had been away. He must have noticed how thin I had become because after giving me the sardines he came back a few minutes later with a bowl of thick soup. It was not borscht or *shchi*, it was not New York pea soup; it was something else. Perhaps it is what Red likes to eat when he is hungry. I thanked him. I told him to give my regards to the captain. I watched his eyes to see if there was a message there, news of mutiny or disaster, the image of a man floating facedown in water, but there was no message. Red gave me the thumbs-up. He left me alone in my cell.

Some nights on the *Stary Bolshevik*, I can hear sounds from outside. I press my ear to the steel and beyond the groans of the ship, the screws loosening and tightening in the walls, I hear gulls. They cry and whistle. Other times I hear whales; I think they are whales; it is a moaning in four colours. My ear is pressed to the steel and I hear this calling that is like many callings folded together. Ancient blues, greys, scarlets, golds, on top of one another, in a chord. One day I will make a piano that plays the echoes of whales.

An odd thing: in my room I sometimes peer through the porthole at the low waves. They are silent. No sounds penetrate the glass. Looking into the blue sky and the bucking ocean, I never see a circling bird.

FIVE

AGE OF CONSENT

AT ITS NEW LOCATION, the Theremin Studio became a zoo-logical garden for like-minded animals. There was still the same procession of pupils—naive amateurs, wealthy dilettantes, scions of Russian-American New York—but also an entourage of artists, scientists, musicians, philosophers, showbiz characters. Awaking in the morning, I turned in my wide bed and wondered what the day would bring, who the day would bring: which men and women would stand in my doorway removing their hats, spilling out introductions. Strangers arrived over breakfast, bowled into the living room after a night of dancing. "Let's go to Theremin's!" they must have said. Like I was the host of a beloved dive.

I gave talks on electricity. I hosted midnight round tables about the latest acoustics research. I taught Somerset Maugham about magnets and Sergei Eisenstein about rust. I served black tea and gingerbread to Maurice Martenot, inventor of the bril-liant but capricious Ondes Martenot organ. He asked for salt and pepper. Schillinger lectured on aesthetics and harmony. The

8

SEAN MICHAELS

brownstone's second floor was for students, the third a workshop, the fourth my personal quarters. The basement had room for storage and a small gym. But the main floor, with its large parlour and low lamps, became a kind of salon. We learned, argued, told ribald jokes. Guests brought bottles of hooch and the liquor cabinet was never empty. While Tommy Dorsey explained his recipe for "Irish spaghetti sauce," Jascha Heifetz would sit arguing with Mischa Elman about tremolo. Glenn Miller would lean by the stairway's banister, flirting with every girl. Isabella Marx used a different insult each time they crossed paths. "You cur," she said. "You rascal." "You wag."

It was 1931. Pash had still not returned. One day a man stopped me at a street corner. Another man, his partner, moved into position. They stood close, their shoulders at my shoulders. They were only slightly larger than I.

The first man looked off across the street and tipped his head forward, like a vulture. "*Good morning, Lev,*" he said, in Russian.

"Hello?" I said, in English.

We stood as a trio while the rest of the pedestrians crossed the street. Soon we were the only ones on the corner. "Would you please come with us," the first man said.

They made me walk slightly ahead of them. I remember noticing that my shoes needed polish. They told me to turn left. They told me to turn right. We passed the entrance to the Waldorf Astoria, completed a few weeks before. Rolls Royces waited patiently, like loyal dogs. We kept moving. We turned left. We turned right. Finally we arrived at L'Aujourd'hui. This was a shabby and grease-stained restaurant, with tabletops the colour of french-fried potatoes. I had been before, but only between the hours of midnight and 8:00 a.m., only after a night of drinking and dancing. Nobody ever called L'Aujourd'hui by its name. We called it after its owner, a cook, Antony Mudolski. We called it

Mud Tony's. By day, the place was missing all of its late-night gaiety. It was a wilted room with sagging banquettes, patronized by ghosts.

The spies took me to Mud Tony's. They ordered three slices of cherry pie and one glass of water, "but hold the water." Into this empty glass they poured a shot of warm, clear vodka.

"Drink," they told me.

I was on one side of the table and the two men sat facing me. One had a moustache with no beard, the other had a beard with no moustache. They wore pale blue suits. I know that all suits are made of cloth but I was struck by the way their suits looked particularly made of cloth.

I had not yet drunk. They stared at me. One of the men folded his hands, threading his fingers together. I could not say why, but this was an extremely intimidating gesture. I picked up the glass of vodka and I drank it. The other man refilled my glass.

"Drink," he told me.

I did not immediately drink. The two men seemed to blink in unison.

The other man folded his hands, threading his fingers together.

I drank. They refilled my glass. I drank again. I had now swallowed three shots of vodka.

We spoke together.

These men were both named Karl. They said they were from Soviet military intelligence. They asked me if I had recently seen Pash. I told them no. They asked me if I had visited with anyone else of interest. I told them no. I asked what had happened to Pash. The vodka had made my tongue slippery. They didn't respond. "We are the same but different," said the Karl with the beard. They asked what I was working on, whom I was working with. I told them anything they wished to know. They were looking after my visa, they said. They gave me papers to sign. They asked about particular contracts and I replied as best I could. "But what of Pash?" I asked again. They told me that he had been reassigned. They said that we would meet every month at Mud Tony's, and I would answer their questions. They said I was a spy and, sooner or later, I would have to spy.

When the bill arrived, they waited patiently until I picked it up.

I DID NOT KNOW IT THEN, but Karl and Karl would be my monthly companions for the next six years. As the rest of my life whirred and dinged, accelerating and decelerating, they were the drag, the margin of error. No matter what else I was doing, I met my handlers at Mud Tony's every two fortnights. I got drunk and spilled my guts. They issued fewer orders than Pash had done, but I understood their orders less. Imagine my life as a barometer; whereas once it moved in slow, deliberate changes, now the dial's needle trembled. For the rest of my time in the United States, even in my most private moments, even longing for you, there was a tiny hesitation. I trained in my basement, working through the four forms; I sparred with Jin at the kwoon; I listened to Haydn and Bach. Still I felt it, thinly travelling in my blood: a wavering.

Yet I found solaces. The studio was a clubhouse, a dugout, a private kingdom. The carpet on the front steps wore out from too many feet. I stood at the stove with Frances, making caramel corn. I began exploring other applications of the radio watchman, devices that lived at once in the visible world and the invisible one, sensing the space that surrounds an object, sensing movement there. I built an alarm system, a wired panel that could be hidden behind a Rembrandt, concealed beneath a topaz. As soon as the thief's gloved hands entered the panel's charged field, like a drop of blood into a pool of water, an alarm sounded. No strings, no codes, no moving parts—the naked perception of presence and absence. I sat at my desk and wrote letters, folded diagrams into envelopes, suggesting that Mrs Pickford, Mr and Mrs McLean trust their Star of Bombay, their Hope and Star of the East diamonds, not to dogs, to sleepy guards, but to the permanent vigilance of electricity.

By return mail, they said: "Perhaps."

I found that I had a thousand things to do, and all these things were distractions from the things that I could not do.

UNTIL ONE THURSDAY I found you waiting on my doorstep.

It had been a long time. Since my conversation with your sister, I had not called again. I did not wish to hear that clear-eyed Clara was out with her tall boyfriend. I did not wish to hear anything like that. I had always known that you had other suitors, but until that talk with Nadia I had never imagined that they could cast a spell on you. You cut too finely. Your gaze was too sure. When I was alone, remembering you, you were never dancing with anyone else.

When I found you on my doorstep in a red coat, leaning against the jamb, you seemed so at ease, so familiar with this place, with the sight of me, smiling, that it felt as if I had been the one who had forgotten you, Clara. You leaned like the hour hand on a clock.

"Hello," I said.

"It's you."

"It's me."

"I did think you lived here."

"Would you like to come in?"

"Should I?"

We kissed on both cheeks and then we were in the parlour. You looked around, you reached absentmindedly toward the bowl of almonds, you used your right hand to take almonds from your left palm and bring them to your mouth.

At the bottom of the staircase, we removed our shoes. You were in stockings. We passed through the second-storey studios. Lucie nodded hello, sliding from F to F sharp to F to F sharp with her right hand. You followed me up one more floor, to the workshop. There were wood shavings on the floor, little piles of nuts and bolts, empty bowls and lonely screwdrivers. Above a chest of drawers was a print of the periodic table of the elements. You gestured toward it. "That looks new."

"Everything's new," I said.

You nodded. You shrugged. I put my hands in my large pockets. Protactinium, hafnium: these elements had not appeared in my childhood encyclopedia. I took your coat. In short sleeves you seemed reinvented. I wanted to lay my lips at your shoulder. In every room you tried to guess what was before you and every time you guessed incorrectly. You took loudspeakers for theremins, fingerboard theremins for loudspeakers.

"And this?" I asked.

"A pocket watch," you said, with a smile.

I set the doll on the ground and it crawled across the carpet to the tips of your toes.

I showed you old televisions and RCA kits, the "whirling watcher," as Henry Solomonoff called it, our machine with perfect pitch. I turned it on and watched the neon light reflect in your eyes. It gyred and flashed but the device was not certain, not sure, in this room where no song was playing. It didn't know which colour to show.

Beside a potted rhododendron lay the rhythmicon I had built for a composer in San Francisco, a piano that played rhythms. Twelve keys: depress one and hear a rough pulse, like a ticking gear or a jagged heartbeat. He had imagined it as accompaniment for an orchestra, a sort of automated timpani. But as I built the machine, raising it from notebook paper into life, I found it was too coarse for this. I used it in other ways. In an empty room I would listen to the rhythmicon's lowest timbre, like a cough, and feel the distant bittersweetness of an undanced waltz. You pressed a key and the rhythmicon barked a beat, and I longed to slip across the floor, with the sun smoothing the rhododendron. I asked, "How are your parents?"

You gave me a long, level look. "How are yours?"

There was a commotion from below and we ran down the stairs. Glenn Miller and Nicholas Slominsky, the journalist, had burst through the front door and collapsed together in the parlour. Lucie had mistaken the lolling for fisticuffs. She'd fetched a bucket of cold water and sloshed it over them. Now they all sat splay-legged on the rug, sodden, laughing their heads off. "Don't be angry!" Glenn shouted as I came down the steps. "There could have been a fire!"

We rolled up the carpet and propped it on the back veranda. Lucie offered to fan it dry, which made Slominsky crack up again. We went back to the living room and sat in a circle, Indian-style, the drunks with towels over their heads. You seemed a little star-struck, Clara, with a stinking Glenn Miller. It was 3:00 p.m. and I needled them for already being so far gone.

"What time did you start?"

"What time would you say, Nick? Eight?"

"Oh, seven. Six-thirty."

"Early birds," Clara murmured.

This provoked another giggling fit. "Honey, are you kidding?" Glenn gasped. "We've been binged since *yesterday*."

They didn't want to sleep. They wanted to make chicken soup. They sent me out for parsnips and when I got back you were crowded around the stove, the four of you, plus Missy and Bugs had shown up, and Rosalyn, and Henry Solomonoff with his pet budgerigar, Hamburger. We must have been a strange sight. Ladies in pearls, chopping carrots and celery; drunks in tuxedos, stirring pots of chicken bones; a yellow bird reeling around the room, chirruping "Bingo!" Bugs and I made tea biscuits, flour splashed on our chests. I remember how you ran the water so I could rinse off my hands. Then we sat at the table, waiting. Slominsky fell asleep. Glenn suggested Rosalyn throw another bucket of water on him. On the radio they were talking about Japan. Missy said, "Let's play some music."

There was one piano on the main floor, one upstairs. Bugs sat down at the first and Glenn clapped his hand on the piano-mover's shoulder. "Play loud, my Negro friend."

Bugs said, "Call me Bugs."

The rest of us clattered to the second storey. Lucie and Rosalyn at space-control theremins, Solomonoff at the fingerboard. "That's enough of the damn theremins!" Glenn yelled. Missy found a trombone. Hamburger was a soloist. Glenn plunked himself down behind the Steinway. "What about you?" he asked.

"Violin?" you said.

I was already on my way upstairs. Under my bed lay two violin cases, like relics. One of the violins was my childhood fiddle; I kept it under my arm. "Here," I said, coming down the steps, and handed you the other case.

"You play?" you said.

"I did."

"'Stardust'!" Glenn declared. "C major!"

"What?" Bugs yelled from below.

"'Stardust'!" Glenn shouted.

"What?"

"'Dust of the Stars'!"

"Dust off the what?"

"'Stars'!"

And Glenn began pounding out the notes.

It was a jubilant cacophony. The theremin players were accustomed to this kind of free-for-all, usually late at night, and they leapt into the fray. So did Bugs and Missy, on piano and trombone, a whole floor between them. But you and I found ourselves waiting, side by side, violins under chins, hesitating in the same moment. The music was beautiful and disastrous. At their standard timbres, my ether devices are not suited to jazz; this "Stardust" sounded as extraterrestrial as its title. I began to laugh but you were not laughing; your eyes were upturned; you were listening. Slowly you raised your bow and began to saw low notes, like a comet losing velocity. I joined you. The theremins wailed the melody. Our violins were steady beneath their glissando, giving Glenn a space to sing.

In the many rooms of the house, amid the salt smell of chicken soup, we played "Stardust." After "Stardust," we played "Everybody Loves My Baby." We played "Blue Skies" and Pachelbel's Canon. My violin felt like something from a past life. Wood from the taiga, gut from a Romanov sheep. I remembered the rooms in which I had been raised, the varnish on the floorboards. The way I sat in bed with a volume of the encyclopedia and imagined moths, Eskimo, the Taj Mahal. I had not known my future. Now my fingers felt clumsily large on its neck. You too were holding another person's violin. You too were courageous. You smiled at me and I realized we had never been

together like this, not in a place like this, a place without spotlights or hidden corners; a place where you are illuminated only
as you are, as bright or as faded. But here we were smiling
together and still in colour.

LATER, WHEN THE LIGHT had changed, and we were sipping
chicken broth from Walter Tower Rosen's fine silver spoons,
Missy asked if you had ever tried the theremin. "I tried," you told
her, although it did not sound sincere. "It's just there is no
tether," you said. Playing violin, the body is a physical connec-
tion between bow and strings. The same with trumpet, with
clarinet, with piano: lips, tongue, hands on mouthpiece, reed,
keys. You are stayed by touch. The theremin player is loose,
untied. There is no tether. So how do you find the note? How do
you find the chord when there is nothing to touch but air?

Lucie said, "You just do."

SOMETIMES I BOB in this maritime cell, lying on my back,
and I can still hear the studio's chatter. I can hear midnight
wingdings and hungover breakfasts, Bugs banging on the door,
Henry Solomonoff knocking over the bottles. Through the *Stary
Bolshevik*'s ventilation grate come toasts, disputes, speeches. I
close my eyes in this stale room and listen to old friends talking
about beauty.

Where are my violins, now? Do they wait for me with Lavinia?
Did she burn them? Are they here on the ship, in the room
across the hallway, packed into the crates with my equipment?
Does Red slip in some nights and take my child's violin from

its case, cradled in his gigantic hands, and play an unhappy ode to Murmansk?

I wish I had given them to you, Clara, as a reminder.

AFTER THAT NIGHT, you came back. You left when it was late and came back the next day. I wondered what I had done to deserve this privilege, and then I realized it was not a question of doing: we liked each other, that's all. That Thursday I worked on the rhythmicon, fingertips stained with flux, and you watched Yolanda Bolotine, ten years old, at the theremin, finding notes in the empty air.

Before your return, I had been dreaming most nights of my upcoming concert at Carnegie Hall. I had played that gilded room before, played it more than once, but now its darkness plagued me. In my dream, the room was too large. We were on stage, me and Rosalyn and Schillinger and the others, sixteen in all, just like we'd planned. There was a grand piano and a double bass, on its side. The loudspeakers stood like scaffolding. Squinting through the footlights, I could see the audience, but it was so far away; the front aisle of the Carnegie was like a dry riverbed, a valley, separating the stage from the crowd. Whole armies could pass on the red floor between us. Beyond the divide, ten thousand faces faded into shadow. The crowd was yelling something, "Bravo!" or "Encore!" or perhaps complicated boos, except we had not yet begun the performance. It didn't matter: we could not make out their barking. In that immense room, the shouting peeled away, emptied out, leaving overtones and echo. The only clear sound was the rhythmicon's count, like an advancing colossus. We remained at our instruments, poised, hands lifted to keyboard theremin and fingerboard theremin and space-control theremin, and we peered into the contorted faces of the distant crowd, silent and roaring, as if they were warning us of doom or a triumph, something we had not seen. At a certain moment I saw Pash among those faces, wordless, pale as a ghost. The two Karls stood on either side of him, just behind, one of their hands resting on each of his shoulders.

In that instant Carnegie Hall's electricity went dead, the room went dark, the dream's whole world flashed out, except for the rhythmicon, the disembodied rhythmicon. It stumbled on, like a wrong heartbeat.

That was the dream. It was ghastly. It visited me two or three times a week as we prepared for the April performance. I glumly referred to the show as "the last hurrah," but my friends pretended it wasn't so: "The best yet," Mitz said, "emphasis on 'yet.'" This time the focus was on my other creations—the keyboard, the fingerboard, the whirling watcher—and not the original theremin. Lucie Rosen and Henry Solomonoff argued about whether we should use the space-control device at all. I tried to stay out of it. I tried to work, to banish the nightmares with thoughts of voltage, resistance, the measurements of wooden joints. And then you returned, and made me dream of other things.

"The Latin name for a gorilla is 'gorilla gorilla gorilla,'" you said. "It's like the zoologist tossed up his hands and said, 'I only have one good idea. Let's use it three times.'"

"Is it really 'gorilla gorilla gorilla'?"

"The thing about you," you said, "is that you have a million good ideas and you use each one only once. Like a tree with a thousand kinds of fruit."

"Apples and plums," I murmured.

"Apples and plums and grapefruit and lemons and grapes and oranges and limes and pomegranates and figs and dates and pears and peaches and apricots and white nectarines," you said. "And light bulbs."

"Light bulbs?"

"All Leon Theremin needs is sunshine and a bit of rain."

ONE SATURDAY AFTERNOON, I was late returning home. Jin and I had spent ninety minutes grappling, clutching each other and then coming apart, directed by sifu. He wanted us to understand this thing of strength, he said; the way a man can come up against a brick wall. In wing chun kung-fu you are taught to pivot, to shift, to adjust your opponent's force by degrees. You do not stand and grapple, straining into each other's shoulders. You do not clench your teeth and push. But sifu told Jin and me to come at each other like this, like sparring grizzly bears, and when we turned he said, "No!" pointing his finger like a dart. "Sometimes it is just strength," he said. "The only answer is persistence." There were red marks on my arms, as if I had been seized by a witch.

After the session I stayed behind to talk with Jin. I did not want to leave the lesson in the silence in which we had spent it. We went for steamed buns at one of the bakeries nearby. Men poured through the shop's doors, calling out orders, dropping money on the counter without checking to see whether it was correct. The room smelled of beef and perfume. Through the windows I watched women pushing carts of Chinese melons and turnips that looked like wedges of timber. We tore at our steamed buns, spilled barbecued pork, bean paste, lotus. Jin talked about his job at the post office, sorting hundreds of letters on which the address was not clear—envelopes sent from Nanchong, east Sichuan province, to "Mrs Chun, Manhattan" or

"Mr Han, Tailor, Mott Street." The addresses were often written in Chinese. "They imagine everyone will know him," Jin said, "Mr Han the tailor."

"They think the city is that small?"

"No! They think Mr Han is so good, so fine a tailor, that of course he will be famous. That the most gifted tailors receive rubies and palaces."

"Does that happen in China?"

Jin laughed. "No. But this is America. The land of opportunity!"

I was late returning home. The chain came off my bicycle and I had to crouch in the street to replace it, trolleys hustling by, horses kicking up clods of earth. I coasted toward the brownstone, standing on the pedals. I assumed Schillinger or Lucie would have come to practise, and each had a key, but when I arrived at West 54th Street I found the worst thing—you, sitting on the steps, waiting for me; and also Sara Hardy, the dancer, leaning her face on her palm. "Clara," I said, skidding to a stop. You stood.

"Hi, Leon."

I assumed Sara was one of your friends and went to shake her hand, then realized my fingers were covered in bicycle grease. I offered a bashful nod instead.

"You must be Dr Theremin," she said. She was a strange-looking woman, so tall in her beige dress. She looked as though someone had held her at head and feet and pulled.

"Sorry to have kept you waiting," I said. My muscles felt overlarge, like clothes I had been wearing for three days.

"I just stopped by on my way to rehearsal," you said. "I wouldn't have waited except I saw this poor girl."

"I'm here for the audition," Sara said.

I leaned the bicycle against the fence. "The aud—? Oh!"

She looked stricken. "Is everything all right?"

"Yes, of course. I'm sorry. I had forgotten. I thought you were Clara's—yes. Just a moment." I unlocked the front door and ushered you both inside. "Let me just . . ." I went leaping up the stairs. I had hauled the dance stage all the way to my rooms on the fourth floor. Nobody was using it and it occupied too much space in the downstairs workshops. Now I set about tidying, clearing away empty tumblers, brushing derelict potato chips from the end tables. Huge spools of wire were sitting on the stage itself and I had to roll these away, round the corner to my bedroom, leaving rail tracks in the carpet.

"All right, all right," I called. You did not hear and I clattered back down. "Welcome," I said to Sara Hardy, the dancer, and also a second time, to you. Your smile made me give a weary laugh.

We climbed to the top floor. Sara seemed bored; she did not even peer around as we alighted on a landing. She had a strange way of breathing through her nose, and I decided between the third and fourth floors that I did not like her. We arrived at the top, and went through a doorway, past my bedroom, and then we were in the "reading room," which was workshop and drafting room and paint cellar, now with an electronic ether dance stage in the centre of its floor. You seemed faintly horrified, Clara. Admittedly the terpsitone was not at its best. Aborted circuits stuck out like insect antennae from its sides; a loop of wire was caught all across its length; the loudspeaker was not yet properly installed and amounted to an oily copper grille that leaned against the bookshelf. Excess wiring spilled from under the platform, like multicoloured grass. "What is it?" you asked.

"The ether wave dance stage," I said, proudly. I gestured to Sara. "Please step aboard."

She wavered on her long legs. "What will it do?"

"Nothing," I said. I snapped the switch on the generator. "Well, it will make a sound."

The room filled with a low hum, as if a bassist was warming up next door. Sara was still hesitating. She looked at you, her new doorstep ally.

"Go on," you said.

Clara, I loved you.

The terpsitone was about the size of a door, perhaps a little larger, upholstered in rosy felt. As she approached, the hum's pitch began to change. The secret was a metal plate, an antenna, fixed beneath the stage. It sensed the conductivity, the movements, of the person who stood upon it. Sara seemed nervous, like a little girl. But she climbed up onto the platform. Cables snaked from the platform to a box near the doorway, a controller station. I adjusted some dials and the hum became much louder, the vibrato tighter, and the terpsitone's drone swooped into midrange.

"All right," I said.

"All right?" she said.

You began to laugh.

Sara Hardy was not the first dancer I had auditioned. She was, in fact, the nineteenth. Six months prior, the terpsitone had sat downstairs, with pride of place in the student workshops. It was my crown jewel, my new infatuation. It felt like an object I had found, an old artifact I had uncovered: dance that makes music. Whereas the theremin reads melody from the gestures of two hands in the air, the terpsitone, the "ether wave dance stage," interprets the movements of the whole body. The performer's gestures have a double meaning—the gestures *as* gestures and the manipulation of sound.

I had been influenced by Martha Graham's dance company,

the way free movement seemed to sing; and also by our hot nights in Harlem, where the trumpeters invented genius one instant at a time. My vision of the terpsitone saw it used in two different ways: by the most skilled choreographers, adapting composed pieces into motion; and by other dancers, volatile and learning, in improvisations.

Yet I could not find performers of either type. Dancers came to my door, pliéed at the doorstep, but when they arrived at the dance stage they were cowed by the electronics, or not cowed enough. I posted notices at ballet schools, backstage at the 48th Street Theatre; these dancers hesitated in the terpsitone's electric field, grimacing at the noise, unable to complete their movements. They started like birds at every change of pitch. Other dancers, avant-gardists referred to me by Schillinger's crèche of choreographers, were too liberated. They whirled and twisted across the stage, whipping sirens from the circuits. I thanked them all and said I would be in touch. Then I collapsed into an easy chair, sighing. Eventually I towed the terpsitone upstairs.

Now Sara Hardy was here, tottering on the charged stage. It was a washout. She moved limply, scared to provoke a sound, provoking sounds all the same. Amid the terpsitone's high *ooooo*, supple and responsive, Sara didn't seem to recognize her own limbs. She lifted her arm and her eyes widened, as if she was horrified by what she had found.

I turned off the generator. As soon as the hum had left the room, Sara seemed to grow five centimetres. She was again a gazelle, on tiptoes.

I showed her out. "Thank you," I said, one hand on the doorknob.

She slung her bag over her shoulder. "It's very hard."

"Yes," I said.

I dragged my feet back up to the fourth floor. I found you crouching on the dance stage, arms loosely resting on your knees. "So much for that," I said. I turned off the room's lights. I did not like you to see my disappointments.

"Hey," you said from the sun-sliced darkness. "Can I try?"

"Try this?" I said.

"Yes."

I left the lights off. The room felt quieter with just sun and shadow. You were silhouetted in the window, still crouching, like a little kid. I squatted beside the generator and flipped the switch. The room filled with sound. You were listening to it. I listened to the sound of the terpsitone as it listened to you listening.

You raised one hand and then the other, paying attention to the changes. You bowed your head and lifted it. You grinned, and the antenna was not sensitive enough to notice. You wiggled your hips. "Here," I said. I plugged another cable into the generator. Now a coloured beam shone onto the dance stage from a spotlight above. It flickered, as if it was being run through a film projector. As you moved your limbs, raising hands and bowing head and wiggling hips, the beam changed colour in accordance with the terpsitone's pitch.

"It shows you the note," you observed.

"Does it help?" I asked.

You came slowly to your feet, the light going rosy. The terpsitone played a C sharp. You pointed at me; your leg swung out in an arc; you showed me your wrist and then the back of your hand. It was not quite a song, but it was a measured, considered singing. Then you laughed and shook out your arms and sent the terpsitone into a shriek. "Well," you said.

"Well?"

We looked at one another. You were on your feet; I was still crouching. We were allies.

"You are better than any dancer," I said.

"At this?"

I nodded yes.

You chewed your bottom lip. "It's interesting," you said after a moment. "Each movement is a choice. Up or down, elbow or knee." You moved your elbow, your knee. "Sixteen bars is like a sequence of decisions."

"Would you play it with us at Carnegie Hall?" I asked.

You seemed surprised. "What? How?"

"You'd learn," I said.

"Leon, I'm a violinist."

I still had bicycle grease on my hands. I said, "Then we will have a violinist playing the terpsitone."

I RECALL ONLY THREE MOMENTS from the last time I played Carnegie Hall.

I remember all of us standing in the wings at the beginning of the show. We were half hidden in folds of black velvet. Albert Stoessel, from Juilliard, spoke at a microphone. He said, "The instruments devised by Dr Theremin are instruments of feeling; they are instruments of the heart." Sixteen friends stood beside me. Ten-year-old Yolanda was the first to go out; she opened the concert alone but for an accompanist, playing Glinka's "Lark." She was as tall as a young maple. I remember I had a screwdriver in my right hand, which I had used to replace one of the fingerboard theremin's vacuum tubes. I dropped it to the stage floor as we all began to applaud.

The second moment was yours. You crouched in black on the terpsitone's platform, as if you were praying, centred in a spotlight. Carlos, the harpist, sat beside you. In the wings, I held my breath.

You stood, slowly, staring into the room's rapt silence. You arched your back. You were a black-barked cherry tree. You were my one true love.

With Carlos you played Bach and Gounod's "Ave Maria." Each note was shown in a beam of light. I had built a loudspeaker, covered it in twill, raised on a simple mount above the stage. Your music pushed like breath against the cloth. It trembled and then sang. You danced, choosing every moment, guiding the melody with a rolled shoulder and the tilt of knee. At the clubs you had not danced like this.

The third moment was hours after the concert, eleven o'clock or midnight. We had just crossed the street, you and I, arm in arm. Our bellies were full of champagne, blini, and chocolate. We were headed to the party at Little Rumania, where we would drink more champagne, toast Wagner and Grieg, listen to old Moskowitz behind the counter, conjuring Gemenc herons on his dulcimer. On the street corner, beside a closed-up newspaper stall, we met a man. He wore an overcoat despite the balmy air. He had a square jaw, wide shoulders. He seemed a full foot taller than I. He had hands like the paddles of a boat.

"Clara!" he said. You stopped and turned. I could not see your face.

"Robert," you replied.

"Late night at the office?" he asked. He gave an isosceles smile.

You said, "Leon, this is my friend Robert Rockmore. Robert—Dr Leon Theremin."

"Pleased to meet you," he said. As we shook hands I imagined pivoting as I stepped forward, raising the elbow of my arm, striking this man across the chest, then releasing his hand, hooking his right leg with my right foot, and shoving him the rest of the way to the ground, to where the pavement was stained black.

I wonder if you felt some tensing of muscles. You did not seem to change but there was a subtle adjustment of body language, a rearrangement of planes, and in that second I sensed that we two were one thing and he was another.

Your hand was on my arm. "Robert," you said, "we need to run."

SIX

CLOSER

BEFORE DAWN THIS MORNING I heard a dog in the passage-way outside my cabin. The sounds were unmistakeable: running, panting, barking. It sounded like an animal of medium size, a pinscher or golden retriever. I pressed my ear to the metal door. The sound came, disappeared, came again. What was a dog doing on a boat? Who would bring a dog to sea?

My room was almost completely dark, just the porthole's disc of morning light at the head of my cot. I strained to imagine the scene outside: the lone animal at the end of the corridor, tail wagging, waiting for something. For its owner? I rattled my locked door. I wanted to take the dog above deck, into the sunrise, to watch the brightening sky. The dog would leap and happily snap. We would be friends. We would be the only two friends on this great iron vessel.

When Red arrived with my meal, hours later, I asked him about the dog.

"What dog?" he said.

"The dog that was here."

Red jerked straighter. "*Here?*" he said, peering around my room.

"Out there." I gestured toward the corridor.

Red looked puzzled. "No," he said.

"I heard it."

"There is no dog," he said.

"I am certain I heard a dog."

He looked at me darkly. "You are making things up."

WHEN I WAS LITTLE I used to carry an alarm clock. Despite my longing for a pocket watch, my mother and father made me wait for my tenth birthday. In the meantime, persistent little Lev convinced his aunt Eva to lend him a square, windup alarm clock, swimming-pool blue, which I carried with me wherever I went, like a talisman.

I couldn't tell you quite what compelled me to haul around the device. At school, with my instructors' tacit approval, I extracted the clock from my bookbag and placed it on my desk. Its ticking tallied the day. It quickened my pace. At home I sat in Father's easy chair and read the newspaper. When the alarm went off, at ten after six, I vacated the seat. "What's the story?" Father would ask as he took off his shoes, and I'd report the day's headline.

I loved the clock's mechanism and I loved to set the clock's alarm. There was enormous satisfaction in the ordered, accurate outcome, the hammer striking its bell. And yet a separate feeling stalked and chased this pleasure. Fear. A trembling, embarrassing, childish terror, like needing to urinate. Despite the clock's ticking it was never *quite* predictable: no second hand, no warning. Once or twice it went off randomly, through some error in the mechanism, for a bleating half a minute. The machine made its invisible countdown and abruptly the whole thing was seized, shrieking, shaking with torsions, until it stopped, or I stopped it, and I sat with heaving breaths, like a man just pulled ashore.

A love of timers' timing, a hatred of alarms' alarms. A stupid circumstance, but I was just a kid. Living with the clock, I would find myself holding my breath, tightening fists, imagining an any-second shrill. Walking down the street, the thing in my bag, I imagined its plain tin shell and the coiled springs inside. I woke from nightmares, heart thumping, and stared at the placid face beside my bed, *tick tick tick*, that harmless metal panic. It was an awful companion.

So at a certain point I stopped setting the alarm. I pretended I simply didn't want to. And a little while after that, I stopped carrying the clock. It was enough to know it was at home, unattended, counting.

IN THE DAYS AFTER you gave up the violin, I wondered whether it had been the same for you with your arm. Had you been frightened of it? Had you carried the fear with you?

We were sitting on the floor in the workshop, legs before us, one of those show-and-tell mornings—leafing through art books, keepsakes, last week's Sunday *Times*. You found my packet of anagram poems; I felt strangely shy.

"What are these?" you asked.

I didn't have a name for them. Silly couplets, the same letters on each line.

I watched you pass from one page to the next.

You said they should be called *leonids*, like the meteor shower.

I was in love, sipping ginger ale. With sunlight folding over us I got up and went to the icebox.

"Here," I said. The ice gave little fizzing sounds as it dropped into our tumblers.

I sat back down beside you. Every time I took a sip, my tongue touched the dusty cold taste of snow.

After a moment I said, "Do you want to visit the North Pole?"

You were staring into your cup, a serious look on your face, as if you were remembering something sad. You raised your eyes. "What?"

"Would you like to visit the North Pole?"

You smiled. "Are you planning something?"

I shook my head.

You felt the rim of the glass with your thumb. "Not by foot," you said. "But maybe by air, like Nobile."

Now I was the one who must have looked serious. You were just naming a man from the newspapers, but Umberto Nobile's name meant more to me than that. His first polar airship, the *Norge*, came through Leningrad on its way to Svalbard. I had stood in its long shadow at Palace Square, watched the foot of its rope ladder wave, magical, above the paving stones. That night there was a reception by the Electro-Technical Society. Amundsen would have been there, and Ellsworth. I was not interested in Norwegian explorers and American tycoons so much as I was by the Italian engineer who was to pilot his own airship to the Pole. But I was knotting my tie when Katia came and asked where I was going, and I said to the Society, and she began to cry. I did not go out. As the adventurers sipped cherry brandy, I nursed a dying thing.

Nobile reached the Pole in his airship. Two years later he returned with the *Italia*, built with the assistance of the city of Milan. This airship was blessed by the Pope. Six hundred miles past the Pole, buffeted by winds, with ice-jammed controls, the dirigible began to plunge. It banked into a spire of blue ice and the Arctic tore up through the floor of the control gondola, at once a blizzard and an electric saw. Nobile and nine others were thrown onto the ice. One man, an Italian mechanic, bled to death as they waited for the rescuers. Six more, trapped in the envelope of the *Italia*, were lifted up, and up, and up, and they disappeared.

But Nobile lived.

I took a sip of ginger ale.

You said, "Leon, I'm not going to play the violin anymore."

I looked at you with a start. "What?"

"It's my arm."

Your arm, your right arm. I stared at it, resting on your thigh. It was docile. It was lovely. You held it out before you, as though someone had taken your hand to kiss. "It hurts," you said.

"It hurts badly?"

"The doctors say it is from when I was an infant. There was not enough to eat, and my bones did not form correctly."

"In Vilnius."

"In Vilnius."

"They can't do anything?"

"It is an old wound."

"They are certain they cannot do anything?"

You circled your wrist with your fingers. "It used to ache when I played. They gave me exercises. The exercises made it worse. The ache became a sting. Bending my elbow, drawing the bow; it's as if there are hot pins in my joints."

"You never told me."

You shook your head. "I'm telling you now."

I asked you, "What will you do?" The ice cubes had melted in my glass.

You flared suddenly. "All these questions!" You climbed to your feet. I got up as well.

"Clara," I said.

You still were not looking at me.

"*Clara*," I said.

"I don't want to talk about it."

"We don't need to talk about it," I said gently.

You were staring at the wallpaper's column of twisting roses.

"Everything's going to be all right."

This sentence made you flinch. Your brow was dark and knit.

"Let's go out," I said.

After a moment you said, "Go out where."

I searched your face for inspiration. It showed me nothing. Strange when a face is bare and yet secret. You were gazing at my painting of a foreign island filled with ruins.

"Connecticut," I said.

Your eyes flicked back to mine.

"Connecticut," I said again.

Your face cracked into a smile. "*Connect-icut?*" you said. I did not know, but I had pronounced it wrong. "You mean 'Connecticut'?"

"Yes," I said.

"Why would we go to Connecticut?"

"We will go and we will find out," I said.

"You're an idiot," you said.

"I will call for a car," I said.

We hired a silver convertible, like the lining of a cloud. Its top speed was very slow. We eased out of New York City and along the bay into New Rochelle. We wove through small towns. We scrutinized hay bales. We passed chimneys and stables and bill-boards reading LOCKSMITHS. Cows loitered, birds cheered. Rivers ran with cold water.

We stopped when we saw horses. You were frightened, frightened of making them run, and you stayed with the car. They were the colours of pecans and walnuts. Their heads were raised, attentive. I padded through the long grass, listening to my breathing, listening to theirs, inhaling the green field smells and the horses' scent, like paprika and clover. I heard you murmur, "Careful . . ."

In Litchfield, Connecticut, we sat in the car and watched a valley disappear. Before it was fully dark, the stars had already come out. I knew the constellations by their Latin names and you knew their English names. Why did we never speak Russian with each other? I think I was trying to build something new, something I had never known before. "Ursa Minor," I said. You replied, "Little Bear."

WE ATE DINNER LATE, at an inn overlooking Lake Waramaug. They brought us plates of raw oysters, sour cherries, radishes with butter. "Such strange food," you said.

"It's the way of Connect-icut," I said.

I had fish chowder and you had a gigantic sirloin steak, a steak bigger than your head, which you attacked with a carnivorous precision I had never beheld in you before. You manoeuvred the fork in your right hand and I saw that there was no hesitation there; no pain flashed in your face. It was not that you could not use that arm: it was that you could not play violin with it. In a way, this seemed an even crueller injury. I asked myself what I would do if someone told me I could no longer be an engineer.

At the table you spoke of your early childhood, before your family came to New York. It was like revisiting the scene of a crime. You remembered the wide cathedral square, holiday processions down Pilies Street. Vilnius was all straight runs, flat lines. You took a heel of bread and ripped it in two. After the Revolution, they closed the city market. You described playing in the empty stalls, skipping with your sister across the speckled earth. You were hungry.

I told you about riding a bicycle through the grounds of the Physico-Technical Institute, about the spray of green leaves and rainbows bending.

You said the weather in Lithuania had always seemed comprehensible; that even as a little girl, you felt the rain coming, saw the sunshine departing. You could intuit the clouds. "In America, what sense do things make?" you said.

I chided you. "You know as well as I."

"It's as if no one here ever learned that there are ways things are supposed to be."

"Yes," I said. "It's why I've stayed."

We spoke of the northern lights. In Leningrad, they streak across the entire winter. In summer there are the white nights, long bright midnights. But after the fall equinox come the gold, green, crimson nights, when glimmers lift out of all that blackness, undeniable, secure, fading. The aurora looks like roads, sometimes; bands of light twisting across hilltops. But the hills are not there, the roads are not there—like the paths of ghosts. You forget their routes as soon as you have glimpsed them.

"Roads less travelled by," you said.

I didn't know you were quoting Robert Frost. "Travelled by whom?" I said.

You hesitated. After a moment, you murmured, "By us."

I used to sit and watch the northern lights from my bedroom window, as a boy, and later, as a man, from my dormitory at Petrograd University. As a husband I watched too. I did not tell you this. I would lean my head against the glass and know that behind me, across the room, Katia lay with her eyes closed.

For dessert you ordered a chocolate parfait. I ordered a cup of coffee. I drank it sweet, with two small spoonfuls of sugar. Someone was playing records, one after another. They all sounded like love songs. You hid your grin as you scraped mousse from the bottom of the parfait glass.

When we went back out into the night, crossing the gravel to the car, I think we both expected to see the aurora. But everything was dark. We expected it to be weaving above us in cold blazing splendour. The sky had clouded over. In the darkness I pulled the convertible roof up over the car and then I went over to you and I kissed you.

I remember how later you swept your hair away from where it lay around your eyes. You stretched your arms as though you were waking. When your wrist touched the window glass there was an instant when your mouth moved, almost smiling, and then you said that you felt outside and inside at the same time.

MUD TONY'S NEVER CHANGED. The walls were an overripe lime green, the tiles a weak milky blue. Cooking oil hung like a fine mist in the air. Every month I hunched in a booth with Karl and Karl and they passed me glasses of vodka and I swallowed them without protest. I spilled my guts. I looked around the diner with sad eyes. The salt shaker was always at the same level. The tabletop was covered in a tacky film.

"And so," asked Karl, the Karl with a moustache, "how are the negotiations with First Bank?"

"Stalled," I said. My tongue felt slick in my mouth.

"Turn the key in the ignition," said the other Karl, "and get somewhere."

I had been in talks with the First Bank of New York about a touchless alarm system. I had been in talks with Brite-Star Toys about a doll that crawled across the floor. I had been in talks with Marzinotto Screws about a theory for preventing corrosion. All of these talks were genuine. They stalled and unstalled. I scored a minor hit with the electric eye, a security device for sleeping children. It was a familiar principle: an electromagnetic field in a ring around the baby's crib. Enter the invisible field, and a bell sounds.

The greatest calamity of Charles Lindbergh's life made me a little rich that summer.

For most of these inventions, full of invisible fields and secret activations, I used the name "teletouch." Teletouch light switches, teletouch alarm systems, teletouch sensors for automatic doors. I had signed a contract with Nate Stone, of Marchands, to develop teletouch window displays. He planned to sell them to uptown department stores: revolving tables and flashing lights whenever a customer passed close by.

The Karls were unmoved. They applauded windfalls, siphoned money from my accounts, but they were not interested in shop-keepers, infants, mechanical amusements. They wanted contracts with major enterprise, corporate skeleton keys. "Have you spoken with General Motors?" they asked. "Have you followed up with Westinghouse?" Even in my intoxication, I knew enough to lead them on, to offer yeses and maybes. I did not believe in their omnipotence, or in the methods of their bosses, but somewhere at the heart of this matter were the best interests of Mother Russia. One day, perhaps, we would want the same things. I might yet be their spy.

ONE DAY YOU SAID, "Can I show you something?"

There were screws in my mouth; my answer came out mumbled. "'V cur . . .'" I was on my back under a plywood display case, mounting bolts along its lower lip, twisting a screwdriver at an awkward upward-tilted angle. I had the vague feeling there might be ants coming up through the floor. Lucie Rosen had said something about ants next door. Something was at my scalp. Was it ants? I did not know.

"You have to come out," you said.

I grunted and began extruding myself from under the case. I was thinking of the ants. I sat up, brushing at my hair and neck. You were standing at the far side of the room, behind a space-control theremin. *DZEEEEOOOoo*, it said. If there were still ants on my head, I forgot them.

Later, you told me how you had come to visit the day before. It was the early evening. You let yourself in but the house seemed empty; there was a breeze coming through the first-floor blinds; nobody was practising. I was away at the kwoon. Sifu was tapping the back of my knees with his stick.

You walked into the living room and found Henry Solomonoff and Charles Ives, waiting for their tea to steep. "Hello!" Henry called out. You removed your hat. They invited you to sit with them, the two composers, and you did; you waited together for the tea to steep. They were talking baseball. *Shortstop*, they said, *RBI*, and after a little while you got up. "I'm going to go upstairs," you told them. On the second floor you wandered through the workshops. You picked through a box of drill bits. You flicked a television screen with your finger. You stood on the inert terpsitone stage, bowed, waved your hand. A theremin sat in the corner, painted flowers on its sides. My former gift to you. You eyed it. "Is everything all right?" asked Solomonoff. He had appeared at the top of the stairs. You looked at him. You were no longer a violinist. You asked him, "Will you show me how to turn this on?"

Now I sat on the floor, astonished. You plucked nineteen notes from the air. The opening bars of "The Swan": just nineteen notes, nothing more. The last of these, set apart, came out wrong—a quivering F instead of high C. In spite of this, in spite of sharps and flats (and you grimaced comically with each mistake), in spite of the way you slid between each note, unable to control glissando, I was dumbstruck. Accuracy with the theremin is a learned thing, a knack that comes with practice. But you showed even in that clumsy playing a delicacy of tone like I had never heard. Every player of the space-control theremin draws his or her music from the same loose current, the same air, the same relationship of hands and antennas. We are all siblings, summoning the same songs. Somehow yours are more beautiful.

"Well?" you asked.

I was speechless.

"Well?" you asked again, a crooked smile spreading.

"Clara Reisenberg," I uttered finally, the only words I could say.

I GAVE YOU LESSONS in how to hold your hands. There are some bends of wrist, positions of fingers, that work better; others less well. "Like this," I said. "Like this." "Like this." You stood beside me and asked, "What about this," touching thumb to forefinger, and it sounded finer than anything I had ever heard.

I sent two theremins to your apartment. The car carried my first gift and a new, modified RCA kit; also a sour cherry tart, a bouquet of jasmine, a bottle of bootlegged gin. I am not sure I knew how to do things by half measures. You practised at home;

you practised with me. After the third lesson we went dancing. We played on the Capitol Club's dance floor, skipping and mirrored, your hair pinned up and me with cufflinks glinting, the whole night glinted, mirroring, and skipped. My hand rested in the fragile strong supple small of your back.

Later, at an automat, I paid a man a dollar and he filled my palm with nickels. The walls had a hundred tiny slots and into these I slipped the coins. Two perfect plates of pie came swinging round on rollers. We poured black coffee from taps, silver spouts shaped like dolphins. We sat side by side. You used a spoon and I used a fork and we ate our pie, speaking of other lemon meringue pies we had eaten, made by bakers in Queens, by hotel chefs, by grandmothers. The automat's recipes, you told me, were kept in safes. The makers of these mechanisms knew the machines were useless without pie, cake, little pots of crème brûlée. Customers want to spend their nickels on delights. I put my hand on yours. The room shone white and felt like the future. You drew the spoon from your mouth, savouring tart and sunbright. There, your inclined jaw. We kissed.

We still had more dancing in us. We caught a cab to the Savoy. Harlem's mixed clubs were our favourites. The air felt thicker, the music better. The big band hollered and you leaned your head into my shoulder. I breathed in, deeply in, gazing into this flowering overgrown throng. We parted. You sparkled on the end of my arm.

We were on the steps outside the Savoy, much later. Lamplight rested on us like a benediction. I could feel the sweat inside my collar, between my shoulder blades, at my wrists. You were tilted away from me. We could hear each other's breathing, still quick from dancing. The cherry trees were full of petals. The sun was rising. It felt yet like moonlight. I looked toward the city and then back toward you. Now there was a sparrow beside you. She stood near your heels. She was small; she pecked at the stones.

When you turned toward me, the sparrow stayed. You did not see her. You showed me your happiness, and your dark eyes, and the curvature of your silhouette. There was a sparrow at your heels. You held out your long hand to me.

"Clara," I said softly.

"Yes?" The word was like a silver link.

"Will you marry me?" I said.

You did not move. You stood on the steps and stared at me with stillness. Your eyes trembled. You began to smile and then you did not smile, but my heart was lifting.

I looked down at the sparrow. The sparrow had gone.

SEVEN

PLAIN TIGER

MY HANDS WERE FLAT on the table at Mud Tony's. Three men sat opposite me; one was a stranger. I had arrived late. I had almost not come at all. There was poison in my chest. There was withering jasmine. There was nothing. I do not know if it was fear that brought me to L'Aujourd'hui or simply the sense that things should have a sequence. This was the sequence. The restaurant smelled of smoke. I had not slept the previous night. Karl smiled, and Karl smiled, but the man sitting between them did not smile.

"So," I said. I almost did not recognize my voice.

"So," said the Karl on the left. "Do you have news to report?"

"No," I said. We were speaking in English. My voice was acrid. It was as if every hidden inside part of me were made of ash, just ash, bare ash.

"Did you meet with Griffiths?" Griffiths was a man from Douglas Aircraft. They had told me to meet with him.

"No."

"Lieutenant Groves?" Lieutenant Groves was a man from the navy. They had told me to meet with him.

"No."

The Karl on the left opened a folder. "Did you deliver the proposal to G.E.?" The proposal was for a long-term teletouch contract. Its smallest print was full of tricks.

"Not yet," I said.

The man in the centre had not spoken. Whereas the Karl on the left had a beard, and the Karl on the right had a moustache, this man had no hair on his face. His head was shaved almost to his scalp. He had square shoulders but a narrow chest. His forearms were like clubs.

The stranger gestured to the waitress. She went into the kitchen. He looked at me with his deep-set eyes. Next to the jocular Karls, this man seemed like a cinder block. I stared back at him. All three men, I realized, had the same kind of eyes.

The waitress came with four empty cups and four slices of pie.

The man in the centre stacked two of the cups and pushed them aside, beside the napkin dispenser. Next he placed one plate of pie on top of another plate of pie. Cherries sludged between the jadite. He stacked all four plates. It was a sickly, stupid mess. He pushed these aside. He placed one empty glass in front of me and one in front of himself. One of the Karls poured vodka into the glasses. These were not the small shots I was used to drinking with the Karls: spirits filled each glass to the brim. "Drink," said the other Karl.

I knew enough to obey. I took it in sips. They waited. My eyes began to water. When I had finished, the man lifted his to his lips. He drank the vodka in one swift movement, as if he was swallowing a cup of water. He put down the empty glass. He stared at me.

"What?" I said.

He took out an eyeglasses case and withdrew a pair of spectacles. They were unfashionable, large and square and thick, like a grandfather would wear. He put these on.

"This week you are going to meet with Howard Griffiths," he said. "You are going to meet with Lieutenant Leslie Groves. You are going to deliver your proposal to Theodore Scott at G.E."

"Yes?" I said.

The man picked up the bottle of vodka. He poured two more glasses. As we drank, he watched me through the thick lenses of his spectacles. The room began to swim. I felt as if there were ball bearings in my joints.

"How long have you been in America, Lev Sergeyvich?"

"Five years."

"Are you here legally?"

"Yes."

"With a visa?"

"Yes."

"How many times has your visa been renewed?"

"Ten?"

"Eleven times," he said. "Who renewed your visa?"

I hesitated. "You did."

"We did." The man lit a cigarette. "We allowed you to come here. We pay your expenses. We keep you from harm."

I wanted to say: *You do not pay my expenses.* I wanted to say: *You have not kept me from harm.*

"What are you working on now?" asked the man.

"Teletouch," I said. "Assorted teletouch applications. These men know—"

"Yes," said the man. "What else?"

"The theremin," I stammered. "Also, a device that can sense metal objects. And the altimeter . . ."

"An altimeter. For aeroplanes?"

"Perhaps," I said.

The man squinted.

"Yes," I said. "Yes, like for aeroplanes."

"Submarines?"

I had not thought of submarines. "Maybe. Different principles would have a bearing, but—"

"What else?"

I took a breath. "Many things."

"'Many things,'" he repeated, without humour. "Where were you yesterday?" I felt as though he was shoving our conversation across the room.

"At my workshop."

"What were you doing there?"

"Many th—" I began to say. "Instructing a student."

"Which student?"

"I don't recall."

"You don't recall?"

"I don't recall."

"Try to recall."

"I need to go," I said. I stood up, unsteadily.

"Sit down," said the man.

I began to edge out of the booth.

"Sit down," the man repeated.

I was in the aisle. The man looked suddenly grotesque, red-lipped, staring at me. His eyes were large behind his square glasses.

"I need to go."

The two Karls stood up. I was walking past them. The one at the edge of the booth followed me. I could hear his footsteps. I could feel his shadow over mine. I imagined his fists swinging at his sides. I swivelled on my heel. "Do not come closer," I murmured.

"Or?" he said.

I replied in Russian. "Or I will knock your head from your shoulders."

Above his little beard, Karl's expression flickered.

The man had not moved from the table. His back was to me. "Your time is not your own, Termen," he called out. He was still using English. "It is a gift from your state."

"I have to go," I said in a hard voice.

"Where are you going? To flee into the hills? To ask Walter Rosen for another loan? To give another music lesson to a Reisenberg?"

At this, I took a step toward him. "What is your name?" I snarled.

"Come here," said the man.

Who was this man whose face I could not see, with the voice of an executioner?

He said, "Come here and I will tell you."

I moved no closer.

The Karls watched me as if I were a wild animal.

The man in the booth stood up. He was my height. He slipped into the aisle, standing at the foot of the table. He turned to look at me. "My name is yours."

"What?"

"It is Lev."

"Lev?"

"My name is Lev."

"Lev what?" I asked.

The man said, "We have given you five years, Lev Sergeyvich. What have you given us? How many months? How much of yourself?"

"I have given you everything," I said.

"You have not."

I clenched my jaw. "Fuck you," I said. It was the first time I had ever said such words in English. "Every idea I have, every invention, I give to the Soviet Union."

He shook his head. "You are a liar."

"What?" I shouted. I was drunk. I jumped onto one of the diner's leather benches. The Karl who had come after me clenched his hands. "What do you call me?" I stood over them, above them. I stared down at this cinder-block Lev. He was a middle-aged man with a receding hairline. I was precarious on the seat, felt precarious inside, but still I knew I could leap across the booth and push the toe of my shoe into this spy's soft jaw. He stood immobile. He had sunken eyes. He shot a glance at the waitress and she disappeared into the kitchen.

"I am a scientist!" I yelled. I took a deep breath. "I am a scientist," I repeated, more quietly. "I study things. I learn, I probe, I assess. But I am here in New York City, two thousand miles from home, two thousand miles from my institute. Why? Why did I come to this city of strangers?" I looked at him. With my gaze, I tried to say, *Answer me.* The man did not answer. "I came because I was *asked*," I shouted. "My countrymen asked; I came. When I arrived I knew only one man. He has disappeared. My friend has disappeared. I have continued to do my work, to meet here with these *olukhi*, to sign their papers and make their deals and give everything to Russia. I have given over everything. Now what am I left with? Alone, two thousand miles from home? Nothing. Nothing! I am abandoned. I am drunk in a dingy restaurant. And you call me a liar." I spat. "Damn you."

I could hear the cars in the street outside. I could hear the murmuring American voices on the kitchen's wireless. The man in glasses wore an expression of sadness. He lowered his eyes and picked up the bottle of vodka. After a moment he put it down. He lifted his gaze to mine. He slipped past the Karl and stepped up onto a banquette, and we were facing each other across the rear of a booth, like two children.

"You're not alone, Lev," he said.

I wondered if his name was really the same as mine.

"We have work for you to do today."

THE MAN HAD TWO PIECES of paper in his pocket, folded into his wallet. The first was a map of the Dolores Building in uptown Manhattan, with a red X on the room numbered 818. The second page was a list of numbers. 3105-GH-4X88L. 3011-MM-2A37B. 3102-TY-1O49B. PERS 07. In all, he said, there were twelve files.

"What is this?" I said.

"They are secrets," he said.

I felt as if my spirit was stumbling through the channels of my body. I was opening and closing my hands. I couldn't distinguish whether I was even truly angry anymore. I wanted to work myself up to make another speech, vehement, full of affirmations; yet my mind just stuttered, racing and seizing, past images of absent Pash, distant Russia, and you. It ran and ran, like unspooling film.

The man put his palm on my shoulder.

I was a ruined mine, caving in.

In a vanishing voice I asked, "Why should I help you?"

He spoke very gently. "We are Russian," he said. "You and I—we are comrades." He left a long silence.

"Yes," I murmured.

"We carry one another, Lev. We stand side by side."

I forced a bitter laugh. "Oh yes?"

"Yes," said the man. He turned his head and I saw the way his eyes were magnified, huge, on the interior of his glasses. "Lev, you are gifted," he said. "You are an exemplar of our people.

Brilliant, with a bold heart, tenacious and brave. Yours is work that no one else can do. You must not doubt for one moment what a treasure you are, for your comrades."

I swallowed. I said nothing.

"You have a meeting at the Dolores Building. We need you to go there and steal some documents."

In my peripheral vision, the Karls seemed to grow fainter.

I told him I had never done anything like this before.

He said it was all right. He gazed at me. He smiled. He muttered something I could not make out. I think he said, "You are a king." I just nodded. I looked at his pages of paper, the columns of letters and numbers. I felt a pang of homesickness for the Cyrillic Ф, the Ж. For the Neva, the Volga, their lifting bridges. I thought of you, Clara. The vodka was still swinging through my heart. I thought of you for a long moment and then I tore my thoughts from that wasteland. I took the pages from him. I folded them. I put them in my jacket pocket. "What else," I said.

He talked of details. My appointment, my alibi, the place where the documents were stored—room 818.

"The meeting with Mr Grimes is at eleven o'clock," the man in glasses said. He looked at his watch. "It is almost ten thirty. It will be lunchtime when you finish. The hallways will be empty."

"Yes," I said.

"Understand that these files are a matter of Russian security." He did not look away from my face. "You are the only operative we have who has a reason to be at the Dolores." He took out a tiny envelope. He slipped out a key and two silver pins. "Take these."

The key was light, sheer, recently cut.

"For 818?" I said.

"Yes."

"And these?" The pins, one flatter than the other.

"For the cabinets."

I shook my head. "I do not know how."

"It will not present you with a problem, Professor Termen."

With two fingers, the man signalled to Mud Tony that we were leaving. The cook nodded his head. He was drying cutlery. He raised a knife to the light.

There was a moment and then I followed.

On the street, the Karls disappeared around the corner. The man named Lev took off his glasses. He scanned up and down the block. I wondered what he was looking for, and dreaded it. A squat Chevrolet pulled up around the bend, Karl and Karl in its front seats.

"So," Lev said. He did not finish the sentence.

I opened the car's rear door. There was a small moment when I thought this man might embrace me.

When I was inside the car, he leaned across the opening. He said, "Go safely, comrade."

"Thank you, comrade," I said, in a dry voice.

He pushed the door shut.

WE PASSED THROUGH MANHATTAN in silence. I felt like a trespasser. Amid traffic, it was as if we were penetrating successive circles of guards. We turned corners, plunged forward, braked. It was cloudy. The sun was a murky searchlight. After a long time, we stopped. Out the window—a great revolving door. The air was cool; I could feel it prickling at my arms. But I was still hot inside, sweat at my upper lip. I was still drunk.

"Take this," said one of the men in front of me. He pushed back a briefcase. There was something inside. The clasps opened in my hands and I saw that it was a pistol. It lay alone at the bottom of the case.

Before I could respond, the first Karl craned round in his seat to look at me. He spoke without mirth. "Don't get caught," he said.

The other turned and looked, too. "It's loaded."

I swallowed. I closed the briefcase. I went out into the street.

In the lobby of the Dolores Building, a man in a uniform sat behind a desk. "Hello," I said, slipping my card across the surface, "Leon Theremin for Bert Grimes. At eleven o'clock." We both looked up at the wall's great clock, saw the gold minute hand tick to eleven. The man smiled and flipped through his appointment book. Even upside down, I could read my name. It looked the same as all the others.

"You can go right on up, Dr Theremin," said the man. He held out a cardboard pass. It was bright green and I pinned it to my chest. The security man did not need a pass; he wore a silver star, like a Wild West sheriff. "Number 372. Third floor."

"Thanks very much," I said, and I strode across the marble to the elevator. In a leather case by my side there hid a gun.

The elevator slid up the centre of the building. I put the briefcase down; put my hands in my pockets. When we reached the third floor, I smiled at the elevator operator, gave him a tip, took my things, and went out onto the navy blue carpet. Right, left, straight ahead; and through the glass doors of suite 372. The secretary said, "Dr Theremin?" and I said, "Indeed," and she said, "Mr Grimes is ready to see you now."

And I said, "Splendid."

Bert Grimes's office was not very big. He stood up to greet me, a round man in a tweed suit, extending his hand the way the man at the deli extends a sandwich. "The wonder-worker himself!" he said. "Thanks for coming."

I called him by his first name. I sat in a comfortable chair across from Bert and for an hour we talked about the factory applications of teletouch technology. He chuckled and clucked. I crossed my legs at the knee. I said, "Exactly, Bert." He showed me papers and we talked about numbers and by the front right foot of my chair there was a briefcase containing a gun.

It was 12:07 p.m. when Bert closed the binder on his desk and offered me another salami sub of a handshake.

"Well there we are."

"Always a pleasure."

"Joanie and I should have you over for dinner. Bring a lady friend."

"Yes," I said, picking up my briefcase.

"You still seeing that blonde? What was her name? Judith?"

I shook Bert's hand again. He walked me to the elevator. We waited for it to open. There was a janitor at the end of the hallway, sweeping. He kept scrutinizing me. I noticed that despite his dusty coveralls he wore polished leather shoes. He swept the floor like a man who did not often sweep the floor. He had eyes like nails.

The elevator opened.

"Good day," Bert Grimes said to me.

I said, "Have a swell one."

The elevator closed. I smiled at the operator, the same one from earlier, a Negro with a birthmark on his chin.

"Hello."

"Hello."

"Thank you."

"Yessir."

We descended. The elevator did not stop at the second floor. As we approached the ground level I slapped my forehead. "Tarnation," I said.

"Sir?"

"I forgot something. Back at 372."

"Wanna go back?"

"Please."

"Yessir." The operator pushed a button and pulled a lever and the elevator bucked in the shaft. We began to rise. I was recalling the map of the Dolores Building, the floor plan folded into the pocket of my jacket, imagining its borders expand and rotate.

"It was important," I said.

"Yessir."

The air in the elevator felt cool and perfect. The operator was in a good mood. He thought we were travelling companions, co-participants in a misadventure. We were not. When we arrived again at the third floor I nodded to him, told him not to wait. "Good luck, sir," he said, and I stepped into the corridor, which was empty, and made as if to walk the twenty steps to Bert Grimes's office: right, left, straight ahead.

Instead, when the elevator's doors closed, I pivoted on my toe. I leaned into the heavy door that led to the stairwell. I unfastened the button of my jacket and I climbed the stairs, briskly, without touching the handrail.

I climbed to the eighth floor.

The walls were painted silver and the floor was made of silver linoleum and the doors were painted in the colours one expects of bank vaults: fiery red, hunter green, lightning silver. I proceeded down a hallway. Each door was marked with a number: 872, 874, 876. Most were closed but through two, wedged open, I saw harmless men eating lunch.

I came to an intersection. I did not need the map folded in eighths in my pocket. I remembered it. I turned left. I held a briefcase concealing a gun. I came to another intersection. I turned right. There were steel doors, glass doors, wooden doors—845, 843, 841. Now the faces behind the doors were of men less harmless-looking. Their eyes flicked up when they saw me pass.

They sat with filing cabinets filled with secrets. I was the wind moving through trees. I turned left and pushed through a door with a decal of the American flag. This corridor was empty. My steps echoed. I walked more softly—826, 824. As I approached 818 I found I was holding my breath. I breathed. With my index finger I brushed a skim of sweat from my upper lip.

I turned a corner and the janitor, the janitor I had seen downstairs, the janitor with eyes like hammered pieces of carbonized steel, was sweeping dust from a clean-swept floor. His head was downturned but when I arrived around the corner his whole body tilted, swivelled, and he was facing me, slightly stooped, with a set jaw.

"Hello," he said.

His shoes were too fine for a janitor.

"Hello," I said.

I was standing in front of the door marked 818. It was grey. The key that Lev had given me was in my hand, cold, like a blade. The janitor had still not looked away. I had still not looked away. I smiled primly. I turned the key in the lock and went into room 818 and I shut the door behind me, standing with my back to it. I listened. There was a thin line of light under the door. I waited. I was silent. I could not hear anything. I could not hear breathing or footsteps or the sweeping of dust. It was pitch black in room 818 and if the janitor was an agent, an agent of something, then at this instant he was listening too. His ear was at the same level as mine, on the other side of this door. He was calculating what I was doing, where I stood, whether I was armed. He was the United States of America and I was the Union of Soviet Socialist Republics. He was reaching into his coveralls and withdrawing a loaded gun.

I crouched in the darkness. The floor tile was coloured by the thin band of hallway light. I placed my briefcase on the floor and

I opened its clasps and they were deafeningly loud and I imagined the janitor kicking through the door and knocking me prone. I imagined bullets. I took the revolver in my hand and I put my hand in my jacket pocket and I stood, and I turned the doorknob. Then I pushed open the door in one swift extraordinary movement and my finger was tensed on the trigger of my gun, concealed in my pocket, and my eyes were trained on the place in the air where I would see a steely stare.

He was not there. The corridor was deserted.

I went back into 818. I turned on the lights. It was a small storage room filled with filing cabinets. There was no way to lock the door from the inside. I picked up the briefcase and I put it on a table in the centre of the room. I placed the gun beside it. I took off my jacket and set my hands flat on the surface of the table, where I stared at them. I stood like that until I had stopped trembling.

Then I raised my head and took the hooked pins from my pocket and read the labels on the locked cabinets whose entrails I had been sent to steal.

SOME THINGS ARE EASY to break: you throw them against a wall, you murmur a few words. Some things are less fragile. They cannot be carelessly ruined. Locks are like this: to break their purpose you must know them fully, as you would know certain faces. You must understand the flick and tick of tumblers, the swivel of nooks in metal. I did not know how to pick a lock. I tapped the first small silver circle. I peered at it. I wondered how long it would be until someone came into this room and found me tampering with boxes that did not belong to me. I had no time for failures. The lock was just a complicated thing that would come undone, like so many complicated things had come undone. I tapped the lock again. I imagined other locks I had seen, the greased fit, and I evaluated the size and style of the mechanism before me. In my hand were my two pins, my lock picks—one like a flattened piece of steel, hooked; one like a strong wire, bent. I considered the way these tools could be used. I took the first and I jammed it into the lock. It remained there, wedged. I fitted the second above it. This movement had no sound. I pushed inside slowly, softly, feeling for a skirting touch. Tiny grooves, sensitive places. The tools were loose in my hands. I found the faintest ridges at the top of this channel. I stroked these ridges with needle-tip. I felt hidden and very strong.

Pins trembled. My hands moved. I sensed precise small changes; pressure, movement. I pressed sideways on the first, larger pick, and the whole lock seemed to quiver. Once more, and a click, and the cabinet's whole deep drawer shuddered out into my chest.

A long row of folders, a thousand sheets of paper.

I worked quickly, searching for the twelve files among reams of typed pages, acetate, mimeograph. There were patents, memos, lists of addresses and employees. There were plans for bridges, the schematics of turbines. Each folder seemed to be marked with a different seal, as if these were the archives of nobles. I wondered who had typed or scrawled in each dossier's code. 1223-BO-1A10E. Was this the riddle of a spy, a bureaucrat, or an engineer? And what was I, now, rifling through a foreign ministry's documents? Had I relinquished something, or gained it?

Four of the files on my list were within the first cabinet. They were slender manila folders, unexceptional. They now lay in a stack beside my loaded gun.

I walked to a second cabinet. Again I inserted my tools into a tiny lock. I listened with my fingers, such a sensitive burglar. I could not help but look back over my shoulder. Every second second I seemed to be looking back over my shoulder. Staring at the closed door, the almost imperceptible line of hallway light. Waiting for shadows or footsteps or the silhouette of an enemy, framed at the doorjamb. The second cabinet opened. Again, a drawer filled with papers. 2988-TY-oH76C, 5297-TY-1T43P, 8196-TY-3U42I, all these untold tales, and finally 3102-TY-1O49B, one of my needles in the haystack. 3102-TY-1O49B was an envelope, not a folder. There was no one to see me; I looked inside. A sheaf of postage stamps. Just postage stamps. I stared at these orange stamps, 3102-TY-1O49B, wondering their secret, wondering whether they tainted or elevated the letters on which they were affixed.

The stack of stolen files got taller. I opened a third cabinet, a fourth. I heard footsteps from the corridor, and I froze—the footsteps moved across the doorway and away. I felt the ventilated air against my rib cage. I left my sweated thumbprints on a creamy carton folder. In this drawer there were thin leather satchels filled with documents. PERS 01, PERS 02, PERS 03. But no PERS 07, the object of my quest, the final file on my list. PERS 04 through PERS 06 were also missing. Had these dossiers been removed? Were they concealed in another cabinet? Again, I scanned the labels of the unopened cabinets. I heard footsteps from the corridor. I froze. The footsteps moved across the doorway and away. I opened a fifth cabinet, tricking the lock with my silver pins. PERS 07 did not hide there either. I opened a sixth cabinet, heard footsteps in the corridor, froze. I looked back over my shoulder and waited. Nothing, nothing. Nothing, and then, as if there were a ghost in the room, the steel drawer of one of the other cabinets slid closed. The sound had a terrifying finality, thundering and also neatly small, like the tick mark on a bureaucrat's checklist, like the cocked hammer on a revolver. A fissure that slides across an airship's engine.

I looked down. PERS 07 lay in the drawer before me. A notebook in white.

I was taking the notebook from its place when the door of room 818 blasted open. It was like the landfall of a cyclone. I jerked around, bumping the drawer with my hand, scraping my knuckle, hearing the mechanism's violent clasp. My gaze was lifting to the doorway, across polished leather shoes but not to the face of the solemn orderly, the adversary I had imagined. Instead, square in the light, like the first figure of an illuminated manuscript, stood Danny Finch. His jacket was unbuttoned. He had blond hair and pale blue eyes and there were no binoculars at his neck. His chest was rising with inhaled breath and my chest rose with inhaled breath, and I did not smile at this man, I did not greet him; I looked at him as if he had already wronged me.

His right hand moved. My eyes darted to my grey gun, quiet on its table, and immediately Danny Finch had glimpsed it too, and he was in motion, lunging, arm outstretched, and I was moving with him toward the same centre of this windowless room. Only I was no longer moving for the gun. I was moving for Danny Finch. There was a table between us and I stepped around it—front-step, my weight on my back leg. I pulled forward with a kick, *jing gerk*, smashing his right knee. He buckled. My fist met his face, knuckles perpendicular to the floor, and I let my hand drop. I pivoted at the hips. I slammed my elbow into his shoulder, a lever at its fulcrum, and he fell sideways. He fell at once. His head clipped the corner of a cabinet and smacked the floor with a sound like a man clapping hands. One clap and there we were, two motionless figures. Danny Finch's limbs were folded near two legs of the table. I was standing in follow-through: bent at the front knee, arms in *jong sao*, tensed and untensed. On the surface of the table, the perfect stack of files. A harmless metal gun. There was a tiny crack in Danny Finch's forehead and a line of blood was now drawing across the tile. I could see part of his brain. I stepped across his body and closed the door. The cabinets were mostly sealed, organized, absolutely inert. Danny Finch was the only mess. I looked at where the edge of a steel shelf had grazed my knuckle. My hands were still. These movements had been efficient and exact, the culmination of study. For a short moment I felt like a kind of master. Then I suppressed the swell of vomit. I realized that I was still drunk. My stomach was swirling and my chest was heaving. I was hot at my temples and collar and wrists. I was a desperate coward. I picked up my jacket from the back of a chair. I picked up my briefcase from the floor, where no blood had touched it. I opened the clasps and put the gun, twelve dossiers, my jacket, inside. Danny Finch was dead at my feet. I had murdered him with my hands. I tried to recall what he had said to me, years ago, when we met. I tried to remember if there had been malice there, the capacity to kill.

I went out of the room, in shirtsleeves, with my briefcase, shutting Danny Finch's body among the archives. The corridor's flooring was like a long line of tundra. I turned one corner and another and in the aftershock of adrenaline I discovered that I was blazingly angry, filled with a fury for Danny Finch and a fury for the Karls and a fury for Pash and a fury for the man who called himself Lev. A roaring wrath, roiling at my heart. I passed the harmless janitor, leaning on a doorjamb, cajoling a secretary; I slipped back by stairs to the third; I thought: *I was alone when I met him in that little room, nobody forced me.*

I remembered the sound of the door blowing open. I remembered the way you had looked at me, Clara, the night before, outside the Savoy, in the barren moment when we parted.

Standing in the elevator, beside the operator with the birthmark on his chin, I said, "Main floor."

He said, "Going down."

EIGHT

HAIR OF THE DOG

I KNOW THE QUESTIONS you are asking. You are asking: Did I have to kill this man? You are asking: What did it feel like? You are asking: Did it destroy you? You are also asking the other questions: Did I make sure Danny Finch was dead? Were my fingerprints not everywhere? What of the security man in the lobby, with his accounting of entrances and exits?

Eventually I learned the answers to some of these questions. Others, I still do not know. When I got into the Karls' grey sedan and we swung away from the Dolores Building, around the block, I did not tell them that I had killed Danny Finch. I opened the briefcase on the seat beside me and they saw the files, saw the gun, and I sat back in silence until we arrived at my home. After they let me out I went down the street to the corner, where a man in a long apron pulled chop suey from a bucket. I scooped the noodles from the plate into my mouth, gnashing, ravenous. When I returned to the house I looked in the mirror. My face was flecked with sauce and scallion, and my eyes were the same as ever.

—

For weeks, I waited for the police to come to take me away. I kept the front door locked. The brownstone on West 54th Street seemed suddenly rickety, vulnerable, easily invaded. They would smash in the door and thunder up the stairs, and I would be rising from my wires and condensers as they descended upon me, nightsticks knowing. Instead, students rang the doorbell; friends snuck in the back. I told them I was afraid of burglars. They rolled their eyes. I received a phone call from a journalist at the *Times*, asking for a quote regarding the composer Edgard Varèse, an acquaintance. "He's very pleasant," I murmured. "Very, very pleasant." I put down the receiver and wondered whether this had been a test, a sting, the call from a team of G-men to determine if I was at home. I went to the window. The street was filled with girls in skirts and dogs on leashes and pigeons like flying oil spots.

Months passed. Inconceivably, whole months passed. Whenever it happened that Danny Finch's body was discovered, his broken skull, there was no story in the paper. No policemen came for me, no detectives took my fingerprints. If there were agents who suspected me, spies and spymasters, these spooks were biding their time, waging a larger war. They must have known, in the shadowlands, that Lev Termen was not the Soviets' only soldier.

I did not feel as if I was a person. If you tore off my hands, ripped off my head, you would find asbestos, chalk dust, tufts of rags. All my blood had been drained away. It lay in an undisturbed pool outside the Savoy. I laughed with my friends and bent over my tools, felt the seasons' skim over New York City, and I was a scientist, an engineer, a man attending meetings, I was the outer part of myself and not the inner. They repealed Prohibition and I sipped a solitary glass of cherry brandy.

Before long it was another year. I went to my monthly meetings with Karl and Karl—they would say I went dutifully, but there was only the semblance of duty, the soldier in automatic lockstep. The Karls made me drunk. I told them the spry nothings that composed my days. Perhaps they thought the booze made me honest. I went to the appointments they assigned—shook hands, signed papers. Now and then they asked me to steal, to take surreptitious photographs, but I bungled these, forgetting to remove the lens cap, taking the wrong document from the wrong folder. These lapses were neither deliberate nor accidental. I do not know what they were. I sat with Schillinger and Frances at *It Happened One Night*, laughing like a donkey, feeling nothing.

"Leon, how are you?" Lucie Rosen asked one day. She was stooped in the foyer, untying her shoes.

"Fine," I said.

She raised her eyes to look at me. "You sure?"

"I am very pleasant," I said.

Nobody wanted my theremins. My meetings with the world's Bert Grimeses were always on the matter of teletouch—my hocus-pocus of invisible sensing. Shop windows that lit up, displays that moved with every passerby. Nate Stone's scheme for Macy's windows had been an enormous hit; he was rich now and kept pestering me for new gimmicks. "Come over," he'd say. "Wanna ask you about something." I'd arrive and face his string of spitballed ideas, half concepts and figments, slung across his marble kitchen table. A secretary perched nearby, hunched over her typewriter.

Spinning windmills, Nate suggested. Books that open and close. "Or electric dogs," he said, "barking over dog food. Wait—cats!"

"Cats barking?" I said.

"Cats meowing."

"Over dog food."

"Over *cat* food."

The typewriter dinged.

I played the dumb Russian because Nate was so boring. His thousand-dollar ideas were for selling cufflinks or toilet paper, each an aesthetic variation on the same root mechanism. It was a decade and a half since I'd invented the radio watchman, and these meetings with Nate and his secretary and that damn dinging typewriter only emphasized the meaninglessness of my present work. I thought with agony of smug, slender Sasha, spending every day in research. "Could you make it rain," Nate said, "when a customer checks out the umbrellas?" While he envisaged commercial magic, I saw just the same old servos, connected to wet buckets.

My half-life went on. Nate's secretary sent me carbon-copied minutes. I sat up all night, taking motors out of windmills, screwing them into hollowed-out books. It was 1934 and this was my livelihood.

I tried not to think of you. When I did think of you, I tried to forget your face. I willed it to blur away, water poured onto a watercolour. You would be just another girl, a silhouette, a skirt. I had known many silhouettes.

When you told me *No*, Clara, it was as if you were rejecting a law. *It is not like this*, you were saying. Denying not my hypothesis but my conclusion. This was not a matter of persuasion. I could not take you back into the Savoy and persuade you that there is no gravity, that there is no death. It was a matter of proof. I needed a lover's proof, incontrovertible. I did not know where to find it. *It is not like this*, you were saying. The particles were not present. The equation did not resolve. I learned that there was another way to interpret the data. This other way is hideous, heartbreaking. A world that is not as it seems.

In this mistaken world, nothing was not fragile. Which principles would be the next to fall? Which truths were false? I was a scientist and a murderer. I was alone. Was I even alive, down deep, in the deepest part, where at night I felt so barren?

I remember one evening, walking home up Seventh Avenue. It was dark. I came up to Lerners—closed up, abandoned until the morning. Lev Sergeyvich Termen, 60 kilograms, a Howell suit, nothing more. I passed the thirteen shop windows and each, one by one, became illuminated.

IT WAS AN EARLY AUTUMN morning when I decided to go see Katia. The sun had not risen. I went down the stairs to make my breakfast and as I entered the kitchen I had a sudden longing for the thick red jam she made every summer. I longed for her jam but I could not even recall which berries she had used. The forgetting humiliated me. I took some slices of ham from the icebox and I sat with a stale piece of bread and this plate of ham. I tried to imagine the taste of Russian raspberries, or cranberries, or bilberries, blueberries, ash berries.

At a booth in Penn Station I bought a ticket to New Jersey. I walked to the platform and thought of the platforms in Leningrad, those proud marble pillars. I had taken hundreds of trains from Nikolayevsky, Oktyabrsky, Leningradsky, that station of many names. I had my *Mandat*, then. A card with the words *Vladimir Ilyich Lenin*. May his memory be illuminated. My equipment packed in its cases and me like an arrow from the Soviet, swift and certain, sent along the rails with word of electricity, indisputable truths. In Kazan and Samara I stood in drafty wooden halls, with boxes full of snaking wire, but there were no deceptions when I showed the townsfolk my machines. I was no charlatan.

I sat with my hands between my thighs, alone in the train car. We were late to leave the station. I had not brought a book. This was my first time underneath the Hudson River. It did not seem like a new place. The walls of the passage were invisible in the dark and you could not hear the river, just the *clack-clack*, *clack-clack* of the train, and I felt as if I were on a ceaseless path into hell. I forgot the tunnel's engineering feat, forgot the years of work plans and careful digging, and when we emerged into daylight I took a long, grateful breath.

We went on, *clack-clack*. I looked out the window at the dull land that ringed the city. Now and then a white barn, a grey river, like the stations on a pilgrimage. I found myself waiting keenly for the ticket inspector, someone who would come in and tear this piece of paper.

The last time I had seen Katia was backstage at Carnegie Hall, four years earlier. A hundred men in pressed black suits, dandies in seersucker, a procession of women in taffeta and jewels, Steinways and Rockefellers, Rosens and Schillingers, the Bolotines and little Yolochka, prawns and devilled eggs, wine and mousse, playbills and coiled cables, and Ekaterina Pavlova Termen, my secret, hidden in a corner, clutching her elbows. Do not imagine that I ignored her. I said hello. I said I was surprised to see her there. I lingered. I wondered if she had come to embarrass me. So many others were waiting for me, around the room. I went away but came back later with a plate of melon and gravlax. She picked at the capers. She wore a plain dress and a gaudy necklace that was not in fashion. When I introduced her to Otis Skinner she nodded at what he said but I do not think she understood him. Her English was not good. I realized that she probably did not even know who he was. In Russian I said, "He's an actor."

"Yes," she replied. "You can tell by how much he talks."

I had not liked Otis Skinner in *Kismet* but he had come to my performance. He told stories of sneezing during the filming of the movie's harem scenes. Katia stood like a faded statuette. After a little while I found a reason to leave her. I glanced back often. Through the glad crowds I glimpsed her arms, her back, the side of her face, always at right angles, as if she had been carved out with a chisel. Then finally she disappeared.

At Newark I changed to the Erie line. I sat across from a father and son. The father was my age. I was not sure of the age of the son; only parents seem to have an instinct for the age of children. He was a boy. He had blond hair and a dark summer tan. He was holding an incandescent light bulb. "Hello," he said to me.

"Hello," I said.

His father gave me a nod.

The boy tapped his light bulb against the carriage window.

"Be careful with that," his father said.

I wondered why the boy had a light bulb, why he was not at school. Where was he going with his father, was the light bulb new or burnt out. The boy tapped the light bulb against the carriage window.

His father glared. "Leon," he said sternly.

The boy sighed. "Yes, Pop."

A boy named Leon, carrying a light bulb through New Jersey.

I rang the hospital from the station in Paterson.

"Can you please connect me to Katia Termen?" I asked the switchboard operator.

"Who?"

"Katia Termen. She is a nurse."

"You mean Catherine Termen?"

"Yes."

"May I ask who is calling?"

"This is Mr Termen."

"Just a moment, please."

Katia answered the telephone in English. She said "Hello" in an elongated way, rising. I scarcely recognized her voice.

"Hello?" I said back.

"Yes?"

"It's Lev."

I told her I was in Paterson. She was not friendly or unfriendly. I said I had come to see her.

"When?" she said.

"Tonight?" I said.

"Lev, I can't. There is a shower tonight for one of the other girls."

We were speaking in English. "Before, then?"

There was a short silence. "At lunchtime, maybe, I have some time."

"Where should I meet you?"

"Come to the sanatorium."

"All right."

"Wait outside."

"Outside the sanatorium."

"Yes, Valley View," she said.

"What?" She had pronounced *valley* like *velly*.

"Valley View."

"*Velly* View?"

"Valley View!" she shouted, angry.

"I'm sorry, I didn't understand you," I said.

I met her outside Valley View, a little after one o'clock. It was a small tuberculosis hospital. There was a measured lawn, empty flower beds. A thousand suspended leaves, red and brown, like old ornaments. A single path led past the gate, through the centre of the grass. A patient drooped in a wheelchair. I looked away. I sat on a bench. The path was made of the sort of dusty gravel that coats your shoes, turns the cuffs of your trousers to parchment. A carriage rattled past, horse kicking up powder, and I imagined my face caked in a thin layer of dust.

Suddenly Katia was standing before me, hands at her sides, in perfect whites. I felt my heart jerk.

I stood. I greeted my wife.

She did not seem to have changed. Her upturned chin and long legs, an oval face like the image on a cameo. A mouth small and elegant. Brown hair, shorter than I had ever seen it, still parted to the right. She had always been small; she was even smaller in her uniform. Slender, compact at the shoulders, a thin belt in a ring at her waist. She was twenty when we were married, ten years ago. Now there were lines around her eyes. These eyes were clear, soft, unlaughing. They matched the season.

She smelled of washing powder and vinegar but also of herself, in a memory I could not place. Snow, books, a new cardigan.

Something twinged in my jaw. I tried to think of New York City. I lifted my head. "If it isn't 'Catherine,'" I said, in English.

Katia shook her head. "You just show up at the train station?" Her voice was as thin as paper. "Why couldn't you call first? You appear. Just like a ghost. I have a job, Lev. I do not have your life—your luxury life. My one break in the day, and here I am meeting you."

"I'm sorry, I . . ." I trailed off.

"Well, what is it? What's wrong?"

I swallowed. "Nothing's wrong."

"Then why are you here, waiting outside a gate?"

"I . . ." I swallowed again. I turned to gaze back through the gate. "The hospital looks like a very good place to work."

"It is not a hospital; it is a sanatorium," Katia said. She brushed a lock of hair behind her ear. She wore two slim bracelets at her wrist. One of them I had given to her, ten years ago. The other I did not recognize. She muttered something to herself, then lifted her eyes to me. "Well let's walk at least."

We set off side by side, and within this parallel movement, strange and familiar, I suddenly glimpsed her wedding ring. There, on her right hand. I stuffed my hands into my pockets. I looked not at her, but up toward the hill. I wished I had brought her something: a flower, a box of chocolates. I had brought her just my bare hands.

Later we were in the rising grass. The conversation was rote: questions about weather, health, family.

"And your brother?" I asked.

She seemed so brittle. "Sasha? You don't even keep in touch with Sasha?"

"Not in a little while."

"A little while?" She snorted. "Two years? Three?" It had been four. "I knew you were not writing to our friends, to my parents; but Sasha—*he's* a *scientist*." She said the word mockingly, as if it were the title of a lord. "You're so busy now that you can't even dictate a letter to one of your colleagues?"

I cleared my throat. "It is not like that."

"What's it like, Lyova?"

I looked at her. She was being deliberately cruel. I didn't blame her. "Tell me how is Sasha."

"He is all right." She took a breath. "Everyone is all right. Just all right. It is a bad time, Lev." She sighed. "You hear stories. The letters feel sometimes like they are being written onto—no, from on *top* of ice."

"Not for people like Sasha, surely."

She shrugged her narrow shoulders. "There are several reasons I do not go back to Russia."

I looked at the earth. "Yes."

"And you?" She gazed at me from under her brown lashes. "Are you going home?"

"To Leningrad?"

"Yes."

"I am staying for now," I said. "I have a great deal to do. Contracts. Inventions. New work every week. Many meetings."

"One of the doctors bought a theremin. He said it was completely impossible."

"Yes, it can be challenging. You must be deft."

"He is a surgeon." She giggled, folded her arms. "He said it was like eating a pie with a shovel."

"These days we are moving on from the theremin to other things."

"Yes," she said.

"Different kinds of sensors based around the electromagnetic resistance of the body, sometimes configured in sequence." She showed no interest. "Or in conjunction with geothermal readings; I am experimenting with naval applications and also aircraft. So long as you understand the principles, there are infinite ways to implement them."

Levelly: "You must get to see a lot of the country."

"There are many, many meetings. Lunches at the Rockefeller Plaza and the Empire State. NYU, MIT, Columbia."

"You're still in midtown?" she murmured.

"Four storeys, and the basement."

She made a thin smile. "The dorm is scarcely big enough for Judy and me. Only one of us can be in the kitchen at a time. If she is making her lunch I have to wait on my bed for her to finish. It's funny. Sometimes I pretend she is my servant. 'Judy, some toast!'"

"I have a very large kitchen," I said. "Do you know Tommy Dorsey?" She showed me she did; in a small way I was surprised. "He comes to dinner parties sometimes. And George and Ira Gershwin. We all just crowd around with the girls, laughing, cooking."

"'With the girls.'"

We had passed into some woods and began climbing a slope. In spite of the incline we were pretending that we were just strolling. Katia was a little ahead of me now. *With the girls.* These words hung in the air. I had known they would hang in the air, before I said them, but I said them anyway. It was as if I wanted to bring us to a particular tree, to look again at an engraving we had carved there.

"Are you seeing anyone?" I asked.

"No," she said.

"You know you can. We agreed, when you arrived here—"

"Yes of course I know. I was seeing someone, now I am not."

"I'm sorry."

"I don't need your 'sorry,'" she said. These could have been bitter words but they weren't. She said them simply, almost lightly. I looked at her, just up the path, the side of her face dappled with light. Straight-backed in her whites. Katia did not need my sorry.

I lowered my head. Ten years ago, I had met her at Sasha's door. A beautiful girl with an armful of tools. A bouquet of tools. We married so quickly. I made a mistake. It was not that I was careless in my calculations; it was that I was seeking the wrong sum. Sasha's little sister, a beautiful girl with an armful of tools, reverent and unhappy. She wanted for us to sip clear borscht at dinner, and then to sit beside me, knitting, as I read the newspaper. She wanted for us to have a dog. She wanted for me to grow bored of my devices, to spend summer afternoons building cabinets in the kitchen, or for us to move to the country: to live alone at the centre of a valley, eating apples from the trees around our dacha.

The second time I went to Paris, I brought her with me. The city of lights and love: perhaps I could salvage my error. We had been married for three years. But she hated the taste of French bread, the dank water dripping down alleyways. She hated the unfamiliar bath and the way the Parisian women looked at her. "Lyova, this is shit," she said.

I gave her money, a map, circled the Louvre, the Eiffel Tower, the Galeries Lafayette. At one of the parties at the Paris Opera I asked a black-haired girl where to go for shoes. She finished her champagne flute in one long swallow. "Rue Meslay," she said. The next day I told Katia: "Meslay Street. Go, buy anything." She came back with a pair of slippers. "Calfskin," she said. I shrugged. She yelled at me: "Aren't you angry?" They had cost three hundred francs. I remember standing under the crystal chandelier in our hotel room, both of us shouting. Then I went out.

"We must end this," I said, the morning I left for America.

She lay in bed and closed her eyes.

When I boarded the *Majestic*, the manifest listed me as a bachelor. I do not know why. I felt somehow vindicated.

When I arrived in New York there was a telegram waiting.

I CANNOT WAIT FOR YOU, it said.

I wrote back, SO DO NOT WAIT.

She came on a ship. It was a deliberate misunderstanding, like she was using her life to make a dark joke.

Now Katia and I had been wed for ten years. She did not need my sorry.

Katia sat down on a rock. "Why are you here?"

I didn't have a quick answer.

"Lev?"

"A visit," I said, "with an old friend."

She looked at her hands. "Are you all right?"

"I am wonderful," I said. "Are you all right?"

I could see her clench her teeth.

"Why are we speaking in English?" I said.

"You are a horrible little man," Katia said. "You are not all right and we are not old friends. Have you come all the way to New Jersey, to a maple forest, to tell me helpless lies? Why are you here? To tell me you love me? To belittle my life? Or is it to tell me you are dying, something like that?"

I swallowed. A squirrel ran across the path and braided between two trees. The wind had fallen away and the air felt very still. Through a break in the trunks I could see down the rise to the sanatorium, the cluster of nearby buildings, a pasture speckled with cows. An eagle wheeled through the empty space.

I rubbed my eyes.

Katia's tone had changed. "Lev?" she said.

I crouched in my suit.

"Lev, I didn't mean . . . Are you sick?"

I picked up a piece of birch bark, like a discarded message. "I am not sick," I said.

She was watching me, just barely moving.

"I am lonely," I said.

I felt the flick of her eyes.

"There was a woman," I said.

Then she straightened, like a building pulled back to standing. The only colour in her face was in her lips and eyes. I could see her choosing what to say.

She stood up.

"I don't care," she said.

She smoothed her skirt with her hands and walked away down the path.

I STAYED IN PATERSON OVERNIGHT. At a church near the guesthouse, a string quartet was performing Haydn. This is a music of astonishing tricks, flourishes that hairpin and buck. The quartet was incompetent. The cellist was graceless; the violinists sounded as if they were golems, made of clay. Only the violist had the capacity for beauty. I wished the other players were dead and it was only that viola, constant, under unilluminated stained glass.

Raspberries, I wondered. Cranberries, bilberries, blueberries, ash berries.

WHEN I GOT BACK to the house in Manhattan, Lucie Rosen was alone on the second floor, practising. It was one of those strange, gloomy mornings: a wet wind, skyscrapers grazing thunderclouds. Lucie had not put on the lights. She stood in darkness with the theremin, repeating two low figures. I came up the stairs and watched her. The gale had come into her face. She seemed fierce, almost stricken.

"Good morning," I said, when she stopped.

"Good morning." She used a wrist to smooth the sweat on her cheek.

"Exceptional tone."

When I said this, Lucie began to cry. Small, contained sobs. I brought her a handkerchief. We stood with the theremin between us. "I'm sorry," she said.

"No, no."

She dabbed her eyes and balled the handkerchief in her hand. For some reason, I was reminded that she owned this house. I felt so tired. I stood beside her, wondering if she and Walter were getting divorced, if she was moving to India or California or Cape Cod. I put my hand on her shoulder. "It's all right," I said.

She swallowed. "Were you there last night?" she said.

"Where? New Jersey—"

"The concert."

I did not understand.

"At Town Hall."

"Here?"

"Clara's concert," Lucie said in a bitter voice.

I did not say anything.

"At Town Hall. She played the theremin." Lucie, my best pupil, seemed about to cry again. "Leon, it was beautiful. It was so beautiful."

There was no thunder, no lightning. It did not rain that day. The clouds passed over and away. Lucie told me about your debut recital, performing works by Beethoven, Tchaikovsky, and Saint-Saëns, on a theremin painted with gold curlicues, pink and red and blue flowers, the finest solo performance that there had ever been.

"She held her hands like this," Lucie said, showing me. "Like this."

WHEN IT WAS WINTER, the streets filled up with snow. The pipes in the house froze. I invented a stand-alone heater that turned on only when it was cold. I sat in my workshop watching its light flicker.

Sifu died. Jin came round to tell me. He asked why I had stopped coming to the kwoon. I told him I had killed a man, and that one day I had found I could not bring myself to go to a room across town to repeat the same motions, in rehearsal. Jin laughed. He thought it was a joke. "You are scared you are getting old!" he said.

I did not go dancing. I did not go to dinner parties with Frances and Schillinger. Tommy Dorsey and George Gershwin did not come over for spaghetti. I missed meetings, lying on my back on my bed, imagining machines that did not work.

I filed for divorce from Ekaterina Pavlova Termen of Paterson, New Jersey.

In February, the doorbell buzzed. It buzzed and buzzed. I did not answer it, but my guest would not be deterred. Whoever it was leaned into the buzzer, letting it sound throughout the brownstone house. Perhaps a kid is being a nuisance, I thought. Perhaps someone rude wants my attention. I refused to move. I lay on my back on my bed. My brow creased.

Then there was a crash. It was the thud of the door being busted in, and broken glass. I sat bolt upright. I could feel my heart in my chest, pounding.

I thought: *Danny Finch's friends.*

I looked around for a weapon, some kind of weapon, a club or knife or a perfect deadly revolver. I would not wait with bare hands. I grabbed a hammer. I padded to the top of the stairs. Someone was coming. Someone very large. I could hear his footfalls, like the first booming of an avalanche. I heard a palm smack the handrail. I shifted my weight to my left leg, bent. I raised my hammer. I breathed, waiting.

Pash appeared around the landing, like a brown bear returning. He seemed twelve feet tall. His hair had thinned a little but his eyes were still pale blue. "Lev Sergeyvich Termen!" he shouted. "King of the Termenvox!" He clapped his eyes on me and held out his paw. I took it, shook it, as if I was checking a door to see if it was locked.

"Pash," I stammered.

He laughed. "Am I a prince of the termenvox, would you say? A baron?"

"Where have you been?"

"Working hard." He was thinner. He smelled like the outdoors, like an evergreen place where a creature would hibernate. "Which is more than we can say for you."

I was speechless. I was breathing like a child. I was a cabin thrown up by a hurricane and then set back down.

Pash looked out over the workshop, curious, appraising, at the same time approving and unsatisfied. He rapped on the surface of a theremin, nudged a disassembled teletouch box. He lifted the skirt of the canvas that hid the cypresses. "My, my," he said, and laughed. A laugh like an old friend. He turned back to me. "I can't tell you how many times I imagined traipsing in here."

"Why didn't you?"

"I was sent away, Lev." He bent to rummage in his bag. My intelligent heater gave a cough and turned on. I had forgotten how much space Pash used up. I had forgotten how much I knew his silhouette—the comfort of a familiar shape, rummaging in a bag. My chest felt tight. With rough movements Pash pulled out a carved wooden eagle, a pair of suede slippers. "For you," he said.

I swallowed. The eagle was smaller than a dessert plate. There was something demented in the bird's face. "E PLURIBUS UNUM," said the chiselled inscription.

"Americans love these patriotic doodads," Pash said. "They can't get enough of 'em." His English seemed looser than it had been, more at home. "This one's from Oklahoma City."

"Thank you?" I said.

"And these aren't slippers." He pressed the suede shoes into my hands. They were soft and pliable, embroidered with tiny mustard-coloured beads. "Moccasins," he said. "Indians wear them so they can sneak up on people."

"And I . . ."

"Well, now you can sneak up on people." He laughed again, powerful and happy. "Right?" But as his laughter subsided, Pash was surveying me. He rubbed his lip. "You all right?"

"Yes," I said.

He clicked his tongue and nodded. "You're all right now, Lev. We're both all right."

I was turning the wooden eagle in my hands.

"Pash, where did you go for all this time?"

For an instant he looked at the floor. I thought he was preparing to make a joke, a feint, but instead his voice seemed scraped bare. "Lev, there is nothing nobler than work. Good work. It's better than fortune and fame. Better than a million girls." His eyes flicked to mine.

In the half-light, I was squinting.

"They called me away," Pash said. He shrugged. "The Crash happened and there were matters that called for my expertise, first in Texas, then Oklahoma. A few years in Florida. Colorado. Union stuff, ports stuff, stuff you don't need to hear about. Our employers needed me there, putting out fires."

"You couldn't have told me?"

"They told me to be discreet," Pash said lightly. "You're not a delicate flower, Lev. You could handle it. I knew you could. And other agents were taking over for me. You were taken care of?"

Taken care of, I thought.

My answer was terse. "It was a disaster. I almost went broke. I almost abandoned everything."

"But here we are," he said. He let out a deep breath. "At the end of it, still, here we are." He seemed distant, then. His eyes rested on the mirror above the mantel. It was as though he was watching some slow construction, waiting for a way to describe it.

"Every single day," Pash said at last, "any of us could give up. Sure we could. But we don't, Lev. Not me. Not you." His gaze slipped back to my cypress loudspeakers, hulking under canvas. "Because we serve. Because there is a good we are doing, an end we're striving for. The nobility of the Soviet dream, yes? And the work itself—let's not forget. You are a genius, Professor Termen, when it comes to the work."

He shrugged. His face was just itself: bright eyes, a small mouth, a nose like a cudgel. He grinned. "You're a lord of the air, remember."

This man I had met in Berlin, with whom my life had been knotted, whom even now I scarcely knew. In that moment I felt as if he understood what I was capable of better than I did; and what I wanted, now that you were gone, Clara; and how all of it could be done.

"I am sorry I disappeared, Lev." He rested his body against the doorjamb. "But I am back now, and despite that lying mirror we're still young men. You've got moccasins and I've got a new telephone number and I say if you're game, then let's finish what we started together. The inventor and his silent partner, masterminds and experts, clever spies, rascals. Ha! Snakes in this million-dollar Manhattan grass."

There was no decision. I simply took a breath. My inhalation was a yes and I felt something heavy lift from my shoulders. I imagined a crane tilting up over the room.

Somewhere in the house, a clock tolled the hour. Pash, still in the doorway, gestured over the workshop floor, past the cypresses, the piano, the flickering intelligent heater, to where a pair of theremins stood tall and side by side, flawlessly assembled.

He said, "I'm rusty as damn, Lev, but do you fancy a duet?"

NINE

RETURN OF THE ROUGHNECKS

FULLY, COMPLETELY, I became a spy. What had been half-hearted became whole. My distractions were cleared away; my mission was clear. I would walk through walls.

Pash had my house cleaned. He called a crew of three women, Romanians in coveralls, hair pinned back. "Go to it," he told them. He took me to the pier; we rode a ferry around the Statue of Liberty. He said: "What are your ideas?"

I asked, "Ideas for what?"

"Ideas for the Americans."

In the clear white daylight, over choppy waves, I found I had ideas. A thousand ideas. "But only teletouch is selling," I said.

"So let's spear some new whales," Pash said.

The studio was quiet. I was not taking new students and I left the veterans to themselves. Lucie nursed her sorrows for two weeks and then began to practise constantly, morning to midnight. I heard her through the floorboards. I did not stand with her. I had my thousand ideas. I was bent over a thousand sheets of paper, with compass and slide rule, crocodile clips on my collar.

I had always been an inventor in New York, but curiosity alone had guided me through the early years: I pursued my flights of fancy and we waited for the telegrams from captains of industry. Now I was more cunning. I knew the places Pash wished to infiltrate, so I imagined what they wanted, and then I built it.

Sometimes I needed help. I went with Pash to a machinist's shop in Boston. I handed the man twenty pages of plans. "Make this," I said. We took the streetcar across town, to a professor's basement office. "Let's talk about the telegraph," I said. I spent six days at the university library, digging through books. Sometimes an idea is like glimpsing a person before she disappears around a corner. You must still learn her full figure. I had no facility with written English but there is a universality to numbers, diagrams, formulas. When I did not understand the text I called a lecturer, a Nobel laureate. I had spent almost a decade in the United States, collecting brilliant men's business cards, tossing them on my desks. The Romanian cleaners had arranged them in a shoebox, alphabetically. When I wanted to know about the railway, I called a senior engineer at Union Pacific. When I wanted to know about aeroplanes, I called MIT's dean of aeronautics. When I wanted to know about the underlying mechanics of the universe, I called Albert Einstein. I called Griffiths from Douglas Aircraft and Lieutenant Groves from the navy.

I sat with Pash in restaurants, opening the molten cheese on French onion soup. "It's a sure thing," I said.

Pash batted away a neighbour's cigarette smoke. "I've heard that before."

After that first night, he never discussed his years away. He was concerned with the present, he said. But I counted his changes. A tan around the neck and at the wrists. Buttons, not cufflinks, at the sleeve. He was gaunter, a little too thin for that great old suit. Yet there weren't any ghosts in his eyes. His hands were steady. His briefcase, clean and unbattered, held the same amount of papers.

I had continued to meet with Karl and Karl, every month, at the little diner. "Tell the men at Mud Tony's anything they want to know," Pash said. He had bigger fish to fry than the ones sizzling in L'Aujourd'hui's kitchen. He was hunting whale. So I sat with the Karls in our customary stall, sipping customary spirits. Despite my protestations, they believed they needed vodka to keep my tongue loose. Yet the other Lev, my bald-headed adversary, did not reappear. I asked Pash if he knew him—described his face, his clothing, the way he carried himself.

"No Lev I know," Pash said.

"Is he called something else?"

Pash changed the subject. Professionally speaking, he and the Karls were distant cousins. "They're parentheses," he told me, "irrelevant." Yet within these parentheses, I had knocked a man down and seen the blood run out of his head. I hadn't told anyone. Neither the Karls nor Pash. It haunted me and yet I did not air my actions. A private killing, an exchange between two men, high on the eighth floor.

I did not know who exactly gave Pash his orders, only that with him I could do anything. I didn't need to be afraid. When I complained that the other operatives got me drunk, that I left my meetings feeling sickly, strings cut, he brought me a pound of butter.

"Eat this," he said, "before."

"Eat this how?"

"With a spoon. Or a knife."

I took out a teaspoon. "All of it?"

"It is the antidote to vodka," Pash said. "A trade secret."

Every two fortnights, I ate a pound of butter. I drank and stared Karl and Karl full in their eyes and felt like my own man.

After a month we went back to Boston, back to the machinist's shop. He showed us the things his crew had made for us: two heavy archways, almost as wide as the garage, packed with electrical components. I walked around them with voltmeters, checking the circuits.

"What they do?" asked one of the men, thin as a pair of long-necked pliers.

"Metal detector," I said.

"What for?"

Pash handed the boss a banker's cheque. "Gangsters."

We loaded the metal detectors into a truck and brought them back to New York, installing them in a warehouse near the Curtiss airfield. We hired actors: men in grey suits and fedoras, packing unloaded heat. We hired catering: rib-eye steaks and layer cake, wardens' food. The officials from Alcatraz came in black limousines. They had sinewy faces and unforgiving handshakes. They grazed the table of red meat and angel food.

"Behold!" I said, as if they did not know what they had come to see. The arches sat like ancient monoliths. The men from Alcatraz had crossed ten states to examine these inventions, to gauge their utility for the country's first super-prison. Now they folded their arms. Pash signalled the actors, our fake gangsters, to walk through the portals. They strutted and sneaked. They couldn't help it—this was their best gig in weeks. Some of them carried no weapons and passed harmlessly through the gates. But the ones with bulges in their suit jackets, secrets tucked behind belt buckles, set off alarms. Their gunmetal tickled the electromagnetic fields.

The wardens wanted to try. They handed me their belts, their watches, their eyeglasses. "Wedding rings, gentlemen," I said, offering my cupped palm. Like obedient school children, they gave up their treasures. Off they went, through the arches, without a sound. I nodded to Pash, who followed.

With him, the alarm went off. He did not smirk. He said: "So you see."

"We see," replied the men from San Francisco, eyeing him.

Their decision came by telegram, a week later. Alcatraz would have Theremin's magic metal detectors. An arch at the cell house, an arch at the dock, an arch outside the dining hall and another straddling the labourers' main access path. We went back to the machinist's shop and this time we paid in advance.

Even as this was happening, we met with the air force, with Boeing, modelling new versions of my altimeter. Their decision came by telegram. The U.S. Army Air Corps would have Theremin's magic aeroplane dial. We met with fire departments about fire alarms, railroad officials about railroad signalling, telegraph bigwigs about my ideas for intercity typewriters. I called up the office of Henry Ford, told them that their cars could have automatic indicators for dwindling batteries, engines needing oil. I had plans for naval signalling, wireless microphones, policemen's private radio sets. As I sketched science, Pash pushed paper, and everyone invited the Russians into their drawing rooms.

FROM THE SKY, CALIFORNIA made me think of a vast, intricate map. A map at seventy percent scale, and me high above it, holding binoculars. It was my first flight and I felt a combination of terror and elation. The reason for the elation was obvious: seventeen thousand pounds of metal, lifted into the air, the earthbound gone flying. I have rarely felt more alive than in that dizzy moment when the aeroplane's wheels left the ground, as if the aluminum craft had simply been picked up. But I was also filled with an engineer's trepidation. Here was a device of great intricacy, a thousand screws, and any number could be loose. In the great fraternity of engineers the shameful central secret is this: we err. We botch and fumble. These words seem funny, harmless, but our failures are not always trifling. There are mistakes we never forgive.

My aeroplane flew from New York to San Francisco and did not crash. I landed and staggered from the genius machine and there was a man with a sign, THEREMIN. "Welcome to California," he said. He handed me an orange. As I took the gift I was caught by an unexpected memory: the clear, clear gaze of Vladimir Ilyich Lenin (may his memory be illuminated), on the day that we met. I cradled the orange in my right hand. My mission continued.

I was here to go to Alcatraz; I went to Alcatraz. A cruel rock floating in the San Francisco Bay. The ferry brought us dumbly, without comment, yet my fingers tightened on the handrail. This was a hideous destination. The engine droned and there was blue in the clouded sky, but I could feel the doom in this grey masonry, the haunted garden that lay in its centre. Our boat came alone.

"Hello, Dr Theremin," the functionaries said. *Hello, hello, hello.* I did not know if it was my imagination seeing pairs of eyes in the high-up grilles. "Hello, Dr Theremin, welcome!" I knelt beside a metal detector, checking the circuits, trimming a wire, guarded by a circle of officials. They laughed, cracked jokes. Beyond their perimeter there was no sound, no movement. I only knew because I had read it: three hundred men, locked in, forbidden from speaking. Pash had asked me to find out about Alcatraz's block assignments—whether the murderers were kept with the spies, the rapists with the bombers, Al Capone sharing a wall with Machine Gun Kelly. This was not an idle curiosity: it was at the heart of this journey, the sort of information that we had built these machines to obtain. But in those hours at Alcatraz I could not bring myself to pry into the affairs of its lodgers; there was no way I could sneak down a hallway to slip files from folders. I snipped the wire. I tested the voltage. I listened for the breathing of the men in their cells. I do not believe in a reckoning, but in the heart of this prison I knew I was tempting fate. I was a murderer and a thief, unshackled, with hands that smelled of orange oil.

Until the ferry took me back to the mainland, and I climbed back into the aeroplane, and I flew away, I kept waiting for a voice that would say, *Hello, Dr Theremin.* A voice that was barbed. It would lead me to a cell. I would lie in my cot, counting hours, until the day I died.

It is different, here on this ship. Here I allow myself to miss you, Clara. To remember every part. I cannot leave my room. Food is brought to me by a stranger. But this journey will not be long. Soon we will arrive at a port whose signs are in my mother tongue. The sailors will unlock my cabin and I will walk the gangplank into Russia, my homeland, where I can enact every dream, if I wish to, and I can openly serve a noble cause. All good things will come, somehow. It is the first law of thermodynamics. Nothing is destroyed.

BOTH OF THE KARLS had notebooks out.

"Centimetres or inches?" asked the one with a moustache.

"Inches," I replied. My hands were palms down on the table.

"How high?"

"Six inches."

They nodded. They were taking these figures down—the dimensions of the mufflers used in Douglas O-43 monoplanes, on contract to the United States Army Air Corps. I was providing Douglas with altimeter prototypes; in the course of this work, I acquired certain aeroplane plans.

The Karl with the beard scrutinized me. "Are you certain of these measurements?"

"Yes."

"You are not even consulting notes."

I nodded in agreement.

"How do you remember the measurements?"

"By remembering," I said.

The Karls did not smile.

One of them took a sheaf of papers from his briefcase. His eyes flicked down its length. There was a long pause.

"Lev, do you wish to stay in the United States?"

I raised my eyes in surprise.

"Yes," I said.

"There is a visa issue," he said.

"Can it be resolved?"

Karl pursed his lips.

"I have much more work to do for our country," I said.

The men exchanged a look. Finally one of them said: "Do you have a woman?"

"A woman?"

"Yes."

"Yes," I replied, defensively, reflexively. I clasped my hands in my lap.

"Then get married," said the Karl with the beard. "It would make matters much easier."

❖

I REMEMBER WATCHING A MAN and a woman waving at each other from opposite street corners. He was in a workman's uniform; she held a bag of shopping. They had different shades of faded brown hair. At first their waves were meant just to say, *I see you*. Then they repeated the waves, almost bashful, out of love. Their waves soon became a kind of joke—bigger and bigger, a caricature of waving. They were laughing, their faces so splendidly happy. Then the crowd swarmed the intersection. I did not see them meet. I wondered if it had been worth the waving.

I felt at that time like an empty cabinet. I was made of good, strong wood. Every morning someone would open my wide doors and slip a new sheaf of papers into a designated place, and the shelves were stacked with so many papers, miles of contracts, yet still I knew this cabinet was empty. Perhaps there was a locked drawer at its heart. Perhaps there was a drawer, perhaps it held something of value, perhaps there was, somewhere, a key. I did not know.

Pash went on with our business. He managed the books. I made things for him to trade away.

In 1937, I heard you on the radio, playing Ravel's "Kaddisch" on the theremin. Your performance was matter-of-fact, dumbfounding. It was finer than any violin performance I had ever heard. The theremin had a purity of tone that made the piece feel like an inherent thing, noumenal and unmediated, a treasure that had always been.

I think I had been waiting for a coincidence.

I called you two days later.

"Is Clara there?"

"It's me," you replied.

"It's Leon Theremin."

"I know."

"You remember me?"

You laughed. "Leon."

I said, "I would like to build you a new instrument."

We met on neutral ground, at Grand Central Station. I waited on the mezzanine. I wanted to see you before you saw me. It is difficult to look for a person from the mezzanine of Grand Central Station. Travellers cross the floor in unique trajectories, like the whirl of dandelion seeds. Every time I tried to pick a person out, a sudden crowd obscured him. It felt like chaos, though I knew it was not. Even these paths, given enough time, could be predicted. Plot the data, pick out its patterns, factor age, occupation, destination. I watched the stirring figures. I wondered if, ultimately, everything could be known.

Stillness separated you from the crowd. A woman in a tilted cloche hat, a three-quarter length coat, unfastened. With small shoulders. Gloves. I came down the stairs, my heart charging in my chest, ten thousand horses galloping across the plain. The windless station hall with all its flat golden light. You raised your hand and waved. You had not changed.

You had not changed, you had not changed.

"Hello," I said.

"Hello, Leon." There was hesitation in your face, something like caution. In a certain way this made me proud. There was memory in the way you looked at me.

"Are you well?" I said.

"Yes. Are you?"

"I brought you this," I said.

You pressed your lips together. You took the rose.

"It is good to see you," I said.

Your eyes flicked up. Each of us took a breath. You finally murmured, "Yes."

I gestured at a marble bench, just there, amid the crowds. "So," I said, gently, "let's talk about staccato."

So we talked about staccato. We had talked about it on the telephone and now we talked about it in the station, like acquaintances and then gradually like old friends, knee to knee. You were a remarkable theremin player but you played approximately the same theremin as everyone else, with components from RCA. There were flowers on the sides but its design was seven years old. Its power supply was unreliable. It failed in humid weather. Its timbre was unsophisticated and its volume control was sluggish, unresponsive. "Like molasses," you said. This was the way with all theremins: they were given to glissando, eliding between notes.

For you I imagined better.

I imagined a theremin that was perfectly made, with custom components for its singular player. A more sensitive theremin, with a more supple volume control. That could sing in a more bewitching voice: a voice like light in leaves, breath in chests, a slender lightning bolt.

"Let me build it for you," I said.

"I will pay," you said.

"It doesn't matter," I said. "I would build it anyway."

You smiled. "And still I would pay you."

I proposed to build it differently than the last, than the one you had; differently than any other theremin in the whole of the world. A theremin with its antennas reversed, for your particular injury: pitch on the left side, for your strong left arm; and volume on the right.

"No."

"No?" I asked.

"It is too late," you said.

With my thumb I traced the centre line of my palm.

"Some things you can't undo," you said.

IF YOU ARE LIKE ME, you dream your life according to perfect conditions. You look at the lines of a proof, the clear symbols of a formula, and you understand the world.

This is dream, not knowledge. Life is not a laboratory; twenty-four imperfect hours make up a day. There is interference, distortion, accident, will. There is also hope. Hope will ruin a thing, or fulfil it.

I had neglected my theremin for a very long time. I had not stared at its coils or wires, had not opened its circuitry to the light. It was early 1937 and a war was stirring in Europe. I lived in Manhattan and considered coils, transformers, pitch oscillators. Every time I dragged the stool to my workbench, I had another idea to improve the device. I met Pash when he asked, dined with his masters of industry, but in every spare moment I was experimenting with new speakers and concentrating coils, tightening and replacing tiny brass screws. I did not call you or send letters. I did not divert the bearing of my work. I did not doubt. My mind and hands were following the directives of my wakeful loosened heart and I was solitary, moving, a free particle that spins, that feels the weak and strong forces exerting gravity upon it.

It is not the same solitude I experience here, aboard the *Stary Bolshevik*. Here I am an idle man in a cabin, writing stories on this typewriter. Leaving rows of sentences, months passing in ellipses. . . . I do not know what forces are in play. I do not see the looming icebergs, the coming storms. Sometimes I wake in the night and I wonder if we are sinking. It would be a long time before I would know that we were sinking. You can become a dead man before you know what you are.

I MET THE KARLS at Mud Tony's.

"How long will it take you to tie up your business here?"

"Why?"

"It is time for you to go."

"No. I have no plans to leave. Is this about visas? I will ask Pash to deal with it."

"He cannot fix this."

"We have too much work," I said. "There is also a woman."

"There are other problems. Has he spoken to you about taxes?"

"Taxes?"

"When was the last time you paid taxes?"

"I left such things to—to . . ."

"There are other problems, too," a Karl said, squinting at the row of cars outside the window.

I WAS FRYING A SAUSAGE in a pan when Lucie Rosen called to me from downstairs. "Someone to see you, Leon!" I did not know whether to take the sausage off the stove or to leave it sizzling. How long would I be downstairs? Would this sausage explode? It gleamed.

I left it. I danced down the steps. "Yes?" I said, peering out across the floor. Lucie was standing with a stranger. He wore an ugly green suit, a bad purple tie. He was one of those men who seem secretly large; a trick of muscles in the neck. He had a wide messy mouth. He was still wearing his hat.

"Dr Leon Theremin?" he said.

"Yes," I said.

"I'm Jim. Can we talk privately?"

"Have we met?" I asked.

"No. I'm here from Commerce and Burr."

"Commerce and Burr?"

The man sighed, as if I were already making him sad. "We're debt collectors, Dr Theremin."

I brought Jim upstairs, as Lucie drilled the back of my head with a very alarmed look. We went into one of the smaller workshop rooms. "Please, sit," I said. Jim sat in a wooden chair with wheels on casters. Throughout our conversation he was moving, slightly, back and forth, like a weaving boxer or a killer shark.

"Thank you for agreeing to meet with me," he said.

I gave him an ironic look.

"Have you seen our letters?"

I had no idea what he was talking about. "What letters?"

Now Jim gave *me* an ironic look. He withdrew a sheaf of papers from his jacket pocket and passed them to me. The letterhead, C&B, in black and red, recalled mortar shells descending upon a city.

"You are president of the Migos Corporation, yes?"

"Er . . ." I said, flipping through the papers. Six months of them, addressed to offices in Manhattan and Queens. A few had been sent to West 54th Street but I had never seen them. *Dr Leon Theremin, President, Migos Corporation; Dr Leon Theremin, President, Theremin Patents Corporation; Dr Leon Theremin, President, Teletouch Holding Corporation.*

"Can you give me an address for Boyd Zinman?" Jim asked.

"For who?"

"Boyd Zinman."

I had never heard of Boyd Zinman. "Who?"

Jim sighed. "Dr Theremin, let's be serious. You have defaulted on debts amounting to almost sixty thousand dollars."

My eyes bulged. "Sixty?"

"Remember Walmor Incorporated, Dr Theremin? Remember International Madison Bank?"

I did not remember these things.

"You should speak to my business manager, Julius Goldberg," I said.

"Ah yes," said Jim, "Mr Goldberg. Could I have his address as well?"

I stammered. "Yes, well, actually no. But let me give you his telephone number."

Jim turned slowly in his chair.

When he departed, he left me with a single typed page. It was an accounting of sixteen separate loans involving six corporations, across nine different lenders. The smallest loan was for $3,000, the largest for $30,001. They dated from as early as 1929. *Commerce and Burr*, read the top of the letter, *WE SETTLE IT.*

I called Pash in a near panic.

"It's under control," he said.

"Sixty thousand dollars?"

"Lev, it's under control."

"What's under control? What is this money?"

"It's our business, Lev."

"Our business?"

"The things we do."

"Who is Boyd Zinman?"

"One of your partners. I introduced you. At the Waldorf."

"I don't remember."

"Clearly. That's why I am occupied with these things and you are not. And I am telling you: it's under control."

"So I don't need to worry?"

"Debt collectors are in the business of fear." He made me take down an address in Harlem. "If they come back, give them that. If Commerce and Burr send you letters, ignore them."

"That's it?"

"Lev, I have work to do. So do you."

I put down the telephone and went back upstairs to my rooms. There was smoke in the air, the smell of pork fat. In terror, I remembered my lunch. I ran to the kitchen, searching for fire. No fire. The sausage still gleamed, hot, in its pan.

IN MAY 1937, the Hindenburg airship burst into flames, killing its captain and thirty-four others. Not long thereafter I completed work on your new theremin. It was perhaps the most perfect thing I had ever made. The cabinet was made of ash; the circuitry was gold, green and silver. Its secrets were concealed within two hinged compartments. From the outside it was a simple wedge on four legs. The pitch antenna rose in a short straight line. The volume antenna looped at the left side, esoteric and in its way ornate. Where the performer stands, there was a small dial: ten numbered settings for ten different timbres. I had not just made the theremin sing more beautifully—I had given it many voices. Darker, higher, deeper, an instrument of caves, or of woods, or of roads less travelled by.

I sent it to you with a note, with a *leonid*:

> *Clara this gentle hid-en hum*
> *all might reach us in the end*

You sent me back an invitation to your performance in Philadelphia on August 14.

You wrote, *I hope you'll come. Bring a friend.*

—

I rang Schillinger. "Clara's playing in Philadelphia."

He said: "So?"

"So I'm going."

"Lev, are you sure—"

"Yes I'm sure."

"Lev. You still—"

"So come with me, Schillinger. Come with me."

I would have gone with Pash but I did not want a defender, a guardian; I wanted simply a companion. Someone to go with me on this journey. I hired a car. Before leaving the apartment I looked at myself in the mirror: forty-one years old. I was a whole man. I was small, steady, younger than my years. I was an inventor and a spy. I loved Russia and Clara Reisenberg.

On the drive to Philadelphia, we talked about old times. We talked about Vinogradov, little Yolanda and the Bolotines, that New Year's Eve in Brooklyn. We were somewhere in the middle of the journey, near Trenton, when he craned in his seat and said, "So. Tonight."

I waited a moment. "Yes?"

"What's the piece?"

I lifted my gaze from the road. "Bloch's 'Schelomo.'"

He nodded his head. "Ah," he said, in a way that was at once friendly and short.

"Do you know it?"

"No."

"Neither do I."

"And she's playing the theremin?"

"Yes," I said. "My new theremin."

He laughed, a little forcedly. "I wish I were so lucky!"

The car was silent. We listened to the clatter of stones on the underside of the carriage.

"Are you still in love with her, Leon?"

I watched the highway into Pennsylvania.

He rubbed his face, then glanced back at me. "You're handsome and clever. You're self-possessed. Generous." He was trying to smile at me, but I was not meeting his eyes. "There are ten thousand women who would gladly join their particles to yours."

He was still trying to get me to look at him. I would not.

"But then I don't need to remind you of that," Schillinger said finally.

We passed a sign on the side of the road, showing a moose, intimating that a moose could step out into the middle of the highway. I wondered whether I would be agile enough to drive around it or whether it would be better to stop the car.

Schillinger took a breath and said, abruptly, "Lev, it is dangerous to hope for impossibilities."

I felt the flick of lines along the middle of the road.

"Impossibilities?" I said.

"That's right."

I said, still without looking at him, "Is that what you tell Frances?"

LATER, AS WE TOOK OUR places in the auditorium, I thought of the first time we saw you play. I had sat in Peveril Hall with Schillinger. We watched the violinist and her sister. This was a different night, now. I knew what you would unveil in my heart. I knew the way the curtain would lift and how we would face each other in this midnight hall, a wind blowing between us.

You would play the most perfect instrument I had made.

There was a large crowd, an orchestra's hundred chairs and music stands. The musicians came and took their seats. The first violinist. Then you, slim and straight, in a white gown fringed with gold. You shook the hand of the first violinist. I wondered if you felt something, shaking hands with your former aspiration. Your hair was pulled back, your face like a drawing. A spotlight illuminated my theremin. You had painted over the ashwood, made it black. You took your place behind the device. *DZEEEEOOOoo*, very softly, and you held your hand suspended in the air. Somewhere on the reverse of the cabinet, a light glowed. This was another new invention; a signal for perfect A. The musicians tuned their instruments. You looked over your shoulder at the first violinist, at the line of double bassists. I sat with Schillinger in the darkness.

You were there to perform "Schelomo," by Ernest Bloch, a rhapsody for cello and orchestra. You presented the complete cello part on theremin. It is a composition of sustained and devastating yearning, a wavering conversation between one voice and the ensemble. Your right hand was a fist. You opened it one finger at a time, asking and withdrawing. The soloist must play in angles, edges, skirting old melodies. You did not close your eyes until the third section, as if suddenly the music was asking something else of you. Only your hands were in motion. In the heart of that hall, you were utterly solitary. I could not have given myself to you even if I had tried.

You used only one of the theremin's voices. And you had painted it black.

At the end of the performance, awkwardly, the conductor turned and made a short speech. He acknowledged the director of the symphony, the attendance of philanthropist Howard Gersheim. Then you said, into a lousy microphone, "And I wish to thank my husband, Robert Rockmore."

TEN

BLANK SHEETS

LAVINIA WAS MUCH MORE beautiful than you.

In the second floor of my home she stood on the terpsitone stage and at first she didn't know what to do with it. Moving, she listened to the way the mechanism's pitch changed. She was alert and present. She made the beginning of something. Then she stepped down and the next girl got up. I turned to Henry Solomonoff. "Who was that?"

"Lavinia Williams."

I said her name back: "Lavinia Williams."

Somehow Solomonoff had become the manager of the American Negro Ballet. He went in to recommend accompanists; he left as their manager. Since then he had not stopped pestering me to bring the dancers to West 54th Street to show them the terpsitone. I told him no. *No, Henry.* I was living underwater, with dreams of floods and taxes. No one had used the stage since you. Then finally one bare morning I did not know why I was saying no, why I was being ruled by dreams, by memory. I brought nine tall graceful women into my home, the vases filled with flowers. (There were also two graceful men.)

Lavinia was one of them. Later, I took the dancers into the kitchen and poured them each a glass of cold water. "*Spasiba*," she said, *Thank you*, and I gave a little turn, surprised.

"*Pazhalsta*," I replied.

She wore a thin dress, lightly violet. "*Do you use the dance stage yourself?*" She was still speaking in Russian.

"*I'm sorry?*"

"*Do you dance on it? To play it?*" Lavinia had no earrings, no bracelets, no necklaces, no rings. I found myself thinking of Schillinger's theories, his multiple formulas of beauty.

She moved her head so; and so; specifically, as if always considering.

"*No, no,*" I said.

"*That's too bad,*" she said, with a half-smile. I wasn't sure if she was making fun of me. She sipped her water. "You don't ever feel like going up and dancing alone? Making a commotion?" Whereas her Russian had a refined cadence, almost regal, her English was casual. It was the softest part of her.

"I'm too busy," I said.

"Or not busy enough," she said. She touched my arm.

I had never met a Negro who spoke Russian. She had learned it from her first dance teacher, in Virginia. She also spoke French, Spanish, Italian and the Haitian language of Creole. She was a good painter and knew how to fish. Her favourite novel was Alexandre Dumas' *The Three Musketeers*. She loved my intelligence, my confidence, the pencil I carried in my shirt pocket. She loved the quiet she saw in me. One week after we met, I took her to watch the boat races in Central Park. Lavinia had a strong chin on a wide face, eyes that narrowed when she saw something that impressed her. The men in their boats swept and swept their oars. Everything was lashed in sunlight. She pointed at one of the smaller boats, tapered, with a blue flag at its prow. "That one looks like a winner," she said. It won, of course it won.

That night we went to a games bar in the Bowery, a cellar where visitors could play checkers against small, severe men. You paid only if you lost. Lavinia and I sat side by side, each of us in a game, each of us playing for free.

LAVINIA AND I WERE married on St. Valentine's Day, 1938. In a hotel room in Montauk, she danced her love song. I sat on the bed, dry-throated, watching the fan of her limbs. She was gorgeous and unreal. Her arabesque, weightless, rose up in the candlelight. Her straight leg pointed back across Long Island Sound. To you. I rose, in the shadows. I simply stood there, waiting for my wife to look me in the eyes.

THEY GAPED AT ME across a plate of toast.

"Who is she?"

Coolly, I drank the poured vodka. "A dancer," I said.

"Russian?"

I snorted. "She is an American."

The Karls did not smile. I measured their expressions. "She supports the class struggle," I said.

I had expected them to be pleased. And yet despite their pleadings for matrimony, their warnings about visas, the men now sat staring at where they had written Lavinia's name in their notebooks.

"You did not consult us," said the Karl with the moustache.

"I spoke to Pash," I said.

Instead of looking chastened, sullen, the Karls seemed merely weary, exchanging glances. "We believe you should leave the country," one of them said.

"I am married now," I said.

"Even so."

My nerves felt as if they were fraying. "There is the new contract with Ossining prison," I said.

"Even so."

I flexed my jaw.

"I do not wish to leave."

Again those weary glances.

I stood up. "I am doing vital work here. Work that is vital to the future of our country. To the Soviet project. Remember the investigations I have done into American aeroplanes, into prisons and railroads. You brought me here to do these things. That's the point of this whole life. How can I replicate such accomplishments from far away?"

"It is not a question of utility," said Karl. "There are other reasons to leave a place. There are questions about your visa. We believe you are under investigation."

"Investigation? For what?"

The handlers exchanged a look. "We're not sure."

"I have friends here," I said. "I have a wife. A family."

"A family?" Bearded Karl raised his eyebrow.

"In a manner of speaking," I said. "Who knows?" Would I now need a son? "My future is tied up in this place. I cannot just disappear."

The men folded their arms.

Darkly, one said, "Tell us more, Lev, about what you can and cannot do."

JUST A WEEK EARLIER, Pash had given us the keys to a Cadillac. He smiled. "Belated wedding present." We went out and stood on the curb. The car was long and low, black, a bullet. I clasped and unclasped my hands. I shook my head. Pash wrapped Lavinia and me in his arms, a business partner with his friends. "A married couple deserves certain privileges."

Now I drove the car home from Mud Tony's. Its engine growled in a way that felt just barely controlled. People watched from the side of the road. I arrived at the house. Lavinia was reading by the front window. She came to me as soon as I walked in the door. She was always so full of desire, tinder on the threshold of flame. "Are you all right?" Her fingertips grazed my cheek. "What's wrong?"

I murmured something wordless. I gazed at the perfect ridge of her shoulder. "Everything's fine," I said.

She laid her nose against my nose. "Pash called."

"Yes?"

"He asked you to meet him at the machine shop."

For a short moment we held hands.

I took the car to Frederick's Garage, where he and I were paying men to assemble metal detectors for Ossining jail, Sing Sing. The wardens wanted arches like the ones at Alcatraz. The contracts were big, but Pash refused to hire a proper manufactory. So I drove across the bridge to Queens, to the deserted end of a dead-end street, where a little Russian garage slouched amid chamomile. As I pulled up, Pash was standing beside a pneumatic lift. One after another, he lifted glass sheets from a crate at his feet, threw them to shatter on the concrete. I approached him gingerly, through the broken glass.

"What are you doing?"

"Breaking glass," he said.

"Why?"

He didn't respond. I watched another strong piece of glass slice through the air and separate into ten thousand shiny pieces.

Finally I said, "You wanted to meet?"

He nodded. He looked at me. "Problems in Frisco."

I tried to give him a smile. *Frisco.* As though we were two cowpokes at a saloon.

He could see there was something else in my face. "What is it?" he said.

I made a vague gesture.

"What's wrong?"

I told him what the Karls had said. About an investigation. About leaving.

"Always with the cut and run."

"It seems different now," I said. "There's something about the visa."

Pash clicked his tongue. "A visa's not *why* you leave. It's *how* you stay."

"I don't know. Maybe the Americans are on to us?"

He snorted. "What reason would they have? You're clean. They're just a gang of skittish lambs. A department of paranoiacs."

"Mm," I said.

Pash turned to me. "You work for me, Lev. I am your champion and protector. I will carry you on my shoulders through the wolves." He lifted up a piece of glass. I waited for him to throw it onto the driveway. He did not.

"All right," I said finally.

"All right?"

"All right."

He heaved the glass sheet. It seemed like it was coming apart before it hit the ground. "The metal detectors aren't working," he said in a level voice.

"What? Where?"

"At Alcatraz. They've stopped working."

"Why?"

He shot me a wry glance. "That's your area of expertise. The ones here are fine. Seem fine. For now."

"What are we going to do?"

"Work out what's wrong," Pash said. "Fix it."

"I'll book a flight."

Pash hesitated. All of a sudden I realized that he was afraid. He had been hiding it very well. There, a brittle fear, at the edges of his eyes. "No, stay here," he said.

"Why?"

"*Why? Why?* I am your protector. Do as I say."

I swallowed. Pash was staring a straight line down the road.

"Is there something I should know?" I said. "Is it those loans?"

"What loans?"

"I don't know. That bank in Wisconsin?"

Pash made a kind of smiling face, without any kind of smile. "Are you in touch with family? Back home?"

"In Leningrad?"

"Yes."

"No, not really," I said.

"You have a sister?"

I pressed my lips together. "Helena."

"You write to her?"

"We're not close," I said. "She's married."

Pash shifted. "Much is happening."

"To whom?" I said.

"Not to us." He drummed his fingers against the rusted lift. "Not to us."

SPRING CAME, and summer came, but they were like visitors in another part of the house. I did not see them, only their signs.

Lavinia planted mint, sage and beans in the window boxes.

At the end of August I had another visit from Commerce and Burr. I had gone with Lavinia to eat at the Plaza Hotel, my old home. Valets parked our car but they gave us a table in the corridor, on the way to the kitchen, as if we were sacks of pota-toes. I was furious. Not from what they did with us, the white man and his coloured wife—from the surprise. "What did you expect?" Lavinia murmured. But there were no warnings, no signs. "If they don't want Negroes, they should say so," I said. "This is a *hotel*."

We ate and came home. I felt my stomach grinding up the Plaza's lentils and quail. As always, the Cadillac felt like some phantom carrier, a spell for moving from place to place. We did not speak in the car. Lavinia was angry with me. When we pulled up in front of the house, a man was at the window, cupping his hands around his eyes, looking in.

I honked the horn. He looked up. He put his hands in his pockets. He smiled. It was Jim, the debt collector.

"Who is that?" Lavinia asked.

"Nobody," I said.

As we got out he sauntered over, as though we were old friends. "Hi, Dr Theremin," he said.

"Hi," I said thinly.

He half-bowed to Lavinia. "Jim Swiss. Commerce and Burr."

"Lavinia," she said.

"Lavinia . . . ?" he asked, leadingly, utterly rude.

"She is my wife," I said.

"Your wife!" Jim exclaimed. He shook his head. "You've been busy, Dr Theremin!" He lightly kicked the tire of the Cadillac. "And that's a nice car."

BLANK SHEETS | 197

"Thank you," I said.

Lavinia led me past him. "Excuse us," she said, "we've had a long day."

"Yes, of course! Who hasn't? What a scorcher. Just wanted to give you this."

"Thank you."

"Oh! And Dr Theremin! Do you have a new number for Julius Goldberg? The old one stopped working!"

"No." We paused on the step.

"No?" Jim asked, with feigned surprise. "I thought he was your business manager?"

"Yes, sorry. Yes. I do have his number. Let me get it for you."

In the parlour I scrawled Pash's new number on a sheet of notepaper. I brought it back out to Jim Swiss, in his ugly green suit. "Hey, thanks," he said. He smacked me on the shoulder. "And that's some pretty girl you found."

I went back inside. I sat on the couch, with Lavinia beside me. I unfolded the letter he had given to me. It was not from Commerce and Burr. It was from the Internal Revenue Service. It advised me that I owed $59,000 in back taxes to the United States government.

"What does it say?" Lavinia asked.

"I need to send in some forms," I said.

In the morning, Walter Tower Rosen came to see me. He rang the bell. He owned the house I lived in but he rang the bell.

"Walter. What a nice surprise."

"Yes," he said. He looked older than the last time I had seen him. I asked myself how long it had been.

"Lucie's going to be round later to practise."

"Good," I said.

His eyes searched the doorway. He cleared his throat. He asked, "Is everything all right, Dr Theremin?"

"Yes," I said, "of course."

"I had a call today from the Internal Revenue Service."

"Oh?"

"Yes," he said.

"I've spoken to them," I said.

"You have?"

"Yes."

"Everything's in order?"

"Oh yes," I said.

He appraised me for a long moment. "Yes?" he asked again.

"Yes. A terrible mix-up," I said.

He nodded. He released a breath. "Well, I'm relieved to hear that. I had been a little—yes, well. Good." He gave another deep breath. "A weight off my shoulders."

I smiled. "Is that all?"

Walter did up his jacket. "Did Lucie talk to you about the new theremin?"

"The new theremin?" I said.

"She said you had designed a new theremin. She wants to commission a model for herself."

"Yes . . ." I said carefully. I had no recollection of this conversation.

He watched me. "I wondered if you needed an advance."

"Oh, there's no need."

"Are you sure?"

"Yes."

"Well, listen," he said. He reached into his pocket. "Here's four hundred dollars all the same. For materials."

I did not immediately accept the bills. Four hundred dollars to make a theremin like yours, Clara.

I took the money. "Thank you."

Walter shook my hand. "Like I said, Lucie will be over later."

"Of course."

"We should have dinner soon," he said. "With your wife."

"That would be nice."

When I reached Pash, he told me to calm down. He gave the same kinds of answers as before. He was taking care of it. The debt was a matter of bank accounts, transferred funds. I told him I thought I understood what had gone wrong at Alcatraz: the tubes were overheating and needed to be changed more often. "Never mind that," he said. "Alcatraz has cancelled the contract."

"But they've been using the arches for months."

"They're ripping them out."

"I said I've solved—"

"The jailers got impatient. Already someone else is installing something. Rivertons, I think. From Chicago."

"Pash—"

"It's all right. We got the information we needed."

"Do we still get paid?" I asked.

Pash laughed. It was a bear's laugh but I couldn't tell if it was easy or forced. I was tired of all these conversations, conversations, conversations. Each one left me with the same nervousness. "It's always about money, these days! We are communists, Lev!"

"Perhaps I'm becoming a capitalist," I said.

Pash clicked his tongue. He paused before answering and when the reply did come, his voice was grimmer, levelled. "No, we're not getting paid," he said. "In fact, we have to pay back the advance."

"What advance?"

"I need to go, Lev. Stop with all this. You'll fall into a pit."

He put down the phone. I kept the receiver to my ear. I felt so angry. The telephone line crackled. Green leaves were quivering on the branches of the trees. "Hello?" I said into the telephone. "Hello?"

❖

IN MY WORKSHOP THAT NIGHT, I raised my hand and made the theremin sing. It sang one note. Lavinia was somewhere far away in the house. The theremin was very quiet, my palm so close to the lower antenna. I had given you ten different voices. I wondered whether you, wherever you were, still used just the first voice.

I made my theremin sing louder, louder. The room was frozen in place. One does not intentionally squander a life; one looks back and finds it squandered. I knew I did not want to make an inventory, but here I was now, counting. One house, crowded with memory, that belonged to someone else. Ten years of work, each patient discovery, amounting to nothing. I had wasted a thousand pencil marks on singsong. On hope. Was this heart worth anything, when you were married to another? When *I* was married to another? Is there any honour, any honour at all, in wanting? In keeping on wanting? I made the theremin sing louder.

Vladimir Ilyich Lenin, may his memory be illuminated, would have said that we can want a better world. That I might redeem my wanting by wanting that.

Through the darkness outside the window I saw my car. A man was standing over it, writing something in a notepad. He seemed a sibling of the grey hedges and the black street and I had never seen him before. He wore a suit, with a pair of binoculars around his neck. He raised them and stared at me, illuminated in my window.

I could see only the black binoculars. Moonlight grazed their lenses.

Suddenly something changed. He had lowered the binoculars, lifted something else, flash flash. A camera, a photograph, silver bromide in a box, my photograph.

The theremin was roaring. With a touch I silenced it. I turned it off. I drew the curtains. I went downstairs, past Lavinia, to the front door. The man was gone. It smelled like garbage outside. At the end of the street I could hear two men fighting. Moths tossed and whirled through the open door into the house.

PASH MET ME AT A BAKERY in Chinatown. We were squashed into a table near the door. Each of us had a tin plate and one almond biscuit. Outside it was so humid, a kind of jungle. Indian summer. Behind the counter someone kept ringing a bell.

"I killed a man," I said. And then I told him about the Dolores Building, room 818, the opening in Danny Finch's brow. He listened with his eyes down. Partly, I had expected him to have known. If he knew, he did not show it. He kept his gaze on the centre of the table. He interrupted only once. "You are sure it was him?" he said.

"Yes."

"Go on," he said.

I described my exit, the elevator ride, the return journey in the Karls' grey car. I stopped talking. Pash picked up his almond biscuit and ate it, chewing each mouthful before he took another. There were no crumbs.

"Five years ago?"

"Yes."

"And you didn't tell them?"

"Who?"

"The others. My counterparts."

"No. I didn't tell anyone."

Pash rubbed his neck.

"Last night," I said, "I looked outside and there was a man examining the Cadillac and he took my photograph."

"Last night?" Pash set his jaw. "Did he look like an agent?" I hesitated and he barked at me. "Come on, Lev. An agent. A suit. FBI, DOI."

"Yes," I said. "What are they looking for?" I did not know if my voice was calm or hysterical. The panic in me felt so tightly contained. "Is it about money? Is it about the murder?" It was the first time I had called it a murder. *Ubíjstvo.* Something had happened nearby—a bus had arrived, a factory had let out; abruptly the bakery was filled with hungry people, bellowing, wedged up against us. I hunched over the table. "What should I do?"

Pash leaned in to meet me. "Don't. Do. Anything," he said severely. "I'll handle it." He sat back and we faced each other. With his fingertips he nudged my plate toward me. I swallowed. I picked up the almond biscuit.

He glanced at me once more, nodded. He stood, squeezed through the bodies, left without saying goodbye.

I craned my neck and through the window saw him step into the steam.

IN RETROSPECT, this was the moment when my world ended. All those tremors and then a quiet catastrophe. Pash disappeared into Manhattan and my life capsized, though I did not yet know it. I came home to an empty house. Lavinia was away at the studio, moving freely. She loved me. I loved Clara Rockmore. I sat at my desk with an apple, a bottle of seltzer water. It was a blazingly beautiful day, gulls dipping through West 54th Street. I gazed at a sheet of white paper. There was nothing on it; I could draw anything.

That night Lavinia and I went to Harlem to see *The Adventures of Robin Hood.* I watched Errol Flynn fire arrows into his enemies.

We went to Ricky's, where they do not sell pizza by the slice. We bought an entire pie, ate it with our hands in the park, burning our fingertips, drying our palms on the grass. We went home and I removed her clothes and she traced me in the darkness; I kissed her ribs, pressed my thumb into the crease beneath her lips, against the rise of her cheekbone. We were travellers, unlit. I wanted everything. We lay, after, in a cold Y, and we felt like branches. I stared at gardenias, in a vase. I circled her wrist with my hand. Every time I moved my lips I was telling a lie.

I AWOKE TO AN EMPTY BED. It was morning. A single 1.5-volt battery sat silhouetted on the windowsill, haloed in dust. Beside my head was a small journal, an oil pencil, for writing ideas in the night. I turned to a random page. *Teletouch mirror: ~~Face~~ Reflection disappears as you approach.* Underneath, a sketch of a sparrow. I got out of bed and pulled on some underpants. "Lavinia?" I said. I went into the other room. More gardenias in vases. I passed the cabinet that held a letter from Commerce and Burr. Everything that was not in shadow was brightly illuminated, sun-streaked.

In the kitchen I put on a pot of coffee. The grains were odourless, like chips of gravel. I leaned into the counter beside the stove, listened to the water boil. From somewhere else in the house I heard a faint noise. "Lavinia?" I called again.

The kettle began to shrill. I poured. I went downstairs, and downstairs, and downstairs, to the grey parlour. It was cold now; the heat wave had passed. The house felt empty. I shivered. "Lavinia?" I murmured. Someone was standing by the barren fireplace. It was not my wife. I found myself in a defensive stance, holding my cup of coffee. The man had his back to me.

"*Hello, Lev,*" he murmured. He was about my height and build, with a collared shirt, his sleeves rolled up.

"*Who's there?*" We were speaking Russian.

He turned. The man in my parlour was the man who also called himself Lev. The man I'd met at Mud Tony's, with Karl and Karl, on the day I committed a murder. His head was shaved. He wore square glasses. I said, "Where is Lavinia?"

He cleared his throat. "Dancing."

"What do you mean, 'dancing'?"

He smiled very, very slowly, as if he was still listening to me speak. "She is at rehearsal."

My voice was level. "How did you get in?"

"I let myself in," he said. He cleared his throat again. I scanned the room, looking for any other men. We were alone. He massaged his right forearm. "You need to leave the country."

"No," I said. "You should talk to Pash."

"I spoke to him yesterday afternoon." He took a breath. "I spoke to him again last night."

"Why isn't he here?"

"He was sent away." Lev pursed his lips. "I do not think you will see him again."

I was still in my defensive stance, left foot leading, right knee bent. I was still holding my cup of coffee, ridiculous. He noticed my pose, gave a kind of laugh. In the next beat his smile hollowed. "It is time to conclude your American adventure."

"If—" I began.

"Lev," he said, with unassailable patience, "it is time."

I gestured at the parlour table—the *Times*, teacups, sheet music, Slominsky's wedding invitation. A pair of Lavinia's ballet shoes curled beside the chair. "How can I leave?"

"Tonight," he replied. "Some men will come this afternoon to collect your work. Others have already been sent to the garage, the storage warehouse. You will collect your papers. Do not use the telephone."

"The telephone? Why?"

"A ship is waiting for you. You are on the crew roster as a captain's assistant. A log keeper. You are not a captain's assistant: you will be confined to your cabin."

I swallowed. "To Leningrad?"

"Yes," Lev said. "Indirectly. It is a six-week journey."

I listened to my breath. They were high, short breaths, as if I were being kept alive by consistency, persistence, the taking and giving of very small things.

"Do not tell anyone that you are leaving," he said.

"My wife," I said.

"We will send for her later."

"When?" I said.

"A fortnight."

I realized that he was lying. I said, "Why not tell her?"

Lev looked at the floor. He pushed his thumb across his lips. "The United States Internal Revenue Service," he said. "The California Detentions Bureau. International Madison Bank. Walmor Incorporated. Isaac and Harry M. Marks. Commerce and Burr. I could go on. You owe a great deal of money. Does she know?"

"No," I said.

He picked up a rock from my mantel, a brick of fossilized limestone that Schillinger had given me.

"Also, I understand that you killed a man from the Federal Bureau of Investigation." He lifted his head. There were bags under his eyes. "Do not tell anyone that you are leaving."

In the next long seconds, we gazed at each other. I didn't say anything. Then I nodded. I looked around the room. None of these things mattered to me anymore.

ONLY A LITTLE WHILE has passed since I stood with serious Lev in the parlour, giving up on America. Sometimes I lie in my bunk and wonder how I conceded; other times I ask myself why it did not happen sooner. Yet I feel calmly certain, writing this log: I had no choice. *I had no choice.* My enemies were too numerous; I had exhausted my reprieves. As a missioned visitor to the United States, I did not belong there. My past and future belong to Russia, where I will wait, loving you, for the fulfilment of all this roving.

Love is strengthened by distance. Dreams have weight and velocity. They are signals, promises. They have a destination. One night we will know no doubts, feel no foreign forces, and our particles will come to rest.

WHEN LEV DEPARTED, I followed him out the door. The air was thick. I watched as he sloughed away up the street, holding out his hand as a goodbye. I saw that my Cadillac was gone. Maybe it was with Pash, on the way to whatever came next. When I came back inside I lit a fire in the hearth, just in case, just in case I needed to burn anything.

Men came to the house that afternoon, as Lev had promised. They were not bungling goons: they were unfussy professionals, efficient. The first car carried chroniclers, note takers; they brought folders, labels, archival boxes. They collected the papers from my filing cabinets and sorted them by topic, sealed the boxes tight. I called Pash. Of course no one answered. Pash had left my life. A large truck arrived with six more men. These ones disassembled equipment, loaded it onto pallets, into pine crates, nailed the crates shut. They asked me, "What is going?" and I answered by pointing. I did not need everything. I needed the first things, the last things, the best things. Some inventions were toys, redundancies, dead ends. But other devices might have a use, tomorrow.

In the cellar I shoved aside old boxes of RCA theremin kits and hauled out a trunk, the same one I had brought from Leningrad. It was the brown of wild horses. When I had come, I had filled it with trousers, shirts, shoes, a tool kit. Now I wanted it to take a million things—photographs, ticket stubs, an automat's receipt for two plates of pie. I looked at the faded corner of the basement where I used to lift weights, complete the four forms. A wooden dummy languished beside a lamp. I had neglected my kung-fu. Perhaps in Leningrad I would resume my practice. I wondered if my broad-shouldered teacher would still be there. If Lughur and Moritz still grappled like rams. I went to the wall, where I had pinned my etching of Leung Jan. He seemed balanced on a precipice. I took it down and put it in the trunk.

Around four o'clock, I took a taxi to the college where Schillinger was teaching. I found his office and waited for him to finish class. He darkened when he saw me. "Lev. Is everything all right?"

Behind his door's frosted glass, I told him I was leaving.

"When?"

"Tonight."

"Bullshit."

This made me laugh. Because he was right: what bullshit. I laughed at its absurdity, and Schillinger watched me laugh, until his grave expression wavered and he began to laugh too. We leaned with our hands on his desk, laughing, laughing, subsiding. It was silent. I stared at my knuckles. What would we say now? What should we say?

"Leningrad?" he murmured.

"Yes."

"I will visit."

"Come for the white nights," I said.

"Yes."

We raised our heads. In an awkward gesture I reached to shake his hand. "I'll call Frances," Schillinger said. "We should have a farewell drink."

"I can't," I said. "There is too much to do."

I saw him looking around the room, searching for a memento to give me, something. Finally, he pulled a book from a stack of papers. "Ah! Here." It was his own new monograph. *The Second Half of History: Art in the Electronic Age.* "Just like one of our conversations," he said, "only you can keep it on your nightstand."

"Wonderful," I said.

"Yes."

We shook hands another time.

"Don't tell anyone I came here," I said.

I TOOK A CAB ACROSS TOWN, unfolding another of the bills Walter Rosen had given me. "Yes, here's fine," I said. I reached forward to pay the driver. As I got out I saw Schillinger's book left behind, on the seat. I closed the door. I watched the taxi glide away.

I stood before the building where you lived with your husband, Robert Rockmore. I lifted the heavy knocker, a brass lion's head, and knocked. I did not expect an answer. This story required me to come here, to knock on the white oak door. It did not require anyone to answer. But then I heard a sound, a man's cough, and the door opened. There he was, younger and taller than I remembered.

"Mr Rockmore," I said.

"Yes?"

My mouth twitched, flinched almost, as if someone had swung at me. "Is your wife at home?"

His gaze tightened.

"I know you," he said.

"Yes."

We faced each other across the threshold.

"I could kill you," I said.

"What?"

"Or I could send her a message and you would never know. It would go right through you."

Something was gathering behind Robert Rockmore's eyes, something weaker than wrath. He worked his lips, choosing a riposte.

I beat him to it. "I am leaving this country," I said. "I will never need to come back."

He took a breath. "She never talks about you," he said.

"Of course she doesn't," I said.

Then he slapped me, strongly, with the palm of his hand. And I punched him in the solar plexus, hard. He doubled over. I shoved him by the head, down into the sidewalk's smears.

There was a moment, and then he said, "I'll call the fucking cops."

I stood over him. My jaw twinged where he'd hit me. I swallowed and felt my heart diving, diving. I wanted to weep, Clara, great grey tears. "Right through you," I repeated, in a thick voice.

It was late that night when my wife came home. She was distracted. She was hungry, angry with her choreographer. On the top floor I prepared an omelette. I chopped onions. She prowled the crowded kitchen, unaware that the house had been excavated, its secrets parcelled up. She ate with knife and fork, talking at me; she did not search my face. Later we lay in bed, side by side. I wondered what I would write in a letter to Henry Solomonoff, to Missy and Bugs Rusk, if I were writing letters. Would I apologize to the Rosens, send them schematics for a new theremin? Would I thank the Bolotines? Lavinia stretched her arm across my chest. I gazed at the ceiling. The clocks were all ticking. "Let's take a holiday to Haiti," she said to me. "For the winter."

We were in a house of dreams. When I was gone, Walter Rosen would take it back.

At 11:28 p.m., into the darkness, the doorbell buzzed. Lavinia stirred. "Ignore it," she said. I remained frozen. After a few minutes, the door buzzed again. I got up. "What is it?" she said.

"The door."

"What time is it?"

"Never mind," I said.

I put on my trousers and belt. I put on the jacket I had set aside. Lavinia shifted. In a parched voice she asked, "Are you getting dressed?"

I tied my shoes. "Yes."

The door buzzed again.

"For the door," I said.

She propped herself up on her elbows. I went downstairs, all the way downstairs, drawing open the door and pulling in all that moonlight. Three men awaited me. "Comrade," they said.

I let out a deep breath. "Here you are," I said. They hesitated when I invited them inside. They wanted to know if I was ready to go.

"Yes," I said, "just a moment."

They said we had to leave. "Yes," I said again. I stood in my parlour, looking around, unsure of what I was seeking, what I was waiting for. I heard Lavinia's voice from upstairs. I called her. I rubbed my face. I gave the men a suitcase that I had hidden in a broom closet. It held more clothes, my shaving things. I gave them a case containing a Skylark Mk II typewriter. They took these things without speaking. Then Lavinia was on the stairs behind us. She wore a shawl across her shoulders. She was long and young, ravishing. She seemed like something borrowed, in that moment; something I had borrowed and was now returning. Her brow was knotted, her wide hazel eyes hardening.

"I have to go," I told her.

"Go where?"

"They are taking me away," I said. "I do not know when I will be back."

"What do you mean?" she said.

"I do not know if I will be back."

She came down the stairs. "What do you mean you do not know if you will be back? Who are these men?"

The men took a step toward me, instantly an entourage.

"We must go," one of them said to me, to her, in accented English.

"*Where are you taking my husband?*" Lavinia demanded, in Russian now.

"Goodbye," I said.

"Lev!"

They had taken me by the arms and were guiding me to the door. She came at us, tried to pull them from my shoulders. She was stronger than they expected and abruptly we were standing together, in the night's halo, the two of us.

"I have to go," I murmured, and I saw her jaw set, saw frozen water at her eyes. "I have to go." With this last speaking, she suddenly became smaller.

She kissed me once, fiercely. She had questions in her face. "I love you," she said. Her glance flicked to the other men.

"Good night," I said. I swallowed.

She grabbed the scruff of my coat and stayed that way, holding me, until one of the men removed her hand.

I went away with them.

WE DROVE THROUGH the city's darkness. Young men on street corners, holding cigarettes. Dogs in the middle of the road. Hobos in doorways, curled on their sides. Neon signs spelled words. POMADE, CABARET, CHOP SUEY, each in red, each somehow a goodbye. The men I was with didn't speak. I wondered whether I had seen my last familiar face? Was I already given over to strangers? New York flickered outside my window. Now I was thirsty for farewells.

We dipped into the Holland Tunnel.

I leaned back in my seat. I looked at the wedding ring on my finger. How long would I wear it? Perhaps they would send for Lavinia after all. Perhaps Lavinia would follow, in a fortnight, her trunk packed with sundresses. Perhaps she would dwell with me in the hills beside Lake Ladoga, planting dill and tarragon, while I strained with wires and tubes and the distance of you.

We emerged in New Jersey, where the sky was pricked with twenty thousand stars. The road lifted us up and set us down and we followed the bend of the water. It was like a sea. Slowly, I remembered: it is a sea, it is a sea. The lights streaked and glittered, New York City across the bay, and then everything beautifully deafened by the roar of a locomotive running beside the road, fine and sparking, iron. I realized I was going home. Home to Russia, the motherland, canyons and cities and three million rivers, rushing. The Physico-Technical Institute. Sasha and Helena. Blini from the stall on Kolokolnaya Street. Springtime and the bitter winter that makes enchantment out of candlelight.

I could see the boats now, in the harbour. They were as big as mountains. One of them was mine. The men in the car were more attentive, roused somehow, looking. The tires beat a rhythm on the road. I folded my hands in my lap. We twisted into the docks, stopped at a sign, wheeled round and into the shadow of the *Stary Bolshevik*. Lights shone down on us. The men got out of the car and I followed them, alive in my shoulders and ankles; the wind was everywhere, whipping, salted. Lev was there, talking to a man in uniform. I shook his hand. I was smiling now, girded. He introduced me to the captain, to the ship's master. "Our log keeper," Lev said. "That is what you are."

"Log keeper," I said.

The captain spoke with a Samaran accent. "Assistant log keeper."

"It is my pleasure," I said, bowing my head.

Lev watched me with a certain skepticism. I did not care about his skepticism; I knew who I was, where I was headed; I knew what I carried in my heart. I was Lev Sergeyvich Termen.

"My equipment is all here?"

"Show him," said the captain.

The man who appeared at my elbow was like a polar bear. "Follow me," Red said, and he led me up the gangplank into the body of the ship. Just as I passed through the bolted doorway I turned and glimpsed Lev with two other men—were they the Karls?—and I think there was a huddled warehouse and the silver imprint of a city spire, and in a certain way there were countless other figures, friends, enemies, and a thousand acquaintances, Katia, Jin and Nate Stone, Rosemary Ilova and

George Gershwin, perhaps Pash, watching from the darkness, as I disappeared into the *Stary Bolshevik*.

I would not come out until we landed. Red would show me the room with my equipment, the theremins packed in crates, the boxes of files, and he would show me the room I am now inside, eggshell blue, with its tidy cot. I remember the key turning in the lock. I remember the heave of the ship as its engines wakened. Like that, so simply, like a folded piece of paper, I was gone.

ONE DAY SOON I WILL arrive at the Leningrad port. I do not know what will await me. I do not know the forces that will swiftly act upon my being. They will let me out of this room and I will go to the mouth of the vessel, shake hands with my captain, feel no more seasickness. After weeks of waves I will wobble on the pier. I will do my duty. I will build new wonders.

I will call to you through the air.

PART TWO

Twelve months of winter
The rest is summer.
Russian saying

ONE

UNICORN

IT IS SNOWING IN MOSCOW. I have spent the past hour in front of this square of window, this square of snowstorm, deciding what to write to you. My headset is around my neck. The machine whirs before me. How does one begin the first letter in eight years? With a greeting? Hello Clara? Dear Clara? Dearest Clara? But then this letter will never reach you. I am almost certain that it will never reach you. I heard your voice again today. I sat at my desk and tried to choose the first line of a letter that you will never read.

It is snowing in Moscow. It has been eight years since I wrote a letter like this, at a desk, to a friend. Is that what you are—a friend? Today I heard your voice through the earpiece, while I bent over my machine. Your voice was hiding in the noise, like a ghost. Like a transmission from the other side of life, from the spring.

When I am finished writing to you I will fold this piece of paper in thirds. I will trade Zaytsev some cigarettes for an envelope. A letter in an envelope, such an easy thing. My plan ends there. There are no mailboxes in Marenko. What is a prisoner to do with a letter? Perhaps I will slip it to a sympathetic guard. Perhaps I will burn it. Perhaps I will keep it forever in my things, forever until a guard discovers it, snatches it from where it hides in a book, tears it into a hundred dry scraps. I remember when this happened to Andrei Markov.

I have a question for you, Clara: What good is a letter that will never be read? What good is a lost message?

I heard your voice in the noise, in the shush of crackling static, on a tape they brought from Spaso House. As I listened to Averell Harriman.

All these new names.

MY NAME IS Lev Sergeyvich Termen, as it always was. My number is L-890. I live in Marenko prison, outside Moscow, with four hundred lawbreakers. We are called *zeks*. It is February 1947, not yet St. Valentine's Day. Nobody in this country celebrates St. Valentine's Day, except perhaps Ambassador Harriman. I am in the attic of a residential building. It is on a side street near the Kremlin; unheated, glacial, but I have known worse cold. I will not ask Beria for a heater. I will not ask Beria for anything. Until he appears in a doorway, with eyes of coal, I will pretend he does not exist.

The reason I am in this place is that when I sit at the small, square window, there is a direct view of another window, four or five hundred metres away, across a red brick wall. I will not tell you who sits behind that window, gazing out across the city.

The attic has a low, angled ceiling. It is all made of wood, like a cabin in the forest. Each corner of the room has a knit of light cobweb, but I have seen no spiders. They are either concealed or they have gone away.

There is a door in the far wall that leads down a back passage to the street. It is not shared with the apartments below, where Kremlin officials live with their families, dine on pork and fresh peaches. I come to this attic twice a week, for fourteen hours. I have never seen my neighbours. I hear them through the floor but only Beria knows I am here.

Sometimes I fear that one of the residents will hear me, and call up to the attic. She will call up to the attic, wondering who is hiding here, and I will not answer, and then my patron will send some NKVD agents to have my neighbours murdered.

There is a desk along one wall of the attic. It has a stack of folders, several writing pads, labels, pens and ink. There is this small typewriter. There are two boxes of magnetic tape. There is my whirring machine, innocuous and painted cream, and another machine, a player, connected to a headset. The first machine has one wire for the power supply and another wire that leads up behind it to the window. It snakes outside through a hole in the wall. On the other side of the glass, a device is fastened to the window frame. The wire leads into this device. The device is black and unusual. It looks like a crow, hunched, gazing out toward the Kremlin.

There is also a gun on the desk beside me. This gun is not for self-defence. If I need to defend myself I will kill my enemy with kung-fu. The gun is not for strangers; it is for me. If I am discovered, I will turn the muzzle of the gun toward myself and pull the trigger, *click*.

I REMEMBER I WAS once a man who conducted the ether.

I am no longer the conductor.

TWO

A PERSON ISN'T SAFE
ANYWHERE THESE DAYS

WHEN I RETURNED FROM the United States, eight years ago, I found Leningrad empty. It was the end of 1938. It was a brilliant winter's day and a huge albino sailor brought me out of my cabin, onto the deck, where the air stung my lungs. The city was like an elegant miniature. Waves skimmed the harbour. I remember seeing the embraces of unfamiliar men and hearing the sound of grinding metal, then later watching a crane hoist my crates from the ship. I remember my fear as the boxes swung in the air, so perilously high: the vision of an overcorrection, a mistake, a slipped hook. For one instant I could see them falling and then the crates would splinter against the ground, explode, all my past destroyed.

The longshoremen lowered the crates so gently, like gifts.

I found myself alone on Neva pier with all my worldly possessions. I did not know where to go. Part of me had expected a government agent to meet me, some delegation or welcome parade. But there was no one. The passengers had disappeared like spiders under doorways. I remember standing on the pier and watching motorcars go round the street corner, one after another, coughing smoke, and the understanding that Leningrad had changed in my absence.

I TOOK A ROOM with Father's little sister, Eva Emilievna. She was a fragile woman now, thin, with watery blue eyes. She had been a soprano; growing up, I thought of her as "the singer." But now my aunt worked at the hospital, wrapping broken legs, making splints. My parents had been dead four years. Eva told me about their funerals, one in the winter and one the next autumn, the pine halls full of friends. "Everyone was crying," she said. "Everyone asked about you." I imagined Mother and Father in their caskets, resting, waiting.

"What were their last words?"

Eva said she didn't know. She touched her cup of tea with the tip of her finger.

I spent each day in a different government office, slumped in a soft chair until my name was called. I met desiccated women from various Soviet agencies. Painted eyebrows, vases full of dried flowers. They added my information to rolls and registers. "You must make sure you are listed with the LNS," one would say. "Check with SSUG." At night I walked home to the apartment, skidding on the frost. Eva arrived later, depleted from her day in the wards. "It is so good to be with family," she would say, turning on a lamp.

My equipment was stored across town, with a friend of Eva's, in a warehouse that safeguarded laundry powder.

At supper we talked about old times. About picnics with Mother, Father, my grandmother, my sister. Mother always made hard-boiled eggs, wrapped them in velvet. Father was in charge of slicing cheese with his pocketknife. Eva remembered the time that each of us, one after another, spilled beets on our fronts. The whole family stained scarlet, like murder victims.

My sister had now moved to Nizhny Novgorod, was married to a mathematician. "Come visit," I wrote, in a letter.

I told Eva about my years in America. I described Manhattan, Brooklyn, the bakeries in Chinatown. I recalled the parties, the brushes with celebrity. "Rachmaninoff," I said, "shucks his own oysters."

She answered every anecdote with wide eyes, wonder. "Did you meet cowboys?" she said.

"I saw one cowboy, from Texas, at the opening of a play. He even wore the hat. But there are not many in New York. Most of them live in the southwest of America."

"In the desert?"

"It is not all desert. I went to California, on the West Coast. They grow oranges."

"I would like to swim in the Pacific Ocean," she said.

"I flew in an aeroplane," I said, "clear over ten united states."

Then Eva tilted her head to one side, with those wide swimming eyes. I thought she was going to ask me about the aeroplane, its shadow streaking the fields.

"I heard about Katia," she said.

I found that my face was frozen.

Gradually I said, "Our divorce?"

"Yes."

Our voices were very plain.

I blinked at the table.

"Yes," I said at last. "I believe she remarried." My smile was small, neat, sad. It was not a performance. Eva watched me with a sympathetic expression, as if she were giving me cards, flowers, a consoling present.

"Did you meet other women?"

The question was uncharacteristically forward. But when I returned her gaze I understood that Eva was not inquiring as my host, as my father's younger sister. She was asking as someone who would soon be elderly, who had never married, who lived alone. A spinster wishing her nephew a certain happiness.

And then I thought of you, standing at that theremin in the afternoon, surprising me.

I thought of you at my door, with snow on your cheek.

I also thought of Lavinia, tall and solemn, in the narrow chapel.

Or later, at the foot of our stairs, as I disappeared into the morning.

Shame skirted my edges, like thin smoke.

I could imagine you so clearly, staring hard at a small article in the paper.

My wife, tearing through my shelves, ringing embassies.

Searching for answers in folders of blueprints.

A hundred carbons with my mute signature.

They had said they would bring her to Russia but they would not, and I had known they would not, and I had disappeared into the morning.

I took so much from this woman and then I took away her husband.

I TRIED TO FIND old friends. In a strange way, it was difficult to recall them. I went to dinners with former colleagues from the Physico-Technical Institute, regaled them with tales of radio waves, factory errors, million-dollar patents. My stories were gilded, full of wealth and opportunity. "And now after all that I have come back. I have come back to work." They responded with an odd reticence, as if I had something in my teeth.

I was penniless. Despite my lofty anecdotes, I did not have a job, a workshop, dispensation from the authorities. I lived in my aunt's apartment. I dreamed of what I did not have. I fastened my cufflinks and raised toasts to Iosif Vissarionovich Stalin, but I was not the prodigal son returned. I was a pauper in a land where I thought poverty had been abolished.

On a Friday afternoon I went to my old workplace. I brought F. Lèle's *Principles of the New Radio*, for Ioffe, carried from America. It was as if I was still twenty-two, clambering aboard the tram, feeling the old bump and shuttle of rails. The carriage was emptier than it used to be. Outside the windows, buildings had been wrecked and rebuilt. Everyone wore heavier coats.

At Finland Station I disembarked. I shed the crowds and walked up the road. Snow was falling. Empty trees stood like turrets. I watched a cyclist press through the snow and grass. A wall topped with barbed wire had been built around a field and I tried to remember if there had ever been anything in that field, if it had even been mowed. Here, the city sounded the same as it used to. Wind, wheels rolling over sleet. Muffled animal sounds, as if dogs had been buried in the snow.

I kept pace with the man on the bicycle. We came to the rise and I looked away into the arboretum, beaten bare by winter. There were still squirrels in the trees. *Who feeds them?* I wondered. Footprints had made paths. One crow. Above my head, white cloud went on uninterrupted.

There was a moment when my boot skidded on ice and I looked up, breathing suddenly hard, and the cyclist had disappeared.

It was almost two hours before I passed across the school's frozen garden, rimmed by new fence. The buildings came into view and I found this was a respite, a gift. They were grand and quiet and I knew them. I went into the western entrance of the institute. My steps echoed in the dim marble hall. I left water footprints. I crossed the floor to Ioffe's office, in the corner, with windows that looked upon the hills and the road, where you could watch the blue sun go down. The office was empty. Not even any furniture: just scratched marks in the floor.

Sasha's room was empty too.

I went to reception. It was a room of strangers. I could not remember the names of the women who had once worked there, with whom I had once joked, but it didn't matter. I spoke to a Tatar secretary. His voice was so quiet that I had to lean across the desk. He gave me the number for Ioffe's new office. I went through the empty hallways, up the stairs, to this door. I knocked. Through the door, he said, "*Da?*" and I went in.

Abram Fedorovich Ioffe, my former supervisor, sat behind a low desk. His hair had turned white. His shoulders were hunched, as if he had been carrying a load. I remembered the way we used to share a samovar of hot water, both of us looking in on it, shepherding it, pouring out two teapots. The big pot of honey that used to sit on his desk. I could not see it here.

I stood in his door, damp and dripping.

There was no recognition in his gaze.

"It is Lev Sergeyvich Termen," I said.

"I know."

The way he spoke, I was afraid he was unhappy to see me.

"How have you been?" I asked.

"Extremely well," he said. His voice was level. His spectacles made him look even older than he was.

I extended the book. "I brought you a gift."

Ioffe straightened. He looked at the spine of the book. He looked at me. I sensed then that it was not ambivalence I was feeling, or hostility. It was caution. Perhaps it was fear. Ioffe smoothed his coarse moustache. He looked at me again. I saw him make a decision. This was a fragile moment. He pushed a hand down his brow and over his face, and stood up, and he crossed the room to embrace me. A bear hug in the office of the director of physics and technology, among ticking clocks and electric eyes.

"*Zdravstvuyte*, Lev," he said, into my shoulder.

"*Zdravstvuyte*, Ioffe."

As we released each other I asked again, "How have you been?"

"Extremely well," he said, and swallowed, and turned away from me.

We spoke for a long time. His office was grey, illuminated by the window's cold reflection. His desk was crowded with papers, thick reports, everything stamped with a seal. The institute had grown and it had shrunk; there were many new responsibilities, he said. Deadlines. Many scientists had left or been sent away.

"I am looking for work," I said.

He looked at his hands. "Are you registered with the planning committee?"

"Of course. But there is some kind of holdup. I thought that if the institute contacted them . . ."

Ioffe gazed at me. It was a steady, heavy stare, as if he were rolling a steel bearing toward me, seeing if I would catch it.

I said, "My research saw many advances, in America."

"Tell me about America," Ioffe murmured.

So I told him about America. Teletouch, Alcatraz, the altimeter, the aeroplane. My adjustments to the theremin, the rhythmicon. My purer research into electric fields, capacitance, signals through the air. He did not interrupt. He listened, leaning back in his chair. I felt the need to be poetic: "With radio," I said, "I feel like an explorer who has only just glimpsed the outline of a continent."

I described to him the time I played before twenty thousand people at Coney Island. "I have many ideas about loudspeakers. Amplification. There are many applications. Not just performances—official announcements, public address systems . . ." Ioffe shifted in his seat. "Or perhaps . . . er . . . military functions . . ." I said.

"What happened with Konstantinov's sister?" he said.

"What—"

"With Sasha's sister."

"Katia?"

"Yes," Ioffe said. He set his elbows on the desk.

"We . . ." I exhaled. "We fell out of love, Abram."

Ioffe looked so sad.

"Is Sasha here?"

"No," he murmured.

"Where is he? It would be good to see him."

"He was arrested."

I was horrified. "Why?"

"Article 58."

"What is Article 58?"

"'Counter-revolutionary activities.'"

"How could Sasha be accused of counter-revolutionary activities?"

Ioffe rose. He stood in silence for a moment. "I do not have work for you here," he said finally. He lifted *Principles of the New Radio*, turned it over in his hands. "I am sorry, Lev."

I swallowed. I got to my feet as well.

"Lev," he said, meeting my eyes. "You must speak less well of your time abroad."

IN MID-FEBRUARY I SOLD a set of tools and bought a train ticket to Moscow. It was a night train. I slept under a thin sheet. When I awoke, someone had stolen my shoes.

I went to Moscow to find employment. To find employers who would petition the planning committee on my behalf. I bought new shoes from a stall at the station. Shiny new shoes. Already my money was almost gone. I checked into a shabby hotel. On a wall in the foyer there was a notice from a travel agency seeking English translators. I made a note on the back of my train ticket. I went up into my minuscule room, like my cabin on the *Stary Bolshevik*. I lay down on the bed, still made, and closed my eyes.

Over the next weeks I took a few small translation jobs. They gave me Russian copy about the Black Sea, the Winter Palace, Kiev's former cathedral. I translated this into the language of Shakespeare and Twain. I remember one sentence, like a treasure I was able to keep: *The columns of Manpupuner will never change, not even in winter.*

I HAD COME TO Moscow with the names of four generals.

These were men I had met more than a decade before. Three years after I showed Lenin the theremin, one year after he died, the Kremlin had once again contacted me, requesting that I demonstrate my work on "distance vision" technology. Television. With Ioffe I had developed a working prototype: a small display, one hundred lines of resolution. It worked relatively well in low light. In a room with very high ceilings, four men crowded around the machine. Their assistants stood in a huddle near the door. I tried to introduce the principles behind the device; the four men just stared at the screen. Eventually they sent me away.

I had taken down their names: Ordzhonikidze, Tukhachevsky, Budennyj, and Voroshilov. Under Tukhachevsky's name, I wrote a sentence, something he had said: *One day, the Red Army will see into tomorrow.*

A few months later I received a message saying Iosif Vissarionovich had been very happy with the device. It would now be developed internally, by army scientists. Send us your notes, the message said. Send us everything.

I was angry. Ioffe advised me to say nothing.

I turned my focus to the theremin.

In Moscow now, I hoped to find these generals. Wherever they were, I would find them. I would tell them: *Let me return to work.*

From Ioffe I had learned that a chemist from the Physico-Technical Institute, a man named Totov, was working as a clerk at the Politburo. "He turned in his vials," Ioffe said. I vaguely remembered Totov: a man shaped like a triangle, wide at the hips but with very compact shoulders. He had sandy hair and glasses. This was all I had, coming to Moscow: four generals' names and Totov, at the Politburo, like a triangle with glasses.

I was persistent, and I located him. On my third visit to the Kremlin's gates, Totov came tottering out. His hair was longer now, like a woman's. There were more lines around his eyes.

"Comrade Totov," I said.

He stopped where he stood. "Who are you?" he said. In the moment's pause I saw the rise of panic.

"Termen," I said, "from Leningrad. Do you remember?"

There was a short beat, then relief splashed over him. "Termen!" he said. "The man with the warbling boxes!"

"Yes," I said. "Yes. Yes, just so."

When he was done work, we met at a café near the library. For a long time we exchanged pleasantries. He did not ask about my past ten years; it was not clear whether he knew I had been to America. I asked him about work and he spoke with a rambunctious, unconvincing enthusiasm. Finally there was a lull in the conversation and I told him why I had come to Moscow. I told him that I was looking for some men who knew my work, who might be able to help me.

"I cannot give you a job," he blurted.

"No, no," I said, "of course not. I wish to continue my research. But I am looking to speak to some men I once met. Generals." I swallowed. "I thought perhaps you could teach me the best way to—to reach . . ."

"Generals?" Totov whispered.

I took the paper from my jacket. "Budennyj, Ordzhonikidze, Tukhachevsky, Voroshilov."

"Is this a joke?"

"No."

"You know these men?" he said.

"I did know them."

Totov quavered in his chair. "I do not know them. I do not know that I can help you."

"What is it?"

His eyes flicked up and down.

"Totov?"

"Ordzhonikidze was in the Politburo. He died a few years ago."

"Yes?"

"Tukhachevsky was executed," he said. "Treason."

"I see. And the others?"

"Budennyj is a marshal."

"A marshal?"

He stared at me, incredulous.

"What?"

"A *marshal*. A marshal of the Union of Soviet Socialist Republics. He is the second-most important soldier in the world."

"I see," I said. "And Voroshilov?"

"*Voroshilov?*" he said. "Voroshilov is *the* most important soldier. He is the first marshal. The hero of the southern front. The commissar for defence. You didn't know this?"

"No."

"Do you remember Luhansk?"

"The city?"

"Now we call it Voroshilovgrad."

I swallowed.

"How did you not know this?" he muttered.

I folded up the paper. "I was not here."

"How did you not know this!" he repeated.

"If I wanted to meet with Voroshilov, how would I do this?"

Totov threw up his hands and squeaked. "How would you meet with Comrade Stalin? How would you meet with the man in the moon?"

I paid for our tea and cakes.

The next day I ironed my suit and went back to the Kremlin. I passed through red-brick Spasskaya Tower and to the entrance of the senate. At reception I said in a quiet voice that I was the scientist Lev Sergeyvich Termen, from Leningrad, and that I wished to have a meeting with First Marshal Kliment Voroshilov. In my message to the first marshal I said that we had met ten years ago, when I had shown him how to see through walls.

I thanked the secretary and sat down and waited.

When visitors' hours ended that night, I returned to the Dnepr Hotel. In the morning I ironed my suit and went back to Spasskaya Tower. I passed through security and crossed the stone streets, past patrolling guards, birds in chirruping oaks, and arrived at the senate. I told the secretary I was the scientist Lev Sergeyvich Termen, from Leningrad, and again I was here to see First Marshal Kliment Voroshilov. I sat down and I waited.

Just as it was turning dark on the other side of the glass, an officer in shoulder boards appeared beside me.

"Comrade Termen?" he said.

He took me upstairs.

I passed through seven sets of closed doors. They checked my identification three times. In all my meetings with military leaders, my meeting with Lenin himself, I had not undergone so much scrutiny. Men surveyed me with faces like attack dogs. The corridors leading to Voroshilov's office were bizarrely arrayed: oil portraits of horses, brown and black, like a parade of derby winners. Although there were also painted cavalrymen, the humans seemed like servants: men-in-waiting, holding the bridles of their leaders.

Finally they led me into a room that was three or four times the size of Eva's apartment, filled with paintings of Iosif Vissarionovich, Voroshilov, Iosif Vissarionovich walking with Voroshilov, and a dozen life-size canvases of Arabians, Tersks, Tchernomor horses. I recognized Voroshilov and immediately felt a sinking feeling. This was the general who had seemed most ambivalent to my research. He had a round face and platinum hair, a moustache like a smear of charcoal dust. His chest was full of medals. His eyes were too near together.

Voroshilov sat. I stood. Between us rested the bronze sculpture of a horse. His desk did not even have a pad of paper: just a single lined sheet, and I could see no pen. Perhaps Voroshilov carried a pen in his pocket, with his military whistle.

"Thank you for meeting with me," I said.

He said, "You are the doctor?"

"I'm sorry?"

"The doctor from Leningrad."

"My name is Lev Sergeyvich Termen. I am a scientist. Yes, from Leningrad. Thank you for meeting with me, Comrade Voroshilov."

"I only have a moment to see you," he said. He did not seem to blink except when other people were talking.

"I know you are very busy. I will try not to take up much of your time." I clasped my hands.

"What is this about?"

"We met ten years ago, when I made a presentation on distance vision."

"Yes?"

I hesitated. I was not sure if he remembered me or not. "So . . . I—since then, I have continued my research in other fields. This brought me to Germany, to France, to England, to America . . ."

He had his eyebrows high, his lips dead flat.

"In New York I collaborated with the NKVD, collecting intelligence for the Union of Soviet Socialist Republics," I said. It was the first time I had ever said such a thing.

"For Beria?" he snapped.

"Who?"

"Comrade Beria."

"No, I worked—for other officers. Now I have returned to the Soviet Union and I am seeking a new project."

"So?"

"So . . ." I began.

"Do you think I am in need of doctors?" he said.

"No, I am a scientist and I thought that as you had—"

"You thought you would come here and dream up some kind of scheme? A swap of favours?"

"What? No! I'm looking for work and—"

"You'd line up and murmur the NKVD's name and abracadabra, some magic powder floats down from the sky—"

"No!" My fingertips fell against the edge of Voroshilov's desk. I had interrupted him. He showed his teeth.

"Comrade, the Union of Soviet Socialist Republics is built on systems. These are plain, practical systems. Sometimes these systems are so plain that they appear ugly. But they are not ugly. They are the most beautiful systems in the world and they function only if the people abide by these systems. Work is the most basic thing. It is the bedrock. If you try to bypass the systems, to exploit some influence in your own self-interest, it is as if you are taking a chisel to the bedrock of the Revolution."

There was a long pause. I said nothing until I realized that he was waiting for me to say something. "Yes, of course," I murmured.

"You say 'of course' as if you were not trying to corrupt the very foundation of the Soviet system," Voroshilov said.

"No, no, I just hoped that—"

"You may go," he said.

"Comrade Voroshilov, I am deeply devoted to the—"

"It is all right; we all make mistakes. Glaunov—show the doctor out."

A man took me by the elbow and then I was outside Voroshilov's office, off-balance among the stallions. "Was he angry?" I said to his assistant.

"What?"

"Was he angry just now?"

"Who?"

"Voroshilov!"

"Oh, no. No."

"Thank you," I said. I fumbled at the buttons of my suit. "Thank you," I repeated.

—

I left the Kremlin and walked along the water. The air was clear and brisk. Night had fallen and I found that I was wandering in straight lines: the path by the river, then across the bridge, and back, and for miles along a road. I passed a silvery concert hall as a children's orchestra streamed out of its doors: boys and girls hauling violins and trumpets and double basses wrapped in cloths. Parents' hands rested on their children's shoulders.

The moon was almost full. The city's glass reflections looked like flashing signals.

I was irritated with Voroshilov but I was more irritated with myself: that I had done no research, that I was so ill-prepared. I was very hungry but in that state of mind where one cannot decide what to eat. I left the river and passed among stalls selling sandwiches, *pelmeni, shashlyk*. Finally, I ducked into a late-night café for a bowl of soup, some bread. I sipped from the bowl. I remember the soup was very peppery. I remember I was wondering whether I should try to meet with the other marshal, Budennyj. I turned this question over in my head.

The waiter asked me if I wanted a piece of apple cake with cream. I shook my head. I did not even say the word *no*. How many thousands of times did I revisit that moment and wish I had said *yes*. How many thousands of times did I long for a piece of apple cake with cream.

I went back to the hotel. I read from a novel about flying in a rocket to the stars. I never finished this book.

I went to sleep on the bed.

In the middle of the night, as is their way, there came a knock at the door.

THREE

PERFUME GARDEN

BUTYRSKAYA WAS MY FIRST PRISON. It was not the worst. I began to tremble as the car approached its gate: uncontrollably, as if I was having a seizure. The guard beside me did nothing. He rode with his truncheon on his lap. I held my jumping hands to my face and tried to slow my breathing, but my heart kept on skipping in my chest like a piece of gravel.

We stopped and someone got out to open the door. I asked the guard again: "What have I done?"

They ordered me out and into a line of other prisoners. The bricks shone in the moonlight. None of us spoke. We searched each other's faces, fearful. Guards yelled commands, cars arrived and sped away, engines shrieked. The prison door creaked open and closed, like the jaws of a trap. From far away it is difficult to write of these things: everything sounds like an exaggeration, a story you have already heard. But I had not heard these stories. I stood in the night, trembling. I did not know it was Butyrskaya. I did not know the names of Moscow prisons. The windows

236 |

were covered with sheet metal and the bricks were the shade of dried blood. The trap creaked open. A man told me to go inside.

Now it has been eight years since I stepped inside these prisons.

In a small room, two guards told me to take off my clothes. I asked them why. Our voices echoed. They repeated the order. I began to unbutton my shirt. I took off my shoes. Razor wire lay coiled beside the exit. I stripped off my jacket and pants, unthreaded the tie from my collar. I stood in my undergarments. "Continue," a guard said. He pointed at my socks, gestured lazily at the rest. I removed my undershirt. I removed my socks. I took off my underpants. Everything was thrown into a bin. The concrete was cold as frost. One guard started sorting through my clothes. He crouched. He set aside my belt, tie, tore the elastic from my underpants. "What are you doing?" I said. The other guard told me to lift my arms and came wearily toward me. He began at my feet, feeling the spaces between my toes, then scraping the backs of my knees with his fingers, and up to my armpits, my splayed hands, and in every touch I felt the grubby casualness of his hands, and I thought of the hundreds of other men he had touched like this, in the middle of the night. I shuddered. He pulled back my ears, rubbing the insides with his thumb. He felt in my hair. He made me close my eyes and pushed at my lids, like a pawing animal. Suddenly his fingers were in my mouth, around my teeth. His hands tasted of vinegar. I gagged. Then he made me take my penis and show that there was nothing else between my legs. He told me to turn and I felt a new dread. But he did not touch me. He ordered me to pull apart my buttocks, to squat, but he did not touch me. He walked back toward the other guard. They told me I could get dressed.

The buttons had been torn from my clothes. My wallet had been taken. My shoes were missing their laces. "Through that door," they said, and I wiped my mouth, and I passed from one circle of hell into the next.

Men in grey uniforms took my photograph.

"What is your name?" someone asked.

"What is my *name*?" I said. "You don't know my *name*?"

"Please state your name."

They pressed my fingers onto inkpads, then onto a shiny card, like a postcard, somewhere to jot a holiday message.

"Profile," someone said, and they took another photograph. My wardens were not monstrous. They seemed tired. They seemed like fathers and brothers. They led me under buzzing electric lights, past painted brick, up and around and through a maze, deeper and deeper, and part of me tried to remember the turns, senselessly, fruitlessly, as if I might escape and run and then be free. We came to a corridor where it said on a plaque, INVESTIGATION–INTERROGATION, and I recoiled, clawed back to where I had come from, and for the first time a guard struck me, hard, across the side of my shoulder. I could have stepped away in *jong sao*, fought, punched my one-inch punch, and pivoted to a kick. Instead I crumpled inward, stumbled, caught the end of my tongue with my teeth. My shirt cuffs fluttered at my wrists. I climbed a metal grille stairway with nets on either side, to catch the suicide attempts. At the top of the stairs I came to a wide desk, like in a draftsman's office. They told me to stop. "Sign," they said. It was a list with the title REGISTERED LIVES. The other lives were hidden by a metal plate. Only one line was visible—a bare strip of paper for me to register my life, and then the metal plate would descend by one line, and my name would be hidden, and the next prisoner would see just the bare space for his or her ink to drop.

Lev Sergeyvich Termen

I went through two more sets of doors and into a cell.

IT IS DIFFICULT TO anticipate what will be our worst thing. Our worst things are not all the same. Hunger, thirst, fatigue. Or fear. I used to think that heartbreak was my worst thing. It is not. In a certain way, heartbreak is a reassurance. There is no reassurance in hunger, in thirst, in fatigue. Or in fear. These things are hollow things, un-things. I have learned that there are certain absences you can keep and hold; and other absences, like lost memories, which you cannot.

I WAITED IN MY cell for a hundred years. I do not know how long it truly was. Time becomes senseless over dilating hours. The room was rectangular and dimly lit. There was a hole in the ground. There was neither bed nor bench and the walls were strafed with rows of iron nails, pointed outward. The nails were to prevent a prisoner from leaning against anything. It seems nightmarish but the reality was so dull, so mundanely cruel. Those nails could have been used to build things.

I stood until I could not stand anymore. Then I sat on the floor, in my sagging and unbuttoned clothes. I sat. I sat. I lay down and turned on my side. In a cell, you gradually begin to count: bricks, tiles, the string of seconds. I began to list primes, counting upward. 223, 227, 229 . . . "What is today?" I asked myself. "It is the morning of Friday, March 10, 1939."

I closed my eyes and cried. I roughly rubbed my face. I clasped my knees and counted. I decided I would not cry again until things got worse.

There was a slot in the cell door through which the guards could look, and it never opened. *Who had brought me here?*

I wondered. *What had brought me here?* Had I betrayed my country somehow? Had I been mistaken for someone else? Was it Totov? Was it Voroshilov? Was it Totov? Was it Voroshilov? Was it Totov? Was it Voroshilov? Was it Totov? Was it Voroshilov?

I did not sleep because I did not think I could sleep but I wish I had slept; I wish I had slept. I wish I had taken that silent and undisturbed century to curl up on the cold floor and dream.

Then the door opened and I was grabbed by the shoulders and dragged, shrieking, down the hall. Most shocking was the suddenness. They grabbed me and lifted me and dragged me, even though I could walk, and this violence tore the wounded shriek from my lungs. They brought me into a room, thrust me onto a chair that was bolted to the floor. A bright light. Two men in silhouette. A ventilation grate breathing hot air from above.

"What is your name?"

"Lev Sergeyvich Termen."

"Do you know where you are?"

"No."

"You are at the heart of Soviet intelligence."

I exhaled. As sifu taught me, I held on to the end of the exhale, extending the moment in silence and stillness before beginning the breath that follows.

"Yes," I said.

"Why do you think you are here?"

"I don't know."

"I will ask the question again: Why do you think you are here?"

"I don't know."

One of the silhouettes moved toward and past me, illegible, and I thought it would strike me. It did not strike me.

INSTEAD, THEY TOOK ME from the room. I was brought to a new cell, this one much larger than the last, with dripping arches and the smell of shit. It was full of bodies. Not corpses, but scarcely people: bodies in spring coats, shirts with buttons torn off. The cell, as big as a classroom, was walled in rust-red brick. There would have been room for a few dozen to sit and rest, but instead the floor was swollen with a hundred men, ashen and dying, or simply fearful; standing, teetering on trembling knees.

The cell door closed. I smelled the bodies, the uncovered toilet, and slipped into these prisoners' woollen folds. I did not understand this room—why we stood like passengers in an elevator, awaiting the next stop. There was hardly room to stand, let alone to sit, but still, but still. And so I sat, with murmuring around me, Indian-style with my knees upraised, until the cell door thudded open and the guard shouldered in, like a cyclops. They must have had peepholes all over, to see one man sitting in the throng. He was huge and dark, with a grotesquely friendly face, and he landed a blow upon my ear, roaring, "ON YOUR FEET."

The other prisoners cowered. When I was standing, the guard was gone. I stood, I stood, trembling.

We were not permitted to talk.

After a long time they hauled me back to the interrogation room. I do not know if the silhouettes were different or the same.

"Why do you think you are here?" they asked.

I swallowed. "It is a mistake," I said.

"What do you think is a mistake?"

"You believe I am a traitor."

"Why do we believe you are a traitor?"

"Because of something I said to Comrade Voroshilov."

"Comrade Voroshilov?"

"Kliment Voroshilov, the first marshal."

"What did you say to Comrade Voroshilov?"

"I said something about America."

"What did you say about America?"

"I don't know."

"Then why do you say you said something?"

"I must have. I don't remember."

"What don't you remember?"

"*I don't remember.*"

"Why did you say something about America?"

"Because I lived in America."

"When did you live in America?"

"From 1927 to 1938."

"Why did you live in America?"

"I—I was a spy."

"You admit you are an American spy?"

"I am a Russian spy!"

"You deny you are an American spy?"

"*Yes!*"

Then, once again, a silhouette moving toward and past me, the terror of impending violence; the door opens; I was taken back to the cell of hollow men.

THEY TORTURED US WITH blunt instruments: hunger, exhaustion, despair. Twice a day we were led down the corridor to a small yard. For twenty minutes we sat on the gravel with a morsel of dry fish, a square of brown bread. Those who conversed were beaten. Those who fell asleep were beaten. The rest of the time we stood huddled in our crowd, trying to learn a way to close our eyes unseen, to lean softly against the murderer or traitor or innocent man next to us and simply rest there, between moments, in slumber.

It was not often possible.

This went on for two days. My interrogators wanted me to admit that I was a foreign agent. How could I admit this? *Clara, I was not a foreign agent.* I write this here, for my own record. *I was not, I was not.* In America, I believed in the Mother Motherland. I served my comrades. I did science; I stole plans; I murdered the man Danny Finch in loyalty to the Union of Soviet Socialist Republics.

After two days they put me on "the conveyor." I learned later that it has a nickname, like you would give to a stray kitten. The guards pulled me out from the shared cell and into an interrogation room and I remained there for days and nights, through mornings and mornings and mornings, with dawns' and dusks' slight light pastelling the window slit. Once you are put on the conveyor you cannot get off. Over and over they asked, "Are you an American spy?" Silhouettes and then men with faces and then silhouettes and then again men. They made me stand at attention, answering questions, blathering about Berlin, London, New York City. For hours I stood and answered, pleading that they talk to Pash or the Karls, or Lev, or to my other associates across the sea. For ten minutes, fifteen, they let me sit on the stool that was bolted to the ground but if I slipped into sleep they slapped me, hauled me up by the armpits, and we began again. The days poured relentlessly on and my interrogators seemed to grow larger, with more limbs and voices, arrayed like shadow puppets. In fatigue you begin to lose moments—whole minutes swallowed up, gone. It is as if reality is acquiring sinkholes, black pits. A tiny part of you begins to panic but the remainder cannot; it is too tired, simply too tired, and so your horrified spirit is like a gagged prisoner, bound in canvas, slowly being lowered into a lake.

"Do you admit you are a foreign spy?"

"I lived in the Plaza Hotel. I shook hands with John D. Rockefeller. I built a television."

"You revealed Soviet technology to the Americans?"

For so long I stood and shouted, incapable of telling lies. It would have been so easy to confess, conceding to these men's reality. But I was a scientist. *Clara, I was a scientist.* All we have is accuracy, transparency, veracity. Only truthful data gives us honest conclusions. So I clung to the shimmering facts, like grasping at fog, until finally I stopped. Finally, I stopped. I swallowed and shook my head and as if waking from a dream, I said: "I was a foreign agent."

I RELINQUISHED SOMETHING when I said that. Something thin and fragile, like a blade of grass. It was so easy to give away. In the relief that followed my concession, my skinny lie, I wondered why I had not relinquished it sooner. They let me sit in a chair and gave me a glass of water. I had relinquished my claim to stand beside Lomonosov, Faraday, Archimedes, Newton— any of them. In that trembling instant, I was grateful to have lost it. I wanted simply to sleep. I wanted to lay down my head and sleep.

It is now eight years later and I am no longer grateful. When I recall my betrayal at Butyrka, those leaning silhouettes, what I feel is wrath. Incandescent wrath and raw, desperate sadness over the thing I gave away. The thing I traded for a sip of water and the right to close my eyes.

BEFORE THEY LET ME sleep, they made me sign a piece of paper. I signed it. Then I lay somewhere, on a bench or on the floor, in my own cell or in a crowd—I don't remember.

THE GUARDS SHOOK ME awake and brought me to a different room. They told me to write the story of my life, my story as a foreign agent. There were four walls, a desk, a cot, a typewriter. A cot! They brought me food on wooden trays. Such generosity from my wardens. "Write the story of your life, your story as a foreign agent." Now that I had confessed, they wanted flesh for the fiction. I slept and I ate and I stared into the dull eyes of my guards. Their patience was not limitless. I sat at the desk, my fingers on the keys, gazing at a wall painted baby blue. I remembered then the cabin in which I had come from overseas. Another locked room, with cot and typewriter. Blue rooms do not have happy endings.

I wrote about my eleven years in America. My arrival and departure, concerts, contracts, meetings, inventions. In a broken, scattered way, I wrote what I recalled. I gave them the plain, tired truth, knowing they would twist it to their uses. I did not know what would happen when I finished writing, so I wrote on. I wrote about breakfasts, patents, sketched tele-touch circuits.

My rebellion was this: I did not write about you. My jailers would have no part of you. I did not write about Katia. I did not write about Danny Finch. I did not write about my wife, Lavinia Williams. In this way I resisted. All of you remained free.

After four days, they took the pages away. They took the typewriter away. Two lieutenants appeared, like scarecrows. The taller read aloud the resolution:

"You, Lev Sergeyvich Termen, born 1896 in Leningrad, non–party member, citizen of the USSR, are found to have been a foreign spy and a member of a fascist organization."

I was not a foreign spy. I was not a member of a fascist organization.

I signed my name.

A MAN LEAVES PURGATORY. The denizens of the place take him somewhere else. It was as if a hidden wall had been drawn up, like a row of teeth: I followed the passageway deeper into Butyrskaya, to a room where only the guilty abide.

A jail is not like other places because you look around and *there* is a thief, *there* is a killer. All these predators, convicted and confessed, four steps from your heart. Criminals and counter-revolutionaries, every one of us a zek, locked in a single cell.

It was not the same as the cell where I first stayed. Here there were rules. There was society—a wrecked world with law and order. The senior zeks slept by the window. I was a new zek: I slept by the fetid latrine. Whereas the simple criminals, the rapists and murderers, were considered allies of the Revolution, and assigned bunks, I was a political prisoner, a class enemy. I came into a brick room and faces turned to examine me. I slept on the floor. None of the zeks had mattresses, pillows, room to breathe. We slept shoulder to shoulder. The blue light stayed on. We were not permitted to sleep when it was day but we were permitted to sleep when it was night. After my torture, all of this was a reprieve. A domain of rules is a system, and I had spent my life taking systems apart, turning them over, intuiting their function. *Finally*, I thought, *a problem I may attempt to solve.* Here was a machine; I would try to figure it out.

So I learned. I learned to find stray threads, to make needles out of matchsticks, to mend my shredded clothes. I learned to rise quickly in the morning to queue for the shower. I learned to use the prisoners' library, Butyrka's sole consolation.

I worried about my aunt Eva.

I made no friends but two enemies.

Their names were Fyodor and Ears. They were criminals, not politicals. They sat on plywood bunks and spat at me. Fyodor was large, with an elongated frame and enormous fists. His face was round, almost cherubic, with shockingly green eyes. Ears was long and skinny, with a cruel look; his namesake parts faced out like cupped hands.

My very first morning in the cell, after we had received our bread, our rotting cabbage, Fyodor demanded my portion. He was crouching beside me, eating his own, chewing. He asked with a gentle, light tone, as if he were asking me to pass the wine. Ears, beside him, stared at me. His stare had a sort of edged curiosity. With his eyes he was inquiring, *What are you going to do?* Fyodor chewed, cleaned his teeth with his tongue. For a moment I felt like a kindly uncle sitting with his nephews. But then the silence stretched on and I understood that this conversation was as cold and unfamiliar as the prison brick. I saw that others were watching us, the newcomer with the teenage thugs. I was sitting a few inches from the toilet. I took a short breath and held out my bowl. Fyodor took it with a bow of the head, a sweet grin. He smirked at Ears. "There's a good friend," he said. "What's your name?"

"Joseph," I said after a moment.

"You're lying."

"No I'm not."

"I heard them say your name when you came in. Lev."

I looked at the palms of my hands. "Yes, it's Lev," I said.

"I am Fyodor. This is Ears. Welcome to Butyrskaya."

"How long have you been here?" I asked.

"Why the fuck should I tell you?" said Fyodor.

They got to their feet. Ears put his hands in his torn pockets and said, "Thanks for the breakfast, old man."

IT WENT ON LIKE THIS. Fyodor and Ears did not claim all of my meals, only some of them. Alive, I was a renewable resource. They crouched beside me, chewing slowly, and I had nowhere to go. Although I was not the only person they picked on, they targeted me with a particular enthusiasm, as if I reminded them of a hated schoolteacher. The other cellmates moved around us in private orbits, each in a different struggle. Even as this life became familiar, waking and queuing and lingering in the prison library, every day brought new terrors. Just after lunch, a guard appears; he calls a name; the prisoner shuffles outside. Minutes later we hear his thin screams. Strong, thin screams, like sheets of glass. Sometimes the prisoner does not return. In a way this was easier than when he did come back, stooped and hobbling, to lie on the planks. This reminder that we were all peers, growing hollower every morning.

In one of our early interactions, I tried denying Fyodor's request for food. Suddenly Ears was showing me a knife. It was an unusual weapon, long and bevelled; it was the kind of object that belongs in a particular workshop, fulfilling a particular function, the tool of a tanner or a woodworker or a bookbinder. In this place it was a blade in a young man's hand. He drew it along my arm, tearing the fabric of my sleeve, nothing more. Fyodor reached for my bowl. "Thanks, Lev," he said. He patted me on the cheek.

Our cell had at least four or five musicians, a doctor, an official I recognized vaguely from the newspaper. There was an acrobat. There was a fortune-teller, an old man who would close his lids and touch the space between your eyes and tell you that you were going to die. Besides Ears and Fyodor, the cell also had other young criminals; they had more or less divided up the prey. Order was maintained by the Rebbe, a Jew and former wrestler, jailed for the murder of his wife's lover. He was a huge, serious man, a little older than me. Through violence or consensus he had become the authority. Whenever Fyodor and Ears claimed their tithe, I saw them glance back through the crowd to where the Rebbe sat watching, near the bright, barred window.

MARKEVICH WAS SMALL AND QUIET; he kept to himself. Like me he was a political prisoner—a former accountant who had done too much work in imports. One day, Fyodor decided that Markevich was an informer. Something had happened to one of Fyodor's friends, a lunkhead with the habit of tearing pages out of library books; he was taken away and didn't come back. The criminals had friends among the guards; they said the paper ripper had been transferred to another prison. Fyodor was furious. He was certain someone had squealed about tattered dictionaries, shredded Pushkin. He blamed Markevich, from whom the goon had once snatched a book. It was arbitrary and petty. I know now that it also betrayed Fyodor's naiveté: we might all be transferred to other prisons, before long. But Fyodor raged, hissing at Markevich, threatening him, stealing his shoes at the showers. "Leave off," I said finally, at once regretting it.

Fyodor pivoted toward me, eyebrows raised. "Oh yes, Lev? What's that? Have some advice? Some helpful advice?"

I shrugged and turned away, but it was too late: now Markevich and I were united in Fyodor's eyes. I went to a corner, slid down with my back to the wall. Then Fyodor was standing at my toes. He was angry, jumpy. Ears hovered behind him.

"So you're a rat too, friend?"

"No," I said patiently. Fyodor reached down and slammed the back of my head into the brick. I heard a *clunk* and the room skewed. For one white moment I wanted to vomit. Then I was swallowing and breathing slowly and looking into Fyodor's pupils. He was smiling. He ruffled my hair. He sauntered away. My vision fogged with tears but across the cell I saw the Rebbe, watching.

So now Fyodor and Ears sat on their bunks and spat at me, spat at Markevich. Someone threw a piece of shit at me in the night. Every morning they crouched beside me, claimed my food. It was even worse for Markevich; they regularly shoved him around, bloodied his face. Gradually everything outside our little drama seemed to disappear. It was as if the cell had become smaller, closer, like a tunnel. I saw Fyodor, Ears, Markevich; I imagined and anticipated them. I held a book in my hands, reading and rereading the same page, distracted by a shrill fear like a ringing in my ears. I did not believe that these boys would do something horrific to me, just that they would do something small and terrible. I dreamed of soldiers, burying me alive.

It was late afternoon when the key clicked in the lock and a guard heaved the cell door open. "Fyodor Solovyov," he shouted. Fyodor's head jerked up. He rose. His face looked as though it hadn't sorted out which expression to use. He shook hands with Ears and wove his way to the door, disappearing. It was from watching Ears, left behind, that I understood this was not a scheduled rendezvous. Ears was nervous. He sat on a bunk, holding his hands. I lowered my eyes to a book about fishing. I was hungry, thirsty, tired, sad. My life in New York had disappeared so easily, replaced with these two things: a book about fishing and the short story of two teenaged thugs. *Sometimes it is just strength*, I said to myself. *The only answer is persistence.* I looked at Ears. I looked at my book.

Fyodor did not return until the next day. I was not there for his arrival. I came back from the library and found him sitting on his bunk, shrunken somehow, reduced. His face seemed emptied out, with bruises on his temples. There were marks on his hands. He noticed me and raised his eyes, and I saw an unexpected, terrible hatred. I saw fury. His face flashed pink and he lowered his gaze. I went to my spot on the floor and sat, encircling my knees with my arms. I had lost interest in my book. Fyodor and Ears were murmuring to each other, just out of view. Markevich stood in a far corner, watching. I was all alone in a Moscow prison. Was Eva Emilievna in a nearby cell, I wondered. Had she been arrested in Leningrad, hauled from her apartment, brought by a Black Maria to an interrogation cell? *Who is Lev Sergeyvich? Tell us about him.* Did she have enough to eat? Had she been hurt?

The evening meal passed undisturbed. Before lights-out, Fyodor appeared beside me. He crouched so silently. He ran his index finger over his lower lip. "I am going to kill you, Lyova," he whispered.

I turned to him abruptly. "What? What are you talking about?"

"I kill rats," he said. "You think you will go on betraying your cellmates? Cowering behind your books?" He snickered. "I *kill* rats."

I swallowed. "I am not a rat."

"When you are being beaten," Fyodor explained, silken, "there is a lot of time to consider who told who what. There is a lot of time to consider who might lie about you to the guards, who might *want* to lie, which zeks in their nice shirts—"

"Why would I speak to them?"

Fyodor did not like being interrupted. His lips went white. I imagined Ears in the shadows, drawing his knife. "There is a lot of time to remember the old man who is always coming and going from the cell, prim and swaggering."

"What about Markevich?" I said, because I am a wretched human being.

"Not this time," he murmured. "I know, Lev. I *know*, you shit, and I will kill you in your sleep."

I did not sleep. All night I listened to the breath and groans and snoring. I smelled the exhalations of imprisoned men. I lay on my back, fists clenched, staring at the hideous blue light bulb, aware of every movement, every voice. There was shouting, far away, through the walls, and men crying. There was wind in the grate, sewer scents. A man rose and urinated into the latrine beside me. Fyodor was motionless in his bunk. I wondered if he had changed his mind.

Men began to stir before dawn, anticipating the competition for the shower. The patrolling guards began their reveille. I crowded with the others by the door, furtive. Fyodor had rolled to sitting. I saw him go over to Ears. For a moment I had the instinct to go over there, to explain myself, to say that I was no informer, just a scientist, a patriot, that I wished them only well. I did not go over. I watched as Ears and Fyodor began to argue, muttering with lowered voices. Fyodor marked his knee with the side of his hand. Ears shook his head. Fyodor became more and more forceful. "*Fyodor,*" I heard Ears say, balefully. "Come *on*, Fyodor."

The guards took us away to the showers.

Fyodor made his move at breakfast. I was sitting stooped over some gruel, my back to where the guards made tea. I heard a sound behind me. I turned. Fyodor was holding a pot of boiling water. The first drops landed scalding on my ear as I swivelled, tore upward, knocking him away. The pot fell, spilling steam and scorching our toes and Fyodor roared forward, wild-eyed, with clawing hands. He was not a fighter. I shoved his arms aside, punched him hard in the side. He wheeled and came at me again. He swung. I ducked. His huge hand grabbed my shoulder and I kneed him hard in the solar plexus, shoved him again. He slipped on his heel, fell, struck his head on a concrete block. His eyes rolled. There was blood.

Where were the guards? I do not know. Why did no one stop us? Because we were all fearful of consequences. But everyone was watching when I killed Fyodor Solovyov. The Rebbe was watching. I was thinking: *My second murder is not unlike my first.* Blood is blood. It pushed into the steaming water.

The crowd parted and the Rebbe stood beside me, the giant former wrestler. He blew out his cheeks. He gave me a very level look, a serious man's look, and he kneeled and touched Fyodor's face, felt for a pulse.

"Get out of here," he said finally, without turning.

I took two steps backward, into the crowd.

The Rebbe stood, bent, grabbed the shoulder of Fyodor's coat, dragged him across the red spray and against the wall. He straightened to assess us.

He said, "The boy slipped on the water."

I WAS NOT BOTHERED again during my time at Butyrka.

The guards did not question me. Of course they did not: Markevich, our informer, did not inform.

One quiet morning, Ears sat down beside me and asked if I played chess. He had a set, made of dried pieces of bread.

Prisoners must cultivate short memories.

ON THE FIFTEENTH OF AUGUST, I was brought into an office and sentenced to eight years in a corrective labour camp.

Eight years, Clara.

It was my forty-third birthday.

FOUR

DISORDER

I HAD NEVER BEEN so hopeful as when Lenin played the theremin. It was 1922. I was twenty-six years old. We were in a conference room, with stooped lamps and tall windows. The trees were bare but Moscow was flooded in bright spring light; the city rose up from the afternoon like a Fabergé miniature, a wonder assembled by human hands.

Fifteen people stood with us around the table. I was wearing a suit under my lab coat, polished shoes. One of Lenin's staff had given me a telescoping metal pointer. I wasn't accustomed to using it, kept opening and closing it in my palm. Kalinin was there, and Nikolayev, the radio commissar. And Lenin! Lenin himself, attentive and present and listening before asking questions, pinching his beard between his fingers. He was compact with a long chest, a surprisingly strong physique. Some sliver of me wondered: Another student of Shaolin?

We began with the radio watchman. I was so nervous, explaining the theory and then delving too deeply into the provenance of the components, opening and closing the silver pointer, citing journal articles by author and title. Finally, Nikolayev said, "But does it work?" and everyone laughed, but Lenin only gently, inclining his head as if inviting me into the joke. I turned on the device and nothing happened, because nothing was supposed to happen. "If someone could cross the perimeter?" I murmured. One of the commissars volunteered; he wrapped a scarf around his face and tiptoed toward the wire-clipped vase, full of poppies. We held our breath. The alarm sounded—a small bell and an illuminated bulb. Such modest magic. But the men exploded in cheers. They slapped the foiled thief on his back. The flowers shook. Lenin said, "Dmitri, I am relieved that you are such a poor burglar."

For the demonstration of the theremin, I was accompanied by Lenin's secretary on piano. Her name was Lydia F. I remember because during that morning's rehearsal, I fell quite instantly in love. Lydia had brown hair to her shoulders, a pointed chin, an awkward bearing. I arrived at the Kremlin in suit and lab coat and realized that I had forgotten to bring an accompanist. I remember standing alone in the conference room, running my hand over my face. It would not have been my first time demonstrating the theremin alone, but this was not some casual demo. This was Lenin. Inside two years, Petrograd, the city where I was raised, would be renamed for him. In Moscow that morning I was panicked and sweating until I muttered something to someone and he returned with Lydia, Lenin's secretary, who had studied piano at the conservatory. She smiled so broadly, sitting down at the keyboard. "Hello, piano," she murmured. "How have you been?"

Three hours later, I flicked a switch on the theremin. It made its sound. I made the appropriate calibrations. I glanced up at Lenin and fourteen of the most powerful men in the Soviet republic. I looked at Lydia, with hair to her shoulders. I nodded to her and lifted my hands and played Saint-Saëns's "Swan," all familiar motions.

Lydia and I met at every chord. With my eyes, I said to her, *Thank you.*

Then I looked at Vladimir Ilyich Lenin. His face was full of wonder. I breathed in and out. I moved slowly, from note to note, conducting. He was listening so carefully. The music showed in his face but so did his astonishment at the principles, the notion of human capacitance and electrical fields. I stood taller. The commissars seemed to sway. Lydia and I played our sad song, slowly, as if we were reorienting objects on a table.

When we were finished, I lowered my arms.

"Go on, go on," Lenin said.

So I swallowed and licked my lips and my heart went *thump, thump* in my chest. "Scriabin," I whispered to Lydia. She smiled, paging through the sheet music. I must have seemed so serious. We played Scriabin's op. 2, no. 1, then Glinka's "The Lark," with its final piano trills. It is a composition that suggests something yet will happen.

The men all applauded. I gestured to Lydia, who stood and curtsied, and they applauded her too. We were all grinning now. I gestured to Lenin and the commissars. Lydia and I offered our own applause. All of us laughed. Someone appeared in the doorway with a cart full of fruit, cookies, tea, but Lenin waved his hands at her. "Wait, wait," he said. "Such hasty refreshments. I'd like to try—Comrade Termen, may I try?"

"Y—yes," I said.

As Lenin joined me at the front of the room I could see that there was no performance in his actions. He was not looking at me, or at Lydia, or at his advisors' bemused expressions. He was not looking at the retreating cart. He was concentrated on the theremin itself, my scattered tools, the dormant box of the radio watchman. Again we shook hands. "Just excellent," he said. "Does it matter what one is wearing?"

I shook my head. "No, no."

"May I try the Glinka piece?"

I was taken aback. It was one thing to fumble through a clumsy swooping scale, but Glinka . . .

He could see me hesitating. "You did say it was simple."

"Yes," I said. "Perhaps I'll just assist you . . ."

"Very well!" Lenin said. He stood beside me like an assistant. Lydia F. was smiling.

"Maybe I will have you remove your jacket," I said.

He did so, draping his jacket over the back of a chair.

I addressed the shirt-sleeved Lenin.

"As I said, this antenna controls the volume, and this the pitch. You see?" I moved my hand away from the left antenna and the instrument increased its sound. Lenin just shook his head.

"Marvellous," he said.

I swallowed. "So I will simply . . ." I moved behind him, took his wrists in my hands. "I hope you don't . . ."

Lenin said nothing. His arms were relaxed. I lifted his left hand away from the volume antenna. "Ah!" he exclaimed, happily. Then I moved the right, adjusting pitch. It was like *chi sao*, the hand dance. I could feel his focus on our movements, the attention in his forearms.

"All right?" I asked.

"All right," he chuckled.

The piano began, softly. And we started. We played our stammering Glinka. I adjusted Lenin's arms and felt him opening and closing his fingers, experimenting with these changes. We made the music louder, softer, high and low. I gradually sensed that he was anticipating the moves, holding his hands in place, lifting or lowering. I withdrew. He sagged for a beat but then he himself was playing the song, deliberate and subtle. I took a step aside. I looked at this wide, warm room, the commissars carefully watching, the pretty girl at the piano. Lenin, Lenin himself, drawing music from the air. He had a narrow smile. He was fumbling and also certain. He was not bad. For a long, strange instant, I saw him posed like a mannequin, frozen, and imagined the way my future might flow out from a single electric note, called and answered; the way I might become Lenin's scientist, Lydia's lover, a friend and colleague to these thoughtful men. Young Termen, building things for the people of the USSR.

When he finished, Lenin lowered his hands.

The theremin wailed and screamed. I dashed in to silence the device as Lenin yelped and everyone laughed, and he shook his head with a mixture of embarrassment and self-satisfaction. There was a twinkle in his eye, maybe in everyone's eyes, that comes from a moment that is ridiculous and excellent. "I didn't know you had been practising," Nikolayev said.

Lenin stayed behind when the others went out for *medianyky*, slices of melon. He peered inside the theremin's cabinet, asked me questions about the circuits. He wanted to know if controls like the theremin's could be used to manipulate an automobile or a telephone. He had ideas I had never even considered: that devices like these could be used by men who had injuries to their hands, soldiers or farmers. "The most powerful application of electricity is not for the strong," Lenin said. "It's for the weak."

Soon we were discussing prostheses—artificial arms and legs, even an artificial heart, powered through the air. "The body itself is electric," I explained. "Our neurons, our brains—"

"Like vacuum tubes," Lenin said.

He asked me about my other projects; we discussed chemistry, physics, astronomy. If my laboratory needed any assistance, he said, I should contact him. "And we must show these inventions to the people."

It was so easy to talk to this man, to ask and answer as Lenin's gaze darted, as he nodded and considered. It was not as if we were friends, but perhaps like old partners, colleagues. Like comrades.

Before I left, at the doorway to his office, Lenin took my hands in his.

"I said earlier that our minds are like vacuum tubes."

"Yes."

"We must remember, Comrade Termen: they are more than this."

It was the first and last time I saw him.

TWO WEEKS LATER, I received an envelope in the mail. Lydia F. had written my name and address in her unadorned hand. Lenin had sent me a *Mandat*—a card entitling the bearer to unrestricted travel on all of Russia's railways. It carried a letter with his signature. *Go out*, he said in his note. *Show your works in Archangelsk, Kem and Samara*. I was instructed to lead a scientific tour, bringing electricity to the people.

Two months later, in May 1922, he suffered his first stroke.

On the night of January 22, 1924, I was working late at the institute. I had travelled by rail to Pskov, Minsk and Yaroslavl, showing the people my inventions. I had come home. The sky was inky in the windows. A charwoman appeared in the laboratory doorway.

She said, "Lenin is dead."

She was ashen.

"What?"

"Lenin is dead."

My mouth closed and opened. I felt as if winter had been let into the room. She held up a sheaf of newsprint. A drawing of his face, partly in shadow, bordered in black.

"Last night," she said.

I put my hands flat on the bench. "Thank you," I said. My eyes watered. The laboratory was quiet except for the buzz from one of the machines.

That night, instead of sleeping, I devised a plan to bring Lenin back to life. It was based on ideas I had had for years. We would freeze his body; we would perfect our techniques until we could repair the organs that had failed. I read and reread the reports of his death. His heart, his brain. We would proceed in a careful, considered fashion. In the morning I rang Rem Sarevko, a former graduate student who now lived in Gorky, where Lenin had expired. "We must save his body," I said. "You must go to the place they are keeping him and explain."

"It's impossible," Sarevko said.

"You are mistaken."

But they had already removed his brain, Sarevko told me. They had cut open Lenin's head and ripped out his mind and put it in a jar, covering it in poison, in alcohol.

"*Why would they do this?*" I asked.

"They wish to preserve it," Sarevko said.

ON THE TRAIN THAT brought me from Butyrskaya prison to Vladivostok, on Russia's Pacific coast, we were loaded like dead animals. They had brought us to the railway in a supply truck marked BREAD. The train car was wrapped in razor wire. They ordered us inside, told us to lie down on three stinking shelves. When no one else could fit, they sealed the door. We lay in darkness. We lay forever, as if in a mass grave. At last, with a sickly sway, the train began to move. A pale light bulb clicked and went on. Around me, several men began to cry.

We were going east, across the entire country, through Omsk and Irkutsk, under mountain and over desert, past Ulan Bator, past China's northern wilderness, forever, to the edge.

For thirty-eight days the rails went *clack clack* and then we reached the sea and things got much worse.

They use boats to take prisoners to Kolyma. These boats are the most terrible places in the entire world. I did not know they would be terrible. I did not know the train would be worse than the prison, that I would ride for five thousand miles in thirst and suffocation, in a car of dying men. I did not know that the transit camp, Vtoraya Rechka, would be worse than the train, that I would squat in the dirt under sheer searing sunlight with ten thousand prisoners, ringed by dogs; that in Vtoraya Rechka you would be shot for standing, shot in the stomach, and dogs with red mouths would lap at your intestines. I did not know that the boats would be worse than the camp, that they are the most terrible places in the entire world. I left the mainland gladly, gliding away from Vtoraya Rechka's wild, roaming cruelty. I thought I was leaving the gangs and the human, inhuman screams. Rifles pointed us up the gangways and onto the cargo ship and, through my wracking thirst, I was glad. I thought I was fleeing something. I was not fleeing anything. I was being poured down a horror's maw.

Lenin's Mandat was one of the items taken from me when I arrived at Butyrskaya prison. Just a piece of card. If it was not burned, it is in Moscow somewhere, with a handful of buttons.

May his memory be illuminated.

The steamer *Tovarishch Stalin* was originally an American vessel. It was covered in painted English words, PORT, AFT, DANGER, messages from a different time. The deck was mopped clean. There were little platforms for men and machine guns. A hatch led down to the hold. That is where the guards took us. At least a thousand prisoners pointed into the darkness. Because of the smell, several people began to vomit. There was very little air. The walls were slick wet metal or slimy grille, splitting the hold into sections. Already, experience had taught us habits: most of us sat or lay on the ground, setting out personal space. The floor was smeared with pitch, mud, feces, and vomit. More and more people were forced into the hold. We spread our legs, so other people could sit in front of us. We could hear the sound of men and women throwing up. There were no women in my section of the hold but you could hear them through the grille. As my eyes accustomed to the darkness I also realized that there was an upper level, a row of plank bunks raised over the floor. The zeks on these bunks did not look like the other men. They were *urki*—professional criminals. Prisoners like us, human cargo, but allowed to rule the camps. Power and deprivation turned these men into animals: cruel, powerful creatures, with tattoos on their chests. As I squinted in the darkness I watched an urka unfasten his belt and begin masturbating. He ejaculated onto the prisoners below. The journey from Vladivostok to Nagayevo took eight days. During this time, the urki spat and urinated onto those of us who sat on the floor. When we complained, they spilled down buckets of shit, fish heads, threats. I watched as a group of urki grinned under their peaked caps, nodding to one another, and slipped down like silverfish to steal a man's coat, his boots, to break his collarbone.

When the guards decided it was time to eat, they opened a hatch in the ceiling and threw down pieces of bread or salted fish. The prisoners clawed in the darkness. Even worse were the moments when they lowered buckets of water, water to quench our thirst; and we stood, gulping breath, following the slow bob of the bucket. I prayed that I would be able to tear through the others, to lap for a moment at whatever the guards had sent us.

Sometimes the urki would turn off the lights. They would descend with fists and knives. They spoke in slang, like nursery rhymes, like characters from folklore. I remember a man with gold in his mouth, the most unkind eyes. I watched him bribe a guard, who allowed a strand of men to pass through one hatch and into another. They raped three women. I knew it was three, because the women called to us, pleading for help, from the other side of the grille.

The boat bucked in the typhoons of the Okhotsk Sea. In seething effluent our bodies knocked against steel and bone, screaming, dying. I was seasick, violently seasick, clutching my ribs and holding a handful of rags to my face, my mouth crowded with bile.

It took eight days to reach a place called Kolyma, in the northeast of the country where I was born. On the journey I remembered you. I remembered Lenin. I remembered every meal I had ever eaten, every kind word or touch. There are no friends on those boats. There is no hope. I knew we were going somewhere, to some unimaginable camp, and I imagined that misery itself could drag our ship through the night. Kolyma, like a magnet, or like Einstein's black hole, a place that draws every sadness toward it. Part of me is surprised that any sorrow can exist away from the camps. Manhattan is 136 longitudes from Kolyma and still we had the folly, there, to cry.

NAGAYEVO IS A WIDE beautiful bay surrounded by an unfinished circle of cliffs. The water is still and silver-blue. It is like a resting coin, a new dime, that reflects the sky.

We came into Nagayevo harbour and they stacked the dead on the pebble beach.

All of us walked away from the corpses. We climbed the hill, blinking in the daylight. The road was made of dirt and then there was a road made of rocks. We looked back at the bay and the *Tovarishch Stalin* sat so smally, so quietly, secreting smoke. It was just one ship in a vast harbour; it was just one ship in a vast harbour. You could found a city there, a little paradise on the sea. Guards pointed the way with rifle barrels. We came up over the rise and the country lay before us, limitless. We were marching at its edge. *Are there deer here?* I wondered. *Wolves?* Later, I learned that there are deer; there are wolves.

We marched until we reached the village of Magadan. It was a young place, tainted by its visitors. They divided us into groups. An officer gazed down at us from a plywood stage. It felt as though we were at the end of our lives, some in-between that follows death. A place of mud and scrub and clouding breath. "This is Kolyma," he said. His voice scraped.

"You are here to work. You are here for crimes against the Soviet state and you will repay your debt with minutes, hours, years. You will repay us with blood and sweat. If you work hard, you will eat. If you do not, you will die. There are no tricks. We need the metal that is buried in the earth; it is your task to extract this metal. If you do not meet your quota, you are a traitor and a saboteur.

"The law is the taiga and the prosecutor is the bear. You will remain here until you leave here. No one escapes."

The man looked us over once more. The sky behind him was endlessly blue. "That is all," he said.

WE WALKED TO OUR CAMP. This was a walk of two weeks. Every day they gave us a fish: a single cooked trout, like a thing from a surrealist painting. Some of us ate the fish at once and some of us ate it little by little, to last the day. We walked and then we slept and the sun crossed the sky. Sometimes it rained.

I remember waking one morning with fog spread over the plateau; it wreathed the sleeping prisoners and the low lichened rocks, the stunted trees, everything except the mountains. The mountains were not hidden and in a way they felt like allies, friends. Only they could not help, could not move. They had withdrawn, our allies. A group of forty-two human beings lay in the day's cold mist.

One afternoon we arrived at the camp. It was near the mouth of a river and you could hear the water whispering over rocks. Mountains surrounded us. A frayed banner hung across the gate: "Work in the USSR Is a Matter of Honesty, Glory, Valour and Heroism!" My clothing was caked black and puke from our time on the boat. The colours had faded in the sun.

We had not died.

They counted us. They counted us again. We stood in uncomprehending formations. I said to myself: *I will remain here for eight years.* It was so cold and our clothing was black and puke and faded. Then they took us to the baths. We stripped naked. With doughy nurses' hands they held us in place and shaved the hair from our arms, legs, from between our legs; they shaved our heads and the beards from our faces. "Lice," they said, but I did not have lice. There was a stove, but we shivered. Then they let us into the other room. We drew our bodies through tepid water. We were grateful even for this. I had never been so dirty. I had never been so deeply thirsty, or hungry. We dried ourselves on rough cloths and they led us to piles of clothes: long underwear, long tunics, quilted jackets and trousers, mittens, rubber boots, hats with ear flaps. These were dead men's clothes. We searched for garments that fit. We looked like scarecrows, rag monsters. Then they took us back outside and they gave us warm broth.

In the day's last light I saw another prisoner kneel. He had found tiny berries hidden in the dry white moss that crackled underfoot; they looked like coral. I had almost forgotten the name. *Brusnika*. Red berries on thin green stalks, with leaves like little tokens. They were everywhere. I lifted three berries to my mouth and they broke against my tongue, sweet and bitter and tasting very faintly of snow.

Winter would come. I knew this: it would come, and then it would go, and then it would come again. And again and again. We would all die in Kolyma, unless we did not. I did not know the trick to living. My hand was dotted with the berries' thin juice and there were guard towers all around, pairs of hollowed eyes, bear turds and wolves' howls, criss-crossed barbed wire. I could not be a block of wood or a slab of chalk, inert. Lev Sergeyvich Termen, come from Leningrad to New York to Kolyma, forty-three years old. The sum of all those years draining away, meaningless, before the empty fact of the present.

I had nothing left to hold.

FIVE

T#E VILLA#E

THE CAMP WAS A CLUTCH of buildings surrounded by fence. The fence was three metres high, wrapped in coils of barbed wire. I never saw anyone touch this fence. The ground was uneven, furrows and rises, as if they had wiped away a rapids and placed us there. The valley's trees had been sheared to build the barracks, the work sheds, the hospital; to erect the administration bloc and the squat cultural-education building, which we rarely visited. The soft grass was littered with brittle shrubs, the sharp shoots of bushes. A misstep would often puncture the sole of your boot. Guard towers stood all around, on the mountaintops, beside the mine shafts' timber adits. You could squint into the flint-coloured distance and see the guess of other towers, the maybe, along those ridges. As the sun crossed the sky the triangular silhouette of a mining tower ticked across the camp. It was an empty landmark: that vein had gone dry, goldless. Old timers called it the gallows tower.

Our camp was like a village. When we were not working we

gathered on steps. We wandered in pairs between buildings of rough grey plywood. This aspect was convivial. No other aspects were convivial. The other aspects were inhuman. We slept on exposed bunks, crammed together, shivering. When it was wet the ground was muddy; when it was dry we lay and listened to hunched men carving dead skin from their heels. At night the barracks filled up with groans, as though the sleeping zeks' souls were being sucked from their jaws. The wind howled like an abandoned child. We strained to hear the cinders in the hearth, a kind of lullaby. We closed our eyes and insects crawled over our faces, moving like scraps of lace. We were awoken before dawn. We rose. We wrapped our rags closer, for warmth, trying to add months to our lives. We went into the frozen morning and lined up for food. Different people were permitted to stand in different lines: the strongest workers, Stakhanovites, who exceeded their daily quotas, received one large ladle of broth, bread, a piece of herring. Those who just met their quotas received one ladle of broth and a piece of bread. And the rest, the ones who fell short of their quotas: they received a little bread, half a ladle of soup. Political prisoners, 58s, were automatically assigned to the poorest category. I held my bowl in trembling hands.

Sometimes the urki would take our food, and sometimes our friends would take our food, and sometimes dying men, mad with hunger, would attempt to take our food; and we would shove them into the snow, fiercely, carefully, because we could not bear to spill a single drop from the brim of the small tin cup.

After we tasted our food we worked for seven hours.

Then we were allowed a portion of cabbage stew.

And we worked for seven more hours.

I was assigned to road duty. This was considered lucky. Most of the men and women of our camp worked in the mines, swallowing dust in darkness, skating toward death. I write this so lightly now, *skating toward death*. During those first weeks, my horror was close to grief. I watched zeks draining away out the camp's high gates. They came back even less alive: thinner, scarcer. As if another year had been shaved from their bones. Huddling in the dinner queue, the prisoners' eyes still reflected the underground. I thought that if I met their gaze I would tumble into it. I could not believe that human beings were being treated in this way. This thought raked over me. As I dragged my cart along the road my face would suddenly contort and I would be crying—not for myself but for this place.

On road duty we died more slowly. The officers watched our dying very closely. Once I had died a certain amount, they would assign me to the mines. I learned this from others as we gathered on the steps, as I wandered past the hospital and the guardhouse.

On road duty the task was this: Drag an empty wheelbarrow for ten kilometres over a ravaged road. The wheelbarrow clanged and caught. We were allowed to talk but we had to remain in single file, flanked by guards. Men would yell conversations until their voices failed. I spoke little. I studied the trees along the road, the way their roots hid in the earth.

The woods parted as we approached the quarry. The road led across a plain to the base of a barren hill. There was a mining tower, two rips in the earth, a giant mountain of dull stone. These rocks and gravel were the detritus of the mine, the wasted part of the diggers' lives. We took cold spades from a pile. Each of us cautiously propped up his wheelbarrow and filled it, lifting stone. Dust rose up like smoke. The more we carried, the more we would eat tomorrow. On the best days, my wheelbarrow held two hundred pounds of flinty rock and dust. When the wheelbarrows were piled heavy, as heavy as we could possibly push, we replaced the spades where we had found them. Sometimes we lay them down and sometimes we threw them. We returned to our barrows and wiped our foreheads on our sleeves and watched the circling brown birds, and we pushed our precarious loads up the slope to the road. At this time we were each permitted to smoke one cigarette.

Our weighted wheelbarrows sank into the road. They tipped and leaned and sometimes they toppled, spilling across the ground. The wheelbarrow's owner would curse, cry, grope with freezing hands to pile the rocks back into the cart. If it was an urka, like Nikola or the Boxer, we would all set down our own wheelbarrows, to go and help. It was not that we would win a favour, but perhaps they would pass us over during a moment of cruelty; their friends might rob someone else. There was a hierarchy among zeks and an even stricter hierarchy among urki. At Kolyma, you could not afford kindness. We helped only the worst men.

After two or three hours we arrived back at base camp. We dumped our stone. It would be used to build the new roads, carrying gold and timber to the harbour.

There were always guards. They always carried rifles. They stood on guardtowers, with crashing spotlights, scanning the grounds and the perimeter. If you went near the fence, the guards would shout and then shoot. If you brawled with another prisoner, not just a swung punch but tooth and claw, they would also sometimes shoot. Sometimes they would not. It depended which zeks were fighting, or if bribes had been paid. Some of the criminals moved around like cats, entitled to milk. You heard stories: a girl crosses the grounds after dark, hurrying to the women's barrack. Men appear around her, like a conjured circle. After a while, the guards yell down: "Come on boys, have some discretion!" They drag her from the cold snow into the shadow of stacked firewood. Later, they take her to the hospital. The urki make sure she is cared for. When she emerges, rested, she goes back to these men. She becomes a sort of prison wife. She is safeguarded. She has found a way to stay alive.

I FIRST MET BIGFOOT beside a grave. Bodies lay in a pit, which we were covering with earth. It was a windless yard. I watched the soil slide from my spade, imagining my own death. The falling earth made only the slightest sound. I did not want to waste my strength. Five of us lifted dry earth and dropped it onto shrouded bodies, proceeding from minute to minute, going on. One man began to pick up the pace. We were shovelling feebly, the rest of us, and this one man picked up his pace, quickened, until soon the clearing's loudest sounds were his inhalations. Fast, clear inhalations, through the nose. His eyes were lowered. He had a thick head of straw-coloured hair, matted at the brow, and a dense beard.

"Did you know these men?" I murmured, after a little while, indicating the grave.

"No," Bigfoot said at once. He lifted his eyes to where I was slowly lowering a clod of earth. "Did you?"

NOW, SEASONS LATER, it feels faintly impossible to be recalling these scenes. I was there; today I am here. Twice a week I come up into this attic, kneel by my machines, listen, type. I transcribe recordings for my masters and I also compose these pages, a little at a time. Sometimes it is hard to imagine I was ever in the taiga; sometimes it feels as if I did not leave. Sometimes I am writing you a letter, Clara, and other times I am just writing, pushing type into paper, making something of my years. There is cruelty to the way a person, a place, can sometimes feel so close, and then the next day far away. You were wearing amber the night we first saw Duke Ellington. Today this memory is beside me. I waited with your sister in the front room of your parents' house and you appeared in a doorway, glowing, in your pale amber slip and with amber around your neck and dark amber curls atop your head. I stood. I kissed your hand. You said, "Hi, Leon."

We went by taxi to the Apollo Club. My heart was whirring in my chest. Silver subway cars poured through the tunnels under Broadway, New York crackled and shone, cranes hoisted whole buildings into the sky.

I remember how we arrived just in time for the first number and how for the whole first half, the horns used mutes. We moved to the strings and brass but Duke's players had hands cupped over their trumpets, plungers over trombones, until at a certain pre-arranged moment everything changed. By chance I had spun you out on your toes. Our arms were at their longest span. At that instant the mutes came off and the brass section bloomed and it was like the clouds had parted, only we hadn't known there were clouds. The room rang gold with it. You were spinning back toward me, hot and amber, and when our bodies touched you murmured, "Hi, Leon." And I thought, *It will be like this.*

Now, in a bare room across the world, I leave commas on the page,,,, like eyelashes.

IN KOLYMA THE GUARDS followed us everywhere, rifles swinging at their sides. They had good boots and good gloves and mostly serious dispositions. Some of them were former prisoners who lived in the village now. Between shifts you could see them come into the work zone, walking freely past the guardhouse, and in their faces there was still something uncomprehending.

Just like their wards, guards were compensated according to production. If a team of zeks exceeded its quota, the escorts took home more rubles. The abuse the guards doled out was functional, pragmatic: walk faster, walk faster, take more stone in your wheelbarrow.

Conversely, the soldiers were punished if one of their prisoners escaped. They could even be accused of counter-revolutionary collusion, get sent to the other side of the perimeter. And so the guards learned to kill the zeks who strayed. In the late day, when our muscles were failing, we had to be especially alert. Anyone who staggered off the road might then stagger into the snow or cedars, sprawling, a bullet between his shoulders. There was a man whose name I don't remember, with red hair, who told me he was going to kill himself. And then he did, almost gracefully, turning his wheelbarrow off the curve of the road and drowsily advancing, toward freedom; Vanya yelled and raised his gun and after two hesitations he pulled the trigger. The redheaded man whose name I do not remember completed the motion he had begun that morning, lifting himself off his knotted plank bunk. He fell forward, into the tundra.

I think I believed I would kill myself, eventually, when the correct moment finally arrived.

The winter came quickly, in place of fall. I lived only barely, by coincidence. At the end of every workday, wrecked, ruined, we trudged back into the camp. We queued for our evening meal: a morsel of herring, a spoonful of pea soup, bread. Someone might steal the soup or fish, but never the scrap of limp brown bread. The prisoners had made this rule themselves. This is humanity, at the end of the world: the refusal to tear away a piece of bread. Once I saw a man try. He was dying of hunger. The whole camp seemed to turn on him, a wolf rising from a pile of leaves. *This you do not do*, they said, kicking the wretched starving man at the places where the skin met his ribs.

My friendship with Bigfoot dawned gradually. We found each other sitting together, one mealtime. We sat in respectful silence. The second time it happened I said, "My name is Lev."

He said, "My name is Maksim. Or Bigfoot."

I said I was a scientist. Once, he said, he had wanted to be an engineer.

We began to walk together, sometimes. Together we observed the camp.

His trust was like a gift.

Bigfoot's feet were not so large, but he had come to Kolyma in enormous fur boots. "My brother made them," he explained. They were brown and white bearskin, as high as his knees. You could hear them, like machines, crunching through the ice to a clearing in the woods. Bigfoot was not on road duty: he and his brigade stripped the felled trees, heaved them into the river. Their mouths gusted steam. At night Bigfoot rolled his boots into a coarse parcel and lay them beneath his head, like a pillow.

Bigfoot's boots did not go unnoticed. He tried to ignore the looks. There was a hard glint to his gaze, something unflinching in his bearing. He had come to Russia from Lvov, in Ukraine, hoping to fight with the Marxists. Instead he was arrested as a spy. I remember joking with him one day, when we had become friends enough that we could joke: "At last, here, you are one of us."

Bigfoot had fought off a few petty thieves but it was different when Nikola came up to him one night, an apparition on the dark field. "Do you play cards?" Nikola murmured.

"No," Bigfoot said.

Nikola had a rough black beard. He kept his hands concealed in a heavy coat. His eyes were hidden under his thick black hair. In some ways Nikola seemed like a serious man. He could have been a professor of Russian literature, a young chess teacher. But there was a certain cheapness to him, a shabby quality to his gestures, that made him frightening. It was not just the 58s who gave Nikola a wide berth: the other urki were vigilant around him, watching him in a room, tracking his movements in their peripheral vision. They let him pass; they did not interrupt him. They rarely saw his eyes.

When Nikola said to Bigfoot, "Come play cards with me," and began to walk toward his barrack, Bigfoot lowered his head and took a slow breath and then followed him.

They played cards. Sitting among Nikola's friends, on other men's bunks. The cards were made with thin scraps of paper, bread-and-water glue.

"What is your stake?" Nikola asked quietly.

"I don't know," Bigfoot said. "Some bread."

"Your boots are your stake," Nikola told him.

Bigfoot won the first two games. He won a half-litre enamel bowl, which meant that at mealtimes he could take his soup first, with those who have their own bowls. Then he won a set of coloured pencils. In the brown of Nikola's eyes you could see he was very angry. His friends were no longer slouched, joking; Bigfoot said he felt them turning their sharpest edges toward him.

Bigfoot lost the next game.

"Did you mean to lose?" I asked.

He didn't answer.

They took Bigfoot's fur boots. Later, he traded the pencils for a pair of leather boots, and he tore strips of cloth from the lining of his jacket, and he wrapped his feet with these. Now Nikola crunched through the ice in Bigfoot's boots, when we walked to the quarry, speaking to no one.

"Do you hate him?" I asked Bigfoot, one early morning.

"Yes," he said.

Being on road crew was easier than working in the mines, or in the trees with Bigfoot, but we were still starving. Our rations were based on our work and we could lift only so many pounds of stone. The most important factor was the number of trips we were capable of making in a day, to and from the quarry. No matter how high we filled our wheelbarrows, it was always more worthwhile to have time for another transit. On a good day we made four journeys. On a snowy day we might make two. And so on the next day we ate about half as much. The slower we worked, the more quickly we would vanish from everyone's memory.

One night I was walking with Bigfoot through the camp. We visited the southeast corner, where white flowers were growing in a pattern behind the latrines. The flowers were illuminated by the floodlights. We walked past the guardhouse, where men were smoking. Above us, towers creaked. The wind in Kolyma did not feel like the wind in other places: it was as if someone had taken her two hands and carefully separated our clothes, parting the fabric, to allow the cold inside. Very few zeks were out at this hour. It was so bitter and dark; and lights-out would come soon. Most would already be sleeping, or staring at the knotted wood above their head, at the thin insects that lay there like pencil marks.

A line of night-blind prisoners staggered across the road. Their blindness was brought on by a vitamin deficiency. All would be normal until the late afternoon: *Go faster*, someone would plead. *Let's get back to camp.* As dusk set in, they were diminished. They became silent and fumbling. After sundown the night-blind were more like ghosts than like men: faltering in their steps, hands fluttering. They searched for their neighbours, for familiar walls, for the world that they remembered. They travelled in flocks, clutching. One zek would stumble and they would all trip after him, like some cruel Buster Keaton routine, collapsing in a skinny pile.

Bigfoot and I stood in the muddy square between the barracks and watched the shambling blind men. We watched zeks carrying water on straining yokes. They drew black water from the well. It was easy to imagine a cavern, a secret reservoir, that yawned beneath the camp, full of smooth black water.

A hundred spruce planks lay stacked in the dirt.

After a moment I said, "I have an idea for the wheelbarrows."

"An idea?"

"To make the work easier."

Bigfoot had a long, plain face, all that straw-coloured hair. He delivered his jokes without smiling.

"Tea with lemon?" he said.

"A track."

"Too much work."

"No." I pointed to the planks. "Nothing elaborate. Slats like those."

"Hmm," he said.

I waited. I wanted Bigfoot to say something more.

He squinted at the guardtower's shifting silhouettes.

"We should get in," he said.

We headed back toward our barracks. The sound of the snow was like pepper crushed in a mortar.

"How far is your walk every day?" he asked me. "Eight kilometres?"

"Each way?"

"Yes."

"I think almost ten."

Bigfoot scrunched up his face. It was a strange expression on a bearded face like his. "How many planks of wood does that take?"

He caught me with this question. We arrived at my door in silence. "Four thousand," I said finally.

He raised his eyebrows just a little. "Four thousand," he repeated.

That was that. I tried to imagine four thousand spruce planks in a mountain behind the hospital. I lowered my eyes. We went inside, to where it smelled like smoke and rot.

In the morning I learned our brigade had finished below quota for the fifth straight day. We were ordered to work an extra two hours. I saw the Boxer exchange a look with Sergey. Both urki seemed to be losing their night vision. Or perhaps I had imagined it. They shook their heads and slumped up the path. It was one of those mornings when you notice the size of the sky, the strange quiet, the endless roll of the land past the wire. You remember that you are at the very edge of things.

I worked all day and for two more hours, pushing my tripping wheelbarrow through the frost. All day, carrying stone.

The group completed only three trips.

That evening I lay in my bunk, on my side, trying to tune out the conversations around me. I was tired and so hungry. I was thinking.

Finally, I rolled off the boards and went searching for Nikola.

THE MAJOR AGREED TO see us before the midday meal.

Vanya, our guard, found me in line.

"Now?" I said.

"Now."

I gazed at the queue ahead of me. I discovered I was ready to give the whole scheme up. None of my grand ideas were worth as much as that ladle of pea soup.

"Did you hear me?" Vanya said.

Bigfoot was watching us from the next queue over.

"Forget it," I said.

"Forget it?" Vanya was short-tempered but not so bad. He always slouched in his uniform, as if the epaulets forced him to lean forward. He stared at me, and the line, gradually comprehending. "You can eat after," he said.

I tried to gauge his honesty.

"Where's Nikola?" I said.

"He's meeting us at the officers' building."

From his place in line, Bigfoot looked worried. I gestured that it was all right.

I still had not left the queue.

"Termen?"

"All right," I snapped. I came away from the line. It was as if I were extruding a sword from my side.

We walked in silence. The grass was stamped down, speckled with snow. Nikola was waiting for us on the steps, hands in pockets. "Hello," I said. He didn't answer.

Vanya rolled his eyes at this little performance. "All right, then?" he said.

Nikola sniffed. He muttered yes.

I nodded.

We followed Vanya inside the building. I had never been through this door. The entranceway was bare and whitewashed. The walls kept the wind out. A bouquet of pale blue blossoms rested in a vase and for a moment we watched them as we walked, Nikola and I, the prisoners.

We came to a door with the major's name. Vanya knocked.

The major said, "Come in."

We huddled into his little office. There were no windows. There was a painting of Red Square and a painting of Stalin and a painting of a peasant woman with a cow. There were pinned-up charts and many typed lists. The major was a young man with a roman nose, long hair pulled back in a tie. He was not thin but he was quite handsome, with a straight clear look. I assumed his long hair was a violation of the military dress code. Like his age, like his assignment, it suggested the major was either very good or very bad at his work.

Vanya saluted.

The major nodded wearily. "All right, junior lieutenant. Proceed."

Vanya hesitated. "If it's all right, sir, I'll let the prisoners speak for themselves."

"Fine. What are your names?" The major took a short breath.

"Lev Sergeyvich Termen."

"Nikola Zharykhin," Nikola said.

"You're both on Junior Lieutenant Bragin's roads team?"

I had become nervous. The major was writing our names on the pad in front of him. This seemed like a record, already; like evidence, liability, a reason somehow to give us each five more years.

I said nothing. Nikola eyed me, disquieted. The major was still waiting for a response. He cleared his throat. "Yes?"

"Yes." I tried to shake off my anxiety. "Wheelbarrows."

The major offered an even smile. "Wheelbarrows." He crossed his arms. "Well, what's this idea?"

Another silence.

I realized no one was going to speak if I did not.

"To improve efficiency," I murmured.

"I'm not going to give you any more food, Termen."

I had noticed the radio on the major's desk, the dish with a piece of sausage, the photograph of two children.

"No," I said. "No, let me explain."

"Yes?"

"Comrade Zharykhin and I were discussing our work and we had a realization. So we consulted with Lieutenant, er, Bragin, and he was very helpful as we—er, distilled this concept into, well—"

"Cut to it."

I swallowed. "The main detriment to our team's production total is the rate at which we travel with our loads between sites."

"The wheelbarrows," the major said drily.

"Yes. Or, really, the roads. In most conditions the transit is very slow."

"I cannot give you new roads, Termen. New roads are what we are trying to *build*."

"Yes sir, but the thought is this: *tracks* for the wheelbarrows. Runners."

"Made of what?"

"Wood. Simple planks. Perhaps with a groove down the centre."

"Hm." The major tapped his pad. Vanya, hunching in his uniform, exhaled.

"These planks would just sit on the road and you would push your wheelbarrows along them?"

"That's right. By my rough estimate, the use of tracks would accelerate each transit by as much as four hundred percent."

The major narrowed his eyes. "By four times?"

I hesitated. "Less in the summer."

The major's lips twitched. "Hm," he said again. But then he realized the obvious thing and he straightened, skeptical. "How far do you travel with these wheelbarrows?"

"About ten kilometres," I said. "I will save you the arithmetic: it would take several thousand runners to line the whole route."

The major said, "So we will cut down a forest? To save you some work?"

"There is another solution."

Nikola shifted beside me.

"It requires just six pieces of wood."

"Is there a section of the route that is particularly precarious?" the major asked.

"No," I said quietly. "We could take three pieces of wood, tied end to end, with a rope handle at the front. One member of the team does not push a wheelbarrow—he lays down this section of track. When all the carts have passed over it, he hauls the track ahead of them."

"One section of rail, advancing with the group."

"Yes. But we do not want to waste time waiting for the track to advance. So we could use two men, each with three lengths of track."

"When the wheelbarrows have passed over the first stretch, that man runs to the front."

"Precisely."

"But it would also remove two men from the work crew." The major picked up his pencil. "So total production would only . . ."

"Six men working at triple capacity still more than doubles the production of eight men."

The major squinted. "If we expand the team from eight men to ten—keeping two for the rails . . ."

I considered for a moment. "Comparing like with like, it improves production by a minimum of 2.4."

The major clicked his tongue. He lifted his eyes to look at Vanya. The junior lieutenant seemed to freeze.

"Very good, Bragin."

Vanya all but melted into the floor.

"And you too, Zharykhin."

Nikola inclined his head.

"And you, Termen, what are you?"

"Sir?"

"An engineer?"

Standing in that sunless room, for the first time in many months, I felt a thing called pride.

"I'm a scientist," I said.

"Termen the scientist." The major made a note on his pad. "Our own little expert."

FOUR DAYS LATER, the Expert began his first experiment. Two men—Volkov and Jansons—were reassigned from another team: they spent a late afternoon assembling two tracks of rails, tying them together, embedding sturdy rope handles. I came back to the camp that night and looked over their handiwork; I was tired, hungry, crumbling. I gazed at this mess of dirty pine and brown cord and understood that it could be another sentence. There would be consequences if my experiment disappointed.

In the morning we learned that Volkov had died during the night, of starvation.

I do not believe in omens.

We went out into the day. Bigfoot was named as Volkov's replacement. I wondered whether I had saved him or doomed him. Bigfoot and Jansons grasped the rope handles and hiked forward into the snow. The wind swept ice crystals over our faces. Unsure, skeptical, we pushed our wheelbarrows onto the planks. There was a trick to keeping them on the track, but it wasn't a difficult trick. Before long we were moving quickly. Jansons would wait for us to leave his track and then scamper ahead of Bigfoot; then Bigfoot would wait for us to leave his track and stride ahead of Jansons. They were the only ones who talked: "All right," they would say, when their boards were level in the snow.

We arrived at the quarry, filled our barrows with stone. The stone was as heavy as ever.

Now, with filled barrows, came the delicate moment. Nikola took a few steps and his wagon almost immediately skidded off the plank, spilling grit. We all stopped, ran over, pulled stones from the snow. Our eyes met, Nikola's and mine. I tried to smile. I was not sure if I should be smiling.

We righted his wheelbarrow and the group moved on. We pushed our wheelbarrows at a steady pace, and Jansons and Bigfoot dashed ahead with their trailing boards, like tails. Nikola's wheelbarrow tipped again, and the Boxer's once, but we pressed on. We arrived at the worksite. We dumped our loads. "What time is it?" I asked.

"It doesn't matter," Vanya said. His mouth was covered with a scarf, as if he were a bandit. "Keep moving."

We raised our wheelbarrows and returned to the quarry. We had almost arrived when the sun broke through the cloud and I realized where it was, how low in the sky, that this plan was working. "What time is it?" I yelled to Vanya.

"Keep moving," he replied, sternly.

We did: to the quarry, and back; to the quarry, and back; to the quarry, and back.

It was noon. We had made four trips. We did not usually complete four trips in an entire day. Everyone was smiling. Even Nikola was smiling, squatting beside Sergey. They laughed and tossed hunks of snow. Vanya pulled his scarf from over his mouth and he was smiling. Bigfoot was standing with me and smiling and he said, "It works."

"We'll see. We'll see," I said. "It's only been half a day." But Jansons called over from where he was talking to two other men. "We've almost reached quota?!" he shouted. "They say we've almost reached our daily quota!" He looked around, incredulous.

"Let's go," Vanya said.

"Let's go *where*?"

"Lunch."

There was a moose standing right there, off the road, on the other side of the ditch. He held his crowned head high. His expression was steady and abiding. We walked right past him, our roads crew, away from this great breathing animal and into the camp, where they gave us each a portion of broth.

AT KOLYMA, THE EXPERT lived a better life than Termen had. For eight weeks, we surpassed our daily quota. Even as the major revised and increased our production targets, we pushed across our wooden rails, exceeding expectations. Because we surpassed these quotas, each of us was classed as a Stakhanovite. We were the first to receive our rations. We received the largest portions. Eventually, other teams adopted the Expert's runners system. I was rewarded with new clothes and an extra allotment of bread. So was Nikola, who the major accepted as co-originator of the scheme.

Junior Lieutenant Vanya Bragin received a promotion, although he remained our patrol guard.

By sharing credit with Nikola, I had won the protection of the urki. The thief knew that there had been no need to include him when I went to see the major. He interpreted my move as a gesture of respect, of deference. Like an offering. I let Bigfoot believe that it had been more desperate. Really the decision was a calculation, nothing more. An arithmetic of risk and reward, made from my hard plywood bed. Finally, in the gulag, I had learned pragmatism. Perhaps it was a gift, perhaps a taking-away.

Because of Nikola I won friends among the urki. Because of Vanya I won friends among the guards. Because so many other workers were improved by my scheme, I won friends in almost every barrack. I had friends everywhere, so many friends. "Expert!" they exclaimed, a good-natured joke, one of the rare good-natured jokes, because in Kolyma the good-natured jokes do not seem safe from the wind.

I had so many friends and these friends could not keep me warm as I pushed my wheelbarrow through the frost. They could not make me younger or stronger. I was happier for a short time but popularity was a hollow solace. You pass a man and exchange a smile, and it is worthless the moment you have stepped away, along the ice-packed path, into the next mud-smudged footprint. I lay in my bunk and watched the bugs squirming in the spruce. My friends had not banished my nightmares. "Expert!" they exclaimed, a greeting said and heard, and then their voices fell away. When you are quickly dying—which we still were, despite the extra herring—it is not thin friends, shambling, night-blind, that give you a reason to live.

Across miles of taiga, so much green and golden country, an ocean, I wondered if you were raising your arms in the air.

THE MAJOR SUMMONED ME one morning, after the prisoners had been counted. His emissary, a Cossack, sent another man to take my place. I resisted: "No, this is my brigade—this is my brigade!" So quickly I became hysterical. I did not want to be sent to the mines. I did not want to be sent to the woods. I did not want to lose my place on this lucky work crew, blessed by technology. "This is my team!" Finally, Vanya exchanged looks with the Cossack, and the Cossack nudged my replacement, and he warned him, "This is only temporary."

I went to see the major in the office with the radio, the piece of sausage, the photograph of a little boy and his older sister.

He told me to sit down. He congratulated me on my scheme. I did not thank him but I said I was proud to have contributed to the Soviet effort in Kolyma.

At first it seemed that the major simply wanted to fine-tune the use of runners. Was an eight-man team, with two rail haulers, the best configuration? Would ten be more efficient? Twelve? Would twelve men require *three* sets of rails?

He asked me to review some calculations. His maths were all right. "Ten men," I agreed, "and two haulers."

The major stretched back in his chair. "You studied at Petrograd University?"

"That's right."

"Mathematics?"

"Physics. And also music theory, at the conservatory."

He nodded. He seemed to be waiting for something.

"Did you attend university?" I asked.

"Horticulture," the major said.

"Plants?"

"Gardens."

"This is not much of a garden," I said.

He observed me, unmoving.

I folded my hands on my lap. "I wondered . . . If you want more help here, in the office . . . Coordinating work groups, or arranging . . ." I trailed off.

The major's face looked like a woodcut.

What was I trying to prolong?

I said, "I have some ideas about telephones. Perhaps the camp could be wired up."

The major shifted in his chair. "Termen," he said, "you are a fifty-eight."

"Yes."

He said, "Politicals do not belong behind our desks."

"Yes of course." I took a breath. I was already dead.

"This is what will happen," the major said. "You will work in the field, work hard, and when you have given eight years to your country, you will be a free man."

"Yes."

"It has already been how long?" he asked. He pulled a piece of paper toward him. He took a beat. "About seven months?"

"Yes."

"Already seven months! So just seven years left. Seven years and five months. Does it feel like a long time?"

"Yes," I said.

He laughed. But he saw that this was not a joke, that it was my life, and he leaned forward, toward me, toward the photograph of his children. "You'll be all right, Termen," he said gently. "You're smart and strong. You'll be on the roads a long while yet."

"Maybe music?" The question jerked out of my throat. I saw a flicker of interest in the major's face and then I did not stop talking, babbling, sketching a scheme that could buy me a few days of warmth. "Maybe I could arrange a concert? Something for the officers? A performance. To help pass the long days. A surprise recital. The officers would be able to—"

"No, not for the officers," the major said. "But perhaps for the workers . . ."

"The workers?"

"Like you."

A concert for the workers would have no purpose except self-delusion. An entertainment for the half disappeared. "What a wonderful idea!" I said. "It would have an excellent effect on morale."

"It's not a bad notion." The major pursed his lips.

I tried to smile as evenly as I could, neither nervous nor overenthusiastic.

"I think there may even be some violins somewhere," he said. "A cello."

That word, *cello*, seemed to lift up into the air. It was like a relic from another time. Cello. I had forgotten that the cello existed.

"I'll think about it," the major said.

My pulse was racing. "All right," I said.

He observed me for a few moments. He picked up the piece of sausage that was sitting on a dish on his desk. "Here," he said. I kept the piece of sausage in my hand until all the doors had closed behind me.

WE WERE BROUGHT TOGETHER two days later: eleven rag-wrapped prisoners, hustled into a room. I knew only one of them, a spindly man called Babu. I recognized a few others. We took a moment to survey each other while the Cossack guard stood with crossed arms. "Go on," he said finally.

I remembered that I was to be the leader. I swallowed. "You're musicians?"

The men and women looked around. They were like skeletons. "Yes," they said.

Four were violinists; two played the cello. Two bassists, a clarinet player, a trumpeter. One thereminist. I do not know how the major found them. The Cossack brought me to a long closet at the back of the cultural-education building, where we were supposed to see films, sometimes. No films were shown while I was at Kolyma. The closet had a box of grimy sheet music and a dark pile of instrument cases. I did not want to know where these instruments had come from. Incredibly, I found four working violins. There was a splendid old cello, like new. A battered double bass. Several cheap trumpets. Although I uncovered a couple of clarinets, the closet contained no reeds. "Do you play anything else?" I asked Babu when I came out.

"Some lousy flute," he said. So he played that.

They gave me an upright piano, on wheels.

How had this piano come to be in Kolyma?

The major allowed us to rehearse for two afternoons. We used the sheet music we had found. Chopin's first piano concerto. Some Mozart. A clumsy arrangement of Pachelbel's Canon. I led from the piano. The bassists and cellists shared parts. It was a hopeful cacophony.

At the end of the second rehearsal, the major listened from a doorway. "Good," he said. "You'll perform tomorrow morning."

I had imagined that we would play at night, in the cultural-education building, for everyone. I had imagined rows of dark faces, silence, then the careful opening notes.

"In the morning," he said, "as everyone goes to work."

The next morning the Cossack wheeled the piano into the no man's land near the fence. The squalid little orchestra stood in the snow. Everything was floodlit; the sun had not risen. There was just the grey sky and the grey earth and the silhouetted wood-line. The prisoners were standing or kneeling with their bowls of soup. They were looking at us with a mixture of fear and elation. Bigfoot was a few feet to my left, like a doting parent. I had not slept the previous night. He could see that I was unsure, my raw hands on the keys. I kept reaching up and pulling my coat around my neck. The orchestra was waiting for my signal. Our audience had fallen silent. Two night birds darted in the space above our heads.

It was cold and I felt that I was about to wrench open an overgrown gate.

"Ready?" I muttered. The violinists' eyes were wide, asking. "One two three, one two . . ." The first notes of Chopin's second movement lifted up. I played a chord. I played a chord and a chord. It was not a beautiful sound so much as it was an orderly sound. There was no bombast, no soaring melody. Looking back, we ought to have played something gay and upbeat. A reel. It would have been a kindness. Instead we played this fragile concerto, snowfall music. It was as though we were filling the work zone with new trees, empty birches and bare white elms. The barracks, the guardhouse became a little harder to see. The stars seemed to come out again, like pinpoints on a map, placeholders. Babu played his lousy flute.

Then the guards said it was time to go, and the brigades began to take formation, and they began to trudge away, through the gate. We kept playing, serenading the workers as they left for their clearings and their pits. I watched my group go—hunched Vanya, tall Sergey, Nikola dragging his fur boots. Bigfoot at the end of the line, gazing back at us. Ten minutes later, when the camp was empty, the Cossack told us to put down our instruments and catch up with our crews.

THE CONCERT WAS A SUCCESS, I suppose. It was a success inasmuch as it gave the performers a few hours away from the wind. The major listened only for a few minutes, standing on the boardwalk, but then he put out a wider call for musicians and there were almost forty of us when we gathered, a week later, in the darkened hall of the cultural-education building. This was no amateur orchestra: there were players from the cities' philharmonics, teachers from the conservatory. Alexander Alexanderovich Gushkin, concertmaster of the Moscow symphony. And I, their leader, at a rickety upright piano.

There were not enough instruments in the little closet. "I'll get you some from the other camps," the major told me. "I want you to play *Boléro*."

"Ravel," I said.

"A Frenchman," he said, as if he were trying to impress me.

"Yes." For a moment I was going to pretend that I was impressed, that the major had proven his knowledge and that we were somehow closer for it. But I did not have the energy for this performance. I felt so tired. "We will need a snare drum."

Then the major said something in French that I didn't understand.

FOUNDERED IN KOLYMA, I led the camp's little orchestra. What did I know of conducting? We performed *Boléro* at night, before a seated audience. I did not play piano; I kept time with a little whittled twig and at the end of the performance the Cossack took it from me, lest I use it as a weapon, lest I use it on myself.

The major had invited officials from neighbouring camps and for the audience, for many of the musicians, it was a joyful event. The booming horns, the weaving woodwinds, the stately percussion. We were not in Kolyma; we were on a Mediterranean hillside, in a Spanish court. We were wearing bright colours, with carafes of red wine. We were in towers, on precipices, part of the major's well-tended garden.

But I was not really with them. I led the little orchestra and I felt as if I was standing near an open window, watching the curtains shift. As the music rose up, it also vanished. Sometimes it is like this, listening to music: the steady bars let you separate from your body, slip your skin, and you are standing before the shuttering slides of memory. Shades of light, skies filled with cloud, old faces.

At the Paris Opera, I was a man with boxes and wires. Ravel himself listened from the darkness. The smell of tobacco. All this electricity, pretending.

On the deck of a ship, I saw a distant bridge. Harpists on the pier. "Mind the step," someone said.

Me on the floor of my parlour, laughing, resting against Schillinger's chair, and all of us passing around a bottle of bootleg rye. Slominsky the journalist—he called it inspiration. *A bottle of inspiration.*

And then, like a change of film, different intensities of colour, memories of you, Clara. Lamplit and candlelit. Sunlit. Sunlit Clara Reisenberg. Tableaux in which you turned and moved, and moved away. Tableaux in which you were visible only in the corner of the scene, almost hidden. I tried to suppress these images, brushing past to other things: Pash, Lavinia, former students. The pages of an old encyclopedia, the one I used to read in bed as a child. *Lepidoptera; Agra; The Mechanical Turk.* I tried to remember other faces. Yet you stayed. I looked away and you stayed. All these other things faded and passed, impermanent. Just fancies, gone. Your face was the strongest thing in all of my heart.

I remember when you said you wouldn't marry me. You looked at me with a face like a question and said nothing. On the steps of a Harlem club, at dawn, with strangers passing on the street. You swallowed. Your hands clenched. I glanced at these small fists but immediately looked back again to your face. I did not want to miss anything. I was smiling like a damn fool. Waiting, smiling, pretending I did not see the way that fear had sprung into your cheeks, like a blush. You were twenty-one and you were not ready to be a wife. Or perhaps you did not love me. Even today it is difficult to write this. In that vital instant I was too ruined to see what was before me. As soon as I saw your clenched hands I was another man, shattered.

THE NEXT MORNING I went to work and I pushed a wheelbarrow full of rocks.

BY DECEMBER, MOST OF OUR living took place in the dark. The few hours of daylight seemed illusory, like silver dreams. We shivered on the road, staring into the circles of our lamps. Sometimes I lifted my eyes and was surprised by an orange sky, a pink sky, my lamplight disappearing into air. But mostly it was darkness, with fine falling snow, temperatures that vacillated and plunged. Men were dying faster. Bigfoot tripped in the ice and tore off two of his toes. He spent two weeks in paradise, in the infirmary, with a hot woodstove and clean white sheets and a nurse who brought him double portions of food, like a hallucination.

He was discharged on a starless morning. The moon always seemed so unkind. Crouched with me, chewing on bread that was nearly frozen, Bigfoot said, quickly, without adornment, "I feel as if I am doomed."

IT WAS INTO THIS PLACE, into this moonlight, that there came a man in a green uniform.

I was returning from a day's work, passing through the gate, when a guard called my name. The word cut through the cold and the darkness like a dart. Each of us has these experiences, three or four times in our lives, when the instant itself feels like a messenger.

"Termen!" shouted the guard.

I walked stiffly toward him, across the crushed snow. "Yes?" I said, through my scarf.

Beside the guard, a man in a green uniform sat on a wooden bench. His greatcoat was unbuttoned. He had black hair and thin lips, a simple face except for the large round nose. I had never seen him before.

"This is Termen," the guard said.

The man in the green uniform mildly considered me, from my face down to my ragged boots. He gave the guard a small nod.

The guard flicked his glove. "You can go."

I pursed my lips, looking between the soldiers.

The Cossack came for me as we were rising the next morning. Someone was banging the pot by the stove and we were all turning on our sides and getting up from our bunks, holding our heads in our hands, wrapping ourselves in cloths. Those who had not slept were staring dead-eyed at their knees.

He appeared beside me and put his hand flat at the nape of my neck. "Let's go," the Cossack said.

I gave a start. "What? Where?"

"Now."

He brought me to the major's room. The office was empty. I stood with the Cossack against the wall. A piece of dried sausage sat on a plate. A picture sat in a frame. I noticed the sleeve of a

78 resting on a bookshelf. A cartoon of a fish at the bottom of the ocean, its lips in an O, a speech bubble with a music note.

The major came in with the man in the green uniform. They both appeared tired. They were holding steaming tin mugs.

"Good, Yemelya, thanks," said the major.

The Cossack saluted and left us.

The major and the man in the green uniform sat down.

"L-890, Lev Sergeyvich Termen. Fifteenth of August, 1896. Yes?"

"Yes," I said.

"Yes," said the major, nodding. He consulted the sheet in front of him. "This is Senior Lieutenant Lapin. Tomorrow he will be taking you back to Moscow."

My voice failed.

"He is already making the journey. After five months at Susuman he has been reassigned, the lucky clod. So he has been ordered as your escort."

"Why am I leaving?" I breathed.

The major shrugged. "You can ask whomever meets you at the other end."

I didn't know what to say. So many times in my life, now, I had been told I was going away. The major and the man in the green uniform, Lapin, were staring at me across the desk. I was grimacing—this wide, strained grimace, tears welling in my eyes. I had understood that I would die in Kolyma. I had understood that I would eke out a knife-edge of life and clasp an old lover's memory to my chest and then die one late afternoon, under a vaulted sky, crumpling into my bootprints.

I felt as if my heart were clutched in someone's hand. "All right," I said finally.

I went out to join my brigade. We worked through the dark morning, in clear air, until around midday a blizzard seemed to rise up from the ground, raw white, and we shoved our wheelbarrows through the smoke-like snow, pulled planks skidding across the ice, felt our faces raked by wind, and the thought I kept having was that I was abandoning these men, my partners, betraying their stooped silhouettes as I dreamed of a hot green locomotive that would carry me westward, from Vladivostok to Moscow, through valleys. In the thick of the storm I could not make out any living things but I pushed my cart of gravel, my last cart of gravel, for the making of roads.

I did not tell Bigfoot until after dinner that night, as we were parting. Near the entrance to his barrack, I said, "I am leaving in the morning."

He simply stared at me.

"I said I'm—"

"I heard you."

We faced each other.

"To Moscow," I said.

"I thought you had eight years."

"It is a transfer."

"To Moscow."

"Yes."

Bigfoot lowered his eyes. He scraped his boot against a small snowbank sprinkled with soot. I had lost him. He looked at me again but he was hunched differently. His eyes were guarded, peering out from his bearded face. His lips were torn from the cold.

"All right," he said.

"You'll be all right," I said, self-conscious that I had repeated his words.

He tipped his chin very slightly.

"We will meet up again, when all this is over. For vodka. For a feast." I took a deep breath. "With your wife. Maybe we will go for a holiday together."

I had lost him. He was not looking at me, not really. He looked so desperately sad.

"Maksim," I said, "you are a good friend."

"You also," he said to me, but I would not accept this gift.

I returned quietly to my own barracks, lay in my bunk. I wondered whether this was a ruse, and Lapin would shoot me when we passed away from the camp.

Or whether I would be shot in Moscow, a hero's welcome.

I lay there, unable to fathom that I would never lie there again. I thought of Bigfoot in his own bunk, staring at the knotted wood, with different thoughts.

Then Nikola came. He was very quiet. "Expert," he muttered.

I turned. His face was level with mine. Nikola's beard was long, curling at the edges. His black hair was smeared against his forehead. His eyes seemed to be reading my own, left to right. He shifted and I heard a rustling sound, like straw.

"What is it?" I murmured.

He rustled again. He was lifting something. He pushed a large bundle onto the bunk beside me. I reached with my hand—long bristles, fur. "What—" I said. I sat up as best I could. It was a coat. Twice-folded, scattered with tiny twigs and flakes of dry leaves. "What is this?"

"Fox," said Nikola.

"I don't understand."

"For your journey. Take it."

"Where did this come from?"

"A hiding place," Nikola said. He gazed at me from under his tangled eyebrows. "Take it," he whispered. "Now, before the others see."

I slid the coat to the other side of the bunk. Nikola nodded. His mouth twitched.

"Wait," I said. He stopped where he was, at the edge of shadow. "Why are you doing this?"

Nikola pushed out his lips—out and sideways, a rough red streak. He was smiling under that sunken look. "Gratitude," he said, softly, as if it was my name.

He tipped his head again. He went away.

The man in the green uniform took me in the morning. As the work crews trooped through the gates, we set off along a different road. I felt as if there should have been buds on the trees, tufts of green grass through snow. There were none of these things. It was all winter. I wore my fox-fur coat and walked with Senior Lieutenant Lapin. "You must be happy to be leaving," he said.

"I am very, very happy," I said, ducking my head to the moon.

WE WERE ALREADY ON the ship when the sun came up. It was a ship like the *Tovarishch Stalin*, steaming from Nagayevo back to Vladivostok. The boat was almost empty, because we were making the return journey. Few come back. I sat with Lapin in the closed upper deck. It still did not feel real. I tried to forget the dripping hold beneath us, where the prisoners would later be brought together, like hideous friends.

We did not linger in Vladivostok. Lapin led me to a train. He clambered into the heated officers' carriage, tipping his cap. I was led away to an empty cattle car. I quickly came to understand that with his coat, Nikola had saved my life. I sat with other prisoners, uncrowded in the carriage, but for three weeks the car was raked by the winter. It was a killing cold. There was room enough to sit and lie and stand, so we behaved like human beings, humane and reasoning. We exchanged weary jokes, the ten of us, rare conversation. We proposed that God existed and that he was a son of a bitch. But gradually a man named Roma froze to death, turning the same colour as the floor. Gradually a man named Timur died, I believe of thirst. We would gather by one side of the car, cupped hands upraised, hoping for the lucky flick of a melting icicle. This was living, I thought. Waiting under an icicle, counting every second.

The train stopped twice a day. They gave us bowls of food, cups of water. They allowed us to urinate, like workmen, into tundra.

Sometimes Lapin appeared. He said to me, "You're still here."

As we made our way west, Timur and Roma remained beside us, growing hard as stone. And I felt myself softening, thawing, warming in my fur coat. My life was growing larger. As we approached Moscow, something in me was stirring. I did not want to acknowledge it; it was easier to be a ruin, inert. The tiniest stone, which cannot be broken into smaller pieces. We passed through villages, past train platforms and silos. The train dragged the dead men to the city and the air was changing, like the introduction of an electric charge. I took it in slow breaths. I stared at civilization, uncomprehending. I huddled in my coat. I was no longer dead. I was roaring on a steamtrain toward the capital, propelled by outside forces. I was in play. I was Lev Sergeyvich Termen, conducted.

SIX

SWIMMING HORSES

THERE'S A STORY I heard in America, at a party, about a silver aeroplane that was skimming the country, five thousand metres up. It flew across a vast and quiet landscape, Utah or Ossetia, until it abruptly exploded. The aeroplane splintered into pieces. A woman came spinning out of this shattering blast. She did not have a parachute. Her hair whipped around her. She fell five thousand metres and landed on the snowy earth, alive, unhurt.

After a motionless moment she must have sat up. There would have been trees, birds, thin clouds.

At the prison called Marenko, all of us were this woman.

WE TELL STORIES AFTER COFFEE, sometimes. We sit in the dormitory, propped on pillows. Usually they are stories of Marenko itself, folklore passed down among the engineers. The time an electrician named Dubinski was found to be keeping a dog, a tiny brown dog, in the closet behind the radio laboratory. He had taught him to wag his tail at the sight of copper wire. The dog was allowed to stay but Dubinski was not.

Or the cleaner who was also a painter, hiding oil portraits at the foot of the east staircase. When he was discovered he was transferred to the design office.

The story of Yegor, who fell in love with one of the free employees. (There were many stories like this.) This woman worked at the checkpoint for the top-secret section, waiting all day for visitors with white or orange passes. It was the most boring of jobs, and Colonel Yukachev had forbidden these attendants from bringing books or puzzles. "You must be watchful!" he boomed. ("He was fatter, then," Rubin said.) Smitten and moony, Yegor wanted nothing more than to linger beside his sweetheart, trading double entendres—or, dare to dream, a kiss. But to approach the checkpoint you had to wield a pass; and so Yegor set about devising secrets, prototype ideas, bringing any conceivable project before Yukachev and asking, with false ambivalence, whether it "really ought to be kept under seal." The story's ending is obvious: the woman was suddenly transferred to another facility; Yegor found himself on the hook for three impossible rocket prototypes.

Although many of us at Marenko spent time in Kolyma— Andrei Markov was there for six years—we rarely discuss it. I do not think it is a matter of humility or out of respect for those who are still there. It is a kind of superstition. Here we are, in uneasy ease, reclining on our goose down; let us not name all the ways we have been spared. Nothing good will come from listing the horrors we have escaped. A little bird might hear, might be reminded. Some spirit might call in a debt.

It is only the new arrivals who ever talk of the trains, the boats.

One night four years ago, a conversation tilted and we were talking of little ingenuities—like Zaytsev's discovery that you could make caramel by boiling a can of condensed milk, or Bairamov's dubious trick of tearing his shirts so he could wear just the collar under his overalls. And I told the story of my stay at Kolyma, about the wheelbarrows and the tracks. At first the others listened quietly but then they all began to roll their eyes. They slapped their knees and laughed. They did not believe me. "What was your laboratory like, at the end of the world?" Rubin exclaimed. "Was there enough solder?"

"Only Termen would claim he revolutionized the Soviet wheelbarrow system."

I protested.

"Just don't tell your story to Yukachev. He'll decide that maybe you invent better when you're hungry."

"Maybe he *does* invent better when he's hungry. Lev would have the beacon up and running tomorrow if we just took away his butter."

Rubin was most scandalized by my recollection of my nickname. "'The Expert'? They called you 'the Expert'?! Were you living in Kolyma or in a children's story?"

MY TRAIN ARRIVED IN MOSCOW and the city seemed vast and thriving, with roaring motorcars and electric lights, clanging trams, flower sellers and vegetable sellers, hills of green apples, children running, clothes swinging on lines, cats and dogs, bare red roofs, shop windows. It presently began to rain and the city was washed blue and still there were children running, rushing cars, dewy radishes in wicker baskets. I felt as though I had tricked death. There had been a diversion and I had darted away, with Lapin, through a break in the forest.

They took me from the train in a Black Maria. Lapin sat in the front of the car but he did not get out when we arrived at Marenko, and so I left without saying goodbye to my saviour. I was bundled away, through gates and fences and up the steps into the building's marble visitors' entrance hall. I was never again permitted into this entrance hall. I remember a long, lumpen chesterfield and a bowl full of cedar shavings and Mignonette. A portrait of Stalin, close to life-size, who neither glowered nor smiled but observed the room, withholding judgment. I was unaccustomed to furniture, to silence, to any kind of hope.

I waited there for twenty minutes, alone except for the riflemen at either door.

Then Yukachev came in and introduced me to the prison for rocket scientists.

MARENKO IS THE NAME of a village approximately ten kilometres east of Moscow. It is also used to refer to the so-called River Laboratory of the Central State Aero-Hydrodynamics Institute, located within Marenko village. This is a five-acre estate comprising three buildings, surrounded by one iron fence, one electric fence, and one wooden fence.

The overall director of the Central State Aero-Hydrodynamics Institute, I am told, is Andrei Nikolayevich Tupolev, creator of the TB-1 bomber. He is at the Kremlin. The director of the River Laboratory, which is to say Marenko, is Colonel Mikhail Vasilyevich Yukachev. We say just Yukachev. The institute and the laboratory are both under the purview of the NKVD. The NKVD is state security. State security works for the man whose portrait hangs in the Marenko entrance hall.

Circles within circles.

Marenko is a *sharashka*, a prison for scientists.

Let me be clear: Marenko is not a jail, with cells and bars and men who sleep with their heads beside the latrine. Marenko is like and unlike Butyrskaya. There is tea and there is coffee, but scientists are not kept here just as coincidence— all the physicists locked away, out of trouble. This is a work camp. Our work is the doing of science. We make radios and rockets, aeroplanes and aeronautic beacons. We build fighter planes and anti-tank ballistics. Every day we go into our laboratories and manipulate instruments, components, blueprints. We test and hypothesize. When we have drawn up our work we give it to Yukachev and it disappears into the open world, like a jet's plume.

The sharashka is a brilliant and effective notion. It is the sort of innovation that only a dictator can implement. Without an electric fence, brilliant scientists will not cooperate with each other. Great engineers stay solo. They are not always proud but they are proud of their ideas; they champion their own solutions, bully others'. Even setting aside questions of fame, name, the glitter of a Stalin Prize, they want for their theories to be celebrated, their proofs remembered. Like mountain goats lowering their craniums—they butt heads.

But it is different in prison. In prison there is no choice. Two great scientists sit at the foot of their beds, dressed in parachutists' overalls. They lean their chins on the heels of their hands. A pawn advances. A knight retreats. These games are so dull. Either they can keep on playing, an idle stalemate, or they can get up together and invent something.

Marenko is driven by tedium, not bayonet. Yes, any abstaining scientist will eventually be shot. Saboteurs, malingerers, serial bunglers—all vanish overnight, into Black Marias. Every zek is just two steps from death. But day to day, over drawn-out breakfasts or in the still hours of the night, fear is not what nudges Marenko's residents back into its labs. Vacuum tubes glint. Puzzles beckon. These prodigious thinkers—damned, done for—making things because they can't help themselves.

Across the USSR, there are a hundred complexes like this. A hundred complexes and hundreds of imprisoned scientists, hundreds or thousands, or perhaps hundreds of thousands, chemists and mathematicians and aeronautical engineers who are 58s, enemies of the state, men and women who betrayed the Soviet by subscribing to French academic journals, by holidaying in Hanover, by co-authoring papers with Oxford dons. Men who did business in New York City, who built arches for Alcatraz, or who suggested once, as Andrei Markov did, that Iosif Vissarionovich Stalin is a "loathsome reptile."

A colony of exiled scientists, grateful to be alive.

Grateful, at least, some of the time.

THE DAY BEGINS AROUND eight o'clock. Bells ring and we roll from our mattresses. There are mattresses at Marenko, and pillows. My dormitory is a high, domed room, with barred little windows. A dozen bunk beds spread out in a fan. We wake and groan, rub our eyes, polish spectacles. Some of us pad to the toilets. Inspection takes place at 8:55. We are counted, as we were at Kolyma, only this time there is no snow, no ice, no darkness. There are no hours of waiting, staggering in despair. For our two guards, the count takes five minutes. Some of us stand; most do not. Some of us drink tea; some rummage in desk drawers. Announcements are made. Wisecracks are wisecracked. Occasionally the floor is opened to complaints. Eli Drageyvich grumbles about the coffee.

At nine o'clock we go to breakfast.

On my first day at Marenko, I was brought into the dining hall around noon. Long wooden tables, swept clean. They told me later that I was trembling. Guards had taken away my Kolyma rags and when they reached for Nikola's coat I fought them, nails tearing, until they clutched me by the shoulders and shouted, "You can keep your coat, Termen! You can keep it!" They just wanted me to put on the prisoner's uniform: thick parachutists' overalls, in navy blue. "We used to wear suits," Andrei Markov said, "until the guards complained that they had no idea who they could shoot."

That first day I squeezed into a seat at the dining table wearing parachutists' overalls and, over top, a rancid, piss-stained fox-fur coat. The man beside me, Korolev, turned with a pinched expression.

"You're new?"

"Yes," I murmured, guarded.

A woman tossed a basket of black bread onto the table before us. Instantly I grabbed for it, teeth clenched, expecting a scramble. My dining partners burst out laughing. Their laughter was loud and forceful, with a little sadness in it. Across the table, Zaytsev said, "Normally I hold out for the *white* bread."

"What is this?" I said, angry somehow.

"You can have as much black bread as you want," Korolev muttered. "The white bread is rationed."

"And the sour cream," complained Zaytsev. "*And* the butter."

"At least you get the full portion," snapped another man, an engineer.

They brought us borscht with vegetables, a piece of pork, potatoes. I was dumbfounded. I stared at my place setting, the knife sitting freely on the wood. My hands were not accustomed to cutlery.

Korolev slid over his plate of meat. "Take it," he said.

Yukachev had told me the nature of this place, its purpose, and he had told me that I was assigned to the instrumentation division, working on dials, meters, counters, but he had not told me that there would be whole pork chops and black bread, one and a half ounces of butter, a little glass of sour cream to scoop, with a spoon, into rich red broth.

"Why me?" I had asked him.

"We found your file," he said. "Very impressive."

I think perhaps he was lying. By Marenko's standards I was not impressive. Over that first lunch I learned a little about the men around me. Bairamov, co-designer of the GIRD-8 rocket. Rubin, a senior physics lecturer from Novgorod. Korolev, former chief of the Jet Propulsion Research Institute—the Soviet space program.

All of these men, traitors now.

OUR LABORATORY WAS A spacious room on the third floor, with vast windows and a dozen cluttered desks, shelves piled high with electronics. It was like a well-funded university office or the lost corner of a corporation—scientists developing their eccentric theories, trading questions through the air. Korolev tuned his radio to symphonies, music epic and thundering, which he would listen to quietly, as if the bombast should be secret. When he was away from his desk, a young engineer, Lupa, commandeered the airwaves and then our lab twinkled with popular song, snare and saxophone; I could never decide whether I enjoyed this stuff, all nostalgic, or whether it was breaking my heart.

We worked all day under Pavla's vigilant eye. She was at once matron, ingénue, and den mother. A free worker assigned to guard the instrumentators, small and straw-blond, she settled our arguments, reminded us to eat, told us when our shirts were buttoned up wrong. Most of the men were in love with her. She was kind to me from the very first day: she had seen so many others like this one, staggering in from Siberia, baffled by comfort. "This is your desk," she said brightly. "Rashi's in charge of the fuses. The hob is over there, for tea. And if your pens go missing, check Bairamov's drawer." At first I assumed she was another prisoner. It was only later they explained the boundary between us, the way Pavla's papers let her pass out of the building, through the gates, into the land of concert halls, cinemas, trams. "She was taught that we are spies and saboteurs," Andrei Markov told me. "I am certain her teachers were adamant." Pavla's bumbling charges were all zeks, after all. Worse, they were 58s, enemies of the people. Her masters wanted her to be watchful for insubordination, mischief, espionage. For lies, sabotage, and smuggled plans. Every night, the woman with the straw-blond hair collected Instrumentation's most sensitive documents and placed them in a safe.

I wonder if Pavla still believes the lessons they have taught her. After all these hours together, are we still traitors? Snakes swishing in grass?

Marenko appeared to be an idyll: the airy lab, books and conversation, black bread in open baskets, science. I tried to adjust to this life. I tried to take my meals slowly, to take in each movement as I lowered my head into a feather-down pillow at night. Instant by instant, I felt for the things I had discarded in Kolyma. My imagination, under the snow. My ambition, between the slats in the barracks wall. On a piece of paper I sketched a circuit that had no purpose; on the roof I peered into Rubin's telescope, squinting at Jupiter. The treasure I had kept hold of, that memory of you—it seemed safe to loosen my grasp, to set it down. A woman who once loved me; there are other things to live for. Aren't there? There was so much work to do.

I HAD BEEN THERE for six months, I think, when I saw Andrei Markov eating alone at the end of a table. He was holding a book in his right hand, a drooping banana in the left. Something about the scene made me pause. "Are you coming?" I asked. I pulled an arm through my cardigan sleeve.

"No," Andrei Markov said.

"Is everything all right?"

"It's Sunday," Andrei Markov said, not lifting his eyes.

I broke into a grin. "We work on Sunday."

"No," he said, "*you* work on Sunday."

"Andrei Markov is exempted?"

"I do not *volunteer*," he said, taking a bite of his banana.

"I don't—" I began, but then I shrugged. I tugged my sweater's collar.

Andrei Markov raised his gaze. He is older than me, with a crown of white hair and a longish beard. "On the second floor," he said over his reading glasses, "at the end of the hall, beside the duty office, there is a list. It is headed, 'Sunday Volunteers.'"

"Yes?"

"Sunday is entitled to us as a free day. Any work is strictly 'voluntary.' Do you know what 'voluntary' means? And yet here is a peculiar thing: every Saturday night, beside the duty office, a list of volunteers is posted. And this list includes the names of every zek at Marenko. For example, Termen, Lev Sergeyvich."

I was not sure if he was joking. "And Markov, Andrei?"

"Markov, Andrei strikes himself from the list."

"Is this permitted?"

Andrei Markov looked at me again, levelly. "How would they punish me, Termen?"

I checked his story later that day. On the second floor of the dormitory building, at the end of the hall, on a wall painted pale green, nine typewritten pages. Dated from the night before: *Sunday Volunteers.* And under M, one name, Markov, had been neatly crossed out, with a pencil-thin line.

The next morning I joined him for breakfast. He sat with his book, silent. Finally I asked, "How many?" This was not a rare question at Marenko.

Andrei Markov turned a page. "A quarter," he said, "and five on the horns."

I could not help but take a breath. Twenty-five years, and five more with diminished rights. "For me, eight years."

"Yes."

"How much do you have left?"

"Eighteen."

"Seven," I said.

Andrei Markov took another spoon of porridge. With a flick of one finger he turned the page of his book.

"You never work on Sundays?" I asked.

Andrei Markov took a moment before answering. Then he set his book face down on the table. The cover said SWIMMING HORSES.

"I am a prisoner." He cleared his throat. "I am a prisoner and you are a prisoner. You remember?" He stared at me.

"Yes," I said.

"It took until my hundredth morning at Marenko for me to remember. We laugh and eat and scribble in our notebooks and we get distracted. We don't notice our jailers. Then one morning I remembered. I looked. We are caged and counting. While our friends die, on the outside, and our wives fall in love with other men, and our children go to school where they are taught lies concerning their fathers, we stay here, frittering away our breath. Every day we get closer to death and every day is wasted, spilled out into the laboratory. This is a theft. This is the most terrible theft. They have taken away my life and it does not matter that my hours are easier here than they were in Kolyma. I will die inside this place. If my life has any meaning, that meaning was made—it must have been made—before they arrested me on February the second, 1933."

"You can still . . ." I began.

"A man has only a slim chance to matter," Andrei Markov said, in a voice that was stony. "A slim chance, like a blade of grass or a poured cup of water. They have taken this from me. They have opened a wound in my side and taken my entrails."

He lowered his head.

"No, I never work on Sundays," he said.

But I did not believe him. Andrei Markov pretended that Marenko was a crevasse, a terrible slit in the earth that had swallowed us up. Marenko was not a crevasse. It was a refuge. In the laboratory, I peered at my voltmeter and consulted with fellow thinkers, all of us in this strange sanctuary, creating things. I said hello to Pavla, and good night. Sometimes, for old times' sake, I did push-ups beside my bunk. I went through the first and second forms, Little Idea and Sinking the Bridge, and the other zeks laughed.

I worked on Sunday, I worked on Sunday, and I worked on Sunday.

Two years passed.

A war raged in Europe.

Every so often we would have a visit from a short man with a small smooth head and round pince-nez glasses. He walked with a slight slouch. His eyes flicked, flicked.

He asked us about our projects. He listened and asked questions.

Yukachev stood beside him, sweating, white as a maggot.

The man's name was Lavrentiy Beria.

SEVEN

TARANTULA

THIS IS WHAT I IMAGINED you were doing while I devised new instruments for Soviet aeroplanes:

I imagined that you went to eat at Rose's and walked home past the stationery shops, a million miles of paper and all those wells full of ink.

I imagined a springtime that was cold at first and then warmer, and you called your sister: "What is *with* this kooky weather?"

I imagined you voted for Franklin D. Roosevelt. You went alone to the voting place and stood behind the screen and toyed with checking the box beside Wendell Willkie's name, just out of mischief, smiling to yourself.

I imagined you played the theremin in Canada, on tour, in a city where they speak French. They said to you: "*Bravo, bravo!*" and "*Enchanté*," and you marvelled that somewhere so close could be so different.

I imagined you ordered a crate of oranges, you and your

husband, but he didn't eat any of them. You ate them all your-self, one a day, cutting them down the centre with a small knife.

I imagined you played the theremin at Carnegie Hall, alone, before velvet sewn with stars.

I imagined there was an article about you in the *Times*. They said you had studied with Dr Leon Theremin. The journalist described your appearance as "luminous." *Rockmore didn't want to discuss her former tutor.*

I imagined you fought with your husband one night, in bed, both of you sitting with your backs to the headboard, your heads to the wall. He said he wanted to have a son. You scraped your fingernails over the duvet. You said, "You live your life and I'll live my life, Robert."

I imagined you sitting in your dressing room after a concert, staring at your reflection in the mirror. You had been in dressing rooms like this before. In front of mirrors like this before. I imagined you were recalling, gently, how close you had come to never playing music again—to becoming a violinist with a tired arm who sits at home with a romance novel and a simmering pot of chicken stock. You looked at your face in the mirror, severe and proud.

I imagined you went to see the ballet, all those dancers throw-ing their partners across the stage.

I imagined you ate the heels of many loaves of bread.

ONE EVENING, LATE, I came out of the laboratory and into Marenko's hallway. I was heading back toward the main stair-case. I was thinking of I-don't-know-what. There were no sounds. I walked. At a certain moment I realized that I was following a path of footprints: a single set of footprints, faintly braiding, the wet footprints of a cat. I knew of no cats in this place. The footprints continued down the centre of the hall and I followed them. I followed them around a corner. I wondered about the story of this cat. This was such a pleasant adventure. I followed the footprints. Then the path abruptly stopped, the path disappeared, as if the cat had been swallowed into thin air.

THIS IS WHAT I imagined you were doing while I was designing rockets with Korolev, furies that would roar into the sky:

I imagined that you went on long walks through the city, through the snow and rain, the sweltering July, seeking something you couldn't remember.

I imagined that you wondered whether your husband would be drafted. Killed on a hill in Egypt, obliterated on a Pacific gunship. "No, Clara," he said, "never." You wondered about the certainty of never. You spoke to girlfriends whose men had gone away, who wrote letters on dusted paper. You thought of a boy from the theatre, an usher, who was in England now.

I imagined that at night you came home and sat with Robert Rockmore, the radio singing.

I imagined one morning you took a cab up to Harlem and got out where we used to get out sometimes, though you didn't realize it until you got out, right into a puddle, looking down at your feet then lifting your gaze up to the orange awning, QUIET BARBERSHOP. "Oh, the Quiet Barbershop," you used to say. "D'you think the barber's name is Sammy Quiet?"

I imagined you walked through Harlem like a wind walking through a million stalks of wheat.

—

This is what I imagined you were doing while I spent sixteen months in Sverdlovsk, a different sharashka, where the furnace clanged, on a team designing radio beacons for submarines:

I imagined the booking of your first overseas tour, London and Paris and Casablanca—you wanted to go to Casablanca. You were packing your cases and practising new material, Stravinsky and Manuel de Falla. I imagined the meetings you had with your girlfriends, giggling over little coffees, thumbing through travelogues at bookshops off Broadway. Then the tour was called off. "Of course it was cancelled!" your husband said. "There's a war on. It was a silly idea in the first place."

Which made you furious. You stood by the window, jaw clenched, staring into the hard wide blue sky. You felt white with rage but also a thin separation, a kind of caul, shame at your pride. "Even in a war," you said, "the world goes on." Silently, you asked Robert to drop the subject, to give it up, to condescend no further. This is what I imagined. And I imagined that you thought of me, as I imagine that you do, and you told yourself: "Lev was worse. He was even worse, Clara."

As I refined submarines at Sverdlovsk, I wondered if I was worse, worse than Robert Rockmore, a monster I did not really know, a man I imagined in grotesque, cruel to him even now; I was cruel even now, ten thousand miles away, building murdering machines.

THEY TRANSFERRED ME BACK to Marenko in 1944. Nothing had changed. Once again I sat with Bairamov and Zaytsev, spreading one and a half ounces of butter onto fourteen ounces of white bread. Once again I worked in instrumentation, flicking dial needles with my fingernail, listening to Korolev's quiet radio, watching the papers flutter under Pavla's elbow. I was building another iteration of the same old machine, another new way to send the same signals home. Andrei Markov waited with an empty bowl, two more rings under his eyes. You were in America, living a life. I was a mid-level engineer. I felt like a glass of water that was slowly evaporating, my atoms fading into sheer air.

"You're all still here," I sighed, my first night back. Around me, men were pulling on regulation pyjamas. I was not sure if it was a thank you I was saying or a mean joke. Old prisoners go nowhere. As I lay down to sleep I found a new feeling in my belly, like a stone. A war was thundering on and Marenko had stayed the same. This changelessness was not without a cost. The cost, I understood, was our freedom.

The blue bulb in the dormitory never went out.

I WROTE, *The blue bulb in the dormitory never went out.*

I feel as if I must pause here for a moment.

I wrote, *The blue bulb in the dormitory never went out*, and then I spent some time doing the thing I am here to do, on this side street in Moscow. I checked the tape reels in my machine, my simple machine, which sits at the edge of this desk. I checked the wires that lead from it to the wall, and out to the emitter/receiver, fastened to the windowpane. I checked the dust—checked to see if it lies as it did yesterday, in the same places. I looked at the boxes of silvery magnetic tape, like tresses. Maybe one day they will destroy me for these spools of silver tape, pierce my throat with a bayonet.

After all this, I slipped on my headset and listened to the other tapes, delivered from Spaso House. To the sound of empty rooms and to the voice of Averell Harriman, American ambassador to the Soviet Union, and to Averell's daughter, Kathy. I adjusted the frequencies, transcribed the pertinent conversations, translated from English to Russian. "We need to ask about that jam," he said. And: "I don't trust the fucking trade commissar, all right?" I made carbon copies. I slipped the transcriptions into their designated folders.

When I came back to this letter, my letter to you, Clara Rockmore, my true love, whatever that can mean, 1234567/////, I saw that I had written, *The blue bulb in the dormitory never went out.* It was one of those moments of precipitous, endless melancholy. Is this despair? The blue bulb in the dormitory never went out and it has still never gone out. It is illuminated now. When I leave Moscow tonight, in a Black Maria, they will bring me to Marenko and I will climb the stairs to the dormitory, and I will find my bed in the cold blue light, murmuring something to Korolev, leaning back in the mattress, staring into the filament that never seems to fade, or fail, and stays.

ONE MORNING, AFTER THE guards did the counting, as I was rinsing my mug in the basin, they came and stood over me. "You have a visitor," the junior lieutenant said.

I quickly raised my head. A visitor. Visitors were very rare at the sharashka, the consequence of an almost impossible ritual. You wrote to a spouse or family member; you prayed the letter was passed through the censors; the relative wrote back; petitions were made; and then one day, suddenly, improbably, a lieutenant announced, "You have a visitor."

I was mystified. A visitor. Who would visit me here? My aunt? My sister? I had never written to either of them. It was not shame or ambivalence that had kept me from contacting them—it was fear. I had listened to enough zeks' stories to know that the sha-rashka's visitor system was often a ruse: a 58 writes a letter to his brother, to his wife, and that very letter becomes evidence of collusion. The brother, the wife, is sentenced to eight years in Kolyma. This letter that begins *My love* is never returned.

On this morning, at the lieutenant's words, I felt a terrible thrill. A visitor! My chest knotted. Just the thought of a remnant, a familiar face, a vestige of my life before. I wanted to tell Eva that her nephew was still alive. I wanted Helena to know that her brother still thought of her. Had one of them found me? Or someone else? Ioffe? Was it you? Could it somehow be you?

Sometimes a zek would persist in writing. Would write so carefully, *My love, my love*, to his wife on the outside. She sends an answer. They make supplications to the state. Thirteen months later, four seasons of nightmares, and finally one morning the lieutenant murmurs, "A visitor." The prisoner exchanges his overalls for a crisp suit, provided by the administration. (These suits, we surmise, are stripped from corpses.) The prisoner keeps his rag shoes—these will be hidden from view, under the visitors table. Then husband and wife are brought together in a room; barred from touching, from embracing, from uttering a single word about where he has been, where he is now, how long he will remain. Perhaps they weep. Perhaps their eyes are clear. The zek in a dead man's suit gazes longingly at his love, his revenant love, saying everything he can possibly say with this look. And his wife says the thing she came to say, asks the thing she did all this in order to ask. She asks, "Will you consent to a divorce?"

She wishes to save her life.

Bairamov always says it is worse to be visited than to be forgotten.

ALL THESE THOUGHTS WERE with me as the lieutenant led me from the dormitory. But almost as soon as we left, I knew that something was not right. We turned right, passed up the stairs and down the hall to the secret area. This was not the visitors section. The guard did not give me a suit to wear. He showed his pass to the attendant and he took me into an alcove, a security station, where he fastened metal cuffs around my wrists. I had not worn shackles in years, not since they brought me from Butyrska to a train car. "What is this?" I said. "Why?"

The guard did not answer.

He led me to a door without a lock. There was a rectangle of frosted glass. He turned the doorknob and the door opened.

"There," he said.

"Who is it?"

"Go inside, Termen."

I nudged the door further with my bound wrists. The room was a long staff kitchen: two stoves, a cupboard, an empty table. Two rectangular white windows—bare windows, ungrilled. I stepped inside.

I turned and saw then that Lavrentiy Beria was sitting beside the washbasin.

"Ah. L-890," he said.

The junior lieutenant pulled the door shut.

I looked around once more, as if someone else might be hidden. I tried to push my breathing down into my belly. To breathe as I was taught—like a child. "Sir," I said softly.

"Citizen Termen," Beria said. Straightaway he rose and came toward me. Delicate and pale, the director of the NKVD, head of internal affairs, king of the gulag, state security, secrets. The birdie in Stalin's ear, faint as shadow. He reached for my wrists and in horror I thought he was about to take my hands, to hold them, intimate. But he just wrapped my right wrist between thumb and middle finger and unlocked the shackle. The key was on a ring. He slipped it into his pocket. He said, "You can call me Lavrentiy."

I swallowed.

"Sit down," he said as he stepped away.

I had met Beria before but never like this: never alone, without a supervisor, without Yukachev, someone else to quiver fearfully beside me. I knew I was supposed to be scared because I had heard all the stories. From Korolev, from Andrei Markov, from gossiping zeks at Kolyma. Deadly little Beria in his snug little suit, his glasses lenses like windowpanes. Beria, who poured vinegar into Kirov's wine. Beria, who drove a nail into Ivan Luchenko's face, as Trotsky's general sat bound before his desk. Beria, whose limousine glides across Nevsky Prospekt, stalking sisters and daughters.

"Do you like it here, Termen?" Beria said.

"Here?"

"The institute."

I swallowed. "Yes, sir."

"You know, you have a very intriguing biography," he said. Beria does not have the voice you expect of a monster. It is a plain tenor voice, matter-of-fact. There is neither the pervert's lilt nor the killer's growl. "I knew I recognized your name—of course, it was from the theremin. You met Lenin?"

"Yes."

"Yes," Beria repeated, nodding. "But you have really had your fingers in many different pies. *Many* different pies. I called up the documents from your work in America . . ." His eyes shifted. "It's very interesting."

"Thank you, sir."

"Your former colleagues say you're brilliant."

Something flickered at my lips. "Who is that, sir?"

"Some former colleagues." He made a vague wave. "Are you?"

"Brilliant?"

"Yes, Termen."

I tried to measure his expression. "I do everything I can for the state."

"Indeed, indeed. And with a history of discretion."

I said nothing. I did not know what he meant.

"I called you here because I require your expertise." Beria exhaled through his nose. He was standing by the stoves. He turned one of the knobs for the burners and I heard the breath of gas escape into the room.

He looked at me.

"Yes sir," I said.

Beria turned back to the stove. He flicked the stove's electric lighter. Snap. Snap, snap. The burners caught. Our empty room with two soft blue flames. "Suppose we had an enemy," he said, "whom we wanted to listen to."

He waited until I answered.

"A microphone," I said.

"A hidden microphone, yes. But suppose this is not a simple enemy, a complacent enemy. Suppose our enemy is sophisticated. Suppose he is wary. Like you, for instance."

"Sir?"

He had an odd little smile. "Suppose the enemy is a man like you. Someone brilliant."

"I don't und—"

"Here is what I am proposing. I require an undetectable way of listening. An eavesdropping bug, yes, that has no exiting wires, no power source, no traditional microphone. Inert. Invisible. Unable to be X-rayed or traced."

"This is not possible."

Beria maintained his peculiar smile. "So quick to say it is impossible. Surely you have not had time to give it proper consideration. The inventor of the radio watchman, the infiltrator of Alcatraz cannot create a radio spy?"

He was plucking at my pride. I knew he was doing it. But I was not the man I had once been. I watched unmoving Beria with his clasped hands, the stove's two fiery ghosts. "As I said, I am quite happy here."

"Who spoke of leaving?"

"My current projects are very stimulating and we are already pressed if we are to meet our deadlines."

"They will get on without you."

"Besides, I am really not sure how you would implement something like this—"

"But you have an idea of where to begin."

I gave a sharp exhale. My hands were flat in my lap. Beria snapped off the burners.

I felt my molars scrape. "Comrade, I am a plain scientist. I have no gift for skulking outside."

"Skulking?"

"In—in concealing. In matters of concealment." I tried a smile. "The dark arts."

Beria was humourless. "Remember who you are speaking to, Termen."

Was I brave now, I wondered?

"I prefer the work I am doing now. I am not a spy."

Beria finally sat down, directly across from me, but far— bizarrely far, the distance of a firing range. "It does not matter what you prefer. It does not matter what you *are*. I have seen your file. You will not pretend, here. You *were* a spy and you will be again, if I ask it. You will dive into the abyss and fetch whatever treasure I require. You will steal, and wash your hands, and steal again. You will be brilliant, and you will be *loyal*, Termen, do you understand?"

I made a beseeching gesture. "I am just a scient—"

"You are a *traitor*, Lev Sergeyvich Termen, sentenced to prison."

"My sentence—"

"Your sentence will end in a pit."

I tried to sit erect. I tried to show that he had not defeated me. I found that I stooped, as if I was being physically beaten.

"It is scarcely a choice," Beria continued. "Either you will disappear, you and your whole world, swallowed up in smoke . . . or else you will serve your country, serve it brilliantly, a weapon in the Soviet's hand, and you will live. Perhaps you will win a Stalin Prize. You will be released, you will live, you will be celebrated for all you have contributed to our mighty and unbreakable union."

Beria said it all with that even cadence, that wicked voice. He leaned back, crossing his legs.

"Are you lying or are you telling the truth?" I said, as if I was brave. My voice was as thin as notepaper.

"Oh I am telling the truth," Beria murmured.

For an instant I imagined leaping from my chair, throwing myself out the open window, a long free leap. I closed my eyes.

It would not really be so different, would it, colluding with Lavrentiy Beria? My life already felt like a remnant of itself. Like a thin dream. Like a habit.

What would change?

Just a new set of orders.

Danny Finch's blood, moving across the floor.

Perhaps this is what Lenin would have wanted: his scientist, listening for the state.

His scientist, going on.

Perhaps I was not giving anything away. A lossless exchange, a chance for redemption. Trading scraps of my present for what we all would require tomorrow, in this war.

I looked at the faded lights behind my closed lids.

I wondered how much a man can make up for the parts he has wasted.

In a small voice, I said: "I want my family."

"What?"

I cleared my throat. "My wife. Lavinia." I straightened in my chair, blinked bloodshot eyes. "They told me they would bring her from America."

Beria looked at me with a frozen expression, lips barely parted.

"I love her," I said, in a tarry voice.

Then his lashes fluttered behind his spectacles and he laughed, hard and flat, key ring jingling in his pocket, because he knew it was not true.

EIGHT

THE MORNING FOG

LET ME DESCRIBE MY LAST DAYS in America.

In Moscow today it is balmy, like summer, a lying summer, and the melting snows rush through the streets like rivers. At my window it is as if I am in the midst of rapids, with the sound of laughing children, and sunlight, dazzling sunlight. Eight years later, let me tell you about my last days in America.

It was like this.

I used to meet with men at a diner called L'Aujourd'hui. The Today. These meetings were gruelling: the tedium of idiots, the brute force of an invisible hand. I hated the appointments, hated the operatives who met me, hated the bland reports they drew from me, like steam from a kettle. And yet in the waning heat of 1938, the early autumn, I spent days and nights alone at that same corner dive, waiting for today to turn into tomorrow.

I have never told anyone this.

I did not want to go home. I didn't want to face the carousel of students, the visits from friends, the expectant eyes of Lavinia Williams, Lavinia Termen, who loved me as if we were young lovers, everything within reach. Instead of facing life and marriage, I hunched in a booth at L'Aujourd'hui, ordering cups of black tea, lemon squares, bowls of potato chips. I sketched plans on paper placemats. I pretended to myself that I was hard at work, waved excuses to Lavinia as I hurried out the door every morning, but there were no revelations on that glossy tabletop. My ideas were desperations. I let them blot salt crumbs and spilled tea.

When the restaurant closed, around midnight, I packed up my things, plinked pencils into my briefcase. I meandered home through the blue streets. Usually Lavinia would be waiting. On the final block I would ask and ask the air for my wife to be asleep, dreaming, folded in sheets. Sometimes I would pass the house and double back, to approach again. *Let her be sleeping. Let her be sleeping.* On many of those nights I would come in and climb the stairs, turn off the lamps, stand at her feet. She always slept on her belly, like something brought in from the shore.

"Hard day?" she'd ask, the other times. She would crouch beside me as I removed my shoes. "You need to take it easier, Lyova."

I was deeply in debt. Even living rent-free in my friends' house, I was drowning in everyday expenses, equipment rentals, interest payments. With money she thought we had, Lavinia bought houseplants, rambling gardenias. Every day our rooms looked more alive, blooming, budding. Every week I searched for someone else to borrow money from, laughing about IOUs, lying about overdue commissions. I owed tens of thousands in taxes. My handlers at L'Aujourd'hui told me I should leave the United States, return to Russia. I refused. I always refused. At

Lavinia's ballet performances I sat with her friends, hands on thighs, watching the dancers twist in the air, watching Lavinia turn from the back of the stage to stare into the dark, the crowd's dark, where we could not be seen.

BERIA GAVE ME A special office in Marenko's secret wing. I had an orange pass with my name and Yukachev's signature. The other engineers asked what I was working on now and I just shrugged, lifted and lowered my shoulders. They let the matter drop. I was not the only zek with a mysterious new commission: Rubin had been transferred to a facility across town, for something to do with hydrogen isotopes.

My work was not with atoms. Every day I showed an attendant my little orange card and entered an almost empty laboratory—four rows of desks, shelves of equipment, an incongruous crystal chandelier. Stalin glowered from a wide, dark painting. I shared the lab with one other engineer, a radar man, and a lanky free worker whose job it was to watch us. We spent our days in separate, silent labour. It never felt like the room had enough air. I ate lunch in the same kitchen where I had sat with Beria, chewing softly beside the stoves. The windows had been closed and locked. If I needed new components, new machines, I submitted a written request. Every requisition was granted.

My task was simple, but then it was not so simple: a bug that required no power source. That required no wires leading in or out. That required no tapes, and scarcely any metal. An invisible, imperceptible, inert device that remembers any secrets that are told to it.

I think it is probably the best thing I ever made.

⁘

ONE MORNING IN NEW YORK the owner of L'Aujourd'hui came up to my table, drying a plate, like a character in a play.

"*Hello,*" he said, in Russian.

"Hello," I said, in English.

He dried his plate.

"Gotta ask," he said. "You okay, bud?"

I did not lift my head from my work. I was drawing a semicircle. "Yes."

Mud Tony shrugged. "All right," he said. He began to move away.

I raised my face and squinted at him. "Can I ask you a question?"

"What's that?"

"Should I go back to Russia?"

He laughed. "How should I know?"

"I'm just asking, " I said.

"Huh." Mud Tony tugged at the ends of his lips. "Is there anything keeping you here?"

"Yes," I said.

I felt my face was very sad. I tried to smile.

The radio was singing a stupid love song.

I saw him see my wedding ring. "Well," he said. He cleared his throat. "No. You should stay."

I looked at the placemat, covered in fragile marks. "Of course," I said.

"At least until things are worked out."

"Of course," I repeated. "Yes."

In early evening, golden hour, I called you from a public telephone. The Plaza Hotel's booths were tucked behind tall windows and there were waving trees, newspaper sellers, a million people pouring past. I took a deep breath and then immediately felt intoxicated.

I said, "Clara?"

You said, "What?

Yes?

Who is this?

I can't hear you."

"It's Leon."

"Leon?"

"Yes."

"Oh! Hello."

"Hello."

"How's it going?"

I said, "Clara, I love you."

"What?"

"I love—"

"What? I can't hear."

"I love you!" I shouted.

"Leon, I'm sorry, I can't—"

I put down the receiver. My breathing was wild and shallow. I went out of the Hotel Plaza and onto Fifth Avenue and I ran straight through the city to your house, down alleys and over fissures, swift as a blazing rocket. I was ragged and sheer and decided. The knocker was a lion's head. I took the lion's head in my hand and banged on your door.

Birds flew up from the eaves.

You did not appear at the door. You appeared on the balcony, above my head, leaning against an iron railing.

"Leon," you said. You were wearing swinging pearl earrings. "What are you doing here?"

Your skirt was the same dark blue as the sky.

"I love you, Clara," I said.

You did not tremble when I said it.

You did not move.

You looked at me.

"I never stopped loving you," I said.

Your fingers tightened around the railing.

"We are *married*, Leon."

"I thought I could escape," I said, in a clear voice. "That we could slip away from each other."

You began to say something.

"But I never *escaped*, Clara. I never did."

"Leon, I was just a kid when I met you."

You trailed off.

"Yes," I said.

I waited for you.

You said into the air, "Your feelings were always so *certain*. Like you already knew. But I didn't know anything yet."

A truck rattled past.

"Run away with me," I said.

"You have a wife."

"I am forty-two years old, Clara, and my heart has never felt real except when I am with you."

You took your hands from the railing. "You're a crazy person."

"*No!*" I shouted. "I'm not, it's not— This is the plainest—"

You were furious then, lips drawn in a line. "You stroll through life like you're indestructible. Like an indestructible—an indestructible *blockhead*, Leon. Immune to everything: to responsibility, to patience. Always wanting, never listening, never—"

"I am not indestructible," I said.

"Like you can just walk away from a life. Like promises don't matter. You are *married*, Leon. *I* am married. *Not* to each other. Wishing doesn't change that."

"I am *not* indestructible!"

"Wishing is just the empty air between people."

"Is it?" My voice was like a piece of lead.

You pushed away from the balcony. "We have to leave some things behind."

The air smelled of exhaust.

I was looking at you but you did not look back at me.

I decided to forget this conversation.

I left America.

IN MAY 1945, I completed work on a radio antenna that could be concealed within a small prepared cavity, with a sensitized diaphragm and tuning post. Nearby sounds made the diaphragm quiver; these modified the charge of the antenna. Operators up to 150 metres away could direct radio beams toward the device and record the reflected signal's modulations. Any modulations could be translated back into sound. Whispers could be stolen.

In July 1945, four young boys from the Lenin All-Union Pioneers attended a presentation by Averell Harriman, American ambassador to the USSR. The boys wore red kerchiefs around their necks. At the end of the reception, after sardines and orange cake, the courteous Pioneers jumbled to the front of the room. Their minders smiled. They lay their sturdy hands on the boys' shoulders. The boys were holding a huge wooden plaque engraved with the proud eagle of the Great Seal of the United States of America. In one talon the eagle clutched an olive branch. In the other, a bundle of arrows. "In honour of the excellent Ambassador Harriman," squeaked a bucktoothed Pioneer, "the Moscow detachment of Young Pioneers offers this gesture of friendship and trust."

Ambassador Harriman was recorded to have answered: "What a kindness."

His government checked the plaque for conventional eavesdropping devices. There were none. It was just a noble bird of prey.

Harriman hung it in his study.

One hundred twenty-one metres away, a radio emitter, affixed to a window frame, pointed toward Spaso House. Separately, a receiver whirred. It recorded noises onto magnetic tape.

I listened.

After the installation of the emitter and receiver, the bugging of Spaso House did not require much upkeep. Beria had men to check the devices, to chase away pigeons, to observe Averell's security staff for signs of suspicion. For a little while I returned to my old work at Marenko, finding ways to regulate the fuel in missiles. But then again one morning, the junior lieutenant said I had a visitor; again I was taken to the kitchen in the top-secret section; again Beria sat waiting for me, patient and evil, hands folded in his lap. A tape machine rested at his feet.

There was a problem with the sound, he said. Although my bug was working, the voices it recorded seemed washed over, almost lost in distortion. NKVD audiologists were accustomed to cleaning audio, extracting intonation and syllable, but my bug did not work like other bugs. My recordings could not be scrubbed with the same processes. "Can you make them clearer?" Beria asked.

"No," I said.

Beria was watching me. He let the moment stretch on. Then he smiled. "Yes, you can."

"No, sir, I cannot."

"You can, Termen. I can see that you can."

"You must be mistaken."

"Listen," he said, reaching down toward the tape machine. He pressed a switch and it began: a blurring gasp of noise, submerged voices, like an alien broadcast.

"Well?" he said.

I shook my head.

Beria licked his lips and then as the recording went dead he began to speak in the same kind of incomprehensible sounds, twinned and smothered words. A weak imitation—in another context I would have laughed—but here his impersonation felt joyless, wrong. I felt as if a river were running over me.

"Please stop," I said.

He stopped. He laughed in a short way.

"When you have made the voices clearer," he said, "write down what they say."

I made my return to the top-secret laboratory, where the air still felt pinched, as though the room were held in a set of needlenose pliers. Every morning an NKVD agent delivered a locked box containing one day's tapes. I set up a listening station, sat with headset and whispering machine, adjusted dials for Hz, KHz, MHz, aW.

There could be no better operator: the bug's solemn English-speaking inventor, sentenced to prison. I began my uneasy relationship with Averell and Kathy; and Mr Capaldi, the ambassador's chief aide; and Snuff, their bearded collie. I listened to Harriman's conversations with himself, late at night, repeating the words of an upcoming speech. I listened to his small talk with the cook, about capers and brown sugar. I listened to the secrets, the United States' state secrets, the conversations between our World War allies as they sat with neglected biscuits, glasses of sparkling water, two folded newspapers. "I am frightened,"

Harriman muttered one morning. "Jack, I don't know that this will all shake out."

YOUR VOICE CAME on a Saturday.

I was sitting in the silent lab. Just two of us there: the free worker and me, paper shifting on paper. I wore a padded, heavy headset. I had a book of lined paper, a typewriter pushed aside. Usually I would transcribe by hand and then retype the pages; the originals went to my guard, who burned them.

For reasons of quiet, the laboratory had no clocks.

I wound back a section of tape that was giving me trouble. Harriman was talking to Capaldi, discussing a meeting with one of Stalin's marshals. He was summing up their plans but he was doing it as he opened the study's door, with scraping wood and a rush of air. "I suppose we'll have to xxxxx xx xxxxx tomorrow," Harriman said, and went out. I rewound. ". . . suppose we'll have to xxxxx xx xxxxx tomorrow." I rewound. ". . . xxxxx xx later tomorrow."

Rewind. ". . . xxxxx xx later," ". . . xxxxx xx," ". . . to xxxxx xx later tomorrow."

I couldn't make it out. "Resolve"? "Call it off"?

I manipulated a panel of switches and dials. The door scrape deepened and then went treble. The voices became airy, aqueous. Certain frequencies became clearer and others slipped away. I imagined lanterns lashed to a pier, shining dimly through fog. ". . . we'll have to susxxxx xx later," Averell said. ". . . have to susxxxx," ". . . have to suspxxx," ". . . have to suspend xx later."

"'Suspend it later,'" I murmured aloud.

The free worker glanced at me.

I wrote down the words.

I wound back the tape for a final pass.

"I understand your point," Harriman said, "so if they do continue down that track I suppose we'll have to suspend it later tomorrow."

And then.

And then there was something else. Buried in the warp and hiss of static.

Suspended like a moonbeam.

After Harriman spoke, or perhaps just ghosted over the grey end of his words, another colour.

Was it the door? Was it Capaldi?

I closed my eyes. I went back and forward.

Distortion?

I went back and forward, searching.

Then, suddenly.

Or maybe it was not suddenly. Maybe it was not suddenly; maybe it was slowly but in the way that only certain changes are slow, slow and very almost, almost sudden. When you stare at a thing that is unfurling and you know it is unfurling, and then finally there is a moment when it is unfurled, strong and present, wide as a sail, or like a new sky, a change that has impossibly slowly suddenly arrived.

It was your voice, unmistakeable and completely hidden, the voice of Clara, who lives in New York City and who said she would not marry me, back when she was young, back before I was wrecked.

You hear a voice in the crowd and you recognize it. Across all the roar of life, through terrible cacophony, you hear the voice you know and you recognize it, catch it in your hands. What were you saying? I did not know. I heard your muffled and secret voice, slowly, suddenly, hidden in the magnetic tape that came from Averell Harriman's study at Spaso House.

I played with dials, switches, filters.

You were saying, "LIFT IT!"

It was so clearly you.

But you were not in the room.

This was not a voice in that room, a voice in Moscow, at Spaso House, some visitor calling from downstairs or out in the street.

"LIFT IT," you said, vibrations caught on a wind.

It was not possible that I should be hearing you.

"Lift it," you said.

It was not possible.

What were you lifting, wherever you were?

I took off my headset. I sat motionless. I stared at the squared blue lines in my notebook, then I rubbed my mouth with the back of my hand.

I wondered if my faculties were failing, hearing a faraway girl in the static of a secret recording.

I took my head in my hands. Yes, my faculties were failing. The air was duping me. You were not there; your voice was not there.

Voices do not stray across the world.

I slid the headset back over my ears, rewound, pushed play.

Lift it, you said.

I WAS NOT ALLOWED TO keep the tape with your voice, nor could I make a copy. Every recording was accounted for, collected by Beria's men at the end of the day. There is no carelessness to espionage. And so I did not leave the laboratory until late that night, listening and relistening to your intonation, your inflection, your sound. I wanted to memorize your voice as I had never done in New York.

Lift it,

lift it,

lifted.

I could not explain how your voice had come to Russia. Acoustic waves can be amplified; electrical fields can be used as catapults. But the calculations were not realistic. Did the Americans have a new kind of loudspeaker? Were you visiting some physics lab at NYU? Perhaps it was a trick of frequencies, an aural illusion?

I rewound the tape.

No. You were there, Clara.

Perhaps you were not so far away, in Sofia or Wien, talking on a radio program. "Lift it," you told the talk show host. And then this signal was caught by a receiver in Moscow.

I did not know.

Finally, it was too late and I stood up from my desk. The free worker took my tapes and placed them in a locked steel container. A guard took the container when we left. I went down the stairs to the dormitory, along the wall, to my bed. I sat there. I had missed dinner. My ears hurt where the headset had pressed against them. I could not stop imagining your clear straight look.

IT WAS NOT LONG after this incident that Beria brought me to the lake.

I do not know which lake it was. Maybe Glubokoye. Maybe Pirogovo. They brought me in a Black Maria. Once again I believed I was being taken to my death. Then the car stopped, the door opened, and I stepped out onto moist grass. There were wide woods and the lake reflected everything, and the sky itself seemed green.

Beria stood in the weeds. "Come here," he said. I padded toward him, into soft mud. It has been months since I was outside, years since I had been in open air like this, wet and open air, with arrowheads of birds running south. There were rich and earthen smells, smells I scarcely remembered, wild raw smells that evoked gardens, boating, my parents' cellar. Battery Park, after horses have scraped up the sod. The low touches of sex. Beria wore a trench coat tied shut. I shivered. They had not given me anything to wear over my overalls. Far behind us, where the driver waited in his compartment, an engine rumbled.

"Citizen Termen," Beria said. He made a sound with his tongue.

I did not say anything.

I wondered if he planned to kill me with his small hands. Would I fight back? After all this, would I fight back?

"You have done excellent work."

I did not thank him. I looked at the beautiful straight line of the horizon and clasped my hands. The lake was interrupted only with minuscule stirrings, fish rising underneath. There was the barest suggestion of fog.

"So, now, something new," he said.

He explained he wanted a bug that did not even require a bug. A way of listening from outside a room, outside the building, without even smuggling something inside. "Microphones on exterior walls," I said, immediately.

"No, no. From a distance. It must be from a distance."

"You could easily conceal a small microphone . . ."

Beria turned. There was a secret in his appeasing smile. "We all have places we cannot go, Termen." His lips twitched. "And we wonder: what is going on inside?"

THERE WAS STILL MUD on my shoes, blades of grass, when I returned to the laboratory. I sat at my desk with a blank sheet of paper. The free worker watched me from across the empty space. A new curiosity hid in his sandy eyes.

I looked at the stray headset, the empty Spaso tape machine. They had taken the last set of recordings away. I knew I was already forgetting the sound of your voice. I felt a hole in my chest. I smoothed the page with my hand.

I told myself you had always been unknowable. Even in New York, when I thought I saw you, when I thought I was listening at your chest, I never knew.

So many signs are meaningless.

I picked up my pencil and began to sketch an idea, in arcs and squares.

How do you listen to a closed room?

MAYBE YOU LIFTED A THEREMIN, maybe a suitcase, maybe a chandelier, maybe a chest, maybe an infant's heavy pine crib.

IT TOOK JUST OVER A WEEK. I handed in my request for materials and watched the free worker's eyes flick down the list. "All right," he said.

A crate arrived. Radio emitters, dishes, lenses, plywood, two thick sheets of glass, in different sizes. I erected the glass in a little room—like a telephone booth, a vestibule. "Could I ask your help?" I asked my guard. "Stand here. Speak."

He stood on the other side of the glass, observed me through the pane. The most difficult part was the fragility of what I was observing: the tiniest changes, smaller than the drawing of breath, the tilt of a head.

"Testing, test," said the lanky, sandy-eyed free worker.

"Yes, like that," I said.

I was not listening to a voice; I was listening to the reflection of the stirrings of a voice.

THE FIRST RECORDINGS of my new device did not sound like *Testing, test, test test testing 1-2 testing test.*

They sounded like *Shhhhhhkhkhkhff shhhh fffmmm m m mmm-mmshhhhhhh shhhhhh ffmmmmmmmmmmmmmmmmmm khhh* and then your voice, I swear it.

You were saying, "Oh, it's that way, Doris."

And then, "Of course I promise."

And then, "Let's go out."

THE NEXT TIME I SAW Beria he came to the laboratory. My radio emitters were set up along one wall, with the booth at the far side. The whirring recording device sat beside my notes.

Beria came in with another man, a pale thin man with a blue tie, who waited beside the portrait of Stalin.

"Sir," I said.

The free worker stood and saluted.

"L-890," Beria murmured. His trench coat was speckled with wet drops. His assistant's dark suit showed that it was snow.

He removed and wiped his spectacles. "It's ready for a demonstration?"

"If you would stand behind the glass," I said.

"No." Beria gestured to the free worker. "You."

The man with sandy eyes walked into the booth.

Beria took a position beside me. "Begin," he said.

I pressed several switches. The emitter hummed. It was now sending radio waves through the room, in a narrow stream.

"Go on," I murmured to the man behind the glass.

"Test, testing, 1-2-3. Testing," he said.

Beside us, a dish was listening to the reflection of radio waves off the surface of the glass. The vibrations were recorded, as sound, on a revolving tape machine.

"Test, test, test," said the free worker.

When he had finished I rewound the tape and played it back through a set of headphones. I adjusted the levels, watched Beria's expression. He showed nothing as he listened. For a long moment I wondered whether the contraption had failed. He was just a bureaucrat listening to an empty tape. Then he raised his gaze. A smile appeared and disappeared on his lips. "Good," he said to me. He made a gesture to his aide, a movement of the hand that looked as if he was saying, *Come here* or *Come here and listen*. His pale accomplice immediately went to where the free worker was standing behind glass, took a silenced revolver from his jacket, and shot him in the chest. It made a sound like a punctured bicycle tire. The man with sandy eyes was saying something but he was unable to say it.

A man becomes heavier when he dies. Beria's guard dragged the body to the door. I gasped at the shooting but then I said nothing else. I wanted very much to burst into tears. How much I wanted to burst into tears, Clara, to show the dead man at least that respect. Danny Finch, young Fyodor, the ones at Kolyma, the free worker with the sandy eyes. My face trembled. I felt as if I was being slowly lowered into a lake.

Beria had the headset around his neck. He said, "This is called Operation Snowstorm. You are never to mention it to anyone. If you even speak its name I will cut off your arms and tear the muscle of your tongue and put you in a cattle car to the taiga."

I was not sure I had any voice left in my throat.

"We will take this thing to Moscow. You will oversee its installation and transcribe its recordings."

"Who are we listening to?" I was like a ghost.

Beria began to remove the headset. He said, "The man in all the portraits."

SNOWSTORM IS RELIABLE at a distance of up to 1,600 feet.

But not in snow.

Not in fog or rain.

ON THE DAYS I AM at Marenko I laugh and kid with Bairamov. I help Zaytsev perfect his recipe for cake. I stroll down the hall with Pavla and ask about her children. In the shared lab, where there are clocks, where there is music, I lean in beside Korolev and we argue about the life span of different vacuum tubes. We rap them, *ping*, against the edge of the desk.

At breakfast I sit with Andrei Markov, stirring a lump of sugar into porridge.

I do not work on Sundays.

ON MONDAYS AND THURSDAYS they bring me to Moscow. I climb the stairs to the attic and sit with the machines. A gun waits beside me.

I write down the words they bring on tapes from Spaso House. Harriman has the same conversations, and different ones. His bearded collie barks.

There is another set of tapes, from the thing perched on my window, which faces the Kremlin, and those words I write down too.

He has a gentle voice, like a music teacher's.

I FIND YOU in every recording.

WHEN IT HAS BEEN RAINING, the tapes they bring me are hours of haze, like listening to clouds form, smoke filling with cinders. The bass notes are great, long presences, like appetites. Spirits wander. Sometimes the silences are like waves rolling and breaking. Sometimes figures coalesce. At the edge of hearing, boundaries fizz and snap. I hear them—forces in the uninterrupted air. Intersecting fields. Loss.

You hear a noise and you think it is a presence; but it is just a shrieking emptiness, interference. You have made a mistake.

I hear your voice speaking and I do not know what I am to do with it. Does it mean that we are touching? Does it mean that we are destined? There is no destiny. There is no touch. My unrequited love, speaking across the sky. You cannot see me hearing. This letter will not reach you. These words will not be read.

Still I hear your voice. It is what I have.

There are nights when I imagine that these bricks and tiles, this glass, this land and city and plain and wood, these towers, these gurgling oceans, and sewers, and the roar of automobiles, of orchestras, aeroplanes spilling bombs, sparrows that land and leave, barracks, pasts, rings, are all distortion. There are only two of us, two real things, two tellers, unseen reflectors, sending signals we cannot carry ourselves, or follow.

Somewhere you are waving your hands in the air.

POSTSCRIPT

Lev Sergeyvich Termen was released from Marenko
on June 27, 1947.

—

Over the next decades his research included work
on rust, piano sustain, rockets, floating bridges, immortality,
UFOs, atomic-bomb detection, long-distance touch, male
impotence and a device that could track the movements
of a musician's eyes.

—

After his release, Termen married Maria Feodorovna Guschina,
a secretary. They had two children together.

—

In 1962, Clara and Robert Rockmore travelled to Moscow.
At a small party, Robert mentioned Termen's name. Agents had
come in the night, Rockmore said, and kidnapped the scientist.
"Oh," replied an acquaintance, "Termen lives near Lubyanka."
Clara was seen to faint.

—

Friends arranged a reunion. The next day, three people met on
a subway platform, under the city. Strangers brushed past.
Robert's arm was over Clara's shoulder. Termen looked at them
without speaking. "Scientists are not supposed to meet with
foreigners," he said at last. "We are being watched."

—

That night, Clara and Robert attended a play at the Bolshoi Theatre. During the intermission, they descended the steps to the street. Termen was waiting in a taxi. They drove together to his home.

—

Robert and Clara sat on a hard divan. Termen stood with Maria, his wife. Outside, it was raining. His daughters played violin. The lamplight fell at strange angles.

—

Robert died in 1963, slipping on ice.

—

Maria died in 1970, of heart disease.

—

In 1991, Lev came to New York and met with Clara. He was ninety-five.

—

He died two years later.

AUTHOR'S NOTE AND ACKNOWLEDGEMENTS

This book is a work of fiction. It is full of distortions, elisions, omissions, and lies. Termen was not a murderer. As far as we know, he did not practise kung-fu. Anyone seeking the true tale of Termen's life must read Albert Glinsky's meticulously researched *Theremin: Ether Music and Espionage*, to which this novel owes an enormous debt. I was only able to play fast and loose with the facts because Glinsky had already so patiently, assiduously, tracked them down.

Us Conductors is also particularly indebted to Stephen Graham's dazzling *New York Nights*, published in 1927; to Chad Heap's *Slumming*; to Anne Applebaum's *Gulag*; Gustaw Herling's *A World Apart*; and Aleksandr Solzhenitsyn's beautiful, terrible, *In the First Circle*. The epigraph for the second part comes from Michael Solomon's *Magadan*. Thank you also to Steven M. Martin for his 1993 documentary, *Theremin: An Electronic Odyssey*.

Bolshoe spasiba to Sergey Kolesnikov, Alexander Zaitsev, Natasha Yarushkina, and Andrey Smirnov, director of the Moscow Conservatory's Theremin Center. Also to my hosts Ivan Cherniavsky in Moscow, Vanya Zhuk in St. Petersburg, and the incomparable Maxim Litvinov and Natasha Kotelnikova in Magadan.

I would also like to thank:

Mollie B. Casey, who introduced me to the story of Lev and Clara, without whom this novel would never have been written.

My parents, Jan and Arlen Michaels, and my sister, Robin Michaels, for more than I will ever remember.

The extended Michaels and Bornstein families, especially: Isaiah Michaels and Jean Bornstein, whom I miss very much; Anne Michaels (for 100 years of inspiration); Jeff Walker; and Jason Bornstein (for chemical know-how).

Dan Beirne, the first person to read this book. He and Jordan Himelfarb, my partners at the music blog *Said the Gramophone*, have taught me more about writing, and listening, than almost anybody else. I am also grateful to our readers over the past eleven years, who wrote, and listened, and who made a small website mean something.

My friends, in particular Maryam Ehteshami, Neale McDavitt-van Fleet, Raphaëlle Aubin, Kit Malo, the novelist Andrew Ladd, Adam Waito, Miranda Campbell, Stephen Ramsay, Catherine McCandless, François Vincent, Basia Bulat, Alexandre Lenot, Marc Rowland (for kung-fu know-how), Helen Ashton and Ramsay Jackson.

The writers whose wisdom, kindness and advice allowed me to come to this place: soul gazers Melissa Bull, Anna Leventhal, Jeff Miller and Michelle Sterling; Carl Wilson; Julian Smith ("also, Information Market"); Drew Nelles; Elisabeth Donnelly; and Pasha Malla.

My fine editors, Anne Collins, Meg Storey and Amanda Lewis.

The Conseil des arts et des lettres du Québec, the Canada Council for the Arts, and Emploi-Québec's *Jeunes volontaires* program.

The kings of the morning: Vince Spinale and everyone at Café Olimpico, and Vito Azzue, now of Café Vito.

My inspiring, steadfast agent, Meredith Kaffel.

And Thea Metcalfe, indescribable, who has changed all the weather.